PRAISE FOR GUNNAR STAALESEN

'A vibrant look at the life, loves and betrayals of the past and the ways in which their tentacles cling, never letting you go'
John Harvey

'Staalesen is one of my very favourite Scandinavian authors, and this is a series with very sharp teeth' Ian Rankin

'The Norwegian Chandler' Jo Nesbø

'As searing and gripping as they come' *New York Times*

'Mature and captivating' *Herald Scotland*

'Every inch the equal of his Nordic confreres, Henning Mankell and Jo Nesbø' *Independent*

'Masterful pacing … moving and uncompromising'
Publishers Weekly

'Not many books hook you in the first chapter – this one did, and never let go!' Mari Hannah

'Almost forty years into the Varg Veum odyssey, Staalesen is at the height of his storytelling powers' Crime Fiction Lover

'Staalesen continually reminds us he is one of the finest of Nordic novelists' *Financial Times*

'Chilling and perilous results – all told in a pleasingly dry style'
Sunday Times

'Employs Chandleresque similes with a Nordic Noir twist'
Wall Street Journal

'Mature and captivating' *Herald Scotland*

'Well worth reading, with the rest of Staalesen's award-winning series' *New York Journal of Books*

'Readers … will feel drawn into the characters and their intertwined lives' *Reviewing the Evidence*

'Haunting, dark and totally noir, a great read' *NB Magazine*

'A vital contribution to the international body of P.I. literature … There are only two other writers that I know of who have achieved the depth of insight in detective writing that Staalesen has: Chandler and Ross MacDonald … Keep doing what you do, Varg. And never die. This weary world needs you more every day'
Mystery Tribune

'Another satisfying addition to this already excellent series, and who knows what awaits Varg Veum in his next investigation … Recommended' Raven Crime Reads

'A dark, brooding, slow-burning murder mystery with vivid descriptions of Bergen and its surrounding regions' Swirl & Thread

'There's a poetic, lyrical quality to Staalesen's writing, he's not all action and fast-paced plot. His ability to produce much more than a thriller, with a beautifully evocative sense of place and masterfully created characters is a joy to read'
Random Things through My Letterbox

'A truly thought-provoking read and definitely recommended'
Jen Med's Book Reviews

'A brilliant example of Nordic Noir, full of dark secrets and chilling characters. I love the way in which Staalesen writes his books, both in terms of his prose and the short chapters, which is just asking for "just one more chapter" when you are trying to put the book down'
Have Books Will Read

'Hints of menace coupled with a chilling climate make this the perfect locational mystery. There is also an emotional element attached to these books … Highly recommended!'
Bibliophile Book Club

'A complex, layered plot in which human tragedy and mystery combine to play out beautifully in a classic Nordic Noir with a touch of Christie to finish' Live & Deadly

'Unexpected and traumatic … what a book!' The Book Trail

'There are some dark and emotional twists and turns … With an addictive plot, believable and relatable characters, this is a novel that I highly recommend' Hooked from Page One

'There is something just so fantastically absorbing about Staalesen's work that I'm always longing to read more … Every time I think I've read the best book I will in a year, Orenda drops a new Gunnar Staalesen that jumps straight to the top of the list' Mumbling About…

**Also in the Varg Veum series
and available from Orenda Books:**
Fallen Angels
We Shall Inherit the Wind
Where Roses Never Die
Wolves in the Dark
Big Sister
Wolves at the Door

Bitter Flowers

ABOUT THE AUTHOR

One of the fathers of Nordic Noir, Gunnar Staalesen was born in Bergen, Norway, in 1947. He made his debut at the age of twenty-two with *Seasons of Innocence* and in 1977 he published the first book in the Varg Veum series. He is the author of over twenty titles, which have been published in twenty-four countries and sold over four million copies. Twelve film adaptations of his Varg Veum crime novels have appeared since 2007, starring the popular Norwegian actor Trond Espen Seim. Staalesen has won three Golden Pistols (including the Prize of Honour). *Where Roses Never Die* won the 2017 Petrona Award for Nordic Crime Fiction, and *Big Sister* was shortlisted for the award in 2019. He lives with his wife in Bergen.

ABOUT THE TRANSLATOR

Don Bartlett completed an MA in Literary Translation at the University of East Anglia in 2000 and has since worked with a wide variety of Danish and Norwegian authors, including Jo Nesbø, Karl Ove Knausgård and Kjell Ola Dahl. He has previously translated *The Consorts of Death, Cold Hearts, We Shall Inherit the Wind, Where Roses Never Die, Wolves in the Dark, Big Sister, Wolves at the Door* and *Fallen Angels* in the Varg Veum series.

Bitter Flowers

GUNNAR STAALESEN

Translated by Don Bartlett

**ORENDA
BOOKS**

Orenda Books
16 Carson Road
West Dulwich
London SE21 8HU
www.orendabooks.co.uk

First published in Norwegian as *Bitre blomster* by Gyldendal, 1991
First published in English by Orenda Books, 2022
Copyright © Gunnar Staalesen 1991
English translation copyright © Don Bartlett 2022
Photograph of Varg Veum statue supplied courtesy of Augon Johnsen

A catalogue record for this book is available from the British Library.
ISBN 978-1-913193-08-9
eISBN 978-1-913193-09-6

The publication of this translation has been made possible through the financial
support of NORLA, Norwegian Literature Abroad.

Typeset in Arno by typesetter.org.uk

Printed and bound by CPI Group (UK) Ltd, Croydon CR0 4YY

For sales and distribution please contact *info@orendabooks.co.uk*

Bergen, Norway

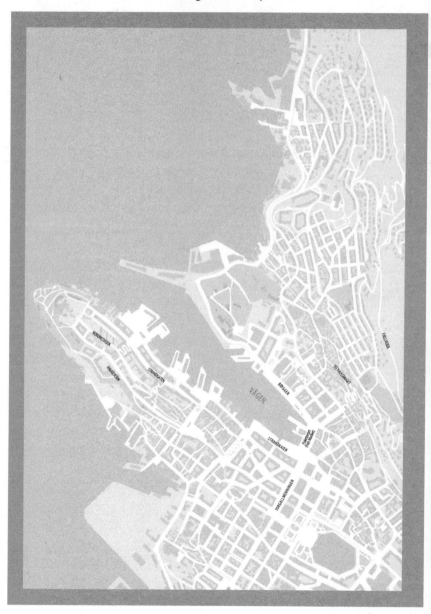

AUTHOR'S NOTE

As there is actually a company in Hilleren, it would be appropriate to point out that the one described in this book, like all the characters, is purely the product of the author's imagination, with no connection to reality.

 —GS.

He who laughs last is the last to laugh.

—Erling T. Gjelsvik

1

It was a quarter to eleven when I parked my car in the drive of the empty house.

A hundred metres away there were two other cars. One was red; the other grey. There was no one in them.

Neither of us spoke.

We got out of the car. Her eyes were the same colour as the darkest patches of the evening sky above us. The air was heavy with fragrance.

'You know they have an indoor swimming pool, don't you?' she said, with a searching gaze in my direction.

'You mean we should have brought our swimming things?'

She smiled suggestively and shrugged her shoulders, as though to say: Do we actually need them?

I met her gaze. It was impenetrable.

In fact, her hands had touched the majority of my body. But that was because she was employed as a physiotherapist at Hjellestad Clinic, where I had spent the past two months; the first as an in-patient, the second as an out-patient. Or, as they prefer to call you in those circles, a client.

'Well, maybe not,' I said casually, opening the gate.

The house had a Kleiva address and was situated on the broad, relatively exclusive peninsula protruding into the north of Nordås bay. It was discreetly set back from the road, on top of a hill and hidden by a small well-tended copse. Roman orgies could have been going on up there and no neighbours would have lost any beauty sleep as a result. And the postman never got further than the gate, where a sign announced with the utmost clarity: *THIS DOG BITES*.

I nodded towards the sign and mumbled: 'I hope it's on holiday, too.'

She smiled. 'At Norway's most luxurious kennels, you can be sure.'

It was one of those light June evenings when the air bursts with summer promise and the stars are still pale. There was a thick scent of bird cherry and lilac. The honeysuckle enticed us with its wet, pungent fingers, and the season's first roses floated like waterlilies on the gentle breeze.

We followed the white gravel path from the gate up to the house. Rhododendrons and apple trees lined our route. Among the small rockeries there were carpets of eager flowers: blue Carpathian harebells, white carnations and yellow-and-violet pansies.

The owners were architects, and the house had been designed for this plot and the surrounding terrain. It bestrode the hilltop, a façade of natural stone, glass and wood, and was probably worth its weight in bankruptcies.

'You should see the view of the sea,' she said.

'From the swimming pool?'

She chuckled. Her hair was short, dark and trim, her nose tanned, her body slim and sinewy. She was dressed for the summer in a white T-shirt and baggy, cream-coloured cotton trousers.

Wearing a shirt and jacket, I was slightly more formally attired. 'Have you got the key?'

She nodded and produced a little key ring. 'There are four keys. Two for this door and two for the side entrance into the cellar. There are security locks on both.'

'Sounds sensible. And what do we do when we're inside? Check all the windows—'

'…switch on the lights, put on a radio, make the house seem occupied…'

'Splash in the pool.'

She angled a glance at me. 'Oh, yes? Would you like to?'

'Let's see,' I said, avoiding her gaze. The only women I had had any contact with over the last six months had been vinmonopol assistants, and I feared Lisbeth Finslo might be too much for me. The thought of sharing a pool with her, as nature intended, produced a dull throb on the deepest bass inside me. But our relationship was professional. She had kneaded me with her restless, muscular fingers and had found me my first job after I had been given a clean bill of health. All I had from my sojourn at Hjellestad was a little scar on my forearm and three tiny stitches, and this job looked like being one of the easiest ever.

She unlocked the door and we went in.

We entered a hallway clad in natural stone. There was green grass in wall niches and there were spotlights in every corner. Sliding doors made of untreated wood hid wardrobes; grey slate tiles covered the floor. The house definitely had character, but I had no sense that this was a home, more like a hallway leading to a study centre for passionate conservationists.

'Pål and Helle have always placed great emphasis on using natural materials,' she said.

'I'm beginning to see that,' I answered.

As she set foot on the stairs to the next floor, she called out: 'Hello?'

No one answered.

'Are you expecting someone to be here?'

She glanced at me. 'What? No. I … It's just a habit I have. I can't shake it off.'

I stared at her neck. It was slim – and tense, and I felt exactly the same. From the instant we had crossed the threshold of the empty house I had sensed it in my body. Something ominous, scary, like when a dog scents death…

We were upstairs. The 'steppe' we entered probably went by the name 'lounge'. Unbleached leather furniture was scattered across a floor covered with rush and burlap rugs. On the walls hung collages of stone, shell and dried flowers, alongside a gigantic painting of a lion family, with the King of the Jungle gazing towards Nordås bay through a glass wall and sliding doors, as though he was musing on all the food swimming around out there. On a knee-height shelf running the length of the room was a selection of expensive art books, and in an alcove decorated mainly with bamboo and glass there was a generous bar cabinet that sent a sigh of nostalgia through me. It was eight weeks since I had last tasted a drop of alcohol.

'Impressed?' she asked.

'I feel like an explorer,' I mumbled. 'Can we afford this safari?'

'*They* can.'

'I thought these were troubled times for architects as well.'

'They worked round the clock in the early eighties and invested wisely. In recent years they've concentrated on special projects and jobs abroad. That's why they have to be in Spain for the next two months.'

'Children?'

'No. I suppose this is a sort of consolation.'

'And where's the swimming pool?'

Her mind seemed to be elsewhere. 'What? Oh, that.' She pointed to a partly open door at the end of the room. There was a dim light shining from below. 'I'll go down and check everything's OK.'

'Don't dive in until you've made sure it's full of water.'

As she left, I reached out a hand and made a grab for her. But I was too late. My fingers brushed against her forearm, unable to hold her.

She felt the touch and half turned to me on her way to the door. The smile she sent me was nervous and her gaze so veiled that it hurt to look at her. But she didn't stop.

I watched her. She fitted into these surroundings. As wary as a gazelle, she crossed Kleiva's African steppe, and when she opened the door wide at the end of the room it was as though she were about to enter a menacing jungle.

Like an echo, I heard her voice on her way down to the pool: 'Hello?'

I went towards the glass wall and looked out.

It was as if Peder Severin Krøyer, the Skagen painter, had visited Norway in the summer and left an unfinished picture, which posterity had done its best to destroy.

If you squinted, the Nordås waters lay like shimmering glass beneath the still-light sky. The verdigris leaves of the trees across the bay stirred in the breeze, and the silhouetted landscape on the other side of the fjord, where Edvard Grieg had played his melodies evoking unsullied Norwegian nature, was blueish black and uninhabited. But if you opened your eyes wide you saw that the glittering water wasn't a reflection of the moon but of a thousand sitting-room windows, and that beyond Troldhaugen, the home of Grieg and his wife, along the southbound motorway, noise barriers sliced through the countryside like a wooden sword fashioned by a talentless thirteen-year-old.

Down on the water, I glimpsed the outline of a man sitting all alone in a little boat, outboard motor switched off, fishing rod in hand and not a sniff of a bite: a Krøyer sketch.

Behind me, I heard a faint noise and spun round towards the door Lisbeth Finslo had just left through. She was back, standing in the doorway. The greenish sheen behind her lent her an almost supernatural appearance, and when she took two unseeing steps into the room, she moved like a ghost. She was pale, transparent, as though the blood inside her had drained away. Her lips moved soundlessly, unable to utter a word.

I ran over to her. When I reached her, she slumped against my chest so heavily that I almost lost my balance.

'What is it, Lisbeth? Are you…?'

She looked up at me, her eyes black. Her face was grey, her

mouth distorted into a hysterical grimace. When she did finally say something, her voice was a toneless staccato. 'H-he's d-dead, Varg. Dead! I had no idea. I didn't understand.'

'Who's dead? Who are you talking about?'

She part turned her head and stared at the door behind her. 'Down there … in the pool.'

I looked at her. Her eyes were spinning and rolled under her eyelids.

I pulled her further into the steppe room. 'Look, sit down here. Breathe calmly and relax until I return. Think about something else.'

She slumped into the deep canvas chair, nodded wearily and looked up at me with an indefinable expression in her eyes.

I stared at her. 'Are you alright?'

She nodded again without speaking.

'Then I'll go…' I gestured towards the door. 'I'll be back in no time.'

She looked at me vacantly, as though she didn't believe me, as though she thought I was going for good.

Then I left her. I bounded down the stairs in long strides.

The room I entered was similar in style to the hall. Around the green swimming pool there were the same grey slate tiles. One wall was clad with untrimmed sawn timber, like a mountain cabin. The others were covered in a wide variety of natural stone, like a topographical map of Norwegian rock from the coast to Jotunheimen. In square wooden boxes there grew a profusion of flowers, enhanced by strategically placed spotlights. On small plinths and in wall niches there were stuffed animals, from weasels to foxes, frozen in motion, with glassy eyes.

Here, too, the whole wall facing the sea was made of glass, but in the lower section there was a metre-high aquarium spanning the length of the room. Silent fish swam around like abandoned fauna, their greys and reddish-yellows contrasting with the blueish-green contours of the landscape on the opposite side of the fjord, visible through the aquarium like the print of a slightly blurred graphic design.

All that was missing was a small glacier up in the right-hand corner and a 'Wedding Procession in Hardanger' video on a screen beneath, then you could have invited a Japanese travel group on a mini-cruise and left them alone for hours. This room was an adventure zone for world-weary ecologists – or architects suffering pangs of guilt about all the shoeboxes they had enlarged and drawn doors and windows on.

But the man at the bottom of the pool was no National Romantic artefact placed there for the benefit of visitors. He was lying face down, like a diver who had come to grief, as lifeless as the stuffed animals surrounding this unusual swimming pool.

I threw off my clothes and dived in. The chlorine gave the water a grainy texture. I didn't reach him at my first attempt, but I did at the second. I grabbed his jacket and dragged him to the surface.

I swam to the edge, got out and pulled him up after me. He was literally a dead weight. He must have swallowed an enormous amount of water.

When, finally, I managed to get him out, I cast a quick glance over him. He was a man in his late thirties, dark-haired after his immersion in the water, with a pale face upon which death had already bestowed blue lips.

Without any hope, but unwilling to reject any possibility of life, I bent back his head, opened his airway, placed my mouth on his cold lips and gave him a few blasts from my lungs. He didn't object.

I searched for a pulse, first on his wrist, then at the side of his neck.

Nothing. He had floated into the beyond.

With difficulty I rose to my feet and looked down at him.

He was casually dressed: an open-necked shirt with short sleeves, a light-blue jacket and faded jeans. On his feet he wore light-brown moccasins. He had definitely not taken the plunge of his own free will.

I quickly dressed and cast a final look around the room. There was nothing to suggest that any crime had taken place. No sign of a struggle, no marks on the dead body.

It was as if the dead man was a natural element in the National Romantic tableau: drowned fisherman brought ashore, or perhaps the last tourist, his garb taken into account.

I shook my head and retraced my steps up the slate staircase.

The door was closed.

I pushed it open and glanced at the chair where Lisbeth Finslo had been sitting. It was empty. The whole room was empty, as though finally the ecological catastrophe had occurred.

'Lisbeth!' I shouted. 'Where are you?'

No one answered.

I crossed the room and ran downstairs to the hallway. The front door was open.

I ran outside. 'Hello? Lisbeth! Are you there?'

Still no answer.

I cast around. The light summer sky had become a sardonic grimace. The breeze through the apple trees sounded like the whisper of evil spirits, and the luxuriant rhododendron bushes stood like darkened mausoleums in the evening air.

I jogged down to the road. My car was where I had left it. But the red saloon had disappeared from the car park a hundred metres away.

I glanced at my watch. It was a quarter past eleven.

In the distance I could hear the wail of sirens.

2

It was darker now, and the scent of jasmine stronger. If you can describe as darkness the gentle dimming of light that is the Nordic summer night. And if you can call it a scent when it rolls over you like the wave of the century.

Up by the Straumeveien turning there was a flash of blue light. I stood by the gate to show them where to go.

They came in two vehicles, a patrol car and a white civilian BMW. Four police officers jumped out of the patrol car, while Hamre and Isachsen got out of the BMW. When Hamre caught sight of me, an expression of acute distaste crossed his face. Isachsen gave a wan smile, one of those you are sent for free because no one else wants it.

Hamre came over to me, nodded dutifully and looked past me, up towards the house. 'Was it you who rang, Veum?'

'No. It must've been Lisbeth. Finslo.' I looked around. 'She must be around somewhere.'

Hamre turned to one of the officers. 'Wasn't it a man who rang?'

A constable with a face like a boy scout's and a reputation as a hoodlum nodded affirmatively. 'Yes.'

Hamre subjected me to a long stare.

I went cold. 'A man? Who was it?'

Hamre nodded to the constable. 'Did he give his name?'

'No. He only said there was a dead body at this address. Then he rang off.'

'You don't remember phoning, Veum?' Hamre said acidly.

'It wasn't me.' And it wasn't the man in the pool. So who was it? And had Lisbeth Finslo left with him, in the red car that was no longer there?

I had goose pimples over my whole body. To distract myself, I turned my attention back to the new arrivals.

Inspector Jakob E. Hamre was a couple of years younger than me. I observed with satisfaction that he had acquired some new wrinkles on his forehead and that the skin round his chin had tightened, making him look older and more marked than he had before. His dark-blond hair was speckled with grey, and he looked resigned, as most Bergen police officers did during the eighties, for understandable reasons.

He was wearing loose leisure clothing: light-brown sandals, white cotton trousers, a short, eggshell-coloured tracksuit jacket with green speed stripes down the sleeves and an open, red-and-white checked shirt.

Police Officer Peder Isachsen displayed less sartorial elegance and dressed according to the economic vicissitudes of Grand Magasin: cheap, brown Terylene trousers, a blazer that had been modern in 1962 and a light-blue peaked cap that would not have looked out of place on a Swedish pensioner driving through Norway on holiday.

'What happened?' Hamre asked.

'I'll tell you everything I know.'

'For a change, eh?'

'It isn't much.'

Hamre sighed. He turned to the other officers and said loudly: 'Let's go up to the house. Veum has something he wants to show us.'

We followed the gravel path upward.

Hamre coughed and looked at me. 'Why's your hair so wet?'

'I had to swim to the bottom of the pool to get the dead body.'

Isachsen stepped on my heels from behind. 'Does that mean you've moved it?'

I half turned. 'You think I should've left him there, do you? Until I was sure he was stone-dead?'

We arrived at the house. Hamre muttered, 'We never get any-where with the sort of people who own houses like this. Because we always end up on the phone, talking to some journalist who feels obliged to interrogate us about police violence.'

'You sound bitter, Hamre.'

'How do you reckon you'd sound if you'd worked for the last ten years in what from the outside resembles a travelling funfair?'

'And from the inside?'

'A nuthouse. We can hardly bend over to tie our shoelaces in a public place for fear that someone will call it police violence.'

'No smoke without fire, Hamre.'

'There's never been a hint of a conflagration, Veum.'

Hamre nodded to one of the constables. 'Sæve, you stay here by the door. Don't let anyone in … or out.'

The constable nodded. He had the proportions of a bouncer, and a midge wouldn't have got through the doorway while he was there.

We went in. Hamre's mood didn't improve at the sight of the hallway, and when we entered the steppe dollar signs and question marks appeared in his eyes. 'Who did you say these people were?'

'Architects.'

He nodded, as though I had confirmed his worst fears. 'Architects and dentists.'

'Where's the body?' Isachsen asked impatiently.

'Through that door over there and downstairs.'

'And what were *you* doing here, Veum?'

I looked at Hamre. 'I'll explain everything.'

He nodded and glared at Isachsen disapprovingly.

We walked down to the swimming pool in single file and the 'wows' grew in volume, as if a group was being shown around and had just spotted the architects' private national park.

The body was lying where I had left it. No one had started to prepare it for taxidermy. Yet.

He was on his back and staring up at the ceiling as though it was all too much for him. This time I noticed something I hadn't seen before: the shadow of bruising under the stubble on his chin.

Hamre knelt down professionally beside the dead man and did what I had done: searched for the pulse that didn't exist. At the same time, he peered up at me. 'Have you any idea who he is?'

'Never seen him before.'

'So, it's not the architect then?'

I shrugged. 'I haven't seen him, either. But from what I've been told he's in Spain with his wife. They work together.'

Hamre patted the man's jacket. Then he put his hand in one of the pockets and took out a sodden wallet.

He opened it and extracted a driving licence. 'Hm. Aslaksen. Tor. Born the fourteenth of the twelfth, forty-nine.' He glanced from the photograph on the card to the dead man's face. 'Well, that's that cleared up.'

He placed the wallet on the floor and stood up. 'We'd better not do anything now until the experts have gone through the room with a fine-tooth comb.' He pointed at one of the officers. 'Will you contact forensics?'

The man nodded and was gone.

Hamre walked to the edge of the pool and looked down. 'So he was lying on the bottom, eh?'

'Yes.'

'And it was you who found him?'

'No.'

He turned to me with an enquiring expression.

'The woman I mentioned. Lisbeth Finslo. She fo—'

He raised a hand with a tired flourish. 'We'll do this upstairs … in the lounge.'

Before leaving, he cast his eyes around the room one more time while slowly shaking his head. 'I haven't seen anything like this since I went to the university museum with the kids. What must it have felt like to splash around in here?'

'Do you know Theodor Kittelsen's painting of the Nix?' I said, leading the way up the stairs.

3

We had sat by the glass wall facing Nordås, as far from the bar with the bamboo furniture as we could. Hamre and Isachsen both had a notebook on their laps. As for me, I could feel a tingling in the little scar on my forearm. I would have given the last two months of my life for a dram.

Jakob E. Hamre faced me with a neutral expression and said: 'Right. Lisbeth Finslo. Who is she? Where is she? And what was she doing here, with you?'

'I can answer the first and the last questions.'

Hamre made a gesture for me to continue.

'She's a physio at Hjellestad, where I was treated for a couple of months.'

Hamre raised his eyebrows, while Isachsen let out a long whistle and exhibited another of his cheap smirks. 'Hjellestad Clinic?' Hamre asked and made a note.

'Exactly.' It didn't bother me to say this aloud. The psychologist there had told me it was the only sensible thing to do: own up to my stay at the clinic openly and honestly to anyone who needed to know.

Not without some sympathy, Hamre added: 'It's been a tough decade for you too, Veum, hasn't it?'

I nodded. 'I hit the wall at Christmas and from then on it was all downhill.'

'But at least you met a woman there,' Isachsen was quick to add.

I ignored him. To Hamre, I said: 'When I was discharged, she got me this job. The owners are abroad, as I told you, and the idea was that I would look after the house. Pop by at various junctures, remove all the junk mail from the post box, switch on the radio and TV, and cut the grass whenever it was necessary. In short, make the house look occupied. A cushy number. One of the easiest I'd ever had. Or so I thought.'

'And how long have you had it?'

'I started today. Lisbeth came up with me, let me in—'

'Just a moment, Veum. She had the keys?'

'Yes, she knows the architects. She's helped them like this for a few years herself, but this time she's going on holiday and anyway...' I gazed across the fjord. 'I think she did it to help me get on my feet. A kind of therapy.'

Isachsen snorted to himself, while Hamre nodded pensively. 'So you haven't met your employers face to face?'

'No.'

'What are their full names?'

'The ones I've been given are Helle and Pål Nielsen. The company's called Embla.'

'Embla?'

'Yes, you know – Ask and Embla. The Adam and Eve of Norse mythology. And in Agnar Mykle's writing.'

Hamre made a note. Then he said: 'And this Lisbeth Finslo ... the relationship between you was...?'

I smiled sheepishly. 'Professional.'

Isachsen snorted again.

'I mean client and therapist. That was all.'

Another snort. I turned to him. 'Is there something wrong with you or what? Have you got nasal polyps? Is there something stuck further up? A pea brain for example?'

Hamre raised his voice. 'And when you got here, what happened?'

'We had a look around. She showed me where things were. Then she went down to the pool.'

'Alone?'

'Er … yes.'

'Why?'

I hesitated for two seconds. 'She wanted to check that everything was in order.' I sent Isachsen an admonitory glare. He didn't utter a sound.

Hamre leaned forward slightly. 'And where were you while she went down?'

'Up here.'

'In here?'

I nodded.

'And you didn't hear anything?'

'Not until she came back up … and was standing in the doorway over there.'

Hamre raised a hand. 'Let's get this clear. When you two came here, everything seemed to be in order. The door was locked?'

'There were two locks.'

'And you didn't notice anyone in the house?'

'No.'

'You didn't hear anything?'

'Correct. But…'

'Yes?'

'Well, it was just a feeling I had. That there was in fact someone here. And she seemed to sense it, too.'

He made a note. 'And then when she came back up…'

'I ran over.' I pointed to the door. 'She seemed shaken. In shock. And she said…' I thought back, trying to reconstruct the conversation.

'Yes?'

'Something like: "He's dead … I had no idea … I didn't understand."'

'Did she say that? She had no idea? She didn't understand?'

'Yes.'

'Right.'

He made another note. '"He's dead". Did that sound like she knew who he was?'

'Ye-es. I think so.'

'I see. And then … What happened then?'

'I put her in that chair and went down to the pool. When I saw him lying at the bottom of the pool I dived in and brought him up.' I cast a fleeting glance at Isachsen and said fiercely: 'Naturally enough, I didn't know how long he'd been there.'

Hamre continued quickly: 'No, of course not. You did the right thing. The first rule is to establish whether the victim is alive. But he wasn't, it seems.'

'No.' I scratched my ear. Years ago, people used to say if your left ear itched, it meant you were being talked about or you would hear some bad news. I feared it would be bad news. 'And when I came back up here, she was gone.'

Hamre stared at me with expressionless eyes. They were blue and cold, with a touch of green glacier. 'Gone?'

'Yes. I called her name, of course. I ran outside. But I couldn't see her anywhere.

'And, so, it wasn't you who rang us?'

'No.'

'And it wasn't her, either,' he said, rapt in thought, and added: 'So who was it then?'

4

The Forensics team arrived, chatting and joking, as unaffected as if they were on a country walk.

Hamre looked at Isachsen. 'Find out where this Lisbeth

Finslo lives. And get someone to go through this house carefully, room by room.'

'And if any more bodies turn up—' I muttered.

Hamre interrupted me. 'Let's go down to the pool.'

'Shall I send an officer to her house?' Isachsen asked.

Hamre gave the question some thought. 'No, I'll go there later. And find the dead man's address as well.'

Isachsen nodded and went out to the cars. I followed Hamre down.

The forensic investigation had started. The body had been photographed, and they were about to divide the room into zones that each of them would examine superficially before conducting a more detailed search.

'Tell us exactly where he was in the pool when you found him,' Hamre said.

I approached the edge of the pool carefully and pointed downward. 'About there. But I doubt you'll find any fingerprints.'

'You'd be surprised to know what our people can find, Veum. My guess is we already have *your* blood type.'

'Yes, but—'

'You were in the water, weren't you?'

I stared at him and he nodded. Then he turned to one of the forensics officers, a small guy with a pointed nose and an elongated neck, who I knew went under the amusing surname of Due – pigeon. 'When the quack comes, tell him I want a report on the cause of death ASAP.'

Due nodded. 'Anything else?'

Hamre surveyed the stuffed animals. 'Reckon we'll get any of them to talk?'

I nodded towards the aquarium. 'The fish have seen everything too, but they won't say a word, either.'

'Who is this man, Veum? What was he doing here? How did he die?' Hamre mumbled.

'A burglar?'

'Who was so alarmed by what he saw down here that he tripped over the edge of the pool and drowned? Did you notice his chin?'

'Yes, either he'd been in a fight with a blunt razor or someone gave him a helping hand.'

'A knockout punch to the chin. Enough to render him sense-less if it was timed well.' He sent me an ironic side glance. 'You didn't hit him, did you, Veum, eh?'

'If I had, I wouldn't be standing here now.'

'What about Lisbeth Finslo? Could she have done it?'

'Hit a man of that size so hard he passed out? She's pretty robust when she has me on the treatment bench, but … Anyway, I'd swear that when she came back upstairs the shock at finding him dead was genuine.'

'But why did she do a bunk? And where did she go afterwards?'

I shrugged. 'Shock? Shouldn't we make an effort to find her and hear what she has to say?'

Hamre nodded decisively. 'What's the time? Five past twelve. We can pay her a visit if Isachsen's found out where she lives.' Hamre's expression changed. 'Unless you know?'

'I'm afraid not. We didn't know each other privately.'

'Yes, you said.'

We exchanged glances, but said nothing.

As we left, I took a final look at Tor Aslaksen. I tried to sear his image onto my brain – dark-blond hair plastered to his skull after the involuntary swim, a straight nose, open mouth with thin lips – to be sure I recognised him the next time we met. Wherever that might be.

We strolled through the steppe to the front door, where the sizable figure of Sæve was posted. Hamre raised his eyebrows.

Sæve shook his head.

We walked past.

It was past midnight, but because it was summertime it would be darker still in half an hour. The night lay around us like a blue blanket sprinkled with oriental oils. From up on Straumeveien came the whoosh of cars passing, but down here it was so quiet you could hear a hedgehog rustling the papers of its supper under one of the bushes.

On our way down to the gate, I said: 'When we arrived, there was a red car over there.' I pointed. 'Half an hour later, when I came out, it was gone.'

'A red car?' He eyed me sceptically. 'What make was it?'

'I'm not sure. It *might* have been an Opel Kadett.'

'Which model?'

'No idea.'

He looked desperate. 'Well, please keep an eye open for a … You're sure of the colour?'

'Oh, yes.'

We met Isachsen down by the cars. While Hamre was conferring with him, passing on the information about the red car, I looked up at the house we had just left.

An hour and a half ago I had come here in the company of a woman who had been talking about a swimming pool. Now there was a dead body lying on the edge of the self-same pool, and the woman had disappeared.

I looked at the sign hanging on the gate: *THIS DOG BITES*. But there hadn't been a single bite mark on Tor Aslaksen.

'I'm taking Veum with me,' Hamre said behind me.

'Why?' Isachsen asked.

'He knows the lady. He can introduce me.'

I chuckled inside. I had always liked Hamre. More than he had ever liked me. And I would happily introduce him as soon as we could find her.

'Follow my car,' Hamre said, getting behind the wheel of the white BMW.

I got into my old Corolla and kept my eyes glued to his tail-lights. They shone red, like the eyes of a predator on the hunt. And it was me it had spotted.

Above us the sky drew the night in like blue ink to blotting paper. Ahead of us Bergen lay like glowing embers at the bottom of an ash pan, drawn from the mountains around the town.

I switched off the radio and drove in silence. I had more than enough to occupy my mind.

5

Lisbeth Finslo lived in Kirkegate, which stretches from Sandviken church to Formannsvei. At the lower end of the street was Sandviken school, which was due to be demolished. Her address was a house at the upper end, a line of rendered, three-storey houses.

We got out of our cars. Now night was at its darkest. The air was heavy with pollen, and above us the sky had broken out in a rash of stars.

One of the season's first cruise ships was moored on Skoltegrunn quay, illuminated like a floating brothel. An ocean-going yacht with three lanterns lit slipped into Byfjord, as cautiously as if it were approaching enemy territory.

From the short cut between Ekrengate and Kirkegate, which the locals called the chicken run, came a middle-aged man wearing a long jacket over a bare chest, Bermudas and white trainers. As soon as he spotted Hamre's white BMW he about-turned and quickly swayed back the way he had come. *He* was definitely one of the locals.

Hamre eyed him sourly. 'The Turkey's into its summer moult.'

I grinned.

'Do you know why they call him the Turkey?'

I said 'no' to allow him the pleasure of telling me.

'Because after he's had a few the most you can get out of him is "gobble, gobble, gobble".'

'I've heard a different story.'

'Oh, yes?'

'He won a turkey once, just before Christmas, in a lottery. In some miraculous way he managed to persuade the shopkeeper who had given him the prize to exchange the turkey for beer. He was the hero of the street for the two hours it took his pals to drink the beer. But the nickname Turkey stuck with him for ever after, like a token of respect.'

Hamre glared at me.

'Gobble, gobble, gobble,' I said, shaking my head.

We walked up to the block of flats where Lisbeth lived. It was painted yellow and reminded me of the dusty Easter chicks you see in shop windows around Whitsun. But the door was green and on one of the nameplates beside the bells we found L. Finslo.

We tried the door. It was locked.

We rang the bell beside her name.

No reaction.

'I've never known the bells in these places to work,' I said.

Hamre examined the nameplate. 'First floor, you reckon?'

I looked at the bell. 'It's no more than an hour and a half since she disappeared. She might still be on her way here.'

'How well did you know her, Veum?'

'Not very. You know how it is. You lie face down on a table, breathing through a hole, and you talk about everyday things. What books you read, what films you like to see, what made my neck muscles so tense. She has a daughter. Fifteen years old, if I remember correctly.'

'No husband?'

'She's a widow.'

Hamre sighed. Then he took out an impressive bunch of keys.

He flicked through them, found one and tried the lock. It opened at once.

I said in an ironic tone: 'How *do* you do that?'

He didn't answer, but motioned for me to follow him in.

'What will you say if we meet someone?' I asked.

'Show them our ID.'

'Mine too?'

We went up a floor. Lisbeth Finslo lived on the right. Her door had square, wired-glass windows and flowery curtains on the inside, about as burglar-proof as paper.

We tried this doorbell, too. We could hear it worked, but no one opened up.

I thought of her firm, strong fingers, how they kneaded and massaged my neck muscles until they softened and turned to butter and silk beneath my skin. I thought of her deep-blue eyes and her tanned nose, and felt a sinking feeling in my stomach. It was a feeling I had experienced before. It never presaged anything good.

Taut-lipped, I found it hard to force out the words. 'Surely you have a search warrant, don't you?'

Hamre sent me an amused look. 'You watch too many American films, Veum. This lady might be suffering from shock. It's our *duty* to enter.'

I watched him feel the lock with his finger, then hesitate between two or three keys and decide on one.

It went in, but not round. He coaxed it, without applying much force, muttering to himself.

I glanced at the neighbour's door. Behind the windows, it was quiet and grey, like a rainy July day.

Hamre tried the next key along. It went in – and round.

There was a faint click in the lock.

Hamre opened the door carefully and stepped inside. 'Hello?'

No answer.

I followed him in, and we closed the door behind us as carefully as we had opened it.

We were in a small, narrow hallway, painted in vibrant colours: green on the walls and yellow on the ceiling. A mirror in a red frame hung on the wall inside the door, and under a hat shelf there was a row of women's outdoor clothing. Nothing masculine here as far as we could see.

Three doors led from the hallway. One was half open. Through it we could see a cramped but attractive kitchen, blue and white with gingham curtains by the windows and a blind with an old Bergen motif, partly rolled down. Behind it we looked out onto the yard at the back of the flats and a steep rock face. The kitchen was so clean and tidy it looked as though it had never been used.

On an impulse I went over and opened the fridge. It was empty and smelt of detergent.

Behind me, Hamre said: 'Didn't you say something about her going on holiday, Veum?'

'Yes, I did, but…'

I walked past him into the hallway and across the hall. I opened the door to the sitting room. 'Lisbeth, are you here?'

Not a sound.

The sitting room was as clean and tidy as the kitchen. The few newspapers there were had been placed in a wooden box beside the fireplace. There were no cut flowers in the vases, and the potted plants looked as if they could survive an environmental catastrophe.

The furniture was simple, the tables were recently polished, the books on the shelves didn't have any conspicuous dust on them, and on the lid of the record player you could even sign your name with a finger and not leave a visible mark.

Hamre led us into the next room, which was where she slept.

There was something cool and aesthetic about the large bed

in the middle of the floor, covered with a shimmering, blue silk quilt and two small ornamental cushions of the same material by the bedhead.

The bed was white, like the rest of the furniture: a dresser, a bedside table and two chairs. One wall was occupied by a wardrobe. A picture, conspicuous by its pastel colours, hung in the centre of the other wall. The motif was a group of pink dianthus superbus on a beach washed clean by a pastel-blue sea that had never heard of seaweed or insoluble nitrates.

The only eye-catching item was a book left on the white bedside table. I went over and read the title page. Cora Sandel, a Norwegian artist and writer. Ah, now my image of Lisbeth was clicking into place.

Hamre opened the door to the last room in the flat and we stepped into a new generation.

It was the archetypal teenager's room. Practical furniture in red. Boxes and boxes of magazines and school books. Shelves of books, not stacked neatly, side by side, but on top of each other, in a jumble, without any system and ready to come crashing down if anyone said a word out of turn. A desk, superficially tidy as if to satisfy a mother, but without a plan or any sense of symmetry. On the walls there were posters of last year's teenage idols, partly stuck over one another as fashions changed. The only stars I recognised were Madonna and Tom Cruise, but neither of them was at the front.

The bed showed signs of a maid's hand: light-blue linen so tight that it would have met with an infantry sergeant's approval.

Again, I felt a sinking feeling in my stomach.

The room told me without any possible ambiguity that this was a child who needed her mother for a few seasons yet. Because it was highly improbable she made the bed herself, and Madonna was no substitute.

'All the birds have flown the nest,' Hamre said.

I looked around. 'What do we do now? Wait here?'

'No. We start a search. I'll write a message asking her to contact me when she gets in.'

When, Hamre said.

If, my gut instinct said.

We pulled the door shut as we left.

'Drop by the station early tomorrow, Veum.'

'Any special time?'

'Shall we say ten, so I can clear my desk first?'

Then we got into our respective cars and left Kirkegate in our respective directions, him to the city centre, me up to the Høyden area of town.

6

I unlocked the front door and switched on the hall light. The old folks on the ground floor were in their mountain cabin in Askøy and I was alone in the building.

I opened the post box. It was empty. Then I took the stairs up to the first floor, unlocked my flat, switched off the light behind me and went in.

I hung my jacket up in the hallway, went into the kitchen and opened a litre bottle of Farris, which I carried into the sitting room.

I sat down in the good chair, facing the dead TV screen, poured the mineral water into a glass and looked around.

The same room. The same old furniture, the same books, the same records, the same pictures on the wall. Only one thing had changed. The contents of the glass.

I knocked it back, poured myself another and stood up. I was uneasy.

It had been a hellish six months. From December to April I had walked through a forest of bottles, and there wasn't a tree left standing behind me.

At the beginning I had walked with my head held high. Then my knees had become weaker and weaker, until they gave way and I sprawled onto all fours. In the end I was flowing through the countryside like a river, until a kindly soul finally picked me up, poured me into a vessel and transported me to Hjellestad.

Up there they received me with sober competence and taught me something I had never learned before: basket-weaving.

They had soft chairs and hard benches.

With the psychologist the chair was soft. I learned to sit with my eyes closed, breathing regularly, my shoulders and arms relaxed. The psychologist had a friendly, somewhat melancholy face and grey, combed-back hair. His name was Andersen. We talked calmly about fathers who died too soon, mothers who died too late and lovers you never saw again. We talked about sons who lived with their mothers, with new fathers, and clients who died while in treatment. And while the psychologist smoked his third cigarette in fifteen minutes, we talked about aquavit. We talked about its smell, its taste and its effect, until the bottom of my mouth was as dry as spruce and my fingers were trembling for lack of something to hold. Something small and round containing something wet and potent. And while we talked the psychologist kept an eye on me through the fog of cigarette smoke, made a few sporadic notes, smiled, chuckled and once in a while tousled his hair with a hand, on which the veins protruded like inverted trenches on a battlefield.

With Lisbeth Finslo the bench was hard. At our first meeting she had shaken hands coolly, introduced herself and told me to remove my top clothing. She hadn't been sun-tanned then, in April, and her hair had been darker. I lay down on my stomach and breathed through the hole in the treatment bench, and her fingers explored my spine and neck. I told her when she hurt me, and her strong fingertips prodded my muscles like millipedes on stilts. Now and then she filled in a form, pressing her biro down hard, and then she told me to turn over. While she charted my chest and stomach in the same way, I kept an eye on her from below. Her chin looked strong from this angle, and I could see the down on her top lip and under her ears. Occasionally her gaze met mine, and once she said: 'So you're a real detective, are you?' 'Well, I'm afraid the *real* bit has faded.' Then she gave me a last, friendly thump to the shoulder: 'Let's see if we can get a bit of colour back in you then.' And the session was over.

There were to be a lot more sessions, and my muscles slowly loosened and then bulked up. She started me off with exercises for the back, neck and stomach, and when she heard I had quite a few kilometres behind me on country roads, she invited me to a jog after work. 'You can be the hare,' I smiled. 'Let's keep to the terminology of the clinic and call it the stimulus,' she responded.

We had run to Store Milde Manor and around the arboretum, under trees full of history, with reddish-brown bark, splintering cones and small light-green plaques that informed us of their provenance.

One run soon turned into many. She was in good enough shape to drag me along at first. But as the weeks on the wagon grew and I slowly felt the strength in my legs and torso return, I was in a position to challenge her.

One warm afternoon in the middle of May, while the sun was playing water polo with the waves in Fana fjord, we sat on a rock by the waterside and recovered our breath after an extra-hard training shift. I had put an arm around her shoulder and, after some initial reticence, she had leaned back against my chest in such a way that I could wrap both my arms around her.

There was a moment's silence as her hair tickled my neck. I had to clear my throat to gain control of my voice as I said: 'I've never asked, but are you … married?' She glanced up at me and shook her head. 'I shouldn't be sitting here with one of my clients though.' After a while she added: 'I'm a widow. And I have a daughter, Kari.' 'How old is she?' 'Fifteen.' 'I have a son of sixteen, Thomas. But I'm divorced.' 'Yes, I know. I could tell by your neck,' she laughed.

Her laughter was infectious. I leaned forward and laughed close to her mouth. She smelt of sweet perspiration, and when we stopped laughing, our lips were our own again. Tentatively, I nibbled at her mouth. Her voice came from a long way away: 'I have a boyfriend. A steady boyfriend.' Then she kissed me hard on the lips, almost like a punishment, before turning her head away and freeing herself from my arms. She stood up and brushed the spruce needles from her track suit as she said: 'We'd better get back. It's time I went home.'

Later, I felt that we were able to talk about most things, as though we had known each other for years. At the same time, we knew this relationship would not develop into anything more. We still ran around the arboretum once or twice a week, but I never kissed her again, and now…

Now she was gone.

I drank another glass of mineral water and tried to reconstruct the sequence of events.

We had spoken about my discharge from the clinic, and she had said: 'I think I can help you, with a job.' 'A job?' 'Yes, a kind of watchman…'

And then, during my last treatment session at Hjellestad she had said: 'I have the keys. If you have the time, I can show you around this evening.'

We had met in town and driven up to Kleiva together. In the car we had talked about … her going on holiday, home to Florø, her and her daughter, but not…

What was his name actually, this boyfriend of hers?

Apart from on that one occasion, she had never spoken about him.

Could that be where she was? With him?

I stared at the telephone. Should I call Hamre, set him on her trail, or...?

No. All of a sudden, I was tired, dog-tired, so tired that the little scar on my forearm was tingling.

I stroked it with a finger.

A few days before I was discharged from Hjellestad the consultant had called me into his office. He was a youthful-looking, dark-haired man with a cordial nature, so much so that you accepted it as part of his profession.

He had leaned across his desk and spoken to me in confidence, as though someone might hear us from behind the sound-insulated doors. 'We've discussed your case in great detail, Veum. You aren't a ... how shall I phrase it? ... a physiological alcoholic. By which, I mean you don't belong to the type who can't touch a drop of alcohol without relapsing into the bad old ways. Nor do we think you are an uncontrolled binge drinker. Your problem is more that you've got used to having a wee dram, all of the time, so often that alcohol has become a perfectly natural ingredient in your life, like Norwegian brown cheese and sheep sausage are to the rest of us. So natural that when you had your traumatic experience earlier this year – an experience I hope your dialogue with Andersen has clarified – that was all you had to lean on. And then it all became too much. Much too much.'

I had nodded and he had continued: 'An important factor in your trauma, if I may call it such, is of course, if you don't mind me saying so, your loneliness.' He paused for a second before going on: 'But we've also observed your ... errmm ... ability to establish bonds of friendship with ... um ... women ... One woman,' he added as though I didn't understand what he was referring to. 'And what you most need in your life, Veum, is exactly that. A stable relationship.' Oh, tell me something I don't know. 'As far as the other problem is concerned, I'd recommend total abstinence for six more months so that by the end of the year you can look back on … well, in fact a whole human gestation period without alcohol.' I could hear the biting sarcasm in my voice as I answered: 'And out of this gestation period a new Veum shall be born?'

He had nodded seriously and carried on: 'To help you through this period we can offer you – well, in fact, we'd recommend it – to have a dose of Antabuse implanted under your skin. That will spare you any decision-making, and it's also a guarantee, both for you and for us, of you keeping, er, our contract.'

I had thought about the bottle I kept in the lowest drawer of my office desk, awaiting my return. I had thought about the bottle gathering dust in my kitchen cabinet and reflecting on the golden days of yore. And I had thought that perhaps it wasn't so stupid what the consultant had said. Not having to make a decision for the next six months was also a decision, now, *then*; and I had taken it.

Afterwards I had felt like a chemical process, unstoppable once it had started; and the scar had become an integral part of me, adapted to my new life, the ticket for the rest of the journey.

I drained the last glass, screwed the top on the Farris bottle, carried it back into the kitchen and went into my bedroom.

I opened the window a fraction to let in the town and the night outside. Distant car horns, the sporadic revving of powerful engines and the whine of tyres as they spun round told me that not everything was dead out there. Not everyone was dead. Only some people.

Then I lay down, in a bed as cold as an ice floe and as deserted as an islet in the Barents Sea, where the fish quotas had been reduced for the next ten years.

7

The police station in Bergen, which is still called 'new' by people of my age and older, was finished in 1965, when police officials tucked their well-used typewriters under their arms and lumbered across the street from the old greyish-green station, soon to be razed to the ground and replaced by a sterile, modern, new Folkets Hus, for the labour movement, with a typical-of-the-period fur shop in the basement; what a convenient arrangement this was for shop stewards in the 1960s. After discussing which polish they preferred for their cars and how large their first mortgage on the house was, they could go down two floors and buy the wife a fur she could wear to her Saturday coffee and cakes that week. And if there were any dubious elements in the ranks they could stroll across the street and discuss their life stories with a chummy officer in the Police Security Service.

Now, a good twenty years later, the police station was already too small. A number of departments had been moved out to rooms in the blocks around Rådstuplass and the old *Morgenavisen* newspaper premises in Allehelgensgate. There were also plans to extend south, onto the site of the former employment agency, which had been moved to the other side of Lille Lungegårdsvann lake, where it was closer to the nearest vinmonopol.

But Jakob E. Hamre was still based in the 'new' building, in an office with tired corners and fraying linoleum, because he was employed by a government department where extra funding was found for new computer equipment and manpower, and the sums earmarked for maintenance were used to seal leaks in the flat roof an architect, probably from the other side of the country, had laid on top of this new-build in Norway's notoriously rainiest town.

But it wasn't raining today. The streets were dry, the sun hung over the town like a magnifying glass, and even at this early hour Hamre had had to open the window to the noise of the traffic and the polluted air. It seemed fresh, but it was not.

When I knocked on the door frame and peeped in through the half-open door he was sitting behind tidy piles of paper, like the loan officer in an average-sized bank that did little more exciting than offer reasonable loans for the purchase of agricultural machinery. He had hung his jacket on the back of the chair and was wearing a short-sleeved shirt with thin blue stripes. His royal-blue tie hung loose.

He beckoned me in and motioned for me to take a seat on one of the free client chairs facing the desk. Then he ran a hand over his regular features and said: 'Right. Sleep well, Veum?'

'Not particularly.'

'And you haven't heard from Lisbeth Finslo…'

I shook my head and watched him expectantly.

'…either?'

'Ah, you haven't, either, then.'

He took a sheet of paper from one pile. 'No. But we've spoken to her sister. She lives in Florø, and Lisbeth's daughter's there. She travelled up a couple of days ago and they were expecting Lisbeth later today. On the express boat.'

'Morning or afternoon one?'

'They weren't sure. But there was one thing I was wondering. When we went through her flat last night, we didn't find a packed suitcase, and you didn't mention her having any baggage with her when you went to Kleiva.'

'She could, of course, have been intending to pack today.'

'But the flat: everything was tidy and ready for departure. I'm pretty sure we should've found a partly packed suitcase there too.'

'You may be right. Have you contacted the Fylkesbaatene ticket office?'

'Yes, she hasn't reserved a seat.'

'And have you tracked down the red car I saw?'

'The one that *might* be an Opel Kadett? No, we haven't.'

'Makes of cars have never been my strong suit, Hamre.'

'It should be in your … erm … profession.'

'I never did any training, like you. What about this Aslaksen? Do you know any more about him?'

He grimaced. 'Do you, Veum?'

I inclined my head. 'If I had, I would've told you yesterday. I'd never seen him before, and I didn't know his name until you read it out from his driving licence. Tor Aslaksen, wasn't it?'

He nodded and took another piece of paper from a pile. 'Engineer. Lives alone.' He glanced up. '"Bachelor" sounds a bit old-fashioned, don't you think? Flat in Fyllingsdalen, employed by a company called Norlon, which…' with a caustic smile he pushed a folded newspaper across the desk to me '…has recently caught the interest of the media.'

I kept my eyes trained on him as I took the newspaper and said: 'Oh, yes?'

He gestured with one hand. 'Read it for yourself.'

I unfolded the newspaper. The company hadn't simply grabbed the media's attention. It was on the front page.

The headline read: 'Environmental Protest in Hilleren'. A large photo showed angry protesters shouting at what looked like a concrete mixer and a large gate, while a few police officers were trying to calm the situation. The caption read: 'Police had to be called when eco-protesters and workers became involved in fights in front of the main gates to A/S Norlon in Hilleren yesterday morning.' There was a link to a full spread on page five.

I flicked through to it. The headings were enough to grasp the gist: 'Clash' – 'Toxic Leak?' – 'Boycott' – 'No Surrender'. Between the headings I worked out that A/S Norlon was producing synthetic polyacrylic fibres from acrylonitrile, formed by combining acetyl with hydrogen cyanide, patented and known as Norlon, which was used to make textiles, furniture material and furnishings, here in Norway and abroad. It was well known that the company had had problems with the safe storage and disposal of toxic waste, and it was when a group of Greenearth activists arrived for an 'unannounced inspection' at the site that the clash erupted.

'The last section is particularly interesting,' Hamre said.

I read: 'From the company side questions have been raised regarding the fact that the so-called "environmental delegation" appeared exactly ten minutes before a vacuum tanker with problematic waste was about to leave the site. There is a suggestion that the cause for this clash could be a deliberate leak from within the company.'

'Do you think that ... Aslaksen...? There's talk of a clash, right enough, but surely not with a fatal outcome.'

Hamre shrugged. 'I doubt I was the first to suggest we'd see casualties at these clashes here in Norway, too. After all, environmental pollution *really* is an issue of life or death, isn't it, for all of us.'

'Absolutely. But nevertheless...'

'There's another interesting angle to all this. The current owner of A/S Norlon – and its business director – is a young man called ... Trygve Schrøder-Olsen.' He let this information sink in before continuing: 'Does that name ring any bells?'

It did, in the distant past. 'Schrøder-Olsen ... Isn't he the one who...? But his name's not...'

'No, but you're on the right track.' He leaned forward, put his finger on the indistinct faces in the newspaper photograph and said: '*Odin* Schrøder-Olsen is his brother and is a leading spokesman for the ecology movement in this region, if not the whole country.'

'But then he's probably the one who leaked...'

'Not necessarily. Everyone at the works must know who he is, so surely they'd take care not to tell him anything. But the connection is clear, and if just one compliant individual inside the company was sympathetic to the environmentalists' case, then…' He shrugged.

'I still don't think that's a strong enough reason to take someone's life.'

'Look at it from the other side, Veum. From that angle, it's not about the environment or environmental protection. It's about money. And people have been killed for money before.'

'You don't need to tell me that.'

'Well, I was thinking that as you don't have any professional qualifications…' He smiled disarmingly.

'This Aslaksen; what did he do?'

'As far as we've been able to ascertain in the little time we've had, he's a mechanical engineer; he's partly responsible for production, and he's in charge of the maintenance and replacement of machinery.'

'Quite high up, in other words?'

'Sort of. A subordinate director, that kind of thing. I'm not completely clear on the organisation's structure.' Then he added mischievously, 'But he's quite high up in other ways too.'

'What do you mean?'

'Privately. He's a member of Bergen Flying Club and he's a skydiver.'

'He's made his last jump now.'

'And with a fatal outcome, unfortunately.'

'What about the Nielsens? Have you managed to get hold of them?'

Hamre coughed and shuffled a piece of paper. 'First of all, another matter, Veum.' He leaned back in his chair, rolled a yellow pencil between his hands and studied me over the top of the pencil. 'When we talked last night you said the relationship between you and Lisbeth Finslo was … You used the word "professional".'

'Yes? Client and therapist.'

'And you stand by that?'

'Yes, we…'

'Yes?' He gave a little cough.

I didn't answer.

He waited. Then he said: 'You see, it's been suggested there was perhaps … a little more. That in fact you're a little closer than you've said.'

'Oh, yes? And who suggested that?'

He smiled gently and studied me with his alert, light-blue eyes.

'Well, they're not completely wrong. I will concede a kind of … friendship grew between us. In the course of a few runs. But nothing else. We weren't even close to anything else, Hamre.'

He arched his eyebrows and inclined his head slightly to one side, as if to say: 'Oh, no?'

'And I definitely don't see what it has to do with this case.'

'She's gone missing, Veum. Surely I don't need to remind you of that.'

'She could be sitting on the boat to Florø this very minute, Hamre.'

'If so, that would be quite foolish of her. Without contacting us first, I mean.'

'And it's Aslaksen who died. Neither Lisb— … Anyway, I didn't know him at all.'

'No, but she might've known him, isn't that true? Do you remember what she said to you when she found him? "I had no idea – I didn't understand" … Don't you agree it's important for us to talk to her?'

I nodded wearily. 'I can help you … search…'

Hamre regarded me with a chilly expression. 'The best help

you can give us, Veum, is to keep your nose out of this. Don't say anything, don't do anything, until the case has been closed. Is that clear?'

'Message received.'

'And I can confirm that we've spoken to the architects. They've never heard of Aslaksen either, they said. They hadn't even heard of you.'

'Strange.'

'But they *had* heard of Lisbeth Finslo.'

'For a moment you actually had me worried there.'

'They were able to confirm everything she'd told you. And they said if Lisbeth Finslo considered you reliable enough to look after the house, then that was fine by them.'

'I suppose they're coming home, are they?'

Hamre gave a resigned nod. 'They'll have to. They have to go through the house in case anything's missing. Any valuables, I mean.'

'A stuffed goldcrest?'

'That sort of thing.'

'But there were no signs of a break-in, were there?'

'No. Even the side door that led directly into the swimming pool showed no signs of forced entry.'

As I got up, he said: 'So we agree then, Veum, do we? Complete understanding?'

'Just ring if you need any further help,' I said drily, with a brief goodbye nod.

Outside the police station I made my way to the nearest kiosk and bought all the newspapers I could get my hands on, to read more about the clash at A/S Norlon in Hilleren.

8

I let myself into the waiting room and went through to my office. It was like returning home after a long holiday. There was a thin coating of dust everywhere as if there had been an explosion in a nearby flour silo and I had been one of the lucky recipients.

I blew the dust from the calendar before changing it to the right month. At least it was showing the right year, which was a distinct improvement on the previous year.

I lifted the telephone receiver and listened to see if there was a dial tone. There was. It had barely noticed I had been gone.

I checked the answer-machine counter. It hadn't moved a millimetre. This must be the only place in the universe where time stands still.

I opened the lowest desk drawer on the left. The bottle inside was empty.

I held it in the air to make sure there wasn't a drop left. I had the feeling I was staring at a photograph of a long-departed ex-lover, with a mixture of melancholy and distance. Then I dropped the bottle into the half-full wastepaper basket. The cleaning lady could take it with her when she came on her annual visit, between Christmas and New Year.

I opened the window. Summer rushed in like a tidal wave, and for a few seconds everything seemed to be floating. A gentle gust of air lifted the dust, only to settle it back down again, over everything, like a slightly messy bridal veil.

It was going to be an unusually hot day. Down in the market-place shoppers had already rolled up their sleeves. Summer-casual women, with Hardanger apples under their blouses, bobbed across the tarmac; the smoked salmon had the indecent hue of racy underwear; and on the vegetable stall the season's first leeks bristled with hormones.

Japanese tourists were out in force, with glasses like telephoto lenses and the continuous whir of video cameras, and over by the railing facing Vågen Bay the day's first shrimps were being peeled slowly before the salty delicacies disappeared between hungry lips. Summer tramped through Bergen's streets like an invisible parade, to the blast of horns from arriving tourist boats. Motorists braked to let pedestrians cross the road, and people sent sudden smiles to total strangers without expecting anything in return. But the air that slowly filled my office was replete with exhaust fumes.

I left the window ajar, sat down behind my desk and read through everything about the conflict at A/S Norlon.

New clashes were expected today, and the police were keeping abreast of developments in the stand-off. At the bottom of one column the company's history was given in brief outline, from its formation in 1949 with the old Milorg resistance fighter, Harald Schrøder-Olsen, at the helm – the father of the present director. He stayed there until his son took over in the autumn of 1979.

Another newspaper commented that Harald Schrøder-Olsen's youngest son, Odin, who would normally be at the forefront of such protests, had stayed discreetly in the background this time, doubtless for family reasons. Odin Schrøder-Olsen had refused to make any kind of comment on the protest and referred everyone who asked to the movement's leader, Håvard Hope.

Hope said that the environmental group Greenearth had selected A/S Norlon as this month's example of a local company that was damaging the environment. He regretted that the confrontation had been so dramatic, but emphasised that this was caused solely by the management's lack of desire for dialogue. He vowed that Greenearth would continue their action until they received a binding promise to deal with the toxic waste more responsibly.

In a leader article, Greenearth was described as one of the more unconventional sectors of the environmental movement. One of the local branch's projects was to build a one-hundred-per cent ecological housing estate at Breistein in Åsane, using exclusively environmentally friendly products and materials, and to be launched under the name Ecoville. The movement was non-party-political and its name had been linked with a number of environmental campaigns and demonstrations in Bergen and Hordaland over the last few years.

I put the newspapers aside. What had this to do with me? I had found a man, dead, in a swimming pool, and this man had worked for A/S Norlon. So what? Had Tor Aslaksen been checking out the Nielsens' house, to see if the swimming pool could be used for the temporary storage of toxic waste? Or was he longing for the fresh air offered by the protected Norwegian countryside as a relief from all the synthetic substances he worked with every day? And, if so, did he prefer the indoor environment in Kleiva to the view from Løvstakken or Lyderhorn, two of the seven mountains around Bergen. But how did he get in if there were no signs of a break-in? And, since the architects had never heard his name before, had he chosen the house at random?

I could have carried on asking myself such questions until eternity, but I had no grounds to ask them, nor any answers, as yet.

Lisbeth Finslo, on the other hand, did have something to do with me. Enough for me to call my old friend at the national registration office, Karin Bjørge, and convince her that I really was back in the saddle.

'That's good to hear, Varg. Is there anything I can do for you?'

I could hear from her intonation that she was expecting a slightly more original answer than the old refrain: 'Erm, there's a name I wonder if you could check out for me.'

Her tone sank as she said: 'And what was the name this time?'

'A woman. Lisbeth Finslo. But actually I'm more interested in her sister…'

'Oh, yes?'

'Who lives in Florø.'

'Is she younger then?'

'I don't actually know. I don't even know if she's called Finslo, but I was thinking that if you spoke to the registration office up there…'

'…It would be easier than if you did it?'

'Mm.'

'I can hear you're well again, Varg.'

'I haven't forgotten who I can thank for that.'

There was silence for a moment. Then she said: 'Oh, when I think of all the things you've done for us, then … Who is this Lisbeth Finslo?'

'She's a physio up at Hjellestad Clinic. And now she's gone missing, or perhaps she's on her way home to her sister's in Florø.' I gave her the little information I had about her: her address in Sandviken and her fifteen-year-old daughter.

'I suppose there's no point asking *why* you're interested in her?'

'It's a long story, Karin. Perhaps we could discuss it over dinner?'

'And when will that be? This side of 2000?'

'What about tomorrow? Unless you're busy.'

'Well, that's a Saturday, as you know. And, no, in fact I'm not.'

'Deal?'

'Wait until I ring you back and see whether I deserve it.'

'Unless I'm much mistaken, I owe you many times over.'

'Well, let's decide on the details later, alright?'

'OK.' But 'later' is like a migratory bird, I told myself, after putting down the phone. You never know exactly when it will come back.

Without giving the dinner date any more thought, I picked up the directory and started to flick through, at first aimlessly, afterwards more systematically.

I looked up Tor Aslaksen, in the safe knowledge that people die more slowly in telephone directories than in most other places. Many survive for a great many editions. His address was in Dag Hammarskjöldsvei, but I didn't dial his number. I heard Lisbeth's voice as she exclaimed: 'He's dead, Varg. Dead! I had no idea. I didn't understand.'

She must have known him. Wouldn't she have expressed herself differently otherwise? 'There's a dead man down here, Varg. Who could it be?'

And then, when I went back up, she had gone, as if gripped not by an impulse, not by shock, but a bad conscience?

Because she had always known that he would be lying there and couldn't continue the sham any longer?

No. Then she wouldn't have said, 'I had no idea. I didn't understand.'

But she must have known something, and she must have had an idea about something. Perhaps she hadn't expected to find him dead, but…

The telephone rang. It was Karin Bjørge.

She got straight to the point: 'Finslo was her maiden name, Varg. And she has a sister in Florø called Jannicke, who has also kept her maiden name. Practical, eh?'

'Very. I feel like I've been transported to Iceland, where people are registered by their first names, both men and women.'

'Have you got something to write with?'

'Just a mo.' I grabbed a notepad and biro. 'OK.'

She read out an address and a telephone number. Then we discussed when to meet the next day.

'I'll pick you up at the bus stop,' I said.

'Pick me up? That sounds slightly improper.'

'Then let's *do* something improper for once.'

'You sound alarmingly well, Varg.'

I glanced down at my scar. 'If only you knew how well my forearm feels.'

'Your forearm?'

'I'll show you when we meet. Bye.'

'Bye.'

I rang off. Yes, I did feel better. All I needed now was the courage to flirt with her face to face as well.

I mused on that before ringing Lisbeth Finslo's sister.

She picked up the phone on the first ring. 'Jannicke here.'

'Jannicke Finslo?'

'Yes, who am I talking to?'

'Varg Veum. I'm calling from Bergen.'

'Uhuh.'

'It's about your sister, Lisbeth.'

'Uhuh.' Now it sounded like an anxious sigh, an expectation that she was going to hear bad news.

We both waited for a reaction, and when we spoke again, we collided in the middle.

'Is there any—?'

'Has she arrived—?'

'...news?'

'...yet?' And then we answered in unison: 'No.'

I took the initiative. 'So, you haven't heard from her, either?'

'No, and we're dreadfully worried, after the police rang, and...'

'What was the arrangement you made?'

'She would come today on the express boat.'

'Which one? Morning or afternoon?'

'She always catches the first one. But she *may*'ve been held up, of course. If the police hadn't rung, I ... Who are *you* by the way? You're not the police, I take it. Are you the guy ... she's with?'

'No.' I almost said *unfortunately*. 'I'm … She fixed me up with a job, to take care of a house, and was showing me round…'

'And then she didn't turn up?'

'No, she did, but things *happened* there. I can't tell you too much. And then she went missing. She did have a boyfriend then?'

'Yes, I think so.'

'Only *think*?'

'We didn't talk much about that sort of thing. Besides, it was quite new, I believe.'

'Her daughter must've known though, mustn't she?'

'Kari? I don't think so … She doesn't know much. Lisbeth's always been shy about … such matters. She doesn't really open up about them. Not as far as I know, at any rate. And Kari's adopted, you know. And she was closer to Erik than Lisbeth.'

'Erik?'

'Erik Larsen, Lisbeth's husband. He was killed in a car accident in 1982. He drove into the fjord, by Solheim.' Her voice broke. 'It was terrible.'

'Mmm. I didn't know.'

'No, she never talks about that, either. That was when she left for the bright lights. To get away.'

'I see. Listen … I'll ring back this evening to find out if she's come on the afternoon boat. Is that OK?'

'Yes, of course.'

I jotted down the names of Lisbeth Finslo's daughter and late husband. Then I wrote the year 1982 and circled it. I had no reason to do it, but sudden deaths have always seemed like a warning triangle to me. I drive past them slowly and keep my eyes peeled.

I tried to imagine the stretch of road alongside Solheim fjord, between Naustdal and Florø. There were many places where you could easily veer over the edge, if it was late at night or the road surface was slippery or you were speeding to get home quickly.

Erik Larsen.

What had he looked like? A woman like Lisbeth Finslo had probably got herself a young-looking husband with a rakish haircut, long, athletic limbs and a loose tie around his neck. A county administrator, or perhaps a doctor, on his way home from a meeting in Førde, driving along a road he knew so well he could have done it blindfold.

And what had he looked like afterwards? When they had fished him out of the fjord?

She should have told me about it. It sounded like she should have talked more in general, about herself and her life. But perhaps that was why she had cleared off – fleeing again from life's brutal realities and yet another sudden death.

I jotted down another name on my notepad, as if there were some connection: *Tor Aslaksen.*

After which I decided to drive out to Hilleren. No one could deny me the right to be inquisitive.

9

Down by the sea, Norlon was like a castle under a siege.

I had followed the main road around Mathopen to the naval base at Haakonsvern, where the NATO submarines lay like slumbering killer whales in their lairs, needing only a sniff of waste oil to mobilise in defence of their land.

The stretch from Mathopen to Kjøkkelvik had been one of Bergen's most popular recreational areas until late in the 1970s, with cabins and boathouses spread in a wide fan around the region's natural counterpoint, Alvøen Manor and the paper factory. Now Bergen had spread its tentacles out here and dragged a trail of concrete buildings with it, along an arterial thoroughfare that was much too narrow to cope with the pressure. On the cliffs the cabins had been replaced by palatial houses, built and occupied by the maharajahs of Mongstad and sheiks of Sture: the oil era's new aristocracy. Personally, I couldn't have afforded to move into even their post boxes.

A big sign for A/S NORLON INDUSTRIES pointed downward and to the left. I indicated and followed the road until I spotted the police vehicle parked by the turn-off. A uniformed officer directed me onto the opposite side of the road, carefully looked both ways and crossed with a polite salute to his cap, then leaned into my open window.

'I'm afraid the entrance to Norlon is closed. Have you got an appointment?'

I looked up at him. He was dark-haired and had a well-groomed little moustache. He resembled a country-and-western singer from Sotra, ready for a photo shoot for the next record cover. Obviously, he had no idea who I was.

I cleared my throat. 'I just wanted to pop into the admin office. Is it impossible to get in?'

'Not if you're on foot. If you have an appointment, that is.' He examined my car suspiciously. 'I assume you're not from the press?'

'No, no.' I put on a disarming smile.

'Because they're not letting any media people in.' He pointed further down the road. 'You can park over there by the Co-op.' Then he straightened up and crossed the road again.

I followed his directions, locked my car and strolled back to take a closer look at the scene.

A/S Norlon was surrounded by a high mesh fence topped with barbed wire. Inside, the factory formed a horseshoe shape around a large, newly tarmacked yard. The three-storey buildings were yellow, the pitched roofs covered with bituminous felt. Behind the factory was the stretch of water known as Vatlestraumen, that carried boats to Bergen. In the middle of the yard stood a large, dark-green vacuum tanker, like some military monster, an overgrown insect. Outside the fence grew birches and aspen trees with dense, green foliage and, above all this, small birds flew around blithely, as though nothing had changed since the dawn of time.

The main gate was closed. Next to the side gate, for pedestrians, stood two police officers and a company guard. In front of the main gate, at an angle to the entrance, there were around twenty demonstrators, all shackled together with chains and padlocks. A further forty or fifty of them were close at hand, ready to take over. Along the road, and up the slope above the factory, tents had been erected, as though the demonstrators were prepared for a long campaign. The whole area was swarming with press and media; there was enough equipment to cover Doomsday. They were all here, from the national broadcasting company, NRK, to local television; from the big national newspapers to the local *Loddefjord Menighetsblad*. Once again, I felt transported to a medieval siege, the attackers a youthful gathering of vagabonds, most of whom would have still been in pre-school during the Battle of Mardøla, the famous uprising against hydro power in 1970.

This was a new generation of activists. For someone who had followed the development of political demonstrations, from the first anti-nuclear weapons marches in the late 1950s, when most demonstrators wore ties, even if with brightly coloured shirts, and the women among them were still *dressed* as women, through the 1960s Vietnam rallies, attended by pale, increasingly long-haired, bearded students in jumpers and cords, to the 1970s *No to the EEC* and the standard-of-living protests, when the pseudo-working class wore jeans and blue gabardine jackets zipped up to the neck, this was a new sartorial collection. The 1980s environmental activists were short-haired and healthy and gave the impression they had just come down from the high-mountain

plateaus, wearing green anoraks, blue parkas lined with yellow artificial fur, military pants with big pockets and high, fur-lined
mountain boots, even though it was the middle of the summer.

A man in his early thirties, conspicuously pale with straight
fair hair, was holding an improvised press conference for the
media vultures. He was distinct from the others in that he wore
shiny, grey Terylene trousers, a white shirt and a tie. I recognised
him from the newspapers: Håvard Hope.

His voice was as wan as the colour of his skin, but what he
said was clear enough: 'It's documented that these toxins, unless
they're stored responsibly, spread from normal waste sites into
nature. Even a layman knows how dangerous hydrogen cyanide
is. Yet for years A/S Norlon has been dumping this poison, first
into the sea, later down a well in this area, and even later into hi-
therto unknown, but definitely not officially approved, waste
sites. It's typical of this company's guilt-ridden management that
they always transport this waste at unsociable hours, late at night
or very early in the morning...'

'Don't you think that's simply the most practical time to do
it, bearing in mind normal operation hours?' one of the journalists asked.

Håvard Hope fixed his gaze on him and answered: 'No. It's a
fact that only very few, highly trusted employees know about this
activity. No one has questioned it and no one's asked where the
waste is taken after it's removed from Norlon's premises. But
today, with the public's ever-increasing awareness of our environment, I feel sure that before very long we'll have the whole of the
workforce behind us.'

'It doesn't seem so – today,' said another journalist, to general
merriment.

Håvard Hope smiled gravely. 'No, perhaps not. But wait and
see. Come back in a month's time and ask me the same question
then.'

'So, you're intending to maintain the pressure for that long?'

'We'll keep going until we've reached an acceptable solution, if it takes a month or even a whole year. First, the directors at Norlon have to agree to have a dialogue. Afterwards we can start talking about dates.'

A murmur ran through the assembled media circus. Some people pointed up the slope, and the photographers moved quickly away from Håvard Hope.

I followed their eyes. A tall, slim, dark-haired man with round glasses was standing in front of a small green tent and had crossed his arms like an American Indian meditating. He was wearing jeans, a dark-brown, tight-fitting leather jacket and white trainers. Like Håvard Hope, he had quite a different and a much more urbane appearance than most of the other demonstrators. Even though I hadn't caught his name, I knew who it was.

As the focus turned to Odin Schrøder-Olsen, only Håvard Hope and I were left behind; him like a fading theatre poster, me like a ticket-dodging spectator.

I looked across the deserted road and met his gaze. It was closed and inscrutable, but the expression on his face told me that he was unlikely to belong to Odin Schrøder-Olsen's innermost circle of friends.

10

I left the media and Håvard Hope, plus his spurned oratory, to their own devices and strolled down to the gate. I gave the 'chain gang' a wide berth and was pursued, every single centimetre of the way, by suspicious stares. But no one voiced their displeasure.

The two police officers watched me with polite interest. It struck me, as if in a sudden acceptance of my age, that they didn't assume I was one of the demonstrators, which would not have been the case ten years ago. To them I was now more like a shabby sales rep with far too many drab hotel rooms behind me.

The man representing the company wore a kind of guard's uniform, blueish-black in colour, police state in design, with a red badge sewn on his right breast pocket displaying the company logo. He was bareheaded with thinning, combed-back hair and a nose that had stewed for too long before someone had stitched it back together with red thread. With the brusque tone of a seasoned guard, he growled: 'Got an appointment?'

'No. I'd like to talk to the personnel manager.'

'Personnel manager? We don't have anything like that here. An office manager maybe? Ulrichsen.'

I nodded. 'Possibly. Ulrichsen then.'

'What's it about?'

I lowered my voice. 'I'd prefer to talk about that with Ulrichsen, face to face.'

'Hm. I'll see if he's free. But as you will appreciate…' He cast an eloquent look at the chain gang and it didn't come back. 'It's pretty hectic here at the moment. Have you ever seen the like of it? Chimps.'

He didn't wait for an answer, but poked an arm through the open window of the small, grey hut, grabbed a push-button telephone and pressed two digits. 'Ulrichsen? There's a man here who'd like to talk to you. No, he didn't say expressly to you. No, I don't think so. Just a moment.' He looked at me and gestured with his eyes. 'What was your name?'

A large passenger plane passed over us, heading towards Flesland airport. I half turned from the two police officers, as though watching the plane. 'Veum,' I said quickly.

'Veum?' he queried, and turned back to the telephone. 'Veum.'

I glanced at the two officers. Neither had reacted. And there was me thinking my name was on everyone's lips at their morning meetings.

The guard nodded into the receiver, as though Ulrichsen could follow him on a monitor. 'Alright, I'll send him up.' He opened the gate for me and let me through. 'He's only got five minutes for you.'

'Thank you. Where will I find him?'

He pointed to a brown door in the centre of a side wall. 'On the first floor. There's a sign saying *Office*.'

I crossed the lawn. Right behind the vacuum tanker I passed a rusty lid over a well. To the right, just inside the gate, there were a handful of reserved parking bays, all unoccupied today; no surprises there.

Before entering I cast a look back. The industrial complex was idyllically situated, set in a natural opening in the rock that must once have been a harbour or a bathing beach. From here I didn't have a view of the sea, but the smell of sea water reached me, like the stench from a recently opened freezer containing untreated animal cadavers.

I was in an old-fashioned stairwell with brown wooden panels on the lower part of the wall, light yellow plaster above. To the left, there was a door with a ridged-glass pane, on which was written *PRODUCTION – LABORATORY*.

I followed the stairs up to the first floor. Old photographs hung on the walls, showing the area before the concern was built, during the construction phase and, at the top, the finished result, which was celebrated with pomp and circumstance, and school-children waving Norwegian flags, as if it were Independence Day. Facing the yard, running the height of the stairwell, was a tall, narrow window. Like a newspaper column, it gave me a view of the spectacle by the main gate, where the chain gang had stood up and was chanting slogans over the fence. I could hear 'No to poison! Down with Norlon!' faintly through the glass.

I opened the office door. Two ladies inside looked up in fear, as if expecting a guerrilla attack from the activists.

I smiled reassuringly. 'Excuse me, but is this where I might find herr Ulrichsen?'

The older of the two ladies nodded to the younger one, who got up and crossed the office to a clear glass door. She knocked, pushed open the door and said something. Then she motioned to me and said I could go in.

I smiled at her as she passed. She gave off a scent of lily of the valley and was cool and fair, like the essence of early summer. Her colleague was more buttoned-up, like an early autumn day with a nip of frost in the air. In a way, this created a kind of balance.

Ulrichsen was one of those people you deposit in a suitable office in their early youth, close the door and never see again. They live in an aura of dust and paper, never let life in through the window, drink black coffee and puff on unfiltered cigarettes until they are smoked inside and out. If they should ever raise their voices, it is because they are speaking on a bad telephone line and, behind them, they leave nothing apart from a set of routines their successors, if they have any, would drop after a minute or two. But they don't have any. They sit there until eternity and survive us all.

Ulrichsen was dressed in a neat grey suit, the previous decade's model. He had pale fingers with bitten-down nails and a face you could have divided into accountancy columns: debit in his eyes and a stroke-of-the-pen smile, like a swift signature under the year's accounts for the chairman of the board.

He had no time for pleasantries. 'Your name's Veum? And this is about?'

I breathed in. 'Tor Aslaksen.'

He looked at me as though I were an unvetted supplement to the statement of accounts. 'He isn't here … today.'

'No, I—'

'And he won't be here tomorrow either.'

'No, but I—'

'He has simply, if I might express myself in this way, *stopped*.' I could sense a kind of triumph in his eyes as if he wanted to say: *That's another item concluded, another expense removed.*

'I know. I even know *why* he's stopped. Not to mention the how of it. What I wanted to know was ... did he have any family?'

'He wasn't married.'

'OK. Parents?'

Ulrichsen impatiently shifted a file. 'If this is about the insurance, I'm sure the names of the relatives have been entered here.'

'I'm sure they have. This isn't about insurance. Erm ... The thing is Aslaksen sold me his car a couple of days ago.'

'So?'

'And a third of the payment is still outstanding ... You see, I had to sell my own car first. Even if he – well, you know – I would of course like to settle up ... with his relatives.'

'Hmmm.' Ulrichsen sent me a disapproving glare, as if he considered this the summit of irresponsible housekeeping.

He got to his feet and went over to a filing cabinet, opened one of the drawers and flicked through to a file. 'I have his details here. There should be ... Ah, I have only his mother, Anne-Marie Aslaksen. She lives in Store Milde, in Mildeveien.' He gave me the house number and slotted the file back in the drawer.

As though he had heard someone shout, he suddenly looked out of the window. From here we could see straight out to the road and right across the sound to Bjorøy and Sotra. The sun was making the water glitter like white, hand-beaten metal. A yacht was coming from Kobbeleia with its sails set, so white they could have been made of paper, unfurled by a nimble-fingered giant. A sudden veil of sadness crossed the office manager's face, as when an imprisoned lifer hears the sound of children playing outside the bars of his cell. 'It must've been a shock for Odin. And in the middle of all this.'

'Odin?' I said cautiously.

He withdrew his eyes from the sea, packed up the five minutes he had given me in a folder, tied some string around it in a tight knot and resumed his position behind the desk. 'Odin Schrøder-Olsen. He and Tor Aslaksen were school friends. They'd known each other for most of their lives.'

That was all he said. But grammatically he was spot on. 'Had known' was the correct tense.

11

The guard with the spider-vein conk let me through the gate. The two officers stood with their hands behind their backs, looking bored. The chain gang by the main gate was still intact, but most of the press had departed back to town, drawn to their deadlines like bees to a jar of honey. Only one of the newspapers had left behind a photographer, like a solo Apache warrior, in case of further disturbances.

The chain-gang reserves had splintered into relaxed groups up the slope above the entrance. Some of them had removed their shirts to get some sun on their winter-pale bodies. The more experienced of them were equipped for a polar expedition or a sudden attack from the police-dog patrol. Some were debating in loud voices. Others sat reading the morning papers; statements issued by Norlon management were quoted between clenched teeth.

Every time I passed a group, a silence descended over them. After I had walked past, the muttering grew louder again and I caught words such as 'cop' and 'wally', but it was water off a duck's back.

As I approached the green tent, two beefcakes in green anoraks stood up and smiled grimly, as if on the front cover of a

Norwegian climbing magazine. 'And where did you think you were going?' one asked.

'On a mountain walk.'

'Then you've taken the wrong path.'

'It's a long time since I've been here. Is Odin Schrøder-Olsen in there?'

'Busy in a meeting. And he doesn't talk to the press or anyone else.'

'This is private.'

'Then it'll have to wait.' He cast an eloquent glance down at the factory. 'We have more important matters to consider.'

'Would you be so kind as to go into the tent and tell Odin Schrøder-Olsen that Veum is waiting for him outside, perhaps until after the meeting? To talk about Tor Aslaksen.'

He eyed me dubiously. He was twenty-something years old, had blond stubble, a nose like a cloven seed potato and a toxic, phosphate-free expression. 'Veum? About Tor Aslaksen? I'll need a little more than that.'

'Tell him it's important. It's literally a matter of life and death.'

'OK. Wait here.' He gestured to his fellow beefcake to indicate that if I tried to force my way into the tent, I could regard myself as the only threatened species of animal they would not protect. He lifted the tent flap, bent down and went in.

I sent a wry smile to his partner, who had a long, reddened face, with sensitive skin where a blunt razor had eventually done its job. He probably used all four sides of the blade to save world resources.

The blond, stubbly beefcake poked his head out of the tent. 'I've been told to ask you if you're a plod or the press.'

'Neither. The first initial's right though. Private—'

He opened his mouth to interrupt me, young and impatient as he was bound to be.

'…investigator.'

He stared at me. Then he poked his head back in and passed on the message.

They laughed out loud in the tent as I shifted my weight from one foot to the other.

The guy with the long face was sure of himself now. I was a threatened species.

Stubbly came back out, still wearing an amused expression.

'You'd better sit down, Veum. Odin will be out as soon as he's free.'

'And how soon will that be?'

'There's no rush, is there? Or have you got a forlorn blonde waiting for you in your office?'

'Not as forlorn as the blond standing in front of me.' I turned round, cast around for a rock to sit on, spotted one four or five metres away and went over and sat down.

The two eco-warriors sat down in front of the tent again. For a while they chuntered together while I concentrated on the view.

From here I could see over the factory and down to the sea. On one side of the sound the smaller Sotra island lay, spread out with all its new-builds, like a doormat to the larger Sotra island, where the highest mountain, Liatårnet, stretched up 341 metres to the aerial masts on top, like a gigantic snail raising its antennae to establish where it is.

To the north of me I had Håkonshella, which had taken its name from King Håkon Adelsteinsfostre. He was born there, according to Snorre Sturluson, the saga writer, and he died there in 961 after the Battle of Fitjar against the sons of Erik Bloodaxe. So the environmentalists were on historical ground.

'Hey, Marlowe,' shouted Stubbly. 'Who commissioned you? Schrøder-Olsen "Supremo", or the Employers' Association?'

I slowly turned round, not entirely sure if he was talking to me or not.

But I didn't have to answer because at that moment Odin Schrøder-Olsen emerged from the tent and looked curiously in my direction.

Stubbly pointed and said: 'There he is, Odin. Shouldn't we stuff him and use him as a mascot in our office?'

Odin Schrøder-Olsen smiled inscrutably, shrugged his shoulders and strolled over to me.

I stood up.

His voice was resonant and agreeable. 'You were asking after me?'

'Yes.' I proffered my hand. 'My name's Veum. Varg Veum. I'm investi— … This is about Tor Aslaksen.'

He immediately shook my hand and said: 'Really? What about him?' His eyes were automatically drawn down to the factory to check, as it were, that the situation down there was unchanged.

'Does that mean you don't know?'

He answered irritably: 'Don't know *what*? I haven't got time to stand around playing guessing games, Veum.'

'And I haven't got time to tell you. I thought you'd been informed.'

'Informed about *what*?! What *is* this about?'

I said as quietly as I could: 'Informed … that Aslaksen's dead.' As I said it, I looked involuntarily over my shoulder to make sure that Jakob E. Hamre wasn't listening to what I was saying. If he was, I feared he would call me in for a much less enjoyable interview than the last one.

Odin Schrøder-Olsen looked at me as though he hadn't completely comprehended what I had said. 'He's dead? Tor?'

As the news sank in, I studied his face. Odin Schrøder-Olsen had delicate features, dark eyebrows and almost feminine, thick eyelashes behind his round glasses. His eyes were blue and his short hair was brown. The visible stubble of his beard cast a shadow over his face like that of a mountain over a snow-covered landscape. The dark leather jacket, the faded jeans and the white trainers made him look like a rep for an international sports shoes company, specialising in long-distance running. Sporty and efficient. He'd tried all the models himself. A front-runner.

But he hadn't signed up for this run, not of his own free will. 'I had no idea ... I haven't been in touch with ... How did it happen?'

'I, erm, think I've already said too much. The police will have to tell you the rest. If you omit to mention that you've heard this from me, I'd...'

He looked right through me as if I wasn't really there. 'It's incomprehensible.' Then he focused on me again. 'You have to tell me how it happened! Was it an accident?'

I nodded reluctantly. 'He drowned.'

'Drowned? But he could swim like a fish.'

'Yes, there are still some issues that need clearing up.'

'But where did it happen? In Milde?'

'No.' I hesitated for a moment, caught between asking a question and giving a complete answer.

He was quicker off the mark. 'Where then?'

'Nordås. Near the bay, that is.'

'Near Nordås bay?'

Then I asked my question. 'Why in Milde?'

'Well, that's where we used to go swimming – years ago. We grew up there, fence to fence, so to speak. His mother still lives there.'

'Yes, that's right. But no, it wasn't there. Were you still good friends?'

He looked past me and down at the factory again. 'Yes, we were. We hadn't seen each other much over the past few years, but ... We always had a chat when we met.'

I followed his eyes. 'You were on opposing sides in the conflict down below?'

He smiled wryly. 'Naturally enough. Not that that was anything special. The *whole* of my family's on the other side to me in this, as you perhaps know.'

'I read about it in the paper. Isn't that a problem for you when this concerns your family?'

He looked me straight in the eye. 'Not when this is the most important matter on the world stage right now. The East-West conflict is cooling. If Gorbachev's allowed to stay in power for a few more years, the international scene may have changed before 1990. But the gap between the north and the south is only getting wider and deeper with every day that passes.' He gesticulated in an arc to include the sea, the sky and the rock we were standing on. 'And this – the air we breathe, the sea we exploit for nutrition, the soil we cultivate – is what we share wherever we live. We can't buy our way out of the toxification of the globe, Veum. Death by suffocation affects us all. So it's important to remove even the slightest cause.'

'Even one as small as Norlon?'

'It's not *that* small. I've worked down there, so I know what I'm talking about.'

'Mhm.'

'But you didn't come here to discuss the environment with me. What was it you actually wanted?'

'No. Actually I've just been down to the factory to find out about Tor Aslaksen's family. And Ulrichsen happened to mention that you two were old friends.'

'And why would you want to know about Tor's family?'

'I was the person who happened to find him. In connection with a job I was about to start.'

'An investigation?'

'As a watchman.'

'I see.'

'And I know from experience that families often want to talk to the person who stumbled over the unfortunate victim. It can often help them in their grief to hear what state he or she was in. So that they don't form their own fantasies of how it was.'

'Right. I see. Well, you'll probably find his mother at home.'

'Yes, I was given her name and address by Ulrichsen, in the office. I was wondering whether…'

'Yes?'

'You don't know if he had any … any close friends? A girlfriend for example?'

'He wasn't married.'

'Yes, so I believe. But he was thirty-eight years old, and if he didn't have any other interests, then…'

He looked at me defiantly. 'I'm the same age and I'm not married, either.'

'Welcome to the club. That makes three of us. But—'

'Anyway, I don't stick my nose into my friends' private lives. If they don't tell me what they're up to, it's their business.'

'So you weren't that close then, I gather.'

'We didn't meet that often in recent years, and it was always by chance. It's not exactly the first question you ask old friends, is it, if they have anyone on the go?'

I swayed my head from side to side. 'In some circles it is.'

'Not in mine. We had more important things to talk about when we met.'

'More important? Information about the activities at Norlon maybe?'

'That, too. Trygve never tells me anything. He just covers it up. Of course, I was interested to hear when they would do something sensible about all the toxic waste they collect over the year.'

'And what they *do* with it?'

He pursed his lips before answering. 'It's not particularly nice to talk about, Veum. If you're really unlucky you get it in small doses, in the food you eat and the water you drink. Imagine, every day, tiny doses of hydrogen cyanide going into your system.'

'The characteristic odour of...'

'...bitter almonds. Exactly. But in such small doses you hardly notice any smell. Or taste. It just accumulates in your system until one day ... One day...'

'Thank you for the information. It's whetted my appetite. You know nothing about Tor Aslaksen though, with regard to...?'

'No,' he said crossly. 'You'll have to ask his mother. I assume he took his girlfriends home and introduced them to her. I have no more to say.' He turned abruptly and took two paces back to his tent.

Then he stopped and turned round. 'By the way, I'll give you one tip. He didn't have any other interests, as you discreetly put it. That much I do know, from the old days.'

I raised a hand. 'Thank you for the tip. That saves me going down one blind alley then.'

He nodded briefly and mumbled something I didn't catch. He gave instructions to the two guards, bent down and went back into the tent.

I watched them. 'Don't forget to take your crap with you when the camping holiday's over, boys.'

Horseface didn't answer, but his blond companion replied: 'Shall we start with you then?'

'Waste of effort. I consist exclusively of biodegradable materials.'

'Earth to earth, rubbish to rubbish?'

I looked at Horseface and nodded to his unshaven pal. 'Newfangled theologian. Enjoy your shift, boys. Don't let a truck pass without sticking a nail in the tyres.'

'What about some solidarity?'

'With the truck? Not likely.'

I stumbled down to the road again. Everything was quiet. The chain gang were chatting like workers on a lunch break. Up in the hills a few more activists had removed their shirts and a couple of girls their bras. The sun shining above us all was the same ball of gas that had lit up Håkon Adelsteinsfostre as he lay dying on the cliff above the sea, and it would be hanging there and shining when we were all gone and no one knew any longer what A/S Norlon had been and there was no one to make a chain gang with.

Until then we all had something to chew on. As for me, I took my thoughts with me into the car and drove them back to Bergen. But they were not at ease on the trip. They kept disturbing me.

12

Bergen was the first town in Norway to charge motorists a toll to drive through the centre. This is because there are so few public parking spaces that it was the only way the authorities could earn some income from the daily flow of traffic that was funnelled through.

I preferred to drive home, park there and walk the ten to fifteen minutes it took me to pass three sets of traffic lights, a crowded fish market and pavements thronged with tourists.

Once in my office, I checked the answerphone to see if anyone had tried to contact me. Strangely enough, no one had. Even though I must have been the town's most sought-after bachelor, after the adolescent Morten Harket of course. Then I leafed through the telephone directory, but not because I had any intention of ringing anyone. Anne-Marie Aslaksen and the

Schrøder-Olsen family did indeed live next door to each other, in Mildeveien. Schrøder-Olsen, father and son, Harald and Trygve, even had the same address, separated only by an A and a B.

While I was at it, I checked Odin's address as well. He had left the beaches alongside Fana fjord and settled in Åsane, in a house in Dalavegen, which runs along the western banks of Dalavatn lake towards Espelid. He could sit there in what remained of the old Åsane countryside and gaze across the water to the new motorway being constructed between Nyborg and Eikås, and thereby gain growing inspiration for continued commitment to the environmental campaign.

Ulrichsen lived in Sædalen, and Jakob E. Hamre's address was in Nybøveien in Nesttun. The very fact that I had looked up the latter two addresses told me that I was running low on ideas.

I went down to the cafeteria on the first floor and ordered a portion of salted meat and potato dumplings, a Vestland favourite. It would have been wonderful, if someone hadn't drowned it, successfully, in fat.

I pushed my plate aside and let the grease congeal into an obituary while I fetched a cup of coffee from the counter.

I thought about Tor Aslaksen, and I thought about Lisbeth Finslo. *I had no idea. I didn't understand.*

What was it that she had no idea about and hadn't understood?

Had she known Aslaksen, and had she perhaps arranged with him to meet us – or rather me – in the house in Kleiva? And, if so, why? Had it had anything to do with the Norlon business, or was it just a coincidence?

Life had taught me not to place much faith in coincidences, but why hadn't she told me straight out that there was someone she wanted me to meet – under somewhat strange circumstances, it was true, but nevertheless...?

And, yes, I had met him, but the circumstances had been tragic rather than strange: at the bottom of a swimming pool. And when I resurfaced, if I can express myself in this way, she was gone. As was the red car.

But who had gone *with* her, where was she and who was the man who had tipped off the police?

I sighed and gazed through the cafeteria window. The afternoon traffic was at its peak. Cars stood stationary in queues, in every conceivable direction. Only the buses that had come into the centre on the other side of Vågen moved blithely forward until the lights in Bryggen brought even that movement to a halt too.

I finished my coffee, ambled down to the tobacconist's further along the quay and bought a couple of evening newspapers, which I took back with me to the office.

While the traffic slowly disappeared from the streets, a discernible stillness descended over the town, the streetcleaners in the market square made a vain attempt to hose the air clean, and I flicked through the papers.

Beyond the Langfjell mountains, to the east, the most coverage Norlon received was a single column in one newspaper and an untitled article in another.

Over there, more important things were happening. A bit-part actor in the National Theatre got married across the entire front page of one newspaper, while a football manager was given the boot over half of another. In fact, the actor had done a summer season in Tønsberg a few years before and the football manager was an ex-international, so the prioritisation was understandable. We were getting enough poisonous gas as it was, without realising it.

I pushed the papers aside. I got up and paced the floor a few times while pondering further on Lisbeth Finslo. Had I known her at all, apart from as the physiotherapist I happened to be assigned to and, a few times, as a running pal? Could she have been keeping all manner of secrets from me, and what actually was my part in her holiday plans?

It was still too early to ring her sister in Florø. Instead, I called the police station.

When I asked after Hamre, I was informed that he wasn't on the premises. When I asked if there was any news regarding Lisbeth Finslo, they asked who was calling.

I rang off without answering.

Deciding not to go home, I crossed the market square, walked up Vetrlidsalmenningen, bought a ticket for the Fløibanen funicular and was transported aloft with a coachload of American tourists.

I went for a quick walk in the mountains, up to the top of Blåmanen and sat amid the cairns staring towards the west.

It was a day with a view of the sea, and the horizon was like a bubble the sun could puncture at any moment. But it was a long time until nightfall. The sun still hung high above, like a thumbprint on the crystal-clear, blue and white sky. The evening would have to pull its light cariole a little further before it dismounted and stabled the horses, their manes sprinkled with stardust and steaming with moonlight. From somewhere in the forest below me a cuckoo laughed derisively at the late sun, as if to say she had laid her eggs in another bird's nest and she would beat it to the call to quarters.

I continued over to Rundemans veien and followed it. Halfway down Midtfjellet a hare crossed in front of me. I stood watching it until it disappeared in the undergrowth, over towards Halvdan Griegs vei.

On arriving home, I made myself comfortable in a chair and rang Jannicke Finslo in Florø. The boat should have arrived by now.

She picked up on the second ring. 'Yes?'

'Veum here.'

'Ohhh,' she said, with falling intonation.

'No news?'

'No. Nothing.'

'So, she didn't arrive on the afternoon boat either?'

Her voice broke. 'No-o.'

'And have you spoken to the police?'

'Yes, they haven't found her, either.'

'Hmmm. Well, we mustn't expect the worst. I'm sure there's a na–tural explanation.' I heard myself hesitate in the middle of the word.

She answered wearily: 'Of course. That's what we have to hope.'

'You didn't ask ... Kari ... if she knows the name of her mother's new friend?'

She lowered her voice. 'First off, she wouldn't talk about it. I think *she* thinks her mother has simply gone off with her new friend. For now she's more hurt than concerned.'

'And?'

'Yes?'

'Has she told you…? Did she know what this friend's name was?'

For a moment I feared she would answer Varg. Then she said: 'She says she doesn't know for *sure*, but she thinks it was ... She had answered the phone a few times when he rang and he had introduced himself as…'

'Yes?'

'Tor.'

The name sank like a depth charge inside me, without exploding. It lay on the bottom, like a dull threat, confirmation of something I had suspected.

'Tor ... Nothing else?'

'No, that was all.' Warily, she added: 'Does the name mean anything to you?'

'Well … When the police rang you asking after Lisbeth, did they say anything else?'

'No. Is there anything else?' There was a new anxiety in her voice.

Hamre would hate me for the rest of his life. 'The thing is that when Lisbeth disappeared … in the place where she disappeared, we found a man. Who had drowned. And his first name was Tor.'

She gasped. 'Does that mean … the same might've happened to her?'

'Hardly. We found him in a swimming pool.'

'But does it mean she's under suspicion?'

'No, no, no. That's not what it means…' But while I was speaking, it struck me that she might well have been. Under suspicion of murdering Tor Aslaksen.

'You have to find her for us, Veum.'

'Eh, what?'

'Could you do that?'

'Well, I can't deny that I do have some experience of such cases.'

'I don't have much money, but—'

'Don't even think about it. After all, she was … I mean, I *knew* her.'

'At least you must take some money for expenses. How much would you need to start with?'

'You mean how much money?'

'Yes.'

'Well … If you send me a cheque for a thousand kroner, that should cover them. I can't rule out the possibility that I might have to travel up to Florø and have a more in-depth conversation with you and Kari. Then I'll give you an itemised bill. Beyond that, I need a photo of Lisbeth if you have one.'

'Yes, I'm sure I have a few amateur snaps.'

'If you could send one asap to my office address: Strandkaien 2, 5013 Bergen. And if you could attach a written confirmation that you have commissioned me to find Lisbeth, that would be very handy. I mean, should the police decide to ask me.'

'Would the police react negatively if I, perhaps, hired you?'

'Not really. With disappearances, they're invariably pleased to have all the help they can get. As you can imagine, they have bigger cases to investigate.'

'This is more than big enough for us, Veum.'

'Of course. I understand that.'

She took a decision. 'That's agreed then. I'll send you what you asked. And I really hope something comes out of this.'

'Me too.' I couldn't promise that she would win the jackpot, but I would definitely do my best to make sure she got her stake back.

After saying goodbye, I sat with the receiver in my hand, staring into the air. Now at least I had a reason to mooch around asking the questions no one would answer, and one reason is better than none. At least it is a start.

13

The next day was Saturday, and still there wasn't a cloud in the sky. It was either a meteorological miracle or the heavens had gone on strike. As though everyone in the weather cookhouse had laid down their utensils and refused to serve us the summer soup we were so used to, in bowls slopping over with rain.

As I placed a foot on the step outside the building where I live, an invisible shimmer of summer night remained in the air, like a concentration of dew. But the light had never been higher and sunshine flowed like a river between the houses.

It was a day to go to the beach with your sweetheart, if you had one. And if you didn't, it was a day for the beach anyway. It was a day you had to know someone with a boat, who could take you all over By fjord and out to the furthest islands. It was a day to drive your car to the northernmost Øygården island, take your fishing rod and hope you don't get a bite. It was a day to climb the mountains, sit with your back against the highest cairn, pour yourself a cup of coffee from a Thermos and fearlessly stare eternity in the eye. It was a day to do exactly what you fancied, with someone you fancied. It was a day to do anything except drive down to the office, find that an express letter from Florø took more than twelve hours (especially when they were night hours), get in your car and follow the arterial road south to visit a place you had hoped you had put behind you for good.

Hjellestad Clinic is situated on the peninsula locals in bygone days used to call Neset, but which most call Milde now, after the bus terminus. It is one of the most fertile areas of land in this part of Vestland; you have to go to Lyse Abbey to see anything comparable. The farm at Milde also used to be run by Dominican monks from the monastery on Holmen in Bergen. There are still maple, box, poplar and walnut trees growing there that were planted by monks in the Middle Ages. A museum – the arboretum and botanical gardens in Milde with their extensive collection of trees and bushes – was built to commemorate them. And it stays open at night.

I parked and got out of the car. I was acquainted enough with the senior consultant to know that he often came in on a Saturday morning to shuffle a few piles of paper in peace and quiet.

The male receptionist had the lugubrious face of a watchdog who always let people in. His face was covered with freckles, and when he opened his mouth to smile, I saw that he had freckles on his teeth as well. 'Haven't you been discharged?' he said, in a resigned tone, as though he was used to patients making an immediate return.

I nodded. 'Is the boss in?'

'Have you got an appointment?'

I made a vague gesture with my head so that no one could say afterwards that I had lied. Then I walked in, past the secretary's empty desk and down the corridor to the closed door bearing the consultant's name.

I knocked. After a moment I heard a voice tell me to come in, and I did as instructed, even if it didn't sound very welcoming.

When I entered, he at first just looked up from his papers distractedly, then down again. And up again quickly, with an expression of acute concern on his features. 'Veum? You haven't…?'

I raised a hand to reassure him. 'No, no, not that soon.'

Then he flashed his boyish smile, ran a hand through his thinning hair, tipped his chair backward and said: 'So, to what do I owe the pleasure of a visit this Saturday morning?'

'I'm … investigating the circumstances surrounding the disappearance of Lisbeth Finslo.'

He examined me with a professional eye and the same stony expression that he wore when sifting through his patients' oddest stories. Tentatively, he said: 'But she's just on holiday … isn't she?'

I shook my head. 'She's gone missing. Her family have no idea where she is. Haven't the police been here?'

'I've been in Denmark for a couple of days. They may've spoken to someone else.'

He subjected me to a probing gaze. Then he leaned across the desk in confidential mode and said gently: 'You know, Veum, she might've asked her family to say they don't know where she is. I mean, if a relationship between a client and a staff member becomes too close, as it can, erm, on occasion, it may be difficult to reject the client, ummm, face to face. Afterwards.'

I smiled calmly. 'I understand where you're going. But the

police were not her clients. And it wasn't such a close relationship between her and me.'

'Really? But she may still have her reasons.'

'There's a death associated with her disappearance.'

He still seemed unmoved, hardened as he was to lies and exaggeration. 'A death? How do you mean?'

'A man. An engineer called Tor Aslaksen. Does the name sound familiar to you?'

'Should it? I don't think he's ever been here.'

'Employed by a company called Norlon. Does *that* ring any bells?'

'None at all. What is it?'

'There's a lot about it in the papers at the moment. In connection with an environmental action group.'

He frowned. 'Hm, now you mention it ... Ah, that company, yes.'

'In addition, I think he might've been Lisbeth's ... Lisbeth Finslo's boyfriend.'

He shrugged. 'It's possible. We have far too many clients with complicated private lives for us to keep up with our staff's.'

'How well did you know her?'

'Lisbeth?' He gazed pensively towards the window and the pine forest outside. 'She's only been here for around eighteen months. Before that she was at a physiotherapy centre in Bergen. She does an excellent job; she's good at creating a bond with clients – and motivating them. You're a case in point. We've never had any reason to complain about what she does, and she doesn't make a fuss. The part of the machinery that never lets you down is the part you notice least.'

'There weren't any other employees she met up with privately?'

'I don't think so. We had the odd get-together of course, up here, or a seminar in Solstrand, for example, and then we got to know each other better. The person she worked most with was Andersen, the psychologist.'

'I don't suppose he's here now?'

'I doubt it.' There was a sudden change of tone: 'You look worried, Veum. Don't let this affect you. I'm not sure this is what you need at this stage of your recovery.'

'Really? I've spent most of my life searching for people who've gone missing. I've found most of them. Alive, I mean. But some…'

I didn't complete what I was going to say.

I could still close my eyes and feel the pressure of her one firm kiss on my lips. I could still hear her breathing as she ran beside me towards the arboretum. It would be a while yet before I was willing to utter the words that finished the sentence.

I got up. 'Then I'd better … look elsewhere.'

The doctor looked up, immersed in thought, already on his way back into his piles of paper. 'You do that, Veum. And good luck … in every way.'

I thanked him. I had a feeling I was going to need it.

14

From the first moment I saw her, I called her the flower girl.

She was kneeling in the grass, halfway up the slope between the wrought-iron gate and the large, dark-brown house, her lap full of wild flowers. The white dress she was wearing was patterned with small flowers, and the way she was sitting with the pleats splayed out and her calves along one side, she reminded me of a baroque porcelain figure. Her fair hair shimmering in the sun fell like tendrils of a flower against her shoulders, and when she looked up at me, her eyes were transparent and unfocused, as though she was finding it difficult to see me in the strong sunlight.

'Are you the father of the little girl?' she asked me in a high, uninflected voice, with some surprise.

'No,' I said. 'You're mixing me up with someone else.'

I glanced up at the brown house. 'Does someone called Schrøder-Olsen live here?'

She nodded and held out her bunch of flowers. 'Look at these I've picked. Wood anemone and bluebells and ... look here ... buttercups and these small violets ... they're cuckoo flowers ... and these red campions.'

She had to be in her twenties, but she spoke like a five-year-old. Her body was heavy under the light dress, and she leaned forward with a conspicuous stoop, like someone bowed under an unrelenting sorrow.

Automatically, I adjusted my language down by several decades. 'How lovely they are.'

She smiled at me, a radiant beam with large, beautiful teeth, but as distant and unfocused as her gaze. 'Aren't they. My name's Siv. Would you like to come to my birthday party?'

I laughed. 'When is it?'

'Today.'

I stopped laughing. 'I'm not sure if I can ... today.'

'Oh, yes, you can. You must.' Spontaneously, she jumped up. Holding the bunch of flowers with one hand to her chest. With the other, she made a grab for mine. 'We're having the cake now. With twenty-six candles.'

I looked up at the substantial house built in a kind of adapted Tirolean style, surrounded by blossoming fruit trees and the buzzing of hundreds of bees. 'I wanted to speak to Trygve Schrøder-Olsen.'

'That's my brother. He's coming, too.'

'Yes, but Siv, you have to understand that I can't ... not like this. What I need to talk to him about is—'

A shadow fell over her fair complexion, and she shouted with a child's defiance: 'You must come! You must! You must!' She squeezed the flowers against her chest even harder, and the grip on my hand tightened.

'Alright then. Thank you. Thank you, Siv,' I said to reassure her. 'Careful with your flowers. Don't crush them.'

She let go of my hand and looked down at the bedraggled bunch. 'Yes, the flowers. Look at these … buttercups and these red campions. I know all the flowers. And the trees. I go for a walk in the arboretum every day at twelve. Would you like to come with me? But not today. Because today's my birthday.'

I sighed. 'Another day then, Siv. I'll go for a walk with you on another day. But now I have to go. I can come one day when you don't have—'

'But you mustn't go. You have to come with me and eat some of my birthday cake. Come on. Here.' She took a few steps up the drive towards the house. Then she turned and looked at me, like a little child looks at a puppy. 'Come on. This way.'

I followed her, mentally holding my head in my hands. I doubted this was the most diplomatic way to introduce myself to the Schrøder-Olsen family.

'That's where Trygve lives. And Bodil.' She pointed to a low, modern house in a late seventies style, with chalk-white brick gables and walls of stained grey timber. It stood in a distant corner of the generous plot, floating on a cloud of rose bushes and moored to terra firma by means of honeysuckle hawsers.

On my way up to the towering house, where an ivy portal marked the entrance to the courtyard garden, I stopped, turned round and surveyed the countryside.

Behind the trees on the other side of the road Fanafjell was reflected in the fjord. The whole mountain seemed to be hovering above the water like an airship. It was one of those weightless days when everything appeared to be able to take flight.

'Come on,' Siv said from behind me. I sighed and continued upward.

We walked beneath the portal and followed a gravel path around the house, which was screened by tall, dark-green hedges and bordered by beds of pansies and some pink, half-opened umbrella-like plants whose name I didn't know.

Siv dashed ahead of me while I reluctantly ambled after her like a son-in-law on his first visit to his wife's family.

We emerged onto a large natural-stone patio at the back of the house. An almost white-haired, dainty little woman in her late sixties was placing the last coffee cups on a white table under a cream parasol. She was wearing a dark, chocolate-coloured blouse with a big bow across her chest and a light-brown skirt. There was something brittle and vulnerable about her features as she looked from Siv to me, and her mouth tautened into a formal rebuff.

'Siv,' she said softly. 'What have you…?'

Siv ran over to her and held up the flowers. 'Look, Mamma, I've picked these. Buttercups and bluebells and look at these … red camp—'

Her mother looked past her and nodded to me, her eyebrows arched in query, as she received the flowers.

I moved and gestured as if to explain.

'This is … He's my guest, Mamma. I've invited him.'

'But Siv…' She smiled apologetically to me. 'You have to understand that…'

I coughed. 'Yes, of course I've been trying to say that … But Siv insisted, so I…'

'He's staying, he's staying, he's staying,' Siv said, her neck reddening.

The mother exchanged glances with me and turned to her daughter.

'It's my day. I've invited him. My birthday, Mamma.' It struck me that her light-blue eyes were dry. Despite the sudden anger, there wasn't a tear in them. She turned abruptly to me: 'What's your name?'

Her mother was quick to say: 'See. You don't even know.'

'What's your name, man?'

'Erm, Veum. Varg Veum.'

'Var-ig?'

'No, Varg.'

Her mother interrupted. 'Right, well, er, hello, herr Veum, may I introduce myself? My name's Aslaug Schrøder-Olsen, and as you appreciate…'

She came towards me, as if to place herself between me and her daughter, but Siv followed right behind us, with her head craned forward, vigilant, level with her mother's shoulder.

'You've already met my daughter and as you might appreciate…' She looked at her daughter shyly. 'She's celebrating her birthday today and we…' She turned round and gestured with one hand. 'We're only going to have a cup of coffee and a piece of cake. Close family, that is.'

'Birthday cake,' Siv said. 'Va-arg.'

Her mother smiled wanly. 'Well, if you have time, and as Siv is so keen, then…'

She walked in front of us towards the white garden furniture, her neck and shoulders slumped in resignation.

Siv tucked her arm under mine and dragged me over, forcefully rather than coquettishly, though not without a certain grace.

'In fact, I had come to see your son.'

Aslaug Schrøder-Olsen's face brightened into a smile, producing laughter lines around her eyes. 'Oh, you know Trygve. But then … He's coming too. Do take a seat, herr Veum, do take a seat.'

I thanked her and perched on a chair, on the very edge, anticipating that she might change her mind at any moment.

I looked around. Broad sliding glass doors led directly into the lounge, where the furniture looked heavy, expensive and antique. A concrete ramp had been built in front of the door so that a wheelchair could enter. Elsewhere the area was laid with flagstones. The light porcelain coffee service was patterned in brown and beige with a delicate base colour. The cutlery was silver, so clean that it was dazzling in the bright sunlight.

'Where's Pappa?' Siv asked.

'He's indoors, my love. You can go and tell him, er, one of the guests has arrived.'

'I've invited him. Varg,' Siv said, looking straight between us, a thin, shimmering film over her bright eyes.

She ran in, and her mother stood watching with a sad expression on her face. Turning to me, she said in a low voice: 'She's so impulsive, the poor sweetheart. Please forgive her. Actually, it was her birthday in April, but these birthday parties are one of the few pleasures she has, so we let her celebrate ... every single month.'

I nodded. 'She obviously thought I was someone else when I arrived.'

'Oh? Who?'

'Well, she asked me if I was the father of the little girl.'

'The little girl? Which one?'

'I don't know. You don't understand, either?'

'No, I...' She sat staring into space, sunk in a reverie. Then she tore herself out of it. 'Right. But you do know Trygve, I gather?'

'No, I ... You see, in fact I don't have...'

A cough came from the corner of the patio, and she gave a start. 'Oh, goodness me, Trygve, you gave me a fright. We were just talking about you. I...' She suddenly realised she was still holding the flowers Siv had given her. Confused, she said: 'I'll just put these in water. Pappa'll be here soon. You already know each other, so...'

She rushed through the open sliding door while Trygve Schrøder-Olsen and I stood looking at each other.

His voice was polite, but measured: 'Do we know each other?'

'No, this is all a misunderstanding.'

'Yes, it must be,' he said coolly, examining me with ill-concealed disapproval.

The two brothers were quite dissimilar in appearance. Trygve was shorter in height, and his face was fuller. He seemed more secure in his masculinity, and his voice had a natural authority that made me grope for support. He had the same pale complexion as Odin and Siv, I noticed, but in his case it seemed neither vulnerable nor transparent, more like a document bearing a final decision. His hair was dark blond and cut in traditional fashion. The crease in his light-coloured trousers was so sharp you could have cut yourself on it, and despite the temperature being around the twenty-eight-degree mark, he was wearing a striped tie and a dark-blue blazer with a Royal Norwegian Automobile Club badge on the breast pocket.

'I brought some roses,' said a sonorous voice as his female companion rounded the corner. She, too, was caught slightly off balance by the presence of a total stranger on the patio.

She was one of those women men of Trygve Schrøder-Olsen's cast like to marry so that on festive occasions they have someone to flaunt and represent them. She was half a head taller than him with luxuriant dark hair cascading in loose curls around an attractive face, deep cheek dimples and such a determined expression around her mouth that I wondered how willing she would actually be to represent him.

'Hi,' she said lightly. 'I don't believe we've met.' She walked past her husband, moved the long-stemmed yellow roses into her left hand, shook my hand with her right and introduced herself with a winsome inclination of the neck. 'I'm Bodil.' Her hand was smooth and cold.

'Varg.'

She raised her eyebrows and said with a rippling laugh: 'Really?'

Her husband realised that perhaps he hadn't quite been as well mannered as his wife, cleared his throat and followed her over. As we shook hands he mumbled: 'Yes, I'm afraid we haven't ... I'm Trygve Schrøder-Olsen.'

'Varg Veum.'

Her laughter rippled again. '*That* too?'

'What...?' Schrøder-Olsen began.

'Siv invited me. I—'

'I see. That explains everything.'

'Not everything perhaps. But at least why I'm here, now. I don't exactly feel...'

Aslaug Schrøder-Olsen returned. Holding a big crystal vase containing Siv's wild flowers. 'Hi, Bodil,' she said, smiling at her daughter-in-law.

'Anything I can do to help?'

'No, now we're just waiting for...' She nodded to Trygve and me. 'Have you had a chat?'

He glanced uncertainly at me. 'Yes, we've...'

I smiled disarmingly. 'Yes, actually I came to have a chat with you, but...'

He quickly assumed command again. 'What about? If it's anything to do with the factory, it will have to wait until after the weekend.'

I stepped closer and lowered my voice. 'It's about ... Tor Aslaksen's death.'

An angel strolled across the tiled patio, smelt Siv's flowers and Bodil's yellow roses and then looked around slowly before thoughtfully merging into the trees that surrounded us. The silence was palpable.

Bodil glanced from me to her husband, then carried on over to her mother-in-law as though she hadn't heard anything.

Trygve Schrøder-Olsen eyed me with an almost offended

expression – because I had taken the liberty of coming here and reminding him of life's realities on a Friday.

His mother looked from one of us to the other, aghast. 'Tor Aslaksen? Surely not Totto?'

'Yes, mother,' Trygve said brusquely. 'He's dead.'

'Dead?' She swayed. 'Totto?'

Her daughter-in-law grabbed her by the arm to support her.

'I thought Pappa had told you…'

'No, I hadn't,' came a sombre, well-modulated voice from the open sliding doors, and a white-haired man with a powerful upper body propelled his wheelchair out, with Siv close behind.

'Is the father of the little girl dead?' Siv asked, gazing around the patio in wonderment.

15

The elderly man manoeuvred the wheelchair expertly between the garden furniture. His blue eyes were focused on me, and he brought his chair to a halt by my legs with an elegant little twist. 'Siv said she'd invited a guest,' he smiled, and proffered his hand. 'Harald Schrøder-Olsen.'

His handshake was firm, as if in a demonstration of his strength.

'Varg Veum.'

He smiled. Harald Schrøder-Olsen made a powerful impression, despite the wheelchair. He was wearing a light-coloured linen suit and a small, somewhat old-fashioned, red-and-grey bow tie. His white hair was combed back and contrasted with his tanned, slightly rugged complexion. He looked as though he had spent the winter in Southern Europe and every available hour of sunshine on the patio behind his house. His eyebrows bordered on white too, and his nose had an aristocratic curve that was noticeably absent in the subsequent generation.

He raised his head a fraction and gazed around. 'Aren't we going to sit at the table?'

His wife said in a shaky voice: 'But Harald, I've only just found out … about Totto.'

The old man's face darkened. 'Yes, that was regrettable. But it's life. We can't stop everything because of that. It's Siv's day today. So, to the table.'

'Odin said he was coming, too.'

I shot a glance at Trygve. He pursed his lips and returned my glance with a hostile stare. 'To be honest, Pappa, we can't have … total strangers here. If Odin comes, too…' He looked at his wife, as if hoping to receive support there.

His father said firmly: 'Veum is Siv's guest. He's staying. And you and Odin keep the peace when your sister has company. Is that understood?'

Trygve blushed with embarrassment, avoided my gaze and answered by turning his back on us all and walking over to examine a rose bush, not that I believed for a second that he was interested in plant life. He reminded me of a boy who had been sent to the naughty corner.

'Then we'd better, erm…' Aslaug Schrøder-Olsen said nervously. 'He can have a piece when he comes. I'll go and get the birthday cake.'

From Mildeveien came the sputtering cough of a twenty-year-old VW. Everyone looked up and nodded to each other.

Trygve said sarcastically: 'Here he comes, our very own eco-warrior in his environmentally friendly vehicle. See for yourselves.'

We did. A greyish-brown cloud of smoke was issuing from the exhaust pipe of Odin Schrøder-Olsen's dusty old Beetle, and it came to a halt in the drive with a stifled yawn and a release of petrol fumes that made the air around it quiver.

Odin stepped out of the car, slammed the door behind him

without bothering to lock it and strode up to the house. He was wearing a faded, light-green T-shirt, threadbare jeans, yellow-brown sandals and nothing else. In one hand he was holding a small red book.

Siv ran past me to meet him halfway. She was laughing out loud like a little child.

Bodil whispered to her mother-in-law: 'I can get the cake. Is it in the kitchen?'

Her mother-in-law sent her a concerned smile. 'Yes. Thank you. And the coffee. It's in the white Thermos.'

Odin and Siv appeared arm-in-arm on the patio. When Odin spotted me, he exclaimed in surprise: 'Veum?'

'Right, so you know each other?' his brother muttered, then resumed his rose studies.

'Yes, we've ... met,' Odin said.

'I invited him,' Siv beamed. 'It's my birthday. Look at the flowers I've picked, Odin. Bluebells and buttercups and ... look ... red campions.'

Odin smiled tenderly at his sister. 'They're lovely. I brought this.' He passed her the leather-bound book. 'Many happy returns.'

She accepted it, surprised, as though unsure quite what to do. Then she opened it, carefully, as though picking a fragile flower. 'Ohhh. Pictures. Flowers.'

He smiled at her. 'It's an old botany book, from early this cent— ... It's almost eighty years old. Look. It has colour plates too.'

Siv slowly turned page after page, mumbling: 'Look at this. Look at them. Look at the flowers...' She read the names hesitantly as though she had just learned them: 'The cow...slip fa... mi...ly. The win...ter... green fa...mi...ly. Look...'

Her brother watched her with a heavy heart. He found it difficult to share her pleasure.

'And here's Bodil with the cake,' her mother said. 'There you are!'

Bodil placed a large cream sponge decorated with fresh strawberries on the table.

'Mmmmm,' Siv shouted and ran to a chair. 'Me first. I want to be first.' She put the book down on the table and concentrated on the cake.

'Take a seat everyone,' the mother said, holding out a chair for me.

On my way to the table Odin whispered in my ear: 'What on earth are you doing here?'

I whispered back: 'I came here to ask your brother a few questions, and then I was shanghaied, as it were, by your sister.'

'Hmm.'

We took our seats around the table.

Siv sat with her father and mother on either side. Bodil and Trygve sat on the left of Harald. Odin and I sat opposite.

The cake was passed around and coffee was poured for everyone except Siv, who drank pop.

I could feel that my back was wet. The sun had risen to the highest point of the day. And the atmosphere around the table was not conducive to cooling anyone down.

'Did you come alone?' Aslaug asked Odin, in a tone that suggested she expected nothing else.

'Yes, it wasn't exactly a success the last time I brought someone,' Odin answered.

Trygve snorted to himself.

Aslaug leaned towards me. 'You see, Veum, I'd like some grandchildren.'

Trygve rolled his eyes. 'Mother!'

She continued regardless. 'But the only ones who could give me some apparently don't have the time.'

Bodil flushed and was about to say something, but Trygve stopped her by placing a reassuring hand on her forearm.

'Of course, I understand them very well,' the elderly woman went on with a venom I would not have believed of her. 'My son has *his* career, my daughter-in-law *hers* to think about. And when she has time off, she goes parachute-jumping. And you know, a pregnant woman in a parachute, now how would that look?'

Trygve snapped: 'Mother! Now you stop it.'

Harald Schrøder-Olsen coughed and ran his gaze slowly around the table, as if to say now let that be an end to *that*.

His wife carried on in a gentle voice: 'Yes, Odin hasn't even married and Siv…' Dolefully, she looked at her daughter, who had cream around her mouth and on the tip of her nose. 'Siv is Siv.' Then she put her silver fork down beside her plate and changed her tone to one of polite conversation. 'And what do you do, herr Veum?'

'I'm a private investigator.'

The angel returned, sat down at the table and helped herself to a large slice of cake.

'Private investigator?' Aslaug choked, as if she had much too big a piece in her mouth.

The angel looked around, slurped her coffee and sent us all a gentle smile.

Odin fixed his eye on his sister-in-law across the table and said mischievously: 'Been spreading your wings recently, Bodil?'

'Skydiving, do you mean?' she answered, as coolly as a refrigerator technician.

'Yes, I didn't mean it in an extramarital sense, even though we have the right man on hand here,' he said, flashing me a look.

'I don't take that kind of case,' I said hastily.

'So comforting to hear,' Trygve said.

His father leaned across and said in his sombre voice: 'What cases do you take then?'

'Erm, disappearances. I—'

Bodil carried on as if she hadn't heard anything: 'Not last week. But there was a meet last Sunday.'

'Yes, we were in Flesland and watched her, all of us,' Harald Schrøder-Olsen said. He moved his eyes up to the blue firmament as though his daughter-in-law was still hanging up there somewhere. 'It was a splendid sight.'

'Bodil did a parachute jump,' Siv said. 'I saw her. There was a plane ... and then ... wheeee...' She gestured with her hand, then spread out her arms and imitated a parachute in the air around her. 'Parachute. I saw you, didn't I, Bodil?'

Bodil nodded.

'Tor Aslaksen. Didn't he do that kind of thing, too?' I asked.

'Yes, he did,' Bodil said curtly.

Her mother-in-law interjected: 'I'm still shaken. I can't understand it. I can't understand how he can be dead.'

No one said anything.

'When did it happen?' she said.

'We found out yesterday,' her husband said at length. 'It was an accident.'

'An accident?'

'He drowned.'

Automatically, her eyes were drawn to the sea. 'Ah, that summer.' As no one made a comment, she added: 'He was always dropping by that summer, when you were young, Odin. Every single day. It must've been a shock for his mother.'

Siv listened to her without focusing her eyes; she had become dreamy and pensive.

Harald Schrøder-Olsen had leaned back in his wheelchair, but his gaze glided across the table like a falcon, from face to face, hunting for prey.

'Was he swimming in the sea?' asked Aslaug.

In a pained tone, Odin said: 'Mamma, let's not talk about this anymore now.'

Then Trygve erupted in an outburst of repressed anger: 'No! Perhaps we should talk about what you've started outside Norlon? You haven't exactly considered family ties there, have you. You ought at least to think about the inheritance.'

'Thank you. I *received* my part several years ago, unless I'm much mistaken.'

'The crap plot of land, is that what you're referring to?'

'Trygve,' Bodil said reprovingly.

Harald Schrøder-Olsen brought his fist down on the table so hard the cups danced on the saucers and his wife had to grab the white Thermos to stop it toppling over. 'I said *no* arguing today. Is that understood?'

Neither of the sons responded.

'*Is that understood?*' he repeated, even more loudly.

'Yes,' Trygve snapped.

'Alright then,' Odin conceded, muttering: 'He treats us like snot-nosed kids…'

'More coffee anyone?' the mother said, hastily filling the cups of those who said yes. The angel must have returned because a profound, oppressive silence had descended over the gathering again.

'Well, that's how it is with us,' Bodil said, looking at me, her dimples almost invisible.

'Listen…' Siv said, still with a dreamy expression on her face.

Everyone listened, but heard nothing except for the birds singing in the trees around us, the insects buzzing in the garden and occasional bursts of laughter from families passing below, on their way to the beach in Grønevika.

'It's the flowers whispering,' Siv carried on, 'telling us to be quiet and stop ar-gu-ing…'

'Oh, Siv,' her mother exclaimed, leaning forward and giving her daughter a hug.

'This is my party. I invited you.' Suddenly she was back, her unfocused eyes were on me for an instant, then she looked at her father. 'Pappa, can't you show Va-arg and me your lovely app… ar…at…uses?'

Her father smiled apologetically in my direction. 'Veum isn't interested in that kind of thing, my love.'

'Yes, he is. And I am, too. Show us, Pappa.'

Harald Schrøder-Olsen scratched his chin and sent her a resigned look. Then he pushed his wheelchair away from the table. 'Well, as this is your party … And as you've never learned to give in. Veum?' He peered up at me with a wry grimace and motioned towards the glass door leading into the house.

I stood up and addressed his wife. 'Well, thank you for the coffee – and cake. It was delicious.'

'There wasn't any hydrogen cyanide in *that* anyway,' Odin remarked.

Harald raised his voice. 'And no arguing because I'm going inside. Is that understood?'

The two brothers nodded dismissively.

'I'll help you to clear the table,' Bodil said. 'Then at least I'm doing something useful.'

Harald Schrøder-Olsen propelled the wheelchair forward with powerful thrusts of his hands while Siv ran ahead of us into the house.

We entered an overfurnished, old-fashioned, upper-class lounge, dominated by burgundy and brown, with flashes of gold and white in the oriental carpets and green in the titles of the leather-bound books on the shelves. In one corner there was a black grand piano and on top a wide selection of family photographs, predominantly children. In another corner there was a TV.

Schrøder-Olsen headed for a staircase with a wheelchair-lift alongside the banister. He quickly moved onto the carpet-clad platform, pressed a button and the lift started. It spiralled downward like a sinking submarine, quietly but inexorably, towards the lower floor.

Siv howled with pleasure at the hi-tech miracle and ran after him on light feet while I courteously brought up the rear, unsure what apparatuses he was going to show me.

We descended into a dark corridor, illuminated only by deep-orange glass dome lights decorated in art nouveau style.

'What does your daughter-in-law do?' I asked Schrøder-Olsen as I followed him along the corridor.

He looked up at me. 'Bodil?'

'Yes.'

'IT specialist … engineer. Now she has a top job in insurance.'

'So, her life insurance's taken care of when she jumps?'

'You can be sure of that, Veum. No exclusion clauses, knowing her.'

He had reached a large, dark-brown door, also in art nouveau style. 'Can you open it, Siv?'

We followed her. Schrøder-Olsen manoeuvred the wheelchair into the centre of the room, swung round and politely gesticulated. 'Welcome to the inner sanctum, Veum. You can try a circuit if you dare.'

16

Harald-Schrøder-Olsen had a fully equipped fitness studio in the cellar. It wasn't even a mini-version. A football team could have trained in here without jostling for space.

With visible pride he showed me his machines. The only difference from a normal gym was the solid bars that led from one piece of equipment to another. He could get out of the wheelchair and 'walk' using his extended arms around the whole circuit, which ended by a door with a rectangular window at the top: a sauna.

The machines were made from nickel-plated steel, the benches upholstered with black leather.

'Show us, Pappa,' Siv said.

Schrøder-Olsen looked up at me. 'Don't you feel like trying?'

I declined graciously. 'No, thank you. I'd rather watch an expert.'

He chuckled, obviously flattered. 'Well, I'm not dressed for this, but I can always give you a quick demonstration.'

He parked the wheelchair by the first piece of equipment, a bench for stretches. With an agility I would not have believed possible for a man of his years, he swung himself up onto the bench and did a few careful stretches while closing his eyes and concentrating on his breathing. Then he sat up and did a few warm-up exercises with his upper body and arms.

Then he swung himself over to the other side of the bench, grabbed the bars and, supporting himself on his arms, moved to the next piece of equipment.

This was a weight trainer. He sat on the seat and grabbed two handles. By pulling he lifted the weights until his arms were at ninety degrees to his body. He kept them there as the veins on his forehead bulged, sweat formed on his top lip and he counted, slowly, internally. Then he allowed the two handles to go back up gently, until the weights had landed, quietly and precisely, like two flying saucers in an American sci-fi film.

He repeated this four times, then let go. 'When I do the full programme, I do it twenty-five times,' he said casually, then moved along the bars like a monkey in a zoo with only limited space to perform its tricks.

The next piece of equipment was for sit-ups, the fourth another weight trainer, this time lying down, the fifth and sixth apparatuses were for thigh and leg muscles, and then there was a rowing machine.

At the end of the circuit was a stationary bike. He gave this one a miss. With a frown, he said, 'This is still too difficult for me.' He looked down. 'I don't have enough strength in my legs. Yet.'

I nodded and asked warily: 'What is actually the matter with you?'

'Ah, the after-effects of a spinal infection I had five years ago. They tell me I'll never completely recover, but it's not in my nature to give up. All my life I've relished challenges. And I don't intend to throw in the towel now.' He looked up at his daughter. 'Not for as long as I have you to look after, eh, Siv?'

But she didn't answer. Once again, she had opened the door to where she kept her dreams concealed, the ones she didn't show anyone.

He sighed and cast a disconsolate glance at me. Then he leaned forward to the sauna door and pushed it open. Inside, another bar led to the bench, but no heat emerged to meet us. 'Finally, I relax here,' he said, letting the door close.

'And how often do you do this programme?'

'Once a day. Sometimes twice. Right.' With another sigh, he tried to shake off the sudden gloom that had gripped him. 'Si-iv! We're going back up. Hello?'

As if approaching us from down a long, long corridor, Siv's face slowly came back to life. and, all of a sudden, her eyes were back, not looking at us, but at least in the same room as us. As though following the flight of a caged bird, her gaze went up and down, high and low, through the room.

'Do you want more cake, Siv?' Schrøder-Olsen asked. 'I'm sure Mamma will give you some.'

'Yes, cake, birthday cake, my birthday cake.' She laughed in an unnaturally loud way, turned on her heel and ran ahead of us out of the room.

I waited until Schrøder-Olsen had made his way back to the wheelchair and held the door open for him.

The lift took him up to the lounge, with me trailing behind him.

As we passed the grand piano, my glance fell on one of the photographs. It was a colour shot of Siv wearing a blue graduation cap.

I stopped by the picture and turned to Schrøder-Olsen. 'Isn't that Siv?'

He stopped. 'Yes, she hasn't always been like ... how you've seen her. She had an accident eight years ago. The year she was graduating from upper secondary. In fact, it's the last photo that was taken of her before...'

I waited for a continuation, which never came. 'What happened?'

A painful expression flitted across his face. 'She fell down a staircase and lost consciousness for too long. Brain damage. I ... There's nothing else to tell. What happened, happened, and can't be changed.' He set off again, quickly, towards the sliding doors and the sunshine.

'Mm, I'm sorry,' I mumbled and set off after him.

On the patio Aslaug Schrøder-Olsen was sitting alone at the table. Her face was raised to the sun, and even though she had rubbed in some sun cream, her skin was so dry that it looked as if it could burn.

'Where is everyone?' her husband asked her irritably.

She eyed him like a hawk. 'Trygve and Bodil went home. He had ... something to do. Odin's indoors cutting Siv a slice of cake.'

They emerged, Siv holding the cake in her hands.

'Oh, Siv,' her mother said. 'Your fingers will get dirty.'

'I'll lick them,' she laughed, with delight, and showed them. Schrøder-Olsen smiled.

'Siv and I are going for a walk in the arboretum,' Odin said.

'That's nice of you, Odin,' his mother said.

'Either of you want to come?'

'No, I'm going to stay here.' She looked at her husband.

He shook his head, still with a dark shadow across his face.

'Va-arg?' Siv asked. 'Would you like to come with us and see the trees?'

I lifted my arm and stared at my watch. 'No, Siv, I don't have any time now. But I can accompany you two down to the road.'

'But you must another time. You promised.'

'Yes, of course,' I said gently. 'Another day I'll go for a walk with you.'

'Now don't you nag herr Veum, Siv. You have to understand that he hasn't got time for that sort of thing,' her mother said.

Siv swallowed the last bit of the cake. Schrøder-Olsen had pushed his wheelchair away from us and was sitting with the Saturday copy of *Aftenposten* spread out on his lap. He seemed older now, as though the demonstration in the cellar had sucked up the last of his vitality.

I spoke up: 'Then I'll be on my way. Thank you. As I said, this was a surprise invitation.'

Schrøder-Olsen looked up and nodded. His wife rose to her feet, like a good hostess, to accompany me to the ivy portal. Neither of them invited me back.

Together with Siv and Odin I strolled down the garden path. I stared at Trygve and Bodil's house. She had changed into an indigo bikini and was unfolding a sun-lounger in front of the house. I couldn't see him anywhere.

Odin noticed where I was looking and smiled. 'So, did you get an answer to your question for Trygve?'

'No, but it was the same one that I asked you yesterday. Did he know anything about the circles Tor Aslaksen moved in?'

He studied Siv's back, who was skipping in front of us.

'I'm not sure Trygve was the right person to ask. Tor was an amateur pilot and my understanding was that he often piloted the plane when Bodil jumped.'

'Do you mean that…?'

'I don't mean anything, Veum, and I haven't said a word. I'm just saying: imagine how that must've looked, from Trygve's angle.'

'Speaking of seeing things from your brother's side, I'm surprised you aren't more involved in the campaign.'

He smirked. 'It's precisely because of him that I'm keeping a low profile this time.'

'Has anything new happened out there?'

'No, but there's going to be another clash if something drastic doesn't happen. They can't store the toxic waste on the premises for ever. And if they decide to transport it elsewhere, then … there'll be hell to pay.'

We had reached the road.

Odin nodded. 'Well, this is where we part company, Veum.'

'For now.'

'Do you think our paths will cross again?'

'Tell me, which is the house Tor Aslaksen grew up in?'

He gestured towards a small, blue house with a well-tended garden near the road. 'There, but don't pester his mother with this, Veum. She's all alone now.'

I nodded sympathetically, but without promising anything.

'You all called him Totto?'

'Yes, from when we were small.'

Siv shouted: 'O-din! Come on.'

'Coming.'

She turned her back on us and walked towards the arboretum. She had already forgotten me, in the same way as she had forgotten the new book she had been given when other thoughts entered her mind.

I stood watching them. He strolled with a relaxed gait while she walked with stiff, slightly angular movements, always a little too fast, as though in a kind of endless, careful fall forward. They reminded me of Christopher Robin and Winnie-the-Pooh walking in Hundred Acre wood.

On the way back to the car park I passed the blue house where Tor Aslaksen had lived. It looked as unoccupied and lifeless as a tool shed in a cemetery early on a Sunday morning.

But this house too reflected a childhood. There had been the sounds of children playing around the white plinth and the blue walls. Boys with grazed knees had climbed trees in the garden, kicked a football on the road and run cheering and laughing to Grønevika to go swimming in the summer. On the fields by the shop, they had learned to ski, and on dark autumn evenings, in the watershed between childhood and puberty, they had sat in Tor Aslaksen's bedroom, playing Beatles records and testing each other on English vocabulary. This house too reflected a childhood someone had smashed and ground to dust, all too prematurely.

Along Mildeveien, cars were parked illegally and so tightly packed together that the bus had to veer into the lane of the oncoming traffic to pass them, a trail of more beachgoers in its wake.

Down in the car park in Mildevågen, cars were so close to one another that you had to breathe in as you threaded your way out to the main road. I left my parking spot to the hordes and heard the bang behind me as two cars tried to race in at the same time. I hoped they were good at conflict resolution. Otherwise, it could be a while before they dipped their toes in the sea.

I inserted a Beach Boys cassette into the player and greeted the summer with music. I had nothing else to offer. Not this side of Christmas.

17

I met Karin Bjørge as arranged, by the bus stop across the street from the old town hall. She was dressed in earthy colours: a skirt and jacket in terracotta and a light-green blouse. Her smile was unable to hide the sorrow that was still etched on her face, but she had let her hair grow again, she had put the nun look behind her and she had outmanoeuvred fate. She was still on the right side of forty – it was too early to roll over and die. There were still a few dinner invitations to enjoy.

We met as old friends. She stretched up and kissed me lightly on the cheek, then hooked her arm inside mine, and we walked to the nearest Chinese restaurant.

While waiting for the food, she leaned across the table and commented confidentially: 'You were going to show me your scar, weren't you?'

I rolled up one shirt sleeve and showed her. She touched it deferentially, as though it were a war wound and not from a thousand empty bottles.

'I thought you'd finished with all that.'

I nodded. 'It's on the way out.' I placed my free hand on hers and squeezed. 'I'm glad you caught me in time.'

She smiled, almost embarrassed. 'Not at all. Besides, I've been on the drugs and alcohol committee at work for years, so I had both the experience and the contacts. I imagine the experience with my daughter, Siren, still haunts me.'

'Well, *skål* anyway,' I said, with a wry grin. I lifted my glass of Farris mineral water while she kept to orange juice, in solidarity. The only way we could possibly become intoxicated was by drinking in the atmosphere between us.

We looked down on the marketplace, where sober tourists were mixing with tottering Vikings weak at the knees from mead. They fitted together like Mongols and Central Europeans during the worst period of tribal migration.

The food arrived on the table, and we ate. 'What actually happened to you this winter, Varg, if you don't mind my asking?'

'I was driving out a demon,' I answered, swallowing a piece of pork in sweet-and-sour sauce. 'I had an old infatuation I needed to exorcise.'

She blushed. 'And did it work?'

'Mhmm. I don't even remember her name.'

She ventured a smile to see if I meant it. And when we left, she invited me back to hers, for a cup of tea.

*

Two hours later we were sitting on her sofa. Through the sitting-room window, the light from the setting sun stroked a golden finger over our skin, and the cups of tea were empty. We were lost in a kiss.

As the sun reddened somewhere above Holsnøy, she lay back on the sofa, her blouse unbuttoned. 'Are you looking at my small breasts?' she asked with the shadow of a smile.

I didn't answer; instead, I leaned forward and kissed them.

She placed her fingers on my neck like soft paws and mumbled into my ear: 'Let's go to the bedroom.'

Inside, she held onto the bedposts as though frightened I would take them with me when I left. A fragrance of ripe apples hovered over her, and I had no intention of leaving. Not for a long, long time.

Before falling asleep I remembered thinking: *Is this the reward?*

But I didn't get an answer to that question, either.

Sunday was like wakening to a new life on an unknown planet. Laughter lurked behind everything we said.

Before we got up, she took my face between her hands and looked at me with a serious expression. 'If this had happened fourteen years ago, what would the rest of our lives have been like?'

I stroked her cheek. 'It's too late to read yesterday's weather forecast, Karin. It's better to see what the weather's like for to-morrow.'

At breakfast she asked me how Thomas was.

'Beate's husband has rented a house in Spain for the summer. I can barely afford the Askøy ferry this year, so he's spending the holiday with them.'

'How old is he now?'

'Sixteen. And I see less and less of myself in him.'

She drained her coffee cup. 'What do you feel like doing now?'

I stroked my chest meditatively, like the echo of a caress. 'What I'd like to do most is stay here.' I looked around. 'However, the sun is still out and we never know how long we will have it for at this time of the year.'

'We can always come back here … afterwards,' she said gently.

*

We walked to the top of Mount Ulriken, sat on a rock with a view of the town, the mountains around it, the fjord, the islands and the sea beyond Bergen – such a broad horizon, it was as if you could sense the curve of the earth. And the newly tuned zither we were holding in our hands was each other's heart strings.

She sat between my legs and leaned back against my stomach and chest. I had my arms around her shoulders and strands of her gossamer hair tickled my face.

It was Sunday, the sky had been cleansed of dirt and only a tiny residue of pollution lay like a coating of dust over the very centre of the town. The sun was making the heather around us steam and emit a fragrance that made your senses reel. Summer had left its mark in the ground and was telling us: this time I'm *staying*.

We sat like this for ages. Afterwards we jogged down to Fløienbakken, gripped by a longing that was bigger and sweeter today because it knew it would be satisfied. Not with a scream. Not with a sigh. But with protracted, playful laughter.

There are lagoons in life, moments of unexpected happiness. This weekend was one such lagoon, and I felt I could drop anchor for good.

But there was still a world outside. In an interval we switched on the television and watched the latest news. I sat up. 'Could you turn up the volume?'

A reporter was standing with a microphone in his hand in front of the factory in Hilleren: '…More drama this weekend as Norlon tried to transport toxic waste from the company's premises on Saturday night.'

The camera swept through the locked gates and into the yard, zooming onto the big, military-coloured vacuum tanker.

'Fighting broke out when a group of employees tried to surge through the chain of demonstrators blocking the exit, and the police had to summon extra manpower to bring the situation under control. The company directors then called off the attempt to force a way past the crowd. There have been no further developments today.'

Afterwards the reporter briefly interviewed Håvard Hope and Trygve Schrøder-Olsen, so briefly that neither of them did any more than state their mutual disagreement. The camera shot rose into the air, caught a flash of sunlight playing on the waves in the fjord and segued naturally into the latest weather forecast.

But we were making our own weather forecasts that evening.

The first night had been frenetic, sudden and notable for a kind of youthful clumsiness. The second night was better.

We had quenched the greatest thirst and could go on long rambles over each other's terrain, smell the summer scents on our skin, hide our faces in moist moss and slake our cravings in new springs.

Resting our heads on the crook of elbows, our fingers caressing the other's face, we exchanged experiences from our tangled lives. Both of us had scars that were so deep, neither of us wanted to venture out yet. And we still had open sores that the sun would need more than a single weekend to heal.

But as night at its darkest enclosed us, we knew each other better than we had done when we met by the old town hall thirty-six hours before.

On Monday morning we launched ourselves into our working week with renewed vigour, me to my office and the first newspapers, Karin to the national registration office.

But Monday morning is a joker. You never know what it might bring.

18

There was an express letter from Florø in my post box. I opened it and took out a photograph of Lisbeth Finslo. That brought me back down to earth with a bump.

It must have been a few years old because her hair was longer, and there was something artificial about her smile, like when a grass widow waves goodbye before the first football league match in spring and knows it will be October before her husband truly returns to her. She was sadder than she had been when I met her.

She was sitting on a step somewhere, in big white shorts and a light-blue blouse. She had one hand behind her neck as if to keep her hair in place, and on the grass in front of her there was a black-and-white blur, which must have been a running kitten.

On the back of the picture her sister had written: *Summer*

1984 (?). And on an enclosed sheet of paper, she had confirmed the commission she had given me.

I sat studying the photograph. It struck me, with greater impact than I had feared, that she was a stranger to me. I was clear now. I didn't know her. I had never known her. She had run past me much too quickly.

I pushed the photograph to the side and concentrated on the newspapers.

The Norlon story was still front-page news, but because the local first-division side had won a football match at the weekend, the coverage was reduced to a single column in one paper, and a corner with a page reference in the other.

However, the papers went into great detail about what had developed into a real free-for-all on Saturday night. The number of demonstrators had trebled in the course of Saturday afternoon, and Håvard Hope had claimed they had evidence from a reliable source that Norlon wasn't even dumping its waste on official public sites. Management, still represented by Trygve Schrøder-Olsen, dismissed such claims as unfounded.

I pushed the papers aside with a sigh. This reminded me more and more of an election battle.

I leaned back in my chair, closed my eyes and thought about Karin. The memory of her body still stirred inside me, a happy satiation, a feeling of bliss. I was a voice that had called in the wilderness, and she had heard me. Perhaps it was her I had been calling all the time, without knowing.

I opened my eyes, turned my hands round and saw my pulse beating through the thin skin. She had kissed me there, first on one hand, then on the other.

The telephone rang. Against my will, I was being drawn back into everyday life. I took the receiver and mumbled: 'Hello.'

'Hamre speaking.' His voice was curt and formal.

'Have you found her?'

'No. You haven't heard from her either, I take it?'

'No.'

'I was wondering if you could pop by, Veum.'

'Oh, yes? Any particular reason?'

'I have something I'd like to show you. How soon can you be here?'

'Well, I'm in the middle of an important conference, but—'

'Fifteen minutes?'

'Fifteen minutes.'

We rang off, and I concluded the conference with the better half of my soul. Then I walked out into the sunshine and strolled down to the police station while imagining what it was that he intended to show me.

I nodded to the duty officer, took the lift up to the right floor and knocked on Hamre's door exactly a quarter of an hour after we had spoken.

He looked up as I entered. 'So you managed to get away?'

I nodded and sat down on the chair he indicated. As if to keep an invisible balance in the office he stood up at the same moment I sat down. Rounding the desk, he pushed a large, blue-and-green nylon suitcase in front of him and into the space between us.

He bored his eyes into mine, like two wall plugs. 'Seen this before, Veum?'

I shook my head. 'Is it ... hers?'

'Why do you think that?'

'Well, I assume you haven't invited me over here to see what you've picked up in the sales.'

He smiled wanly. 'No. But yes, we do think it's hers. It contains mostly clothes, and apart from them, some toiletries and a couple of books. In the wash bag there was a prescription made out to her.'

'Where did you find it?'

The plugs expanded a few millimetres. 'In a storage locker. In

Strandkaien. Two minutes from your office.' He let the words sink in while keeping his eyes on mine.

'Well, that's where the express boat to Nordfjord leaves, so it's not exactly a surprise, is it.'

'No, maybe not. But it means, which you will also appreciate, that she never caught the boat.'

'Was the locker locked?'

He nodded. 'We routinely examine any lockers that exceed the twenty-four-hour deadline. The rest took care of itself.'

I held up my arms. 'You can frisk me if you suspect I have the key.'

He scrutinised me for a while. Then he looked away, turned, walked around the desk and sat down again. He left the suitcase where it was, like an unpleasant admonition between us.

'Is that all you've found?' I asked cautiously.

'No.' He weighed his words like gold nuggets. 'We've found … that is, we think we've found … the red car.'

'Aha. Where?'

'In the car park by the Oasen shopping centre in Fyllingsdalen. It *was* a Kadett, Veum. And it belonged to … Tor Aslaksen.'

'Yes. But I hardly think it was him who parked it there.'

'Hardly.'

'What about…? Was it locked? Was there a key in it?'

He examined me with an amused twinkle in his eye. 'Yes, Veum. It was locked. And, no, there wasn't a key inside. It's missing. And if we find someone walking around with it in their pocket, then we have pretty incontrovertible evidence.'

'What about … any other clues?'

'The car's being thoroughly inspected now. That's all I can say.'

'And Lisbeth? Have you found anyone who's seen her?'

'No. We've done a house-to-house search in Kleiva. No one has seen anything; no one has heard anything. Her daughter is still mystified. We've tried to trace who she was with…'

'Tor Aslaksen,' I said softly.

He leaned closer. 'Are you sure?'

'No, I'm afraid not. But his name was definitely Tor. Someone who had been ringing her quite often recently.'

'Did the daughter tell you that?'

'The sister. But she got it from the daughter. Nothing was cast-iron though. Lisbeth seems to have been keeping her cards close to her chest, even within her family.'

'Strange, don't you think?'

'Maybe. Maybe not. We might find out if you checked Aslaksen's circle of acquaintances.'

'If only he had one. Apart from work and the skydiving community, we haven't come across anyone he contacted regularly. The neighbours were barely on nodding terms with him. He never took anyone home to his mother. A loner, if you ask me.'

'"A burned child shies away from the fire", as we say?'

'What do you mean? Are you thinking of a specific event or person?'

I didn't answer, and he carried on: 'Do you know something more, Veum?'

I threw up my hands. 'No, but thirty years old and still unmarried? He must've been burned at some point.'

'Or he had very expensive fire insurance,' Hamre commented tersely.

We looked at each other for a few seconds, like two hardened poker players, still unsure how good the cards were in the opponent's hand.

I coughed. 'Perhaps I should tell you…'

'Yes, you should,' he answered.

'Her sister, Jannicke, has asked me to search for her, too.'

Hamre smiled patronisingly. 'Well, if she has nothing better to spend her money on, fine. With our network and your budget, I'm afraid you'll be getting the short straw. But I appreciate your telling me, Veum – in case we should meet, covering the same ground, if I can put it like that.' There was a dangerous glint in his eyes. 'And I hardly need add that if you should run across vital information, it's your duty to inform us.'

I nodded. 'Have you anything to offer me in return?'

He ignored the question. 'Where did you meet that evening, you and her?'

'In Strandkaien, by the corner of the Harbitz building.'

'In other words, she could've dropped off the suitcase in left-luggage and gone straight to meet you. Even though she wasn't going to travel until the following day. And we both saw how tidy her flat was. What does that suggest to you?'

'She was intending to spend the night somewhere else?'

'Exactly.' Again, his eyes shone. 'Do you spontaneously invite ladies home for the night if they're angling for it?'

'But she wasn't. She wasn't angling for anything.'

'Sure, Veum? What was she actually checking down by the pool? To see if the water was warm enough?'

'Listen—'

'Did you have your swimming things with you, Veum?'

'No.'

'Did *she*?'

'I don't think so, but—'

'Do you understand what it sounds like if two people, sexually mature, go for a swim together – naked – all alone in a house where it's very unlikely anyone will disturb them?'

'Honestly—'

'Imagine the following scenario, Veum: Lisbeth Finslo is with Tor Aslaksen, but fancies a swim, with you. Aslaksen follows you and surprises you while you're in the early stages of … foreplay. A situation arises and you punch Aslaksen on the chin. He falls into the pool … and sinks.'

'How did he get in?'

'You left the door open.'

'He was there when we arrived.'

'Lisbeth Finslo had a key. If they really were an item, he could easily have had a copy made.'

'And after I'd let him sink, I told Lisbeth to disappear into thin air, so that I could call the police and say I'd found a body?'

'Why not?'

'Besides, it wasn't me who called. It was a man – *another* man. And who was that, Hamre? Can you work that one out with your enormous network?'

He laughed disarmingly. 'I said "imagine the following scenario", Veum. I'm not saying it's correct. But I can imagine several of my colleagues would buy it, without even looking at the price.'

'So, in other words, we're back where we started?'

'Not necessarily.' His gaze was ominous. 'There's one aspect I haven't yet mentioned.'

'Oh, yes? And that is?'

He shuffled the papers in front of him, as though unsure quite how to express himself. 'Tell me … what do you remember about the Camilla Case, Veum?'

The hairs on my neck stood on end. 'Camilla … Do you mean *the* Camilla Case?'

He nodded.

'What does it have to do with this?'

'I shall tell you, Veum.'

19

The Camilla Case started as a routine investigation, but ended as a nightmare. It was one of those cases that leave a stain on the nation's conscience, for which we all, in some way or other, bear the guilt. The case had never been solved.

I looked at Jakob E. Hamre. 'That's quite a few years ago now.'
'1979.'

'Eight years already, my God.'

He watched me, waiting.

'A little girl, seven or eight years old…'

'Seven.'

'…who disappeared from her home under mysterious circumstances and was never found again.'

'In a nutshell. Do you remember any more details?'

'Let me think. It was in Bjørndal forest, wasn't it?'

He nodded. 'The clearing there, to be precise.'

'I can visualise the full-page spread now. The terraced house where they lived and a portrait of the little girl the papers used alongside their headlines for months afterwards.'

'They still write about it, at least once a year, when they summarise unsolved crimes – or when related cases appear in other parts of the country.'

'I've seen. Camilla … what was her surname?'

'Farang.'

'I remember her parents making a desperate appeal on the front page of most of the national dailies.'

'They're divorced now.'

'The strain was too much?'

'Mm, yes. And the circumstances. There was something not right about this case from the start. There still is, for that matter – it hasn't been cleared up.'

'What was the problem?'

'I'll try and stick to what I know. Camilla was put to bed after watching children's TV and having supper – and before the TV news. So seven-thirty, at the latest. At some point during the news, she called for her mother, who went in to talk to her. At around seven-forty-five, she calculated. She poked her head around the door one more time, at eight-forty-five approximately. She was asleep by then. And that was the last time anyone we spoke to saw of little Camilla.'

'OK. That's what I remember. What usually happens in cases like this is that the child wanders away from the house … and doesn't return home, right?'

'Exactly.'

'So the investigation concentrated on the situation at home?'

'Mm. It did. But let's keep to the facts. The mother discovered her daughter was missing when she decided to turn in herself. At eleven-twenty. She checked the bedroom to make sure her daughter was sleeping as sweetly as before. But her bed was empty. At first, of course, she thought she'd gone to the loo, but she wasn't there, either. The bedrooms in these houses are on the ground floor and there's a door from the child's room to a patch of garden behind the house. This door was open.'

'Open?'

'Yes.'

'Any signs of a break-in?'

'No.'

'But it must've been locked?'

'Probably. But the mother wasn't sure. They may've forgotten to close the top catch because Camilla often used this door when she went out to play. They usually closed it when they put her to bed, but she couldn't swear she had that evening.'

'And if it *was* locked, the catch was so high up that a girl of seven wouldn't have been able to reach it?'

'Yes, not without a ladder, and there wasn't one in the room.'

'What did the mother do?'

'She was in a state of shock, of course. The first thing she thought was that her daughter must've been sleepwalking or something like that. She ran out of the house and searched for her, pretty erratically from what we could gather. She only called the police after ten minutes. Her call was recorded at twenty-three thirty-four. A search was quickly organised, but, as you know, without success.'

'No clues at all?'

'None. Over the many months the investigation lasted we didn't find a single one. There was a lot of circumstantial evidence, of course, loads of calls from the general public, searches of some houses around Bjørndal and other parts of town, including those of several known paedophiles.'

'You made an arrest too, didn't you?'

'Yes, but it was an impetuous decision. We had nothing on him. It was all based on circumstantial evidence that didn't hold water. The famous burgundy-coloured car, which turned out to ... Well, we got to the bottom of that too. And banged our heads against a wall again.'

'What about the domestic situation?'

'That was what we concentrated on. You always have to tread carefully with parents caught up in something like this. Very soon there are inexactitudes and misunderstandings because of the colossal emotional strain. Anyone with children will understand that. So, it took a while before we could pinpoint the contradictions in the mother's statement.'

'You didn't mention where the father was that day.'

'He was inland, doing some business or other.'

'Some business?'

'Or a course. He worked for an IT firm. At any rate, he was at a course centre outside Oslo, with a watertight alibi. He had no idea what had happened when he was rung the following morning.'

'I see.'

'You can imagine the rest?'

I nodded.

'That was when it came out that the mother had seen Camilla a second time. At eight-forty-five, more or less. And she'd been asleep apparently.'

'At a quarter to nine.'

'Then the mother went into her bedroom – with a friend.'

I sighed. 'And, naturally enough, it wasn't so easy to admit that, even in such a dramatic situation as this.'

'You can imagine it – the guilt. If she'd been in the sitting room watching TV, no one would've blamed her. But in the adjacent room, in bed with another man...' He gestured expressively with his hands.

'And this man...'

'Left the house at eleven. He should've been at work by then, but ... time flew and he had to rush off.'

'And he couldn't have...?'

Hamre shook his head. 'He wasn't alone for a moment while he was there. We have the mother's word on that, and we had no reason not to trust her by that point. Besides, we went through his car with a fine-tooth comb. Their car, I mean. And there was absolutely nothing that indicated a crime.'

'*Their* car?'

He nodded gloomily. 'That was where we went wrong. The man's car was being repaired so he'd come to the house by bus. When he had to leave in a hurry, fru Farang – her first name was Vibeke – offered him their car, so long as he took it into the garage, because it was due for a service the following morning. A burgundy Opel Kapitän estate. Which was seen by a witness leaving the area at approximately eleven. When we ran a check on the relevant brands and models of cars in that colour, we came across an ex-con. To make sure no evidence slipped through our fingers, we arrested the man and thoroughly examined the car, his flat, and the attic and cellar of the building where he lived. We found nothing, but unfortunately the press had caught wind of what we were doing. I'm sure you remember the headlines: 'Camilla Case Arrest'. And the whole country breathed out, until the following day, when we had to announce that we'd let him go because there were inadequate grounds for suspicion.'

'I remember that. What happened then?'

'We went down other avenues. Combed the whole area around her house. The forest, drains, rock faces. Searched lakes, rivers etc, all the way down to Bjørndalspollen. House-to-house searches, again and again. The bigger papers followed up with comprehensive reports, reconstructing events in that part of town, minute by minute. TV put out a reconstruction on the two big news programmes at peak viewing time. Nothing. It was hopeless. In the end, after several months of intense work, the case was gradually wound down. After six months it was on the back-burner, and a year after the little girl had disappeared, it was officially closed. With the proviso that it would be reopened if fresh evidence came to light.'

'And has it?'

'Not of any significance – until today.'

I leaned forward. 'I still don't see any connection between these two cases. Where's the link?'

'The man who visited Vibeke Farang the night her daughter disappeared was Tor Aslaksen.'

20

I let the information sink in as my mind raced, like the revolving images on a one-armed bandit. When they finally stopped, the three images were: Tor Aslaksen at the bottom of the pool, Lisbeth Finslo shouting, 'I had no idea. I didn't understand,' and the vague memory I had of the newspaper photograph of a little girl.

'And the job he was rushing to that night was at Norlon?'

Hamre nodded. 'Yes.'

'How did you find this out?'

'I had a vague feeling I'd come across his name before. I hadn't been at the centre of the Camilla Case. Other officers led the investigation, and I was never involved in the interviews with Aslaksen. But I fed his name into the databank and it came up with this.'

'And what more can you tell me?'

He reached out for a pile of documents and picked up three or four sheets of paper stapled together. 'I have a summary of the interview here. When Vibeke Farang finally came clean and gave us a name, there was no reason for him to deny anything. And he wasn't married.'

'And?'

'They'd met at a fitness studio – Health and Beauty – where she was on the staff. The relationship lasted six months, off and on, all depending on where herr Farang was in the country. And everything had taken place after Camilla had gone to bed. No one – not even the nosiest neighbours – had observed what was going on. The husband had no idea. Tor Aslaksen hadn't bragged about it to anyone. If it hadn't been for what happened to Camilla, nothing would've ever surfaced about it, I suppose.'

'I don't remember seeing any of this in the press.'

'No, it didn't leak out. We managed to keep a lid on this particular part of the case. There were a couple of journalists with centrally placed sources, let me put it like that, who were on our backs. But we managed to shut them up, partly to protect the investigation, but also to ensure peaceful private lives.'

'And what did Aslaksen have to say about the evening?'

'Nothing that took us any further. Broadly, he confirmed everything that Vibeke Farang had said; but then he'd had plenty of time to prepare. He'd arrived, through the main door, at around eight. They'd drunk a cup of coffee and chatted for a while before they got down to business. He then found himself

pressed for time and they hastily arranged that he would borrow
the family car, as I've already explained. He drove to Norlon,
where he was called to a meeting regarding the technical side of
the transportation of a substantial amount of waste. Toxic waste,
I should add, bearing in mind the present stand-off there. The
following morning, he took the car to the garage for a service
and, still unaware of the connection, read about a little girl who
had disappeared: no names were released to the press that day.
It was only the following day that they were made public; according to his statement it was a terrible shock. So terrible that
he was rendered speechless…'

'Isn't that what I said? He *had* had his fingers burned, Hamre.'

'So speechless that he didn't even think of contacting the
police. It was Vibeke Farang who brought his name to our attention.'

'Hm. Were any of the girl's clothes missing?'

'Was she dressed, you mean?' He frowned as he thumbed
through the piles of paper. 'As far as I remember, the mother said
no clothes were missing except for the pyjamas she'd been
wearing in bed.'

'And what time of the year was this?'

'April. End of the month.'

I gave this some careful thought. 'Well, naturally, I can't
imagine that I'll come across anything you haven't found during
six months of investigation. It isn't immediately clear what the
motive could be, either. A jealous partner can, of course, devise
the most unpleasant things, but Farang's alibi was, if I understand you correctly, rock solid?'

'Not a flaw in it.'

'And Aslaksen – did he say anything about the girl at all?'

'The night she disappeared, she was barely mentioned. On
earlier visits he'd heard her voice a few times, if she hadn't fallen
asleep by the time he arrived. Once he'd met her in town with

her mother, and he'd said hello, the way you do to the children of friends. Otherwise, he never talked about her.'

I scratched my head. 'And where are they all today?'

'Well, we know where Aslaksen is. Vibeke Farang lives in Sotra and still works in this fitness studio in town. Except that she's changed its name.'

'To what?'

'Body & Soul, whatever that might mean. Her ex-husband, Bård Farang, has remarried and lives in Hardanger.'

'Tell me, Hamre, why have you told me all this? You guys aren't usually so generous with information when I drop in.'

Hamre leaned forward and eyed me gravely. 'Because the Camilla Case is one we'll never shelve until it's solved, Veum. And we need all the help we can get, from what the press calls "the great detective" – the general public. In this connection, you can regard yourself as the public. If you uncover anything at all that might cast light on this eight-year-old case, we'll be very grateful.'

I clapped quietly. 'Congratulations.'

He watched me.

'You didn't run any other names through your databank, did you, Hamre? Such as Lisbeth Finslo?'

'Yes, in fact I did.'

'And?'

'Nothing. The cleanest record imaginable. Not so much as an unpaid TV licence.'

'She comes from Florø, you know.'

'And what's that supposed to mean? They don't have anything to entertain themselves with up there?'

'No, no. I was thinking perhaps she isn't on the same register or—'

'No, she is. Though not with respect to minor offences. I'll ask the Florø police to check their local registers, not that I think it will take us a millimetre further.'

'So, basically, we're back to where we started – square one?'

'Life is a board game.' He waved wearily. 'Go back to Start, Veum.'

I stood up and made for the door.

'But don't forget … If you should find anything, then…'

'I know quite a few papers that would pay considerable sums for it. I'm on my way to one now.'

'Oh, yes?' He arched his eyebrows.

'To read through their archives. On the Camilla Case.'

21

Great circles of white light marked out the edges of houses in Bergen's narrow streets. Mount Fløifjell lay on its back, lazily breathing into a green mantle of foliage, almost reflected in a sky that had not been bluer since Noah's ark beached and the waters slowly began to sink. I felt like the first animal coming ashore.

With every year that passed, I thought: women are more attractive this year. And younger. And a little more inaccessible.

When I entered Paul Finckel's office I realised that he was suffering from the same longings. He was poring over an English tabloid newspaper open at page three, where a Welsh Valkyrie was displaying her charms to such devastating effect that even a hardened voyeur like Paul Finckel had fallen victim to idle fantasies.

Every time I saw him, I thought he had become even fatter. And older. And a little more unappetising. And it didn't escape my attention for a minute that we were exactly the same age.

He looked up at me gloomily, ran a podgy hand over his straggly beard and grinned torpidly. 'Varg the outcast, lean and fast.'

'And you…?' I nodded towards the Welsh torpedoes. 'Dreaming of happier days?'

He snorted into his beard. 'One of Maggie Thatcher's bell-cows. In a week she'll be telling the general public she's slept with a minister. In two she'll be forgotten. That's how they increase circulation.'

'While you do your best to keep it down?'

He smiled. 'If we're still talking about circulation, then yes. I've done my bit though, as the bride said on her wedding night.'

'Was it you who wrote about the Camilla Case – many moons ago?'

There was a glint in his eyes, like diamonds in a pool of dirty water. 'The Camilla Case. Have you got a sniff of something, Varg?'

I looked around his tiny office. It seemed smaller than ever, but that was because he had become bigger and still hadn't emptied the boxes of newspapers he'd had the last time I was here, half an aeon ago. One of them was in front of the open door, which couldn't be closed without shifting considerable piles of material.

I lowered my voice. 'I won't deny there's a chance the case might become front-page news again. You couldn't let me have a look at the archives, could you?'

He rolled his eyes. 'How much time have you got?'

'As much as I need.'

He grabbed the phone and dialled an internal number. 'Sol? Moon here ... Ha ha ... The Camilla Case. All the folders ... Under C? ... Yes.' He rang off. 'Sol will cast her rays over us as soon as she has time. Tell me what this is about.'

'I can't. For the time being I just want to get up to speed. It's been mentioned in connection with another case I'm on. You will, of course, be the first to hear when I have something.'

He grinned mischievously. 'You've said that before, Varg. But by the time it comes to my ears – through the usual channels – they'll be grilling you at the police station.'

'Well, you know how it is. Those boys like to stake a prior claim to everything.'

A tall blonde with gravestone teeth appeared in the doorway, carrying eight bulging, yellowish-brown folders. She ploughed a way through the mess and dropped the folders on Finckel's desk, sending up clouds of dust and some press cuttings. 'Next time fetch them yourself,' she snapped, and left, without dignifying me with a glance.

'Sol, don't let the sun go down on me,' Finckel complained as she left.

He pushed the folders over towards me dismissively. 'Do what you have to do, Varg. I'll see if I can squeeze a few lines out of the computer in the meantime.' He swung his chair round and stared gloomily at the blind screen, which was pleading for input.

I concentrated on the archive folders.

Broadly speaking, the material was organised chronologically. However, there had been a good deal of delving into the folders before, so in some places the chronology had been muddled, not that this upset the whole picture.

The very first article appeared the day after she disappeared. The cutting was dated 27th April, 1979. The heading read 'Police Search in Bjørndalen'. The text itself didn't tell me anything I didn't already know, while the photo showed four or five people in uniforms combing the small forest.

The next was more dramatic: 'Where's Camilla?' The typography told me she had moved to the front page, where she would stay for months. The article was illustrated with a picture of Camilla, obviously taken from a colour photo, and a caption suggesting the police had started to fear a criminal act.

I sat studying her face, a grainy raster image from the mists of time. She had blonde hair in a bob, with a bow above one ear. There was a pallid smile on her lips, as though she was becoming heartily sick of the photographer's repartee. Her eyes were large, her face was round, and she was wearing a dress or a blouse with a white lace collar. She had been seven years old in 1979. Today she would be fifteen, if she was still out there, somewhere.

I raised my head and stared pensively at the backyard Finckel's office looked out on.

Finckel looked up. 'Well? Find anything?'

'No. I was just thinking…'

'Mhm?'

'These children who go missing – what happens to them? Does Peter Pan take them to Neverland, never to return? Or do they live with new parents who themselves have been childless?'

'You can forget the latter, as she was so old when she vanished. Infants maybe. But her…' He grimaced cynically. 'The best-case scenario is she went to sea. But it's more likely that she's buried somewhere no one will ever dig.'

'They made an arrest at one point, didn't they?'

'Correct. An old friend of the police. Raymond Sørensen. But he'd never done anything *so* serious. They were like dolls for him. He liked to dress and undress them. A harmless fellow, but an absolute pest to those he molested. He's out again now, by the way.'

'Out again?'

'Yes. They nabbed him for something else, eighteen months after the Camilla Case. Molestation and abduction. A girl of six. He's out on licence now after serving five years.'

'Raymond Sørensen?' I noted down the name.

'Is he the one you're after?'

'I don't think so.'

I leafed through the cuttings. On one I saw an aerial photo of the whole residential area where she had lived, with a white circle around one house. 'Has Anyone Seen Camilla?'

Every so often there were detailed summaries of events and

the investigation so far. In connection with one of them Camilla's parents appeared on the front page. Their faces looked harrowed from lack of sleep. 'Give Us Camilla Back!'

Bård Farang had thick dark hair that fell in untidy curls around his skeletal face. Vibeke Farang seemed younger than him; her hair was straight and lifeless, and she had dark bags under her eyes, like a child who has been allowed to stay up for too long.

I showed the cutting to Finckel. 'They got divorced later.'

He glanced at it, uninterested. 'Yes. The stress was probably too much for them. Modern marriages aren't built for that sort of strain. The builders have bodged and the contractor's gone bankrupt.'

'Did you meet them?'

He pulled at his grizzled beard. 'What do I get as commission, Varg? A dram on Judgement Day?'

'If you think you need one.'

'It'll have to be one on the rocks. Yes, I met them. If you can make out the signature, you'll see it was me who wrote the article. But it was at a press conference, with no chance of anything personal, although it was heart-rending enough, even for a hardened hack like me. Later I had a more personal interview with the mother. Alone.'

'Not with the father?'

'No. He shunned the spotlight. It was probably his way of gaining some distance from everything. Whereas she never gave up; she seemed to throw herself into the scrum again and again. It's no more than eight or nine months since she was interviewed by one of the weeklies.' He wrote the headline in the air: CAMILLA'S MOTHER NEVER GIVES UP HOPE. A heart-wrenching interview with the mother of the missing girl.

'So, you think there's a chance she'd talk to me, too?'

'And what would you talk to her about? The lover?'

'Ah, you know?'

He smirked. 'Of course, I do. She had a man in the house and was humping him while her daughter went missing from the adjacent room.'

'But why did you never write about it?'

'Privacy, Varg. Besides, how do you think I would've fared with my sources at the police station if I'd gone public with information like that? They would've dried up as fast as the booze at a vinmonopol sale, my lad.' He slumped back in his chair. 'So that was what you thought you'd discovered. Sorry, Varg. Old hat in these parts.'

'You know the name of the lover, do you?'

His eyes flickered. 'Well, I heard the name once, but it turned out ... It doesn't matter. Do *you* know?'

'It definitely wasn't me. Listen, since you know the case firsthand, have you got any personal theories as to what might've happened that night?'

He scrutinised me with a hangdog expression, the way a Catholic priest would regard a sinner come to confess. 'It's chance that rules our lives, Varg. I think she crossed the path of a dangerous and capricious person at the wrong time. One of Raymond Sørensen's kind, only worse and more cunning. Someone who struck when the opportunity offered itself, spontaneously, without forethought.'

'And the opportunity was...?'

'The first time a small child experiences sexuality in a brutally raw form, it's frightening. Imagine little Camilla being woken by the noise coming from the neighbouring room. Screams and hoarse groans. She goes out of her bedroom, tiptoes over to the door, peeps in through a crack and sees her mother with another man.' His darkened eyes are moist. 'What does she do? Does she run in shouting "hey, hey, leave my mamma alone"? While her mother is writhing under him groaning "yes, yes, yes"? Or does she run blindly into the street, as far away as she can get? And then…' He paused. 'I don't know, Varg. A theory, as you said.'

'And this person who would have picked her up came out of the darkness and disappeared into it, without being seen?'

'It's exactly what happens in all cases like this. Unfortunately, the Camilla Case is not the only one. Children are so vulnerable when they are exposed to someone malevolent.'

'In other words, you don't think this case will be solved?'

'After so many years? No, I don't, unless new information comes to light. What are you sitting on, Varg?'

I smiled sheepishly. 'A chair.'

He leaned forward. 'The next time you ask to see the archives, I'll send you to Norwegian Children's Comics.'

'No need. I collect them. Okay then. I'll tell you the little I know. But I can assure you your police sources will not only dry up if you print any of this, they will turn to sand beneath your feet.'

'Come on then. Spit it out.'

'There was a death reported in the papers on Saturday. A man drowned in an indoor swimming pool up by Nordås bay.'

'An accident, wasn't it?'

'The police are investigating it and are searching for witnesses who might've seen anyone or anything unusual near the crime scene. One woman in particular. By the name of Lisbeth Finslo.'

'And?'

'Well, it might not have been an accident after all. The man who died was Vibeke Farang's friend from 1979.'

Finckel let out a long whistle. 'And you think this death might have something to do with the Camilla Case?'

'I don't think anything. I don't know anywhere near enough to form an opinion. I'm trying to find Lisbeth Finslo, but while I was at it my attention was drawn to this connection.'

He looked down at his hands and glanced up at the screen. 'That was all?'

'That was all.'

'Let me know if you find anything more concrete? In the meantime, I'll read up on the death and the missing woman. What did you say the dead man's name was?'

'Aslaksen. Tor Aslaksen.'

He settled his gaze on the archive folders. 'And you can leave them there. I'll flick through them myself now you've whetted my appetite.'

22

I walked back to the office and tried to contact Bodil Schrøder-Olsen.

She worked in an insurance company, her father-in-law had said. I consulted the Yellow Pages, under 'Insurance'. The telephone directory in Bergen was in *nynorsk* even though the majority of the population spoke *bokmål*. This was what you called county democracy, which must not on any account be confused with the normal usage of the word 'democracy'. Many people wrote furious letters to the newspapers about the issue. As for me, I had never been able to see it as anything other than amusing – spicing up humdrum, everyday life. And for those on their final journey it hardly mattered whether you were categorised under 'Funerals' or something in *nynorsk*. So, with an indulgent smile, I looked up the *bokmål* word for insurance, was told to look under T for the *nynorsk* word, and did as I was instructed.

I started at the top of the pyramid, with the companies that had the biggest deficits in their annual accounts and the top managers who paid no more in tax than a pre-school teacher. I didn't find her there.

I worked my way down the list, past the companies that had

just been bought up by Swedish investors and those that had merged with bankruptcy-threatened banks or other insurance companies with tax-efficient investment needs, to one of the smallest and therefore also the most solid, regional companies.

I found her there, good-natured and charming, until I said who I was. Then the temperature plummeted at once, and she said in a chilled tone: 'And what kind of insurance are you after?'

'Life insurance, literally.'

'Delightful.'

'I have a few questions to ask you without the family present, if I may.'

'Sorry, I'm busy.'

'For how long?'

'All day. I'm on my way out of the door to a big conference in Sandsli, and from there I'm going direct to Flesland airport.'

'Are you going abroad?'

'No, I'm going to do a parachute jump.'

'Ah, I see. And when will you land?'

'By then it'll be time to eat, and this evening I'm busy.'

'I wouldn't wish to have to drop by and ask my questions over a meal…'

'Are you threatening me?'

'I'm making you an offer. In other words, I would appreciate it if you could find time for me somewhere. It won't take long. I could maybe drive you to Sandsli?'

'I can drive myself, thank you very much. And I have a briefing on the cassette player. The only time I can see you is if you join me in the plane.'

'OK. When?'

'Meet me in Flesland, in the small planes area, at four-thirty, sharp. Now I have to go. Be punctual. I won't wait.'

She rang off, no superfluous civilities. I put down the receiver slowly, wondering what I should ask her.

They had fish on the menu in the first-floor cafeteria, but that fish hadn't seen the sea from the inside for many weeks. On the other hand, it was saltier than pickled herring and the meat was paler than a dead deacon.

At the table beside me sat four pensioners discussing the weekend's pools results. They had this week's coupons spread out in front of them, like a horoscope for the rest of their lives. So they were confident that they would also see this Saturday.

After the meal I felt like a Mormon on the banks of the Great Salt Lake, and I had to go to the counter for another jug of water so as not to turn into cured meat on my way to Flesland.

I drove via Paradis, but there was nothing heavenly about the temperature. The thermometer was approaching thirty, as though the heat from the queue of dense traffic was sending the temperature soaring.

I put the fan on the highest setting and rolled down the window, not that that gave me more than an illusion of cool air. The sky above the amputated motorway between Hop and Rådalen was like a glowing metal plate, a blue flame from a soldering lamp. If you looked into the sun, you risked going blind.

I parked by the gates to the airport for private planes. I had hardly come to a halt when Bodil Schrøder-Olsen drove up alongside in her smart, little red Lamborghini, so close to my tarmac-grey Toyota that on a rainy day we could have crawled through the side-windows to each other without getting our hair wet.

She nodded curtly, walked ahead of me to the gates and unlocked them. I followed her. Neither of us said a word.

She was wearing a black leather skirt, a short-sleeved white blouse and pretty black shoes. Over one shoulder she carried a tightly woven, Indian pattern red-and-brown bag. In her other hand, she held an indigo briefcase with bright-red hinges.

In front of one of the hangars a blond, well-built young man with a decorative oil-smear on one cheek was preparing the plane. Bodil gave him a hug and walked towards the hangar. 'I'll get changed and check the equipment.' To me she said, as if I were her chauffeur: 'Wait here.'

'But…' I shrugged and turned to the pilot. 'Hi, my name's Varg Veum. She's invited me to fly with her.'

He smiled youthfully and measured my strength with a supple, muscular handshake. 'Petter Svardal.'

'I thought Tor Aslaksen was usually her pilot.'

'Not recently,' Petter Svardal said lightly, gazing upward as if to judge the direction of the wind.

'No? For how long?'

He shrugged. 'A few months. I'm not sure.'

'And you were on the reserves bench and offered your services?'

His gaze returned to earth, blue and implacable. He stepped closer. 'I didn't catch … your name. What was it?'

'Veum. Varg Veum. She's invited me along.'

'I did catch that bit.' He turned abruptly, took a cotton rag from the back pocket of his faded jeans and walked towards the aircraft to clean an imaginary stain on the tailplane.

The plane was painted blue and white with a silver stripe in between. One door was open, and I could see into the passenger cabin, where the seats were upholstered in bluish-grey imitation leather, perhaps made by Norlon in Hilleren.

I stepped closer. 'What make is this plane?' I asked his slim neck.

He glanced over his shoulder while continuing to clean. 'A Cessna 117. 1979 model but as good as gold.'

'As trim as a trapeze artist?'

He turned right round. 'Eh?'

I gesticulated. 'Have you been a pilot long?'

'Six years.'

'Is it your plane?'

He gaped at me, his mouth half open. 'This one? No. It's hers. Surely you know that. I just fly it for her.'

'Does she fly as well?'

'Of course. But it's a bit difficult to fly it after you've jumped.'

'I can see the problem. Have you got your own plane?'

He shook his head. 'Can't afford one, yet. But I'm saving up. In the meantime, I fly for others. I've flown tourists to the Hardanger glacier ten to twelve times this summer already.'

His gaze slid past me, to the hangar gates, the way a dog looks up when it sees its lord and master coming through the door. If he'd had a tail, he would have wagged it.

I turned and followed his gaze.

She had changed into something more practical: a light, greyish overall, white helmet with the plane's colours on the side, a flash of a white T-shirt at the neck and high, light-brown boots with solid soles. The parachute was attached to her back by tight straps, which crossed her chest down to a broad camouflage belt. Her dimples deepened as she threw me a spare parachute and said: 'Take this one, Veum.'

I caught the light packet and felt my stomach sink. 'But I'm not going to…'

'Really?' she answered sarcastically and took a large stride up into the plane.

'Have you jumped before?' Petter Svardal asked me curiously, as though he was from the local radio station and was going to interview me before the big jump.

'Blessed are the meek,' I answered. 'For they shall inherit a parachute.' Then I followed Bodil Schrøder-Olsen into the plane.

The heat outside made the smell inside stronger. Oil and leather mingled with the perfume on her skin, becoming a mixture unlikely to be sold in the elegant department stores of Paris.

I dropped the parachute onto the floor and mumbled: 'You're not getting me to try anything like this … without training.'

'Wuss, are you, Veum?' she said provocatively, adjusting the straps around her thighs. 'And you the big, tough 'tec?'

Petter Svardal looked at me sharply as he passed, but said nothing.

There was no partition between the pilot's seat and the cabin, so I said softly: 'How can I ask you private questions like this?'

She sent a disdainful glance at the pilot's seat. 'Petter won't say anything. Besides…' She raised her voice. 'Petter.'

He turned.

'After you've received the "clear for take-off" signal from the tower, keep your headphones on for a bit, while Veum and I have a frank exchange of opinions. Alright?'

He nodded, like the well-trained poodle he was, put on the headset and started checking the instruments, then called the control tower.

Bodil followed the take-off procedure intently, and it was only when the plane was taxiing down the runway that she leaned back in her seat, buckled her belt and directed a gaze at me. 'You have ten minutes, Veum. Not a second more.'

Petter Svardal's headset crackled and we increased speed. To the east of us were the terminal buildings; to the west the mountains on Sotra rose as a barrier between us and the horizon.

'I'm interested to hear what you know about Tor Aslaksen and why he died.'

She took a deep breath, annoyed. 'First up, I have no idea why he died. And second—'

'But you knew he was dead?'

'Of course. Trygve told me.'

'When did he find out?'

'Friday morning. The police told him. As soon as they'd found out who he was and where he worked.'

'And you?'

'Trygve rang me, in my office. It was a bit of a shock.'

'You were … close friends?'

Her dark eyes flashed. '*Second* up, that has nothing whatsoever to do with you, Veum. My husband had known Tor since his childhood – he was also a colleague and a subordinate; but it was only after I met Trygve and was introduced to Tor through him that we got to talking up here … in the flying club.'

'You had common interests?'

'He was an engineer. He'd always been fascinated by flying. For me it was a challenge, as with IT. To master a skill like men. To show I'm their equal in another area to which they think they have an exclusive right.'

'A kind of symbolic battle of the sexes, you mean?'

Her smile was tinged with steel. 'You could call it that, yes.'

'When did you meet your husband?'

'Trygve? In … 1981.'

'And when did you get married?'

'Two years later.'

'And when did you start – please don't take this amiss – flying with Tor Aslaksen?'

'Another two years later, I'd guess. Around eighty-five.'

'And how long did it last?'

'What do you mean *last*?'

I nodded towards the pilot. 'You have a new pilot now.'

As if on cue, Petter Svardal accelerated, pulled back the control column and forced the plane into the air with an elegant, upward swallow-dive into the turquoise summer's day. The sound west of Flesland became a belt of sunlight dividing the countryside into two. We rose like a shuttlecock struck by a heavenly racquet, and before we knew it the islands of Lille Sotra and Askøy, Hilleren and Kvarven, and then By fjord, lay beneath us like glossy stickers in an album.

'Listen, Veum. Who I fly with on these jumps is as far from your business as it's possible to get. Sometimes it was Tor, sometimes it's Petter, other times it may be someone else. The key is it must be someone I can trust. You'd never be invited.'

'You're so kind. But it's been a while since you've flown with Tor, from what I gather.'

She cast a stern glare at Petter Svardal's neck. 'Where did you gather that?'

I stared out of the window. 'Just something I picked up.'

Bergen and the seven mountains unfolded beneath us. Nordness headland pointed north, as if showing us the broad path to perdition. The Fløien, Ulriken, Løvstakken and Damsgård mountains enclosed Bergen's central parts, unable to prevent the town from sneaking through Løvstakken's legs and down into the valley of Fyllingsdalen, around the corner of Damsgård to Loddefjord and along the beachy edge of the Sandvik mountain towards the districts of Åsane and Arna. And to the south the gates were open to Fana.

'Anyway, it's rubbish,' she hissed. 'I'd fly with Tor tomorrow if that was on the programme.' And added: 'If it were possible,' in a different tone of voice.

She looked at her watch and glanced at the altitude meter on the instrument panel. 'Five more minutes, Veum.'

We were still climbing. The mountains below were shrinking until they were behind us and we were over the flatter terrain of Fana. The agricultural areas by Stend and along Lake Kaland cut yellow swathes through the green, now with rashes of new-builds from Nordås to Flesland, around the Klokkervannet lake, towards Hamre bridge, and up both the wooded sides of Vallahei.

I leaned over to her. 'What does the name Lisbeth Finslo mean to you?'

'Lisbeth Finslo? Nothing. What's it supposed to mean to me?'

I scrutinised her. Her face revealed nothing apart from irritation, but perhaps poker was another of the sports where she wanted to challenge men.

I went a step further. 'What about the Camilla Case?'

Now irritation gave way to uncertainty. 'The Camilla Case? What do you mean?'

'Do you remember the Camilla Case?'

'Naturally. Who doesn't? Besides ... But what has it to do with all this?'

'With Tor Aslaksen, you mean?'

'Yes?'

I ignored the question. 'You said ... "besides". What were you about to say?'

She shrugged. 'I worked with her father for a couple of years.'

'Camilla's father?'

'Yes. Bård Farang. In fact, when he left, I took over his job. We were colleagues.'

'When did he leave?'

'End of 1980, start of eighty-one. Eighteen months after ... It must've been terrible for him. For them.'

'Why did he leave?'

She gestured vaguely. 'Apparently he had a ... religious awakening.'

'Oh, yes?'

'He left town. I'm not sure where to. Back to nature or something.'

I pondered. 'Tor Aslaksen. You got to know him later, didn't you?'

'Yes, I told you I did.'

'And he never mentioned anything about the Camilla Case?'

She looked around. The plane was circling over the marshes north-east of Flesland.

She checked the parachute harness. 'Why on earth would he?' she mumbled distractedly.

'Well, I…'

She fixed her eyes on mine. 'The offer's still open, Veum.'

'The offer?'

She patted Petter Svardal lightly on the shoulder, unbuckled her safety belt, walked over to the door through which we had entered and pushed it open with a determined shove.

A gust of wind blew into the cabin, a frosty finger stroked my neck, and I automatically gripped the arms of the seat to make sure I wasn't going anywhere. The din of the engine rose like a storm around us.

She gesticulated towards the shimmering blue sky. 'Maiden jump, Veum. It's now or never,' she shouted.

'Never,' I shouted back.

She appraised me, the way an experienced fisherman looks at a minnow before chucking it back. Then she shouted a last message to Petter Svardal: 'I'll land on C.'

One second she was there, arms outstretched, like a diver in a competition, ready to launch herself. The next she was gone. The blue sky outside the door waved at me like a white flag.

Petter Svardal removed his headset and half turned. 'Shut the door, will you, Veum.'

I leaned over, grabbed the door with both hands and closed it after her, the way you shut the gate of a burial chamber.

The plane banked and I looked out.

Far, far below, a blue-and-white parachute had opened, as if a gigantic mushroom had grown up through the grey-and-green landscape.

I leaned forward to Petter Svardal and said in a low voice: 'Have you been to bed with her?'

He sat stupefied for a few seconds as a deep crimson spread up his neck. Then he turned around and said in a barely controlled voice: 'That's none of your … Do you want me to go on autopilot and forcibly eject you?'

'Autopilot? In a plane of this size? She was definitely sleeping with Tor Aslaksen.'

'I mean it.'

Our eyes locked in hopeless combat, then he concentrated on the route ahead and down, while I leaned back in my seat, alone with all my fumbling thoughts.

The rest of the flight passed in total silence.

The plane landed elegantly and taxied at great speed towards the hangar. When it came to a stop I unbuckled the belt, pushed the door aside and jumped down onto the tarmac. Behind me I heard Petter Svardal say: 'Veum, wait…'

I turned and waited.

The first punch I parried with my palm, the second with my left forearm. He made a very obvious move to kick me in the groin, so obvious that I had all the time in the world to perform a toreador's flourish and shimmy away.

He stamped the ground and raised his fists in a desperate attempt to look ferocious. Only partially succeeding.

'You've raised your pennant and flown it high enough now, Petter,' I said with an ironic smile. 'Don't force me to dub you a knight, because I'll leave you sprawled on the ground for quite a while.'

He lowered his arms and spat on the ground in front of me. 'I'll go and look for her,' he muttered as he passed me heading towards the gates.

'Look for C,' I shouted after him, then slowly followed in the same direction.

I didn't go to C. I got in my car and drove the shortest route to B.

23

I passed Straume bridge and followed Straumeveien inland. The windy old road that had been infamous for traffic congestion had become the smoothest-flowing arterial road ever. If your mind was elsewhere while you were driving you would be doing ninety before you knew it.

At the Kleiva turn-off I abruptly swung down to the right, on a sudden impulse. A fast fibre-glass boat ploughed through the white-foamed waters down in Nordås bay, the birds were singing as though desperate, the flowers were sporting feverish, gawdy colours and a smell of concentrated heat wafted over from the set-back façades of houses. I was soaked in sweat.

I parked the car and got out. I had half a mind to fan myself with the car door. The sky hung low over everything, like blue adhesive paste. The heat was on the verge of reaching a tipping point, into something reminiscent of a climate catastrophe, a delayed echo of Chernobyl.

The THIS DOG BITES sign was still on the gate.

I bared my teeth. 'If it bites me, I'll bite it back,' I muttered as I pushed open the gate. But no Hound of the Baskervilles appeared. Perhaps it was dead too.

I walked up to the door and rang the bell. At length I heard some faint sounds coming from inside. Then the door opened, slowly, as if it were made of lead.

The man who opened the door was wearing shorts that were too big for him. But then he was a bit too big for himself too, at least from the chest down. The shorts were a faded blue, as though they had been left on the washing line in the sun for too long. He wasn't wearing anything on top, and his hairless skin was dark brown and taut, with some white tears in the veneer, almost like birth marks. His hair was grey with a black kernel, which could have been dampness, and he had combed it over

his forehead in an attempt to look youthful. Instead he resembled a fallen senator from the Roman Empire's very last days.
On his smooth-shaven top lip there were beads of sweat, and his
voice was heavy with condensation. 'What is it you want?'

'The name's Veum. Nielsen?'

'Yeah.'

'I was here the other night, with Lisb—'

'Yes, so I was informed. Come in. A terrible business. Have
they found her yet?'

I shook my head and followed him into the hallway.

'We're sitting out the back with refreshments. Join us.' His
smile was ingrained, but that was the only boyish thing about
him, so far.

With mixed pleasure, I again saw the African steppe lounge.
He waded through without comment.

Half of the glass wall facing Nordås bay had been pushed
aside, and on the patio two faded, canvas deck chairs faced the
water. From the side of one chair protruded a relaxed, freckled
female arm, holding a glass.

The man coughed. 'Helle. We have a guest.'

The voice matched the arm. It was equally relaxed and slurred
from alcohol. 'Oh, who?'

I walked around the chair and proffered my hand. 'Varg
Veum.'

She pushed her dark-green sunglasses onto her forehead and
stared at me with eyes that were as golden-brown as the contents
of her glass. Her handshake was limp and uninterested. 'I'm
Helle. Nielsen.'

She was attired in the same way as her husband – topless and
in oversized shorts. But hers were yellow.

Her nut-brown breasts were large and somewhat sagging, the
nipples pointing gloomily south. I had the uneasy feeling she
was watching me with three pairs of eyes: the sunglasses on her

forehead, the light-brown eyes in the middle and the red areolas at the bottom. She gave no indication that she wished to cover up. It was probably how she was used to sitting on the patio in Spain.

'Would you like a drink, Veum?' Nielsen asked.

'A Farris, please.'

'Get a chair for him, Pål,' his wife added. 'Sit yourself down then,' she said, pointing to the free chair.

Her husband disappeared and I carefully took a seat.

Her hair was big and copper red, and her face, neck and shoulders were covered with freckles. Her lips were big and full and pink. She reminded me of a polished Cadillac with visible rust spots – she had spread her lipstick extra thick in one corner of her mouth, hoping to cover the scab over a cut.

'So you're the man who was going to look after our house while we were away?' She made it sound like an accusation.

'Yes, but I hadn't even started when this happened. Lisbeth was supposed to show me around and then—'

She dismissed me with a lazy wave of her hand. 'Yes, we know all that. How did you know Lisbeth?'

'She, er, hired me.'

'Not personally then?'

'No.'

'And you take jobs like that. I mean, house surveillance?'

'Yes. And you – how did you know her?'

Pål Nielsen returned. On a small tray there was a bottle of Farris and a tall glass containing ice cubes. In his other hand he was carrying a little folding chair, this too with faded canvas and a wooden frame. 'Here I am with something refreshing to drink. Are you driving, herr Veum?'

I nodded. 'But let's keep things informal. It's too hot to be on formal terms.'

He smiled quickly. 'OK.'

He filled my glass, unfolded the chair, took his own glass from the small table where he had left it and then leaned over as far as he could, as far as his stomach allowed. 'Now you'll have to tell us everything, Veum. What actually happened?'

'Haven't the police told you?'

'Yes, yes. But you never know. They have to stick to the official version. You … erm … don't have to?'

'I'm afraid my version is fairly similar to the official one. I just asked your wife how you two knew Lisbeth Finslo.'

'Lisbeth? Oh, she treated a friend of ours. Sometimes he used our pool … Well, you've … And then he combined it with physio treatment here.'

He motioned to the glasses and the bottle of Farris. 'We're outgoing types, easy to get to know. We invited her for a drink, sat chatting … Later she came again, not in a professional capacity.' An expression of tenderness crossed his face. 'I think she liked it here. Needed someone to talk to.'

'She lost her husband in a terrible way,' his wife slurred.

'Yes, a car accident, wasn't it?'

'Yes, without any warning. And now this. Where can she be, Pål?'

Pål Nielsen looked at her shyly and rolled his shoulders. 'If only we knew.'

'She … Did she always come alone when she came here? She didn't have anyone with her?'

Helle Nielsen revealed a pink tongue between her pink lips. 'No … always alone. As though she didn't want to make us … jealous.'

'Erm, what did actually happen, Veum?' her husband hastened to ask.

I slowly shifted my gaze from him and back to her. 'Jealous? What do you mean?'

'Helle…' her husband cautioned.

But she had a bit too much drink on board to listen properly. She parted her legs to stroke the inside of one thigh. 'There are many ways three people can have a nice time, Veum,' she slurred and looked at me with all three pairs of eyes.

Her husband glanced at her apologetically. 'Don't listen to her, Veum. Her tongue's run away with her…'

'Run away with me?' Helle continued with the same lazy doggedness. 'You were on your knees…'

'It's too hot here. And you've had too much to drink. Let me hear Veum tell us what happened that evening. Ready?'

She raised her eyes and stared straight at him with a provocative expression. Then she repositioned her green glasses on her nose, as though she was pulling down the blinds. 'Sorry, I'm sure,' she said submissively.

Pål Nielsen glared at her. Then he brushed some imaginary dust from his bare knees, coughed and repeated: 'Let's hear what happened that evening, Veum.'

I looked at him with new eyes. We were definitely back in Rome. I heard the grating undertone in my voice as I said: 'So that's why she never brought anyone with her. Tor Aslaksen perhaps wouldn't have liked it here.'

'Tor … Aslaksen?'

'The man who drowned in the pool.'

'Ah.'

His wife chuckled behind the green sunglasses as though amused by something private. He looked daggers at her.

'You two never met him?'

'Who? This … Aslaksen? I'd never even heard the name before, Veum. Was he…?'

'Her friend? Maybe. What do I know? What do we know about anyone?'

He leaned forward confidentially. 'Listen, Veum. Don't judge her too harshly. There are so many ways to show your need for affection. There are so many emotional signals. You'd be surprised at what we—'

'And where were you two that night, Nielsen?' I interrupted.

'Us?' He smiled wanly. 'You already know. We were in Spain, Veum – busy on our big project down there.'

'With a glass in each hand, eh?'

Her laughter rippled, she pushed her sunglasses up for a second and pouted her lips into a kiss for me. Then her sunglasses fell back onto her nose.

'Which project is that, Nielsen?'

'Are you really interested?' he answered sarcastically.

'Very.'

He coughed and looked around, as if to make sure there were no other listeners. 'Well, it's … one of our nature projects.'

'One of your nature projects? I don't follow you.'

'Yes, the thing is … What modern man longs for most now is genuine, unspoiled nature. We have several of these projects on the go in Norway: one on the Møre coast, one in Jotunheimen, and now … we're expanding our repertoire. You know what the term "time-share" means, don't you?'

'You buy into holiday accommodation, such as flats, without owning them, but you're guaranteed a stay at a specific time every year?'

'Exactly. And this is what we're building now, for lovers of unspoiled nature.'

'But then it's no longer unspoiled.'

'Yes, it is. Because we build with respect for nature and in sympathy with whatever structure is already there. So, in Jotunheimen, we've used the old, summer mountain farms, in Møre the fishing cabins, and in Spain … in Spain we've found a place high up in the mountains, far from the usual tourist centres, and there we're constructing in adobe – sun-dried clay brick.'

'With a built-in shower and mini-bar plus key?'

'Ermm, we do have modern facilities of course, but the *experience*, Veum, that's primordial.'

'You can save the clichés for the sales brochures, Nielsen. So, last Thursday, you were in Spain?'

'Ask your friends at the police station, Veum. They've probably checked our alibi with the local *policía*.'

'Don Pedro Calamare,' his wife added theatrically. 'The local sniffer dog with a moustache like a vibrator brush ... Hum-hum-hummm.'

I could feel the muscles tightening in my jaw.

With taut vocal cords, I asked: 'And how often did Lisbeth come here?'

Pål Nielsen puckered his lips in a way that was reminiscent of a demure wine-taster. 'Mm, well ... A few times a month, in the short time we've known ... we knew her.'

'You don't expect to see her again?'

'After this? Hardly.'

'Tell me, Nielsen, how far down the age range do you go with these people you ... feel affection for?'

He quickly licked his lips. 'Age range? I'm not sure I understand...'

'You two don't have any children?'

'No we—'

'...don't,' his wife chimed in, like a practised choral part in a classical opera.

I heaved a heavy sigh. I had a question on the tip of my tongue, but this wasn't the right moment to ask. Instead, I said: 'You mentioned a friend of the family Lisbeth was treating.'

'I did?' Pål Nielsen said curtly.

'Who was that?'

'It ... An old friend of ours. Schrøder-Olsen.'

'Harald Schrøder-Olsen?'

'Yes. Do you know him?'

'But he's in a wheelchair.'

He smiled condescendingly. 'Why do you think she was treating him?'

'But how did he get down the stairs to the pool?'

'We pushed him in through the side door, Veum. Straight from the garden path. You have no idea how good swimming is for people in his situation. It went without saying that he could use the pool, as often as he wanted.'

'So, Lisbeth Finslo treated Harald Schrøder-Olsen…?'

'Yes, is there anything strange about that?'

'No, nothing strange. Just two intersecting roads from out of nowhere.'

Helle Nielsen tapped a long index-fingernail on her empty glass. 'Pål … refill time.'

He got up, took her glass and went inside.

After he had gone, she raised her sunglasses again. The look she sent me was arch. She spread her thighs a little more and stroked the place where they met with both hands. Despite the heat, I saw the tips of her nipples stiffen and stand up. Her voice was like sandpaper as she said: 'You have a standing invitation, Veum.' When I didn't answer, she added: 'If you're the lonely type, you're welcome to come one day when Pål isn't at home. I like … the cut of your jaw.'

I drank my mineral water in silence. The ice cubes had long melted, so the glass didn't make any sound either.

She curled her lips and rolled her eyes as though unable to comprehend that anyone could say no.

Then her husband returned with a drink that was so dark brown, it could have been mixed with furniture polish. He gave her the glass and sat down, with an irked expression on his face.

'Where's this side door, Nielsen?'

He thumbed over his shoulder, without bothering to turn. 'Round the corner.'

I craned my neck. Correct. I could see the fish in the aquarium inside the panoramic windows. They were swimming around as if nothing had ever happened, as though the world hadn't changed one iota from when the most active of their predecessors had placed their fins on the sandy ground and crawled ashore to become mammals. And here, at evolution's terminus, were we, God's gift to the world: humanity.

'Feel like a swim, Veum?' Helle Nielsen sent me a moist smile from the top of her glass.

'The last time anyone suggested that … No, thanks.'

'Shame…'

Her husband glared at her. 'Tell us what happened that evening, Veum.'

'Not much happened. We arrived. She unlocked the door and was going to show me around. In the pool we found a body. When I went back to the lounge she'd gone. No one's seen her since.'

'But … how did she get away?' He pointed to Løvstakken mountain at the top of Straumeveien. 'You can't exactly walk anywhere, can you.'

'Exactly. She must've met someone outside. Probably the same person that Tor Aslaksen had met in the pool.'

He went pale. 'But what was this Aslaksen doing in our house, on his own?'

I shifted my gaze to his wife again. '*You'd* never met him either? Tor Aslaksen?'

She looked up from her glass and frowned. 'Who? Me?' she replied, as innocent as a tax dodger.

Her husband was looking at her too, now. 'Yes, you. Helle?'

She took a big swig, slowly licked her lips and said, with total rejection in her eyes: 'I've never heard of him. That's the truth.'

I glanced at Nielsen. His face had turned jowly and bloated, and the boyishness resembled retarded development. I could see that it was many years since he had stopped trusting anything at all she said.

I sighed and looked around. The birds singing, the ornamental shrubs around us, the green mountainside and the blue sky, Nordås bay below and the rumble of the motorway on the opposite side, like the buzzing of large bumblebees behind the noise barriers. We were in the Garden of Eden, but they hadn't met the rental obligations and had been told by the landlord to move out. I sat there like Archangel Michael, with an extinguished sword of flames in my hands, and they were Adam and Eve, somewhat over-age, overfed on the forbidden fruit, wallowing in cholesterol and with little more than a spiritual wilderness to look forward to, east of Eden.

I rose to my feet. 'I'll be off then.'

They were still staring at each other, like two hypnotised snakes, poised for a duel.

Then Pål Nielsen slowly got up from his seat, still glaring at his wife. 'I'll see you to the door.'

She raised her glass and fixed her eyes on me again. 'Come again, another time,' she said and winked at me. A drop of sweat slid slowly down between her breasts. Her nipples were flat again. The great, big, ugly wolf was on his way out.

In the hallway, Pål Nielsen mumbled with embarrassment: 'You'll have to forgive Helle, Veum. She's a bit intoxicated today. She isn't usually like this.'

'No? When will you be going back?'

'To Spain? As soon as the police allow. But, of course, we'd like to know that all's well with Lisbeth before we go.' He half turned to the house. 'Would you still be interested in the same job?'

'House surveillance?'

'Yes. What else?'

'I don't think so. Thank you, anyway.'

'OK, fine,' he said nonchalantly. 'Then we'll have to find someone else.'

'Do that,' I said, taking my leave.

I glanced at the sign as I passed. It struck me that I hadn't seen any dog. No one had tried to bite me, either. But that was perhaps because they hadn't come near enough. I was keeping all possibilities open.

24

I parked in Tårn plass and walked down to my office. It was six o'clock in the evening and the town had been invaded by tourists. They took snaps of the most unusual things, which made me wonder about the towns they had come from. The Japanese tour group that photographed, en masse, the city hall tower block must have confused it with one of the mountains surrounding the town; and those who immortalised the doorman outside Børs Café must have had strange expectations of local customs and costumes, if they thought he was a guard standing at ease in front of the mayor's flat.

In my office I got down to business.

I rang Karin Bjørge, at home, to say hello, but no one picked up.

Then I rang Florø and spoke to Jannicke Finslo. Her voice was faint and toneless, as though she was on strong medication. There was no news about her sister.

'I was wondering whether to travel up tomorrow.'

'Here? To Florø?'

'I'd like to speak to Kari.'

'I see.' After a while she said: 'So you don't have any news, either?'

'No, but the police have found her suitcase.'

'Yes, they told me. That was when I…' She mumbled something or other I couldn't catch.

'So, I'll let you know if I'm not coming.'

'Is there any point?'

'As long as there's life there's … hope,' I said, catching the boomerang effect of my words before I had even finished speaking.

'That's the whole point,' she said, and after a short pause, rang off.

I looked out of the window, to the north, as though I could see all the way to Florø. I hope she had someone to take proper care of her.

I took out a sheet of paper and wrote down the names of Camilla's parents.

I flicked through the telephone directory. I found no Vibeke Farang in Bergen. So, I searched through the nearest surrounding districts, and in Sotra I found one. I jotted down the address and telephone number.

Then I called Enquiries, where a cheerful Lærdal voice answered. I could clearly imagine her: big and energetic with a mass of auburn locks around her head.

'I was wondering if I could bother you with a little problem,' I said.

She spoke the same language as the telephone directory. 'As long as it's only about telephone numbers, fine,' she said, and I realised we were on the same wavelength.

'I'm searching for a man, that is, the number of a man called Bård Farang, who probably lives somewhere in Hardanger.'

'Just a moment. No problem. If he has a phone,' she nynorsked.

I listened to the stratospheric noises for a few seconds, as though she was sifting through the heavenly archives. Then she was back: 'Here he is. Farang, Bård. You'll find him under Kvam municipality. Do you want his number?'

'Yes, please.'

I wrote it down. 'And how are things in Lærdal?' I asked.

'Oh, thanks for asking. It's up and down. But it's like that everywhere, isn't it? Have a good evening,' said Televerket's representative, before moving on to other enquiries from the district whose telephone network she had full IT access to.

I looked in the directory under Kvam and found Farang with an address in Jondal.

I sat looking at the two telephone numbers: Vibeke and Bård Farang. She had kept the surname, possibly for convenience. They both lived at a reasonable distance from Bergen, she a little closer than him, as though the tragedy they had experienced had pushed them away from town, but not so far that they couldn't return at the drop of a hat if someone called them. Camilla, for example.

Vibeke had sought the sea. Bård, one of the fjords hidden behind the mountains. Neither of them had any interest in continuing to live in Bjørndal.

He had known Bodil Schrøder-Olsen.

She had known Tor Aslaksen.

But had either of them known Pål and Helle Nielsen? The rest of the Schrøder-Olsen family? Lisbeth Finslo?

Who had killed Tor Aslaksen? And why had Lisbeth Finslo disappeared? Did it have any connection with Camilla Farang's disappearance eight years before?

There were too many questions, and I had no idea who to ask.

I should talk to both Vibeke and Bård Farang, but not yet. The first person I should talk to was Lisbeth Finslo, but she was, literally, out of reach.

Others?

I racked my brains.

What was it Siv Schrøder-Olsen had said to me when I met her at the gates? *Are you the little girl's father?* Which little girl was she thinking about? Camilla?

And hadn't she said something similar later, during the conversation on the patio? But even if it was Camilla she was referring to, it wasn't Bård Farang who was dead but Tor Aslaksen. And why on earth would she talk about Camilla at all? Were there any other connections apart from Tor Aslaksen having worked at Norlon and Bård Farang knowing Bodil before she became a Schrøder-Olsen?

At any rate I had promised Siv I would go for a walk with her in the arboretum one day. Perhaps I should keep my promise tomorrow before going to Florø?

I dialled Karin Bjørge's number a last time.

After a long ring she picked up the phone with an abrupt: 'Yes? Hello?'

'Hi.'

'Is that you, Varg? I was in the shower. Sorry for being a bit slow.'

'It's for that sort of reason that I'm looking forward to phones with screens.'

'Mhm. Are you coming up?'

'While you're still in the shower? I have to pack. I'm going to Florø tomorrow afternoon, and early tomorrow I'm off to Store Milde.'

'Come on, I'll put some water on for a cup of tea…'

'OK.'

I went. It was much too early in the relationship to say no.

I packed my notepad, switched off the office light and walked out into the summer evening with a faint smile on my lips, like a herald of good news, a harbinger of better times. I hoped she would like the news I was bringing her and that she hadn't enjoyed the better times for so long that she would soon begin to get bored.

25

A new relationship is like finding gold. In the car heading for Store Milde the next day I could feel the gold dust from another night of love settling at the bottom of my riverbed, like a promise of more finds. To stay in the mood, I hummed: '*In a cavern, by a canyon, excavating for a mine...*' And belted out the refrain across the grassy slopes of Blomsterdalen valley – '*Oh, my darling, oh my darling, oh my darling Clementine*' – until the last line held me in its grip like a melancholy afterthought: '*Thou art lost and gone forever, oh, my darling, Clementine...*'

The sky was again cloud-free and so blue that blisters were beginning to form. On Fana fjord a yacht was running lazily before the off-shore breeze, and along the road into the arboretum came the squawks from a thousand bird nests, with the season's loudest demands: *More food!* Summer lay like a lagoon around us and it was miles and miles to the first autumnal storm.

It was Tuesday morning and everything was still and peaceful as I strolled up the gravel path to the Schrøder-Olsen's old Tyrolean-style house. In the background was Trygve and Bodil's single-storey detached house, closed and deserted, and the only sound to be heard as I rounded the corner to the flagstone patio was the flapping of a newspaper as a page was slowly turned.

In his wheelchair sat Harald Schrøder-Olsen, alone, reading the *Aftenposten*. He didn't seem surprised to see me. 'Well ... good morning, herr Veum.' He stared at me from under his thick white eyebrows.

'Good morning. I promised Siv to go for a walk with her in the arboretum.'

His eyes didn't leave me for a second. 'She's there already. With her mother.'

He rested his elbow on the garden table and the saucer rattled under the only coffee cup there.

I didn't move, slightly unsure of myself, as though I had come to apply for a post and didn't know whether to stay on my feet or sit down. I cleared my throat. 'I've heard … It's my understanding that … you know Lisbeth Finslo.'

'Yes, and?'

'She's a physiotherapist and was treating you?'

'And what does that have to do with you?'

'You know she's gone missing?'

'Missing? Stuff and nonsense. She's on holiday. She has someone to cover…' He noticed my expression and paused. 'What do you mean?'

'She disappeared on Thursday. The same day that … And since then no one's seen her.'

'She was going to Florø, she told me.'

'She never arrived. Did you know that she and Tor Aslaksen were in a relationship?'

'Aslaksen? I've never … in which case that must be very recent. Otherwise Trygve or Bodil would've said. How do you know?'

'I don't.'

'Does that mean …? Is she suspected of having had something to do with the death?'

'Until she resurfaces … yes.'

He slowly shook his head. 'Inconceivable.'

'Was she a good physiotherapist?'

'The best I've ever had.'

'How long has she been treating you?'

'For three and a half years. At my wish, she carried on even after she started at Hjellestad. It was a perfect set-up. Geographically speaking, I mean.'

'She treated you in the pool, I understand?'

He sent me a sharp look. 'Tell me, am I being investigated, Veum? If so, it would perhaps be better if we called the police at once.'

'No, no, no. I just heard by chance. At Pål and Helle Nielsen's. Aslaksen drowned in their pool.'

'Really? The papers said it was in Bønes.'

'Somewhat inaccurate reporting.'

'Why has no one told me that?'

'To spare you?'

'I don't need to be spared,' he snapped. 'My God, I'm the toughest nut in the family.'

'How well did you know Tor Aslaksen?'

'How well? I employed him. He'd been a friend of the boys since childhood. One of my closest employees for many years. But privately?' Automatically he looked down the road at the house where Tor Aslaksen grew up. 'He never married. He was too restless when he was young and too much of a loner later in life. I don't know. I didn't know him in that way.'

'But professionally…?'

'Professionally, he was brilliant. One of the best at finding new chemical bonds that became harmless when they dissolved.' And added, with heavy sarcasm in his voice: 'The pressure of the ecological movement…'

'And Lisbeth Finslo, how well did you know her?'

'You don't know your physiotherapist, Veum; she knows you.'

'So, she never told you anything about herself?'

'No more than the bare minimum. I gathered that she lived alone. She was a widow, she said. And she had a daughter, isn't that right?'

I nodded. 'So, you didn't meet privately?'

'Privately? What do you mean by that?'

'I mean … you went to the Nielsens' place to swim…'

'As part of the treatment, yes. I paid for every minute.'

'But you went there too when the Nielsens were away?'

'They let us use the pool, yes.'

'And you did?'

'Yes. Several times.'

'How did you get in?'

'I was given the key to the side door. The one that leads straight into the pool.'

'Have you still got it?'

'The key? Of course.'

'Can I see it?'

'Why?' he asked with obvious irritation. 'It's in the key cupboard in the hallway. But it's not necessary, Veum. I know it's there.'

I regarded him pensively. 'Alright. And what did this … therapy involve?'

'I swam to and fro. Did some exercises in the water. The main aim was to strengthen my back and stomach muscles.'

'And did Lisbeth swim too?'

'Naturally,' he said sarcastically. 'She needed to help with some of the exercises.'

'Hmmm.'

He suddenly leaned forward, his face as gaunt as a donkey's. 'Listen, if you're trying to suggest by these questions that I had … some kind of sexual congress with Lisbeth Finslo, you're utterly mistaken, Veum. Look at me. I'm not so young any more. And it's not only my legs that are paralysed.' He leaned back in the wheelchair. 'So now you know.' At once he looked weary; weary and old and decrepit. 'Shouldn't you…?' He gestured weakly with his hand.

'Yes, you're right. Thank you for the information, thus far. Goodbye.'

He watched me cross the patio. 'Goodbye. And Veum…'

I stopped. 'Yes?'

'If you see my wife … I hope you're not going to plague her with … these things.'

I smiled thinly. 'No, I wasn't intending to.' I left him there, in the warm glow of a new summer. He was an ambassador of the previous autumn though, exiled in a foreign land and ready for sending home. But still enjoying the privileges of a kind of diplomatic status in life.

As for me, I crossed the border to the arboretum and wasn't stopped at passport control either.

26

I found them sitting on a bench by Lake Mørke, which looked like a pond, but had a seemingly invisible, overgrown connection with the fjord to the north.

A cool, sombre atmosphere hung over the place, like in a cathedral. It was as though you could still see the shadows of the ancient monks wandering among the trees, deep in meditation. Siv and her mother were staring at a little green island in the black water. Pines and birch trees grew on it while around them the forest consisted of tall dark-green spruce trees and Asiatic conifers of various kinds. A handful of dark-red, almost burgundy, water lilies were floating in the water, which emphasised the sacred feel of the place.

The two women appeared to be in silent prayer next to each other. Siv was wearing a light-blue dress, as maidenly as the one she had worn the last time I saw her, and she was holding another bunch of flowers. Her blonde hair had caught the sun, while her mother's had turned to snow: white and trim. Aslaug Schrøder-Olsen was dressed in green today, a moss-coloured outfit with a light-brown cameo brooch on her chest and dark-brown walking shoes on her feet.

'Hi,' I said cheerfully as I approached them. 'So, this is where you are.'

They gave a start and looked up at me with very different expressions: Siv, open and expectant; her mother, anxious and suspicious.

'I promised to go for a walk with you,' I smiled at Siv. 'But your father told me you were here with your mother.'

'Have you spoken to Harald?' fru Schrøder-Olsen asked spikily.

I nodded.

Siv held out a hand. Her fingers were holding the little bunch of flowers much too tightly. The life nerve of the bluebells was already broken and their heads were hanging, the wood anemones were gasping for oxygen, with open petals, and only the tormentil, with its long, muscular stems, pulsed with life and sought the sun, which filtered down in health-friendly doses through the compact foliage above us. Even after a week of sunny weather an unremitting smell of damp rose from the forest floor, and it struck me, more than ever, that we were in a rainforest. Which was protected, what was more.

'Look at the flowers,' Siv said, with a nervous enthusiasm in her voice. 'Eggs and bacon, tormentil, wood anemone and bluebells.'

'Mhm. They're lovely,' I replied with a smile.

The look she sent me was dazzling, and blank: a glass wall with a roving light behind it, but the glass was matt, and you couldn't see if the light was a presence or only a reflection.

'I'm sure Veum knows their names,' her mother said cautiously.

'Varg. Your name's Varg,' Siv continued, as though she hadn't heard anything.

'So, you recognised me?'

She nodded vigorously and held out the bunch of flowers again. 'Eggs and bacon, tormentil, wood anemone and ... bluebells.'

Her mother sighed. 'Siv,' she said softly. 'See if you can find some more that you can show him. I'll wait here.'

Siv jumped up with a big smile, nodded excitedly, pointed to the dark water and said: 'But not those. Waterlilies are dangerous. The water's dangerous. Pick flowers in the forest.' She ran off with light, child-like steps. My gaze was held involuntarily by the cardinal-red lilies. If you half closed your eyes, they turned into bloodstains on the water.

Then I shifted my gaze and watched Siv again. She was already crouched down between the trunks of some gnarled pine trees. She turned her head and shouted to us: 'Arctic starflower. Lots of them.'

Aslaug Schrøder-Olsen didn't take her eyes off her daughter. Then she said sadly: 'Having children is a lottery. It's like sowing bulbs in November. You never know what will come up. Some will be killed by the frost. And those that come up are very often completely different from what you'd imagined.'

'What actually happened to Siv?' I asked warily.

She gazed across the lake with that distant expression people adopt when it isn't the actual surroundings they are focusing on, but the past.

'I saw her graduation photo. On the piano, in your house. Harald said she fell down a staircase.'

She was almost seventy years old. Nonetheless, it was easy to see she had been an attractive woman all her life. Even if the years had left their marks on her features and a veil of past time over her face, she still was. But now her beauty seemed to be crumbling in front of my eyes, her age lay like sawdust in her wrinkles, and she was transformed into a monument to everything that had gone sour in her life – to all the forks in the road where she had made the wrong decision.

Her gaze slipped back to Siv, who was squatting down in her light-blue dress, picking white starflowers from the moss-green heaven she dominated like a goddess. 'She hasn't always been like this, Veum. She was the apple of our eyes. The liveliest, happiest girl you could ever imagine.'

I nodded encouragingly. 'So I understand. Your husband said the same.'

'Now she's how she was when she was four or five. She adores flowers, as she used to. She's as spontaneous and giving as she used to be. There wasn't a day in the summer when she didn't come home with flowers for us. Even when she was in upper secondary, she brought flowers from the kerbside, on her way from the bus stop. We always had fresh flowers on the lunch table.'

'Mhm.'

'She was the typical graduation princess. I mean ... would have been. Now they don't do that anymore. She was outgoing, always in a cheery mood, helpful at home. She had refreshing infatuations – I mean ones that didn't frighten us, because she knew what she was doing, and the boys she went with ... they were nice boys, Veum.'

Her gaze drifted to the other side of the lake, as though the nice boys from the past were somewhere on the bank. 'But afterwards ... Afterwards they kept their distance, bit by bit, all of them. The boys first. Then her girlfriends. Now no one comes to visit her ... apart from Odin of course, but he doesn't count.'

Again, I had to watch Siv. She had moved a little deeper into the forest and higher up. But this wasn't the girl of four or five I saw. Now it was the lonely woman of twenty-six who had only the faces of flowers to look into.

'We loved her so much, all of us. Trygve and Odin ... even if they probably thought it a bit embarrassing when I became pregnant again. Odin was twelve. Trygve was fourteen. Old Bergensians have a beautiful name for such children born late in a marriage. They call them "winter fruit".' Her eyes moistened as she watched Siv again. 'She was our winter fruit, but she wasn't short of nutrition. It was the branch she grew on that was cut down.'

I cleared my throat. 'I never found out ... What actually happened?'

She continued as though she hadn't heard me: 'When she was big enough to go to dances, her brothers drove her, there and back … and the whole crowd of girlfriends. Then, after they moved out, or had other interests, Harald had to step in. And in the last year, the odd admirer, old enough to have a driving licence. But that was rare. Usually it was Harald.'

I waited. I had a feeling she was gently circling around what she had to say, getting closer, but with reluctance.

'On her eighteenth birthday she got her driving licence as a present. But we didn't buy her a car. We didn't want to spoil her. She would have to save up, if she wanted one. But we paid for her licence, and on her birthday she took the test … and passed with flying colours. I can see her now, running up from the gates. It was in the middle of April, a beautiful sunny day, but she out-shone the sun. She hadn't even stopped to pick some flowers, so keen was she to tell us.'

The memory evoked a smile on her face again and she spoke with more warmth as she continued: 'She borrowed our car, of course, when she needed it, and when it was free. She was so proud the first time she drove off, alone, to visit an admirer.'

'Did she have many, erm, admirers?'

'Yes and no. Lots of nice boys. There were always new voices on the phone. But there was never anything serious with any of them … I think.'

'You think?'

She turned sharply to me, almost angrily. 'Yes, we weren't watching her every move, naturally enough. She was entitled to her own private life.'

'Yes, yes, of course. I didn't mean to imply anything.'

'But then…'

'Yes?'

'Then everything came to a sudden end.' She bit her lip and turned away.

Siv had stood up among the trees. She was surveying the black, glistening waters with an attentive expression on her face, as though she too was listening to bygone voices, all the nice boys...

'How did it happen?' I asked again, as resolute as a tin soldier.

She was staring into middle distance so that I saw her face in profile, clearly outlined, pale, like a silhouette on a brooch. 'One evening Harald was called to the office. Quite late. An important conference. Something had come up – afterwards it was so unimportant, I don't even remember ... He'd had a drink, and to be on the safe side, he asked Siv if she would dr-drive.'

'Oh, yes? And she did?'

'She did.'

We had reached the difficult part now. She weighed every word she said and she was finding it difficult to find the right ones. 'They arrived, and Siv parked. Harald went ahead, up to the office. When he was almost there, he heard...'

She paused. 'That's what's so terrible. No one saw what happened. There were no witnesses. And, of course, she couldn't ... afterwards.'

'But what did your husband hear?'

'He heard her scream something, as though in desperation, and then ... a bang.'

'A *bang*?'

'Yes, I mean ... on the stairs. She fell.'

'Down the stairs?'

'Yes, she was on her way up and then ... something happened ... and she fell. And then total silence.' She swallowed and carried on: 'Harald ran down, as fast as he could – this was before his illness, you know. And when he reached the bottom, there she was. Lifeless. He tried to lift her, to wake her, but he definitely shouldn't have done that. It turned out later that she'd broken her neck. She was unconscious for several days before she came to. At first, we thought she would be paralysed, but the doctors did a fantastic job on her. The only physical disability she has is on her left side. You can see she has a limp, like after a stroke. But *psychologically* … she's never returned to us. It was so bitter. This was just before her final exams. In the final mocks she had nothing but top grades. But she never sat the exams.'

'When did this happen?'

She stared blankly. 'In 1979. April. 26th of April.'

I fell silent. There were no more questions to ask, and those that came to mind, seemed insultingly direct. My brain was working at top speed, trying to sort the information, to imagine the scene and, not least, the unknown factors. One of them forced itself to the surface: 'Tell me, when your husband was on his way down the staircase, did he meet anyone? Or was there any evidence of another person?'

'Was she pushed, you mean?'

I nodded.

'How many times have we asked ourselves the same question, do you think? But there was no one. There was no one in the building apart from those who should have been there, and they were in the conference room waiting for Harald.'

'And they were…?'

'The boys of course. Trygve and Odin.'

'Odin too?'

'He was working there at the time. Tor Aslaksen, and the foreman – I don't remember his name; someone else, not sure who. But they were definitely up there, all of them.'

'But the case was investigated, I assume?'

'Investigated? By whom?'

'By the police of course. Who else?'

'It was an *accident*, Veum. An accident,' she said in muted tones, then added: 'Shhh. No more now.' I followed her gaze. Siv was on her way back to us. I straightened up. *No more now.* Well, I agreed. It was more than enough anyway. A completely new perspective, a chain of events as intricate and unsolved as those I had met earlier this week. And this, too, with the same name, the same common denominator: Tor Aslaksen.

27

Siv's bunch of flowers had grown. Proudly, she held it up for us. 'Look at the flowers. Eggs and bacon, tormentil, wood anemone and bluebells. Arctic starflower, cowslip and clover. And butter-cups. I found all of them. For the bunch.'

I no longer saw her as she was now. As if through tracing paper, I saw the images of the person she had been before: the girl who had picked flowers on her way home from school; the graduation princess with five admirers on each hand, but none of them serious; the eighteen-year-old falling headlong down the stairs, and finally the image of her lying lifeless at the bottom. Siv five times over, but only one of them was *here*, now.

'They're lovely,' I said. 'You love flowers, don't you.'

She nodded and smiled. 'Yes. I do. They tell me who I am.'

'Tell you who you are?'

'Yes. Eggs and bacon, tormentil, wood anemone and blue-bells. Arctic starflower and ... cowsl ... clo-clo ...ver.' With that she seemed to fall into a kind of trance over the colourful flowers, as if nature had hypnotised her into a wakeful doze, with the aid of a bewitching spectrum of tallow and blue, white and violet.

Aslaug Schrøder-Olsen looked at her slim, gold watch. 'Siv ... I think we have to go home now.'

'Just a little more,' Siv answered from faraway.

'But you know, Pappa...' She angled a glance at me. 'My

husband becomes so … impatient if he doesn't have his one o'clock cup of tea on time.'

'I'll accompany Siv, so you can go ahead if you want. I'll make sure she gets home in one piece.'

She examined me carefully, as though wondering if one of the nice boys had returned, but without quite recognising him. 'Perhaps you'd like a cup of tea too?' she said with less than convincing hospitality.

'Yes, please,' I answered.

We stood up, and she held out a hand to Siv. 'Come on, my love. We have to go.'

Siv looked up, first at her mother, then at me. She got to her feet, mumbling: 'I dreamt I was the little girl.'

Tears sprang from her eyes with the force of a wellspring.

Her mother pulled her close and wrapped her arms around her. 'There, there, my lovely, there, there. It's nothing. You're here with your mother now. It's all fine. Everything's fine now.'

Siv was shaking with sobs, and her mother looked over her shoulder at me. She shook her head disconsolately. 'Sometimes she has dreams like this. She can wake up in the middle of the night, screaming with terror. I think … her poor, tormented brain … So much of life unlived wants to come out.'

I felt ill at ease, as though they were naked or I was an intruder, peering in on a scene I had no right to see.

I leaned back and looked up, past the tall, dark tree trunks, the thick canopies above, the jungle-like foliage – up to where the sky arched, blue and pure, and pierced by the sun. Between the sky and me two birds were dancing on the breeze: a mating ceremony for the gallery, where the lonely hearts' club had their annual meeting. Oh, yes, Aslaug was right: having children was a lottery.

The sobbing subsided. With her free hand Siv stroked the tears from her cheeks. Her mother produced a handkerchief and dried them with soft, gentle dabs. Siv looked at me through red-rimmed eyes. As she held out the bunch of flowers she said: 'I told Totto everything.'

I opened my mouth to answer, but her mother spoke up first. 'Now we have to go, Siv. Pappa's waiting.'

'Mhm. Pappa's waiting. I'll give him the flowers. Eggs and bacon, tormentil and wood anemone...' She ran off in front of us, humming the new variant of her refrain.

Her mother watched her and said in a bitter undertone: 'Some people lose their children when they die – or go missing. Others lose them while they're still alive.'

'Go missing? Are you thinking of the Camilla Case?'

She sent me a puzzled look. 'The Camilla Case? Who's Camilla?'

'Well, I...' I changed the topic. 'Totto, that's Tor Aslaksen, isn't it?'

'Yes, we never called him anything else,' she replied with a turn of her head.

In silence we followed the narrow gravel path up to the little arboretum and the oak Crown Prince Harald had planted when the botanical garden opened in May 1971. We passed noble firs and Japanese umbrella pines, pines and larches, holly bushes and rhododendrons, alders and maples.

At one point Aslaug Schrøder-Olsen raised her head and took a breath, deep into her lungs. After exhaling, she said: 'This is the best air I know ... in this forest. It's like ... like having an extra pair of lungs. And this scent, of resin and life.' She fixed me with a serious expression. 'For me this is a sacred grove, Veum. Here I meet God. Here I understand that the earth is a forest floor and we're the world's smallest insects. Some of us are trodden on when fate is afoot. Others are spared until their time comes.'

Siv turned to us and waved as though she was listening to what her mother was saying.

I waved back, and her mother concluded with a reflective: 'Ah.'

We were there. Harald Schrøder-Olsen was sitting on the patio, impatiently rustling his newspaper. He looked up peevishly when we appeared.

'Tea will be ready in five minutes, my love,' his wife said hurriedly as she ran into the house.

Siv held up the bunch of flowers for her father. 'Look at the flowers. Eggs and bacon and clover, wood anemone and...'

'Yes, yes, yes,' her father said, in a brusquer tone than I remembered him using with her before. 'Go inside and put them in water, Siv.'

'I have to put them in water, you know. Put them in water.' She laughed with delight at her own cleverness and ran in.

Once again, I was alone with Harald Schrøder-Olsen.

For a few long seconds we appraised each other, like two duellists at dawn, after the seconds have withdrawn.

'You found them, I see.'

'Yes. Your wife's invited me to a cup of tea.'

'Oh, has she now?'

'There was something I was wondering.'

Sarcasm dripped from his voice: 'Oh, yes?'

'About Siv.'

He arched his eyebrows. 'Right. About Siv this time?'

'Yes, Your wife told me about what happened when she ... About the accident.'

Unconsciously he cast a glance at the door leading into the house. 'Did she now ... Her too?'

'It was obviously ... tragic.'

'I've heard that word mentioned, yes.'

I ignored his tone. 'I've been there, to Norlon, and I've seen the ... erm ... crime scene. Where did it actually happen?' As he didn't answer, I continued: 'On the staircase leading to the office?'

He nodded, against his better judgement.

'Tell me … I'm not sure if I remember correctly. On the ground floor there was another door … to the left? It leads to the production hall and lab, doesn't it?'

He nodded again.

'The offices are on the first floor. Was that where you were going to this meeting your wife mentioned?'

'No, it was on the second floor, in the conference room. I was just about to open the door when I heard her.'

'You heard her scream?'

An expression of pain drifted across his face. 'Yes.'

'And where was she then?'

'On the landing between the ground floor and first floor. That is, she must've been roughly at the top of the stairs when she fell.'

'And you ran down when you heard her?'

'Yes, of course.'

'And you didn't meet anyone?'

'Who would I meet? Father Christmas? I thought Aslaug told you everything?'

'But let's imagine … *If* there'd been anyone there, with her, this person *could* have come out of the admin offices, pushed her down the stairs and then run out of the building or back into the office?'

He studied me with boundless irritation in his eyes. 'And who would *that* be? There was no one else in the area apart from us. It was late at night.'

'A burglar maybe?'

'A burglar?'

'Yes? Imagine the following situation: Siv's on her way up the stairs after parking the car. Suddenly she meets a total stranger coming down the stairs, perhaps carrying stolen goods. She screams. The man, if it is a man, pushes her, she falls … Most murders in Norway, apart from crimes of passion, happen like this.'

'But there was no sign of a break-in, Veum.'

'No?'

'No. Don't you think we would've reported it to the police if there had been?'

'Would you?'

'I mean…'

'What about the people in the conference room? Was there another staircase between the second and first floors, apart from the one you used?'

'There was a fire escape of course, at the back, but—'

'And from there you could go down to the offices and onto the main staircase … and perhaps *back* the same way?'

'Ye-ah,' he said dismissively. 'But no one did. No one left the conference room. They were waiting for me, weren't they.'

'Are you sure? That no one left, I mean.'

'Don't you think I asked afterwards? Don't you think we checked every possibility when it was all over?'

'But did you do that yourselves? You didn't leave it to the police?'

He leaned forward in his wheelchair. 'This wasn't police business, Veum. Don't you understand? It's never been a police matter.'

I sighed. 'This is exactly what I'm wondering. I mean … *why*? What was the meeting about?'

He leaned back again. 'Internal affairs. Nothing to do with any of this.'

'No? Who was present?'

He eyed me with a sudden weariness. Then he stroked his forehead with a brawny hand. 'Trygve, Odin, Tor Aslaksen, the chief shop steward, the foreman.'

'That was all?'

'There was no one else. So, you see it was a very clear situation.'

'What were the names of the workers?'

'Clausen and ... it was probably Thomassen. I don't re-member. Thomassen's dead and Clausen's left. Trygve can tell you if ... if it's of any interest. But it isn't.' Gradually his fire was returning. 'In fact, I think you should go now, Veum. I'm tired of you sniffing around and asking questions here, there and every-where. What are you really after?'

From the lounge came a nervous clink of thin porcelain cups, like a sheepish fanfare. Then Aslaug Schrøder-Olsen appeared with a tray in her hands. On it were matt tea cups, a white teapot, sugar and slices of lemon, a bowl of scones and a set of silver spoons, as shiny as on Siv's birthday. 'Here I am,' she twit-tered.

I glanced down at my watch. It was five minutes past one. The scandal was a fact.

Behind her came Siv. She was carrying a tall glass of red juice with ice cubes in. 'Juice,' she said to me, as though I was from an alien planet and had never seen anything like it before.

Harald Schrøder-Olsen glowered furiously at me while his wife placed the cups on the table, but he was well mannered enough not to repeat the alternative invitation while his wife and daughter were present.

Aslaug Schrøder-Olsen poured the tea and asked if I wanted sugar or lemon.

'Only lemon, thank you.'

In the silence we sipped tea. It had a faint tang of smoke, like the smell of burnt forest, with a tarry after-taste.

Fru Schrøder-Olsen passed me the bowl of scones. 'One of my home-made scones, Veum? It's a British recipe.'

I helped myself and sank my teeth into the pastry. It was solid British artisanship, as compact as wood chip and filled with raisins. I was going to be full for hours.

Siv had brought a rag doll with her. Now she was sitting and chatting into its ear. The doll was a girl, dressed in blue with a white pinafore, like Alice in Wonderland. All we needed now was a rabbit, and the mad tea party would be complete.

I put down my cup. 'Which of your sons was friends with Tor Aslaksen?'

'Odin and Totto were the same age—' said Aslaug Schrøder-Olsen before her husband interrupted her:

'We're not talking about this anymore.'

She looked enquiringly at him. Then she lowered her gaze, reconciled to her fate.

'Life on the forest floor,' I muttered.

'What did you say?' Schrøder-Olsen barked.

Siv's face rose with a thoughtful expression on it. 'Totto said there was no problem. Everything would be fine.'

He turned to her. 'What?'

'I told Totto everything. He said that—'

'Enough, enough.' He rolled his eyes. 'This is too much for one day. I'm afraid, Veum, you'll have to go.'

'But Harald—' his wife said, outraged by this lack of manners.

'I can't stand your bloody face any longer.'

Undismayed, I stood up and said quietly: 'To tell the truth, that's the most cultured way anyone has told me to go to hell before.' I bowed to his wife. 'Thank you, fru Schrøder-Olsen. The tea and scone were excellent.' I turned my gaze. 'Siv…'

She looked up.

'Take care of yourself, Siv,' I said gently.

She smiled, but said nothing. For a second or two she was in fact present, a reflection of her actual self, illuminated by a ray of sun.

Then the moment was over and I left. Behind me was total silence, as though the whole tea party had been a hallucination, which was suddenly gone.

Down by my car I stopped and looked up at the blue house

where Tor Aslaksen had grown up. In the garden in front of the house an elderly woman was on her knees, tending a rose bed.

I left the car and walked over to her garden. I knocked lightly on the gate and said: 'Fru Aslaksen?'

She didn't react.

Slightly louder, I repeated: 'Fru Aslaksen?'

She peered up at me.

She didn't need to say anything. It was her. She had a face set in grief, a gravestone to her son, chiselled in marble.

I pointed to the garden path and asked if I could come in.

She nodded helplessly and I opened the gate.

28

She stood up slowly, like a plant growing on time-lapse film. But she would never bear any flowers. She had withered, for ever.

She was dressed for gardening, wearing old-fashioned, brown gabardine trousers, a green jumper that had seen its best days a quarter of a century ago and rubber gloves, so as not to dirty her hands. In one, she was holding a small blue rake; in the other, an insecticide spray.

She had hidden her hair under a brown kerchief, wound around her head and tied over her forehead, like an old-fashioned charlady. She was probably younger than Aslaug Schrøder-Olsen, but in a much worse state of health, ravaged by sorrows of an earlier vintage than the sudden death of her son. Her lips were taut and thin, there was no suggestion of any make-up, and her complexion was like rough marble: sharp at the edges, with lots of cracks and stained by liver spots, like spattered mud after a heavy downpour. Her eyes were blue and pallid, as though all the colours of her body had been diluted over time.

'Anne-Marie Aslaksen?' I asked.

She nodded and moved her lips soundlessly.

'My name's Veum. My condolences.'

She inclined her head and mouthed a thank-you, still no sound.

'I don't know if I … if you feel like a chat? It was me who found him, your son, Tor.'

I paused and looked for life in her stiff facial features.

Her eyes moistened, and she instinctively raised a rubber-gloved finger and stroked their corners. She pointed to a small, white garden table with her other hand. I nodded and she led the way.

We sat down, her on a bench with her back to the wall, me on a chair with the sun on my neck. She leaned over and put down the spray and the rake. Then she carefully unrolled the gloves from her fingers, as if she'd just performed an operation. Perhaps the operation had been on her vocal cords because now there was some sound issuing from them. 'Veum?'

I nodded again.

Her voice was thin and fragile, like cracked porcelain, as she continued: 'Yes, the police mentioned … You were some kind of night watchman, weren't you?'

'Yes.' She was right. That was exactly what I was. A night watchman in broad daylight.

'Tell me how you found him. I can take it now.'

I told her as gently as possible, without adding any unnecessary details, such as Lisbeth Finslo. I told her how I had found her son at the bottom of a swimming pool in the house I had been responsible for, how I had dived in, dragged him out and unsuccessfully given him mouth-to-mouth resuscitation.

I didn't say a word about Lisbeth. I'd leave that to the police. I didn't even mention his car or where it had been found. And I took great care not to touch on the Camilla Case.

The whole time I kept a vigilant eye on her, as if checking for unexpected reactions. But there were none. There were no reactions at all. She sat like an iron monument in a graveyard, forged by the sun, corroded by time and with no other external signs of grief.

'Then I called the police,' I said, rounding off the report. 'And that was it. I thought you'd want to hear this from me personally.'

She nodded gently. 'H-how did he look?'

I hesitated. 'Normal. He hadn't been in the water for long. If you hadn't known you would've thought he was asleep.'

'Did he seem to be at peace?'

I looked at the blue timber wall as if it was the colour of peace. 'Peace? Yes, I think you could say that. There were no signs of pain or terror, or anything like that.'

'No, death erases that,' she said drily. 'My husband, when he died, had a long, painful illness behind him. In the last month he refused to let Tor visit him. He was no more than thirteen then, and Jan Peder, my husband, said he wanted the boy to remember him the way he had been when he was healthy, before decay had reduced him to a living corpse, as he put it. But he was beautiful in death, despite all his depressing thoughts. He had such a strong sense that he was dying prematurely, with so much unachieved. He thought about us, how we would be after he'd gone. But we received some help,' she quietly concluded, looking at the Schrøder-Olsens' Tyrolean-style house.

I followed her gaze. 'He was good friends with the Schrøder-Olsen boys, wasn't he?'

'With Odin mostly. Trygve was always more distant. Older. But their father was decent. He supported Tor through his studies, let him work at the factory during the holidays and do the weekend night watch, for good money. And afterwards, when he'd finished, he employed him, gave him a good job. Jan Peder would've been proud of him.'

I hesitated for a moment. 'He ... he was a total stranger to me. When I found him, I mean. But now, afterwards, it is as if death has bound us together. I've thought about him ever since it happened. I feel that ... I would have liked to know him.'

She searched my face, apparently seeing through me at once. 'Would have liked to know him? You?'

I angled my head and nodded gently, so as not to exaggerate.

'Hmmm,' she said, examining me and waiting for a more convincing justification.

But I didn't have one to give her. A bumble bee flew by, with summer in big yellow saddlebags between its legs. It hummed contentedly as it seduced a rose and flew cheerily on to its next victim, which opened its stamens for the impudent suitor, drunk on nectar from a thousand novices.

Pained thoughts compressed her mouth into a line. 'And this, after he'd finally found someone.'

'Someone...?'

She quickly licked her lips, as if to soothe them. 'He didn't have a happy life.'

I waited, silent. She would have to find her own way to an elucidation.

'I've often thought that because his father died so young, he was too attached to me. So I always encouraged him to look for ... a substitute.' She shifted her gaze again. 'Like Schrøder-Olsen over there. Like ... his pal's elder brother.'

'Trygve?'

'Yes, in a way. He became his boss later of course. Tor lived here for a long time. Grew up here. But he never brought a girl-friend home. As though he didn't want to offend me.'

'But he did have girlfriends?'

She closed her eyes and opened them again. 'In the end, I urged him to move out. I told him to leave home and find himself somewhere to live.'

'The flat in Fyllingsdalen?'

'Yes, that was in 1975. When he was twenty-six years old. But he remained alone. He sacrificed everything for his job.'

'But he did have friends? After all, he was a member of a small flying club, wasn't he?'

She looked up and said quietly: 'Can you imagine anything lonelier than the big blue void up there? All on his own, in a little aircraft making so much noise you can't talk to anyone without shouting?'

'Did you go up with him?'

She nodded and an unconscious tremble went through her. 'He took me once. Later I refused. Floating up there like ... like butterflies on needles ... it isn't natural.'

'But didn't you say he'd found...'

'Yes. I could see it. You know, the way a mother can, although he never said a word about it. And now I don't suppose I'll ever meet her.'

An unpleasant thought reared its head from under a rock inside me: *No, maybe not. Unless...*

'But you think he had a girlfriend?'

She nodded calmly. 'For the last four or five months, yes. I could see it in his eyes when he came to visit me and in the set of his mouth ... He'd finally met someone ... finally satisfied a longing ... an expression he'd never had before. I could see that a couple of times he'd been on the point of telling me. Like when he was small and had been in the shop in Nesttun and bought a Christmas present for me and could barely keep the surprise to himself. He'd been so proud ... and now he was the same.'

So proud of Lisbeth Finslo? *But I have a friend*, she had said. *A steady boyfriend.* Tor Aslaksen?

'So ... no name?'

She shook her head.

'No pictures?'

'No.'

'Hmmm.' Another bumble bee passed by, unless it was the same one, with its saddlebag full and pollen on its hairs, dizzy and buzzing, as if the sun had smothered it with kisses. From above it was being observed by a dragonfly, a MIG fighter on a mission on behalf of our moral guardians, for whom summer is an abomination and winter the only purity, the calendar's ultima Thule.

'Trygve and Odin's sister, Siv – it's my understanding that he was like a brother to her as well?'

'Oh, yes.' For the first time there was something vaguely reminiscent of a smile around her mouth. 'The poor thing. But she was so small. It was Siv who started calling him Totto. Later that became his name.'

'He kept in touch with her, even after the accident, I'm told?'

'Yes, they were like brother and sister. If the accident hadn't taken place, then maybe *they*…'

I weighed my words carefully before I uttered them. 'Do you think that … Was there any kind of contact between them, on that level, before she had the accident?'

She sent me a stern look. '"On that level"? You don't mean … Oh, no, it was more like an afterthought – a mother's dreams of a child she no longer…' she swallowed '…has.'

I didn't say any more. It was five days since her son's death and I couldn't ask her about the Camilla Case. I didn't have the heart.

I got up and thanked her.

She accompanied me past the rose bed she had been busy with when I came. She stopped and said: 'I've planted this rose bush for him. It will grow here for as long as I live. I'll take care of it as if it were a living person. The only one I have left.' She angled a glance at me, her neck bent. 'But this is just nonsense, isn't it, Veum. As if roses could be as alive as people. As if the life of the smallest human being wasn't worth more than even the most beautiful flower.'

The smallest human being rang in my ears as I politely took my leave, closed the gate behind me and walked over to the car.

When I drove off, she was on her knees by the newly planted rose bush, like a devout Catholic in front of a private saint's image. In my heart I wondered if she called it Tor.

With my head full of thoughts, I left Store Milde. Three hours later I was sitting on the express boat to Florø.

29

Florø lies on a peninsula on the coast between Nordfjord and Sunnfjord. With its white timber houses on low-lying rock formations it is reminiscent of a Sørland town, which has been banished for unknown reasons to Vestland. On an early summer's day, with the sun shimmering over the town, you expect to be addressed with soft consonants. In late September, with storms rolling off the sea, it is warmer in Siberia.

For those who live in the country & western district of Sogn and Fjordane, Florø is in Alaska. It is the district's Klondyke except that there is no gold. Unless the black stuff they are pumping up from the sea off the coast is gold. On glass-clear winter nights, with darkness as a reflector, you can see the mirror-image of the gold out there in the western sky, like the Soria Moria Castle of Norwegian folk tales. It is only a shame for the town that the fairy-tale character of Askeladden is now an oil field in the North Sea, and on his way to Mongstand and Møre with his pipelines, he bypassed Florø.

It was still light when I stepped ashore on the express-boat quay. In the golden evening sun Florø lay like a peaceful mix of schools and commerce, with markets and everything you could expect, from shops selling American branded clothes to Chinese restaurants with discounted lunches. Between the original timber builds the 1980s had invaded with their concrete blocks constructed with insurance money and bank shares – as safe as ant hills now that economic conditions had changed with the wind and were blowing cold, hard gusts down your neck. Time to sell. Time to board up the windows and lock the front door for good. Creditors arrived and good luck to all the latecomers. They will never build a railway line to Florø. They missed the boat on that one a long time ago. In that sense Florø is a piece of Norway in miniature, somewhere you will always feel at home.

Jannicke Finslo lived at the top of Livius Smithgaten, in a little, white timber house not far from Florø church.

Jannicke Finslo – Per Bruheim the sign said on the door, like an engagement notice.

I rang the bell, vaguely wondering who Livius Smith was. Klondyke's last gold prospector or & Wesson's partner?

Then Jannicke Finslo opened the door and I knew at once it was her. The family likeness was striking, even if her hair was longer and lighter than Lisbeth's. Her facial features had the same mix of seriousness and sincerity, and although they were marked by resignation now, the lines beside her eyes revealed that laughter was not far away, if life gave her a reason.

'Veum?'

'That's me.'

'You'd better come in.'

I hung up my coat in a well-lit blue hallway and followed her to a spacious kitchen with a view of the harbour. On the worktop was a plate of home-made open sandwiches covered with aluminium foil, and a Thermos of coffee. 'I thought you'd be hungry,' she mumbled, pulling out a nickel-plate chair with a red, imitation-leather seat.

I sat down. She placed the sandwiches on the table and poured some coffee into a white mug. She didn't ask whether I wanted anything else. They don't drink tea in Sogn and Fjordane.

As for her, she leaned against the worktop with a half-full mug in one hand. She was wearing a dark-blue blouse with a red anchor on a breast pocket, unbleached jeans and sealskin slippers with a Sami pattern. Her face was pale and narrow, and she had dark bags under her eyes.

'Per's doing overtime,' she said.

'Where?'

'In Ankerløkken.'

'And Kari?'

'She's gone to the cinema. I'm happy she has her mind on something else.'

I nodded and took a mutton sausage and cucumber sandwich.

Then we both spoke at the same time: 'And there's still…?'

We stopped and I continued alone: 'I'm afraid not. None here, either, I take it?'

She shook her head. Then she gesticulated with her free hand. 'I don't understand what can have happened. I simply don't understand.'

'There were no hints beforehand that something was brewing?'

'None. We'd made a clear arrangement. Kari would come up here as soon as school finished and Lisbeth the following weekend. We've got a cabin in Askrova, and as neither Per nor I have any holiday before July, she and Kari would use it the first two weeks of the school holiday. The last week they'd stay here and look after the house for us, and after that there was talk of Kari maybe having a friend up here to stay for a while, when Lisbeth had started work again.'

'Hm. How is she taking it – Kari?'

Jannicke Finslo pointed to the plate, telling me to help myself. 'She … I don't think it's really sunk in what's happened. The un-certainty. She's in a kind of latent shock which I'm frightened will deepen when … there's certainty.'

I took a sandwich with sardines in tomato sauce. 'You fear the worst?'

She nodded gravely. 'I do. I know my sister. I know she'd never subject Kari to something like this, voluntarily.'

The sardines swelled in my throat, and I had to use my muscles to swallow them. 'Yesterday, on the phone, you said that Kari was adopted.'

'Yes.'

'When did that happen?'

'The adoption?'

'Yes.'

'Oh ... she was quite old. Her real mother was a drug addict, and she'd lived with foster parents from when she was an infant. But for some reason her foster parents were removed and she was put in an institution until Lisbeth and Erik took her.'

'An institution?'

'Yes, a children's home. There's nothing wrong with her if that's what you're thinking.'

'Quite old, did you say? How old?'

'I don't remember exactly. We were living all over the place at that time, if you understand what I mean. Per was working for Rosenberg in Stavanger, and Lisbeth and Erik spent a year in Spain, in connection with his architecture studies. We didn't move up here until my mother died and we took over this house. And that was in ... 1979. In the summer. The year Kari started school.'

'1979? And that was the first time you met her?'

'Er ... Kari?'

I nodded.

'Yes, it probably was. They'd only had her for a couple of years then.'

'And you hadn't seen any photos of her?'

'Oh, yes. We received Christmas cards with a photo ... I think. Why on earth are you asking me about all this?'

I hesitated. 'Let me put it like this. When you do a jigsaw, some people like to put pieces together from the first moment; others collect them first. I belong to the latter group. When I have all the pieces, then I start the picture. But there are invariably some pieces I can't make fit. I just have to live with that.'

'I don't understand a word you're saying.'

I changed the topic. 'Have you got children?'

Her eyes released me at once, and a distant winter stroked a cold finger across her forehead and left its mark. 'No,' she said bluntly. 'It seems we're not able to have children.'

I was about to help myself to another sandwich with Roquefort and red pepper when the front door went.

We looked at each other.

'It's Kari,' she whispered.

We heard hurried footsteps, and Kari stood in the doorway, scouring the room with her eyes. 'Is Mamma...?' she asked, hardly daring to look at me.

'No, I'm afraid not,' said Jannicke Finslo in a gentle tone. 'But this is Veum. He's trying to find her.'

'Hi,' I said.

'Hi,' came the muted response.

She was dressed the way young girls did this year, in slightly oversized, cream flannel trousers, baggy at the back like a farm-worker's, a short, green leather jacket and loose, tallow T-shirt. Her build and hair colour were quite different from those of the two Finslos I had met. She was robust and red-haired, with light-brown freckles over her nose and cheeks, and a curious little mouth that was reminiscent of a flower bud that hadn't yet opened.

'Was it a good film?' her aunt asked.

She wrinkled her nose.

'Did you meet anyone?'

She shook her head and shrugged her shoulders, which I interpreted as: *No one I'm going to tell you about.*

'Do you want to hang up your jacket and take a seat?' I said in a friendly voice.

She looked at the plate of sandwiches and nodded. Then she went into the hallway while Jannicke Finslo opened a green fridge door and took out a carton of semi-skimmed milk. She filled a large mug.

Kari returned. She slumped down on a free chair, helped herself to a sandwich, took a swig of milk, rested her forearms on the table and looked past me out of the window.

I coughed. 'As your aunt said, I'm looking for your mother.'

She didn't react, but her eyes glazed over, and I could see her lips tightening.

She wore a lot of make-up, on her mouth and around her eyes, and the contrast with her red hair was emphasised by the white powder on her face.

'I'm trying to gather any information that might help me find her.' I let that sink in before continuing: 'What we're all keen to know, of course, is whether she may, consciously or unconsciously, have indicated that something unusual was going on in her life recently.'

She nodded mutely, as a sign that she had understood. But she didn't say anything.

'I know it's hard to talk about such things when it's about your mother. But I'm used to these situations. I'm a trained social worker and have worked with children and teenagers for many years. You can trust me, Kari. Whatever you say will remain between us.'

Jannicke Finslo stirred uneasily, and I looked up at her. I continued: 'Perhaps you'd prefer to talk to me alone?'

Jannicke Finslo opened her mouth and Kari whispered: 'Yes.'

Her aunt looked at her with injured pride in her eyes. Then she turned away, walked to the door and said in an unsteady voice: 'I'll go in and see if there's anything on TV.'

She closed the door firmly behind her. Then we were alone.

Kari raised her gaze and looked at me: 'She was frightened.'

A chill hand squeezed my heart. 'Frightened? Your mother?'

She nodded. 'I noticed. During the last few weeks. There was something she was worried about and sometimes…'

'Yes?'

'She put the phone down when I came home. Interrupted the conversation – "we can talk about it later" – and rang off.'

'And she didn't say anything to you, anything that might've suggested *what* she was frightened of?'

'No. But one evening…'

'Yes?'

'One evening – late … after I'd gone to bed – the phone rang again. I had to go to the loo, and the door was open, so I couldn't help hearing what she said.'

'Right. And you heard?'

'I don't remember the precise words, but it was something like: "Don't get involved in all this, Tor. It might be dangerous."'

'Tor? Did she really say "Tor"?'

'Yes. He phoned a few times and asked after her. I've told the police as well: "Tor here. Is your mother at home?"'

'"Don't get involved in all this, Tor. It might be dangerous." Anything else?'

'"OK. I'll see if I can fix that." And then at the end something like: "Yes, as discreetly as possible. I'll see what I can do, but you be careful now, alright." Then she rang off.'

I made a note. '"I'll see if I can fix that. As discreetly as possible, I'll see what I can do?"'

She nodded.

'This could be a huge leap forward in the investigation, Kari. But why didn't you say this before? To the police, I mean.'

She shifted uneasily. Then she said, in such a low voice that I barely caught the words: 'I'm so scared of being abandoned again. If Mamma goes missing too, it'll be the fourth time someone's left me. It's as though … as though no one wants me.'

I straightened up. 'The fourth…? Do you remember when you were sent to … your parents?'

'Just about.'

'How old were you?'

'Four.'

'And when was that?'

'When I was four?' She calculated quickly. '1976.'

'1976? And that was to Erik and Lisbeth?'

'Yes?' She sent me a puzzled look.

'Fine.' I didn't pursue this line any further. 'There are no other details you can remember? This Tor, do you know anything else about him?'

'He never came to ours.'

'But she must've mentioned him?'

'Only indirectly. To say she was meeting him on such and such an evening.'

'And how long, more or less, had he been ringing?'

'I can only remember his name coming up a couple of times over the last few months. She could've known him for longer.'

'Your father – Erik – died in 1982, didn't he?'

Her mouth tightened. 'Yes.'

'And you moved to Bergen the same year?'

She nodded.

'Five years ago.' I groped my way forward. 'Do you know …? Has your mother had any other … friends since then?'

She stared into the distance. Again, her eyes glazed over. 'Not as far as I know. No one she brought home. But I was always scared … I mean, she was still so young and pretty that … it would be strange if…'

'…someone wasn't interested in her?'

'Yes.'

'And you were scared of that? That it might happen?'

'Scared?'

'You used the word.'

'Did I? But I didn't mean it like that. Only of what I said before. Of being left alone again.'

'But you had a good, warm relationship with your mother? That was my understanding.'

'Did you know her?'

I nodded. 'Superficially. She gave me physio.'

'Backache?'

'Neck.'

She nodded, suddenly mundane. 'That's what affects most people. The back and the neck.'

'And the bit upstairs, if you ask me. Between the ears, to put it another way. What I wanted to say was … Surely you don't think your mother would've left you because she'd met another man, do you?'

'Nooo.' She demurred, like a small child, not quite sure about what she knows or wants.

I sighed. 'So, you didn't hear this Tor's surname mentioned?'

'No. Auntie Jannicke said something about … Has this Tor gone missing too?'

I mused as I watched her. I reckoned she could take it. So, I nodded and answered: 'Gone missing in the sense of dead, yes.'

Her eyes glazed over again, but this time the glass was thicker. I didn't observe any other reaction.

That was as far as we got. We called Auntie Jannicke back, and a few more sandwiches and a cup of coffee were forced upon me before I made tracks for the accommodation I had booked at one of the town's overnight establishments suited to my lifestyle and one which would undoubtedly make a thoroughly solid impression on my clients: a mission hotel.

Before I fell asleep, I flicked through the book on the bedside table and consoled myself with Matthew 7:7: 'Seek and ye shall find'. If nothing else, my trip to Florø had given me at least a couple of new pieces for the jigsaw. Now all I had to do was find the board so that I could see if they fitted.

I slept poorly and woke up early, afraid I might miss the morning boat, which left Norway's westernmost town at 8.30.

In the morning mist, light and golden like champagne foam, we ploughed through the Vestland's skerry waters, passing landmarks such as the island of Alden and Mount Lifjell, and feasting our eyes on the municipalities of Sula and Gulen before Lure fjord swept us past towards the narrow strait of Alversund and By fjord revealed Bergen in all its summer splendour, like Japanese pastel art on rustling rice paper. Somewhere there seemed to be a hole in the sky, letting good weather leak through, unless it was the depleted ozone layer, which could no longer keep ultraviolet light at bay.

When I stepped ashore on Strandkaien it was 11.30.

On the vegetable stalls lay the season's fruits in a wide spectrum of colours, from white, yellow and orange, to dark red and every variation of green. In the flower market the summer's fireworks lit the square with colours we barely had the vision to do justice. Above Mount Fløi's green façade the sky opened wide. We were airing after the winter and cleaning every nook and cranny.

I walked up to the office and unlocked the door.

There was a message on the answerphone. I rewound the tape and played it again. A metallic voice said: 'Message from Bergen Police Station. You're requested to contact Inspector Hamre at once. I repeat: at once.' And as if they weren't confident of the recipient's mental faculties, they repeated the message again.

There were no other messages.

I switched off the answerphone, lifted the receiver and dialled the police station number. I reached Hamre, and he spoke on inhaled and exhaled air: 'Where the hell have you been, Veum?'

'Not far. Florø.'

'And what the devil were you doing there?'

'Well, I didn't meet him there. But I did meet Lisbeth Finslo's family.'

He went quiet for a few seconds. 'Her sister and daughter?'

'Yes. I told you her sister commissioned me to keep searching, didn't I?'

'Well … you can stop now.'

'Have you—?'

He interrupted me: 'We've found her. Can you come over at once?'

'Yes, of course, but I—'

'*At once*, Veum.'

'Is she … dead?'

'What do you think, Veum?' Jakob E. Hamre said, and put down the telephone.

30

Images, thoughts and questions raced through my mind as I ran the short distance from my office up to the police station: Jannicke Finslo, who didn't understand what had happened; Kari, who was so afraid of being abandoned again; the car hoisted out of Solheim fjord with a body inside, in 1982; and Tor Aslaksen at the bottom of a swimming pool, last Thursday. The newspaper pictures of little Camilla Farang, missing since 1979; Siv Schrøder-Olsen with her hands full of flowers; the chain of demonstrators in front of the main gates in Hilleren; Lisbeth Finslo running ahead of me along the paths in the arboretum, her lips against mine; her face when she came up the stairs from the swimming pool: *I had no idea. I didn't understand*; Lisbeth, who had been missing for as long as Tor Aslaksen had been dead. Where had they found her? In what state and what had happened to her?

Hamre was waiting in his office. He peered up and growled: 'You didn't waste any time.'

I nodded.

'Take a seat.'

I did as he said.

He leaned across his desk and fixed his eyes on mine, as he was wont.

I waited.

'As I said, Veum. We've found her. Unfortunately, and fortunately. All depending on how you see things.'

'In other words, she's dead?'

'Yes.'

I digested the news. While I had been making my way here, I had felt the metallic taste of certainty in my mouth. The taste of death, as irrevocable as autumn, as sure as a blood infection.

'Was she murdered?'

'Yes. Strangled. And it was quick.'

I shook my head. I was unable to visualise it. All I could see now, with total clarity, was Kari.

'When did you find her?'

'This morning. A man was walking his dog.'

'Where?'

He bided his time. 'We have to ask you a favour, Veum.'

'Shoot.'

'We need a print of your car tyres and of the soles of the shoes you were wearing the evening she disappeared … To rule you out of our enquiries,' he hastened to add.

'Of course,' I said. 'That's fine. Do you need my consent in writing?'

'No, thank you.' There was a glint of a smile.

'So, where?'

He rubbed his hands, a dry, creaking sound, like paper rubbing. 'In Bønestoppen. Set back from the road. She's been there the whole time. We're pretty certain about that.'

'And no one's seen her?'

'She was well hidden. In a drainage ditch, with last autumn's leaves and branches spread over her.'

I was beginning to *see* her now that he was going into detail. 'In other words, the man who may have been waiting for her outside the house in Kleiva, strangled her there and then, drove straight to Bønestoppen, got rid of her body and drove back home?'

'Or on to Oasen, in Tor Aslaksen's car. That's the theory, yes. Forensics are already working on her body, of course. We'll have to wait for their findings.'

'No signs of a sexually motivated attack?'

'Nothing to suggest it. Her clothes were untouched, let me put it that way.'

'In other words, it looks like the two murders are connected?'

'Have you ever doubted it?'

'No, not really. Kari, her daughter, had the impression she was frightened of something, before.'

'Frightened? What of?'

'She didn't know. But she overheard a phone conversation her mother had been having with someone called Tor…'

'Oh, yes?'

'In which her mother told him not to get involved in anything, it was too dangerous. Later she said she would try to fix something, possibly arrange a meeting, as discreetly as possible, and then she told him to be careful again.'

Hamre wrote this down with his scratchy pen. 'Why the hell didn't she say this before?'

'Would it have helped? Her mother, I mean.'

'Nevertheless.'

'Perhaps she preferred my way of asking to the police's. I've always had a way with children and old ladies.'

'Yes, I'm sure that's the reason. At any rate, it's useful information. We'll talk to her as well, later, but for now...'

'Have you informed the family?'

He nodded. 'The Florø police are taking care of that. The police and the priest.'

I was back in the white timber house, in the modern kitchen, with the woman and the girl in Livius Smithgate in Florø. The news was definitive now, what they had both been expecting and fearing. And the pathologist's verdict was ... dead.

'Have you any leads?' I asked.

Hamre looked at me. 'I hope so.'

'Is it possible to visit the crime scene?'

He looked at me again, with even greater intensity. 'Maybe. I'm going there myself.' He grabbed a piece of paper. 'Where's your car parked, Veum?'

I explained.

'And your shoes?'

I pointed downwards. 'The very same.'

'Good. Let's sort this out first, and once it's done, we can drive to Bønestoppen together.'

'Like two old lovers on a drive down memory lane?' I said ironically.

'More like two rejected suitors.'

'You're right. Death took the bride. We were weighed and found wanting. This time.'

'Exactly, Veum. This time.'

We rose to our feet and left, like two clowns in a rehearsed sketch. But there was no laughter and no applause. All we had was each other's company, and we had tired of that long ago.

31

A crime scene is a crime scene is a crime scene.

It was at the bottom of the cul-de-sac known as Bønesheia, on a steep slope covered with pine trees. The whole area was cordoned off with red-and-white tape tied from tree to tree in a wide circle around the corpse.

We parked the car behind a handful of civilian vehicles and a patrol car. Two or three photographers and journalists made a bee-line for us, and Hamre held up a hand. 'No comment. There'll be a press conference at four.'

'But at least you could say *who* you've found?' said a reporter who looked so young, I suspected he was writing for a school newspaper.

Hamre shook his head, stepped over the cordon and motioned for me to follow. 'You lot stay there,' he said to the press and ignored the fact that a couple of the photographers had already taken enough pictures of him and me to paper the walls of the royal mansion in Bergen.

We stepped over the high kerbstone separating the carriageway from the undergrowth and stood looking down. A couple of officers came to Hamre to report, but he silenced them like a second Moses with the stone tablets on his way down Mount Sinai.

In a pine tree, a little way down the slope, some kids had built a cabin with old formwork boards. Further down, the hillside became steeper towards Bønes school and Upper Kråkenes, which were well hidden behind the compact wall of vigorous pines. Before us the suburb of Fana spread out in all its munificence, from Natland and Landåsfjellet in the north-east to the axis of Fanafjellet to Flesland in the south. Below us lay Nordås bay with the same coruscating innocence as the previous week. A romantic bridge curved between the Marmor islands, and on the other side of Nordås bay the urban sprawl had spread like an epidemic during the last decade, so that now there was almost no break between the old town limits and Sandsli.

I turned and looked across the road, where lines of terraced houses, so new that they smelt of mortgages even from here, pointed towards Mount Løvstakken's forest-clad southern side. It was being eaten up by the 1980s' hunger for building plots too. It was an exposed place to get rid of a body, one would have thought, but just here the rear wall of a garage was staring with blind concrete eyes onto Nordås bay.

I nodded towards the terraced houses. 'No one there see anything?'

Hamre shrugged. 'We've already started door-to-door enquiries. But lots of people are at work and a good number are probably on holiday, so it could be quite a while before we've spoken to everyone.'

'Where was she?'

He pointed down to some juniper bushes, where several familiar faces from forensics were already well under way with their investigations.

'And she's been there all the time?'

'Presumably.'

I nodded towards the cabin in the tree. 'Isn't it odd that no one's seen her?'

Hamre sent me a scowl. 'Once again, the school holidays are working against us, Veum. I don't suppose there have been any kids in the tree house over the last few days. She would have been completely visible from there. From here it wouldn't actually have been possible to see her, behind the bushes.'

'How was she … I mean, was she carried down here?'

'We assume he parked by the roadside, in the most protected spot, because of the garage up there. He probably dumped her over the concrete kerb and let her roll down. The marks on the corpse would suggest that.'

I shuddered and clenched my teeth, so hard it hurt. It was as though I could feel her fingertips on my neck again, as cold as ice.

'And then?'

'He followed her down, perhaps to push her over the bushes; at any rate to camouflage her with any branches, twigs and foliage he could find. But once your attention had been caught, she was easy enough to see. We found some footprints down there, which we hope will give us something concrete to go on.'

'You're sure it's a man?'

'If it isn't, she's a very strong woman.'

'It's impossible to get any tyre prints from tarmac, isn't it?'

'Well, there's a turning area further up, with quite a bit of dust from concreting work. We've cordoned that area off, too, and we're making casts of the tracks we've found.' He gestured towards where the body was. 'The most important thing is that we've found her, Veum. Experience tells us that where we find a body, we'll find clues.' His eyes narrowed. 'Somewhere inside the barricade tape we'll probably find the clue or clues that will ultimately lead us to the murderer.'

I felt thoroughly depressed. What once had been a living person, Lisbeth Finslo, with organs that pumped and filtered, muscles that stretched and contracted, hair that fluttered in the wind, pores that opened and closed, eyes that met other eyes, lips that ... Now she was no more than a discarded corpse, a fly paper for clues, a numbered file, a legal case, a meal for the pathologists and finally: ashes in an urn, placed in the ground, a name carved into stone and a memory for those who would still remember her after a few years, until the memories faded and there was nothing much left apart from a moss-covered headstone and a crime scene.

For crime scenes always survive. From crime scenes, blood rails against the heavens and reminds us of our fates. To crime scenes you can always return.

I followed Hamre down to the juniper bushes where she had been found. The forensics officers were crouched down with their plastic bags, their spoons and trowels, their adhesive labels and cameras, like at an archaeological dig. But all they found here was the remnants of a destroyed life, a truncated career and a mute scream.

In the juniper bushes the berries were green, like unlived lives. Around us here was a strong smell of forest floor and resin. Ants were swarming around our feet, like a main street in a metropolis at lunchtime. Birds were boring their trills into our heads, without closing the holes afterwards. On the breeze came scattered organ notes, like an accompaniment to a distant funeral.

For Lisbeth, Bønesheia was the last cul-de-sac she entered. For us, it was about how we found our way out again.

Hamre eyed me, ashen-faced. 'I assume you've noted that this is *our* case now, Veum – one hundred per cent?'

I nodded and muttered: 'I'll focus on the Camilla Case. So I have something else to think about.'

'You do that. The trail from that case has gone so cold it'd be hard to do anything wrong.'

I cast around apathetically. 'Was that the reason you had me come out here?'

'To make you face up to reality, Veum. And to see how you reacted to the crime scene.'

'And when will I be presented with the conclusions of this psychological test?'

'We'll send them to you in writing, Veum. In duplicate. One copy for you and one for your doctor.'

'And if I don't have one?'

'Send them to the refuse department. It'll serve the same purpose.'

He gave a strained smile. He had never liked me and never

tried to make a secret of it. But his way of expressing himself was still preferable to that of his colleague Dankert Muus. I suppose it was what you might call charm. Either you have it or you don't. Personally, I paid far too high a price for the modicum of charm I had inherited.

'I'll get someone to drive you back. I have to stay here for a while.'

He was about to shout to one of the uniformed officers, but I pre-empted him. 'No need. I'll catch the bus.'

'As you wish, Veum. You support public transport, do you?'

'All too seldom, I'm afraid. But when I do, I no longer feel so alone.'

'Have a good trip then.'

'And the same to you.'

We parted on these terms, like two casual acquaintances: our mouths full of polite phrases; our heads full of corpses.

A crime scene is a crime scene is a crime scene. At least there is never any dissonance here.

32

Fjell town hall in Straume stands like a down-payment on the 1990s, waiting for better times. From its strategic position in the middle of Lille Sotra island it keeps watch over Sartor shopping centre, the built-up area in Hjelteryggen, the traffic link south and tax rates.

The Camilla Case was eight years old, but it still opened doors today. The office assistant in the property registry took out official records heavier than the municipal social budget and flicked through to the right pages without so much as asking for a stamp tax in compensation for the bother. He straightened his horn-rim glasses, stroked the long red fringe from his brow and moistened his fingers on a damper pad with every page he turned. He had a meticulous tie knot and a winning charm, so much so that he was to stay an office assistant in Fjell municipality for the rest of his life.

Vibeke Farang had inherited a property north of Sekkingstad from her parents. Six years ago, she had turned the former summer cabin into year-round accommodation. I sketched a quick map in my notepad, thanked the assistant for his help and left just as they closed the doors for the day. It was four o'clock and the council were hurrying home to eat.

The sun was shining like an Egyptian curse. I almost drove by the Bible school in Bildøy for a swift confession, but I resisted the temptation and followed the road west, hoping the sea would offer a cooling breeze for my afternoon coffee.

I found Vibeke Farang's name on a green post box by the kerb, five or six kilometres south of Eide, where the sea opens up and washes its hair with foaming shampoo in the strait between Dyrøy and Algrøy, which lies, like a north Norwegian fishing station, on the most fertile soil at the northernmost tip of the island.

I parked my car behind a ten-year-old Opel Kapitän estate the same colour as turbid red wine. Then I followed a modest footpath down to the sea, over clumps of hardy, yellowish-green grass, rocks washed clean by sea spray and westerlies, and cracks and hollows filled with gravel and pebbles to ease access. Rather inappropriately, the path ended in a wire fence and a gate with a sign saying: *Private property. No admittance.*

It was not in my nature to let empty threats hinder me, so I opened the gate and passed through without stepping on any landmines. The only searchlight to shine on me was the sun.

I continued along the path until I came to a cliff face falling steeply to the sea. Concrete steps led down to the house, which I saw from almost directly above it.

The roof was covered with bituminous waterproofing and the walls were stained a bluey-grey with dark-red frames and doors. I could hear music, but I couldn't see anyone.

For a moment I scanned the horizon, from south to north.

I had been in these parts before. During the summer of 1981 I had spent the whole of my holiday here, in a cabin owned by a distant relative. A couple of years later I had gone to a cabin a little further north on the island, tracking a guy who had vanished into thin air. And if I continued further north, to Øygården, what I had experienced there six months ago was beyond belief. So Sotra had become a kind of theme in my life, a place I returned to more and more often.

I looked down at the house again. The music from below sounded canned and insistent, like old marching tunes in new packaging.

With my hands in my pockets, and at a stroll, as if to signal to the whole world that I was coming in peace, I walked down the concrete steps towards the back of the house.

If I had dreamed about a cool breeze, I was disappointed. The rock face behind me reflected the sun onto my neck, making the sweat run between my shoulder blades and my head sway from its moorings, like a balloon before it takes off.

The music was louder now, coming from the front of the house. I followed the noise and called out 'Hello-o' as I rounded the corner.

There was a concrete patio on two levels in front of the house with a mini-version of Babylon's hanging gardens, created with sweet peas, in the division between the two levels. The music came from the lower patio, from two platter-shaped speakers in a rectangular, black cassette player.

The woman down there was moving to the music, but in a kind of delayed rhythm, slow and charged, which both reflected and challenged the driving beat of the tune. I recognised some of the exercises from my reticent youth, a kind of syncopated yoga, but I would never have been able to perform any of them now.

She was as supple as a snake, with trained muscles like woven wicker. They rippled under her dark-brown skin, dividing and fragmenting her body into groups of muscles, sinews, diaphragms and membranes, like a demonstration dummy used to train new medical students.

The tight-fitting bikini was in cream and would have been quite attractive, had it not been for the grease marks left by the oil. Her hair was short at the front, streaked and tied into a knot at the top with a green elastic band.

She was a typical bodybuilder, glistening with luxurious oils, ready to perform in any championship. And she had done most of the work herself. God may have been the architect and opportunity the builder, but she had taken responsibility for the basic entrepreneurial work. Her body was so muscular that, but for the bikini top and the width of her hips, it would have been difficult to determine her gender.

But I recognised her face. It was tanned and excessive exposure to the sun had given her a network of premature wrinkles. Nevertheless, she stared at me from eight-year-old newspaper cuttings with eyes that were as bottomless and sombre as they had been then.

'Ermmm,' I coughed. 'Vibeke Farang?'

She looked up at me, in mid-movement. For a second, she paused. Then she completed the movement, let her head fall forward and sat utterly still for a few seconds while only her diaphragm moved – slow, deep breaths.

Afterwards she unfolded her legs beneath her and stood up straight, without any help from her arms. She bounced over to the cassette recorder and switched it off with her big toe. And turned to me in a relaxed defensive pose, ready for an attack if I chose to try anything, and she was fairly confident of a favourable outcome, judging by her facial expression.

'And you are?'

'Veum. Varg Veum. I'm here on account of ... Camilla.'

Her face lit up as though I were an angel from aloft and she had been waiting eight years for the news I would bring her. 'Is there anything new?' she asked in a tremulous voice.

I quickly shook my head. 'No, I'm afraid not. Sorry. Nothing like that.'

Her gaze became vacant for a moment. Then it returned, as alert as before. I saw her muscles tense in her calves, and her arms hung by her sides, like a cowboy ready for the shoot-out on the last reel of a western. 'Who are you?'

Behind her, a gull dived down to the sea, like a fragment of the sun that had broken free. It pierced the surface of the water and seconds later rose again, flapping its wings furiously towards the sky, a flailing fish in its beak.

'Veum, as I told you. I'm a private investigator.'

'Does that mean that someone has commissioned you? Is it ... Bård?'

'No, no, no. I was on another case that suddenly developed a link with the Ca ... the case concerning your daughter.'

'And which link was that?'

'Tor Aslaksen.'

As the gull melted away in the sky above us, so the name melted in her eyes. But I could follow its passage for quite a long time.

In the end, she said quietly: 'Yes, I saw he'd had an accident.' We stood in silence for a moment. I was soaked in sweat.

To get some air to my skin, I pulled my shirt out of my trousers and opened the top buttons.

'Would you like something to drink?' she asked. 'Orange juice?'

'Please. And a jug of fresh air, if you have any.'

She looked at her watch. 'We can go for a walk along the sea, if you like. While we talk.'

'That sounds good.'

'I'll just put on some clothes,' she said, walked up the few steps to the patio where I was and past me, so close that I could have touched her. But she wasn't on her guard any more. I had been categorised as harmless.

33

I looked around.

Beside the cassette player, there were two dumbbells, a sun-lounger and an open paperback, the front cover facing upward. A woman with a plunging neckline was being embraced by a man with a high hairline, and the pastel letters of the title gave a further hint to the tone of the writing. On top of the cassette player was a pair of sunglasses with a light-green frame.

On the top patio there was some white garden furniture, and extra deck chairs had been folded up and placed against the wall under the roof.

The shadows were sharp and the sun burned down on my neck like a glowing coin. I took a deep, deep breath and stretched up on my toes in my light shoes, as if that would help.

She came back out, wearing a loose, blue-checked summer shirt over her bikini. On a dark-green plastic tray she had two glasses and a big jug of orange juice with ice cubes in.

She slipped her feet into white canvas sandals and filled the glasses. 'There you are.'

I took one glass, lifted it to my mouth and drained it in one long, ill-mannered swig. The ice cubes stayed at the bottom of the glass and I could see them shrinking in front of my eyes. I opened my mouth and swallowed them too.

She sent me a wry look and refilled my glass. 'Was it good?'

'It was wonderful.' I stared across the sea. 'It's incredibly hot.'

'Climate change,' she said, as dispassionately as if she was commenting on a change of wind direction.

'Change? It's been unchanged for more than a week now.'

'Yes, but the extremes. We're going to have warmer winters, heat waves in the summer, and heavier storms in the autumn and late winter. The polar ice caps are going to melt and the seas will rise.'

'At least you'll be safe at this height.'

'That's what happens when child-like humans think they're grown-ups and play with things they don't understand.'

I finished the second glass and put it down on the table. 'Shall we go?'

She pointed. 'There's a path down to the sea, below the patio.'

I nodded and went down the steps to the lower level. I gestured towards the cassette player and the dumbbells. 'You're in training?'

'It's my job,' she said.

'Oh, yes. Where?'

'I'm an instructor at a fitness studio. Besides, I've been doing bodybuilding since I was a young girl.'

'That's obvious.'

'Thank you, if that was meant as a compliment.'

'Don't you usually get compliments?'

'Yes, but not everywhere. Not everyone views the human body as part of the same sacred nature surrounding us. It has to be nursed and tended and spared unnecessary strain.'

We descended the last home-made concrete steps onto a jetty where there was a little wooden boat without an engine. 'So, I don't smoke or drink, and I keep to a sensible diet, train regularly, and if I go in a boat...' She pointed.

'Then you row.'

'Precisely. If you walk across the jetty, you'll find the path on the other side.'

I did as she said. There was a narrow, well-worn path along a little shelf in the rock. Short, yellow grass grew along it, and along the edges tiny, dry rock flowers, some yellow, some pale red. With every step we took I felt, miraculously, the first breaths of an invisible sea breeze, so quiet it was barely more than an exhalation from someone standing near you, but, nevertheless, it did cool me.

She came up beside me. 'What actually happened … to Tor?'

I glanced at her. 'He drowned. Have you had any contact with him, recently?'

'Oh no, never. Not since … you know.' She hesitated before carrying on: 'I don't know how much you've heard.'

'About what?'

'About Tor and me.'

'Well…'

'But how did you connect his death to Camilla?'

'Are you up to talking about it?'

'About Camilla?'

'Yes.'

We had climbed onto a high rock. The breeze, moist with salty water, caressed our hair. Beyond, we saw the sea, like a dark circus ring. Above it the horizon stretched like a shimmering silver tightrope, and a ship balanced on top, leaving us spectators in breathless excitement, as impotent as clowns banished to ringside seats.

She said softly: 'I don't think anyone can understand what happens to people who go through such an experience.'

I looked at her without saying anything.

'It's one thing to lose a child in a natural way. After an accident or an illness. But when a child goes missing and you never see her again … My life stopped the day Camilla vanished. In the eight years that have gone by since then, there hasn't been a minute when I haven't thought about her.'

I nodded, still not speaking.

'During the first few days, even if everything was chaos and confusion, at least you had some hope. That she would reappear. That they would find her and she hadn't suffered too much. We do hear about people who haven't had children themselves, who...'

She faltered.

'Then came the long weeks, when you just prayed to God you would get her back, whatever they'd done to her, you could console her, you could hug her and bring her back to life, you would have her back with you. The appalling images in your mind, the dreadful imaginings of what they might've done to her, the abuse they'd subjected your little girl to and finally – perhaps – how they just discarded her. I started searching in bigger and bigger circles around where we lived. Even though they had combed the area and done all they could. I couldn't stop myself. I walked past lakes and ponds, stared into them to see if I could spot anything that shouldn't be there. I looked under tree roots, under big rocks, lifted bushes, stepped into ditches half-full of water ... in ever greater circles. Whenever I crossed roads, I wondered: is that what happened? Perhaps a car hit her and the driver took her and just dumped her ... somewhere else? That would've been more humane, wouldn't it. A better death for Camilla than someone...' her voice broke off '... using her and disposing of her.'

She scanned the open land and seascape around us, the cliff down to the sea, the smooth rocks, the islets, the houses on Algrøy, the sun glittering on the sea, the on-shore breeze, the piercing blue of the sky above us. 'Children are like untouched nature. Until adults sully them. With their dirty lives.'

I still didn't say anything. This was a race she would have to run to the end; then I would stand by the finishing line with bananas and a foil blanket.

'Now I think: today she's fifteen. I don't think *would have been*; I think *is*. I can see her, living a different life, separate from us, but still the same girl. Camilla. *My* Camilla.'

She had arrived. She raised her head and looked at me, with deep, horizontal lines in her brow. Her eyes were blind and transparent, like an ice sculpture. 'What was it you wanted to know?'

I searched for the right words that could lead me onto the right path through the dark forest that still surrounded her. 'I was just wondering about a few details. Something you can remember from the night she disappeared.'

She stared at me vacantly. 'That night? In a way it has gone for me. I don't know if what I remember is that night or it's just how it's stuck in my imagination. It's all so unreal. Still.'

'But Tor Aslaksen did visit you?'

She nodded, and her eyes shifted to the horizon again. The ship had gone now. I hoped it had reached the other side of the world, and if not, there had been a safety net in place.'

'How did you get to know him?'

'At the fitness studio. He came to train now and then.'

'A meeting place for muscles?' I said in an attempt to strike a lighter note.

'You could say that,' she answered in a monotone. After a short pause, she carried on: 'He was nice. Modest, but someone you could talk to. He invited me out. I told him I was married, but…' In a lower voice she said: 'Bård was away a lot. One day Tor invited me to his place. It became a…'

'Relationship?'

'A friendship.'

'But you…?'

'Yes, we did.'

'And the night Camilla disappeared?'

She nodded and swallowed. 'Yes, then too. I popped my head round her door before we went into the bedroom. She was there then. She was asleep, like a little angel with her head on the pillow. And that was the last ... the last I saw of her.' The tears fell suddenly, like drops of rain from a cloudless sky. Angrily, she wiped them away with a cupped hand.

'And you two ... you hadn't heard anything?'

She shook her head vigorously. 'No, no, no. But we ... The back door was unlocked. She must've woken up, looked in ... at us, understood – or not; run off, outside and straight into ... eternity. Into the darkness where something evil and dangerous was waiting for her.'

'And afterwards?'

'Afterwards?'

'Yes, I mean, Tor Aslaksen had left when you discovered that Camilla had gone, hadn't he?'

'Yes, we ... I saw him to the door, said goodbye, and then before going back to bed I nipped into her room to see if she was still asleep. When I saw she wasn't there, I was stunned at first. I went into the toilet to see if she was there. Then I ran through the whole house before I realised that the back door was open. I ran out, behind the house and called her name. No answer. I ran around the houses shouting my head off. Then I went back in and called the police.'

'Where was this back door?'

'In Camilla's room.'

'Did you see anything of Tor Aslaksen later?'

'No, we ... Never again. Of course, I talked to him a few times afterwards, during the investigation. About the car that he took to the garage for me. But otherwise it was a total break. He was as desperate as I was about everything. In a way, we both felt it was our fault, kind of. And, of course, it was. Anyway, he never came to the fitness studio again, and I never met him again.'

'And your husband?'

'That finished of course. He found out about everything, didn't he.'

'Yes, but anyway. A tragedy of these dimensions would over-shadow even the—'

'Some relationships seem to be strengthened by adversity. Others break up. Ours had already begun to develop cracks. Stuff like Tor and me doesn't happen for no reason, does it.'

'No, I suppose not.'

'So, when the initial drama was over and we'd begun to calm down, sort of, young herr Farang packed his bags and headed for the hills.'

'The hills?'

'Away. Away from civilisation, evil, stress, everything. Searching for the idyll. Now he lives on a mountain farm in some god-forsaken bloody place deep into Hardanger fjord, with a wife and kids and what-have-you.'

'Are you still in touch with him?'

'Haven't been for a long time.'

I hesitated. 'He was out of town when this happened?'

'Yes, at a *seminar*,' she said, with such bitterness that it dripped with sulphur and acid.

'If I mention a few names…'

She looked at her watch. 'We'll have to start back.'

'Are you expecting someone?'

She nodded.

'Lisbeth Finslo. Does that name mean anything to you?'

Her expression was blank. 'Who's that?'

'It doesn't ring a bell?'

She shook her head.

'Bodil Schrøder-Olsen?'

'No.'

'But her name was different then of course.'

'Who is it?'

'An ex-colleague of your husband's.'

'Bodil? No, I don't remember … Has she got anything to do with Odin Schrøder-Olsen?'

'Yes, she married his brother. Do you know Odin?'

'Everyone knows who he is. Besides, he trains with us.'

'Right. Did he train with Tor Aslaksen?'

'No, that was a long time ago … He's only been with us for two or three years. Did Odin and Tor know each other?'

I smiled, unable to ignore the mythological parallel, Odin and Thor. 'Like father and son. They were childhood pals and former colleagues.'

'Hm. There are lots of intersecting lines, I can see.'

'Far too many,' I said, trying to draw a mental chart of the key connections.

We had reached the end of the path now. She bent down and picked one of the pale red flowers. She turned to me and said with a sudden ferocity in her voice. 'Do you know what this flower's called, Veum?'

'No. Botany was never my strongest suit.'

'Nor mine. But they've always grown here. The only difference is that when I was small, they had a wonderful bitter-sweet smell.' She wrinkled her nose. 'Now they just smell bitter.' She threw the flower down, and it lay like a mutilated body on the rocky ground. 'As if the pollution in the sea has reached all the way up here.'

I gazed across the sea, which looked like oil, it was so calm. 'Not impossible.'

'Do you know…?' She chewed her lower lip.

'Yes?'

She studied the flower. 'Whenever I pick one of these flowers, I think about … It's like I get a guilty conscience.'

'What about?'

'It's as if…' Her eyes became moist again. 'As if Camilla's in the flower. As though she's come back to life, in a new form, and then…' she was almost whispering '…I picked her.'

I felt a knot in my stomach, and with a tentative smile I stretched out a hand, grabbed her shoulder and squeezed it gently as if to say: *I understand you, Vibeke. I'll be with you on Judgement Day. I'll put in a good word for you.*

Without another word, we moved on.

As we climbed down to the jetty, I mumbled: 'Perhaps I was here / at the dawn of time / as white Spiraea / waiting to be found.'

She looked up at me. 'Eh?'

'Knut Hamsun. A poem.'

'For some reason it reminded me of Simon and Garfunkel.'

'You may be right. But I think it was Norway's answer to them, Tobben and Ero.'

We crossed the jetty and started the climb to her house.

'How long did you stay in Bjørndal?' I asked her from behind.

She stopped. 'A few years. Actually, I didn't want to. But I didn't dare to move either. Sometimes I thought, when I was sitting there alone, in the evening, months after she vanished, I thought: now she's coming. Suddenly she'll tap on the glass in the back door and want to come in. And then it'll be as if she's only been away a short while and has finally found her way home. But she never came back.'

As she was walking up, she said: 'I'd taken this place over from my parents. At the same time as … In the following years I spent as much of my free time as I could working here, turning it into a winter home. I've done the majority of it myself. It became a kind of mania, a form of systematic desensitisation. Doing something the whole time, hard training or grafting here, *while* thinking about her, until I could finally think about her without bursting into tears.'

We were up on the lower patio now.

From the patio above came a gentle cough, and the man there was looking at his watch at the same time as Vibeke Farang.

I had seen him before, when he was holding a press conference outside the gates to Norlon A/S. It was Håvard Hope, from Greenearth.

34

Håvard Hope stroked his straight fair hair with its diagonal fringe. The bright sunlight made his pallor seem unnatural, almost albino-like. 'A bit later and I wouldn't have been here,' he said to Vibeke Farang.

'I'm sorry, but I went for a walk with Veum here.' She walked towards him while I stood still, partly waiting and partly to be discreet.

We formed a kind of triangle: him on the patio above, me down here and her on the way up the stairs between us.

'I don't know if you've met...'

He shifted his focus to me. 'No, I don't think so.' He sent me a measured nod.

I nodded back. 'My name's Veum. Varg Veum. I was present at your press conference at Norlon the other day.'

'Which one?' he said acidly.

'Last Friday.'

He shrugged. 'There have been so many. So, are you a journalist?'

'If the Salvation Army are detectives, I'm a journalist.'

'What kind of answer is that?'

'He is one,' Vibeke Farang interrupted. 'A private detective.'

The yellow teeth Håvard Hope revealed could have done with a thorough examination. I quickly pre-empted any comment from him: 'Private *investigator*.'

He half turned to Vibeke Farang, who said quietly: 'It's about Camilla.'

'Will you never get any peace?' he muttered dejectedly.

She placed a hand on his arm. 'I'll go in and get dressed.'

He nodded, and she took the empty glasses and the jug of orange juice inside.

There was a silence that left us both feeling uncomfortable. We tried to break it simultaneously.

'What—?'

'How—?'

We stopped, and he motioned me to speak.

'How's it going at Norlon?'

He tautened his lips before answering: 'There are signs that we're moving towards another serious confrontation, either this weekend or the beginning of next week.'

'And you're standing by your guns?'

He shifted uneasily. 'Naturally.'

'How are the police reacting?'

'So long as we stay outside the factory premises, we're on public ground, and as long as we don't impede general traffic in the area, which is as good as zero, they'll stay on the margins and wait.'

'But they'll intervene if the confrontation becomes physical?'

'I would think so. In reality, this is a political matter. Someone at a higher level of authority should be giving clear instructions as to how they deal with their toxic waste. That's all we're asking.'

'In other words, you're up for a negotiated solution?'

He shifted his feet again. 'There are of course differing views, but in general we're agreed. At any rate, *I'm* in favour of a negotiated solution,' he concluded, straightening his back.

'And Odin Schrøder-Olsen?'

'For obvious reasons he's keeping in the background this time. Originally, in fact, he was *against* the whole action.'

'Yes, but he's an experienced activist. Don't tell me he hasn't had a word to say regarding strategy. After all, he's on home ground here, if I can put it like that.'

'I'm not trying to pull the wool over your eyes,' Håvard Hope said, with a face like a sullen schoolgirl.

'Do you work out as well?'

'Work out? What do you mean? Does it look like it?'

I looked at the thin white arms sticking out of his dark-blue, light cotton shirt like tentacles. 'Well, not at the gym, at any rate. I was just thinking, as you're clearly good chums with Vibeke Far—'

I stopped as the person in question re-emerged from the house. She had changed into jeans and a T-shirt. Otherwise, there were no obvious changes. 'I'll just take...' She nodded towards the cassette player, the book and the other equipment on the lower patio.

I bent down and picked up the dumbbells. They were pretty heavy. I would have had problems doing twenty reps.

As she passed me carrying the cassette player, I caught the scent of lily of the valley. That hadn't been there before.

I followed her inside.

'Just put them on the floor,' she said.

I put down the dumbbells and cast a quick look around. The interior was still like a cabin, with natural-coloured wooden panels on the walls, rag rugs on the floors, landscape paintings and pine furniture with woven upholstery. In one corner there was a small electric organ and from the top of a book case an unnaturally large and frighteningly vivid photograph of little Camilla stared at me. It was in subdued colours and developed on linen paper, like an old painting, which seemed to make her more alive than a standard photograph.

Vibeke Farang had delved deeper into the house, to the kitchen, judging by the sounds. I looked at Camilla, seven years old in 1979, four or five when this picture was taken. Her hair was longer than I remembered from the newspapers, and the ribbon bigger and whiter. Her eyes were large and full of wonder, and a smile played on her lips, it too imprinted with the same wonder children have when they watch adults' strange doings.

It caused me physical pain to gaze at the picture. I had to tear myself away and went back to the sun and Håvard Hope.

He growled at me: 'It is possible to get to know people in other places than a gym , you know.'

'Of course.'

'Vibeke's an active member of the movement.'

'Greenearth?'

'That's how we got to know each other.'

'And who got her interested? Odin Schrøder-Olsen?'

'Does it matter who?'

'No. And you're "just good friends", as the magazines phrase it?'

'I came here to pick her up. We're going to the … er … night shift.'

I smiled thinly. 'You're on shifts already? Sounds well organised.'

'Strength through organisation, Veum,' he said, as though he had been sent by the TUC. 'We have to be rested for when the great battle commences.'

'Call in King Arthur and the knights of the round fable,' I said.

'Table, you mean.'

'*Fable*. We are talking about politics, aren't we?'

He sighed. He looked tired. He reminded me of an undergraduate a week and a half before their final exams. As a student with whom I had shared a bed for a day or two had said: 'Finals aren't difficult. They're just a lot of work.'

Then Vibeke Farang came out and said it was time for his oral. In other words, she was ready to go.

On the way up from the house I asked if she lived here without a car.

'I have an old banger, but…'

'We have to limit parking at Norlon,' Hårvard Hope said curtly. 'And one car pollutes less than two.'

'Besides, we have to pick up another couple in Hjelteryggen,' she added.

'And, besides, it would look a bit conspicuous if all the eco-warriors turned up in their own cars, wouldn't it,' I opined.

No more was said until we were on the main road. Håvard Hope drove an environmentally friendly, soot-coloured Volvo that did a kilometre a litre and was constructed long before the words 'catalytic converter' came into being. The burgundy Opel Kapitän was hers.

I pointed to the Opel. 'Is that the same…?'

She nodded. 'I've never been able to afford a new car, and it has a sentimental value too.'

'Hmm.'

Before getting into the Volvo, she said: 'If you should find out something … about Camilla … don't hesitate to contact me at any time of the day or night. *Any time*, OK?' She was staring at me with such gravity I was frightened I looked ill.

I nodded. 'Of course.' I proffered a hand. 'Thank you for being so kind.'

She didn't smile, but she shook my hand and pressed it gently, the way a woman seeking a separation would have pressed the hand of a public arbitrator.

Håvard Hope leaned out of the Volvo window. 'Are you coming or…?'

She was, and I waited for a couple of minutes after they had left before getting into my own car and driving in the same direction. I have never been that fond of following a bridal couple with a veil of exhaust fumes flapping in the wind behind them.

35

I took the scenic route around Hilleren. It was like returning to a faded version of the previous Friday.

Håvard Hope's Volvo was parked by the Co-op up the hill, but I couldn't see either him or Vibeke Farang in the vicinity. By the entrance to Norlon there were two new officers, gesticulating that I wasn't to drive down.

I nodded to tell them I knew, parked by the kerb and looked out through the rolled-down window.

The media circus had relented. They had been invited to other opening days. There wasn't so much as a portable Puddefjord Radio tape recorder in sight, and the only cameras I saw were for personal use.

But the chain gang was still there, closer together, with more people than five days before and even more sparsely clad. There wasn't a green anorak to be seen and many of them had their chests bared. If the campaign lasted a few more weeks, they would all be sun-tanned. That would save them the autumn trip to Gran Canaria.

The officer nearer to me, a stout teenager in his forties, winked at me and said: 'If you want to join in, grab the chain.'

'Not today, thank you. I have to go home and do some baking,' I said, started up, signalled left, looked in the mirror and reversed into Hillerenveien.

I stopped at the main gates to Haakonsvern naval base with my nose facing outwards so that I wouldn't be arrested on suspicion of espionage.

I took out my notepad and flicked through to a page entitled 'Camilla'.

I ticked Vibeke Farang's name and stared at Bård Farang's until I decided it was too late in the day to drive to Hardanger and back.

So, I moved my finger down until it pointed to a third name: Raymond Sørensen. Arrested in 1979, but released the following day without charge.

Nevertheless...

Raymond Sørensen lived in Daniel Hansens gate, the heart of what used to be called Nedre Nygård, but which events had re-christened Little Manhattan. I drove that way home.

The building he occupied, known as a 'chimney house', because of the high risk of a fire, was next to St Jakob's church and surrounded by skyscrapers.

The stairs in the block of flats were worn and in bad condition; the area had lain under threat of demolition for many years. Like a grey-and-white layer of dust, the remnants of winter still covered these buildings, where even in the middle of summer there was no more than a gentle thaw indoors.

On a piece of cardboard fixed to a second-floor door with a rusty drawing pin *R. Sørensen* was written – in round, childish letters in biro.

I rang the doorbell. Half a minute later the door opened a fraction. From above a solid security chain a section of a long, melancholy face peered out at me. 'What is it?'

'Raymond Sørensen?'

His eyes were pale and watery. 'What about him?'

'Is that you?'

He had to give this some thought. Then he nodded. 'So?'

'May I come in?'

'What is it? No one passes this door. Not Jehovah. Nor the electricity people.'

'I'd like to talk to you about an old case.'

He moved to close the door, but I already had my foot in. 'The Camilla Case.'

'I'm not talking to anyone about that.'

'I know you were innocent.'

His smooth pate glistened. 'Why do you want to talk to me then?'

'I just wanted a general frame of reference.'

He eyed me suspiciously. 'A what?'

I sighed. 'The patterns of behaviour that lie … I mean, what makes people do things like that.'

He blushed. 'I've never done anything like that. I only stroked 'em.'

'Stroked?'

'I've never kidnapped anyone. It's always been of their own free will.'

'Free will? I don't know any details of the cases you've been convicted of, but … You *used* to have a burgundy car at that time, didn't you?'

'I said I don't want to talk to you. Who the hell do you think you are? In fact, who are you – another bloody parasite?'

'You've had visits from them before, have you?'

'I can smell you from here.'

'But I'm not one of them. My name's Veum, and I'm a private investigator.'

'A private what? You can go to hell with all your private bollocks, as far as I'm concerned.'

'Listen.' I looked around demonstratively. 'Wouldn't it be better if we had this conversation in your flat?'

'No one comes in here.' He looked down. 'And if you don't shift that foot sharpish, I'll go and get an axe.'

'You have one to hand in case you have to chop up the furniture, do you?'

He glared at me.

'Come on, Raymond. Give me a couple of minutes.'

'I'll give you what for, I will. Will you lot never understand how simple it is?'

'Simple?'

'The postman did it, for Christ's sake.'

'The postman?' I was so surprised I pulled my foot back.

He jumped at the opportunity and slammed the door shut.

I stared at the peeling, dark-brown door. *The postman?*

I stood for a few minutes, waiting to see if anything happened, but I knew I'd had my chips.

If necessary, I could return another time.

Deep in thought, I walked down the stairs and into the daylight. *The postman?*

I drove slowly back to my office. *The postman.* Somewhere a distant bell was ringing.

At the office I found Bård Farang's telephone number and dialled it.

A child's voice answered. 'Hello?'

'Hello. Is your father at home?'

'Yes. Who shall I say it is?'

'My name's Veum. But he doesn't know me.'

'Who are you then?'

I was growing weary. 'Can I speak to your father?!'

I heard the sound of water draining down a plughole. Further away, the same child shouted: 'Pappa. There's a grumpy old man on the phone for you.'

Soon after, a measured voice said: 'Hello?'

I oozed charm. 'Ah, hello, is that Bård Farang I'm talking to?'

'Speaking. Who's that?'

'My name's Veum. Varg Veum. You don't know me. I'm a ... er ... private investigator. I've discovered a connection with the ... Camilla Case in some work I'm doing.'

There was a silence. 'I see. What are you after?'

'I have a few questions I'd like to ask you. I was wondering if I could drive over – tomorrow, perhaps.'

Another silence. 'Have you spoken to anyone else?

'I've spoken to your wi— ... to your ex-wife, if that's what you were referring to.'

'Yes, it was.'

'And she was very accommodating. But I need more perspectives on the case, if I can put it like that.'

'Well, I don't want to stand in your way. What was the name again?'

'Veum.'

'Are you afraid of heights, Veum?'

'Not particularly.'

'Then I'll pick you up by boat in Røyrvik. Do you know where that is?'

'No.'

'Halfway between Tørvikbygd and Strandebarm. What time shall we say?'

'As early as possible. I have to be back in Bergen by four.'

'Could you be there for eleven?'

'That should be OK. See you then?'

'See you then.'

I put down the receiver and dialled the number for Norlon A/S. A woman who sounded uncannily like the autumn lady from the admin office answered.

I assumed an administrative tone and made a vain attempt to speak like someone from eastern Norway. I sounded like a de-racinated western Norwegian. 'Health Executive here. Berge. I'm looking for a herr Clausen. He was an employee at Norlon.'

'*Monrad* Clausen?' came the sharp retort.

'Yes. He was the, ermm, let me see, the foreman there. Could that be right?'

'Yes, that's Monrad. But he retired ages ago.'

'I see ... Well, it must be him. You wouldn't have his address by any chance, would you?'

'I think he moved back to ... Just a moment.'

I waited, hoping he hadn't moved back to Kirkenes in the far north.

She came back on the line, pleased with herself. 'It's what I thought. He's moved to Vaksdal. Would you like his precise address?'

'Yes, please.' I breathed a sigh of relief and noted it down. I could actually call on him after I had been to see Bård Farang, if that visit didn't take too long.

So far, so good.

I slumped back in the chair. I needed a dram.

But I knew now. Days like today were the reason I'd had an Antabuse implant, which rendered me incapable of drinking anything stronger than coffee. I felt like an old grey blanket, covered in muck and crap, ready to be thrown on the dump at the first opportunity.

The day had been one long succession of mental short circuits. I couldn't stop thinking about Kari and how she must feel now that she knew about her mother's fate. Or about Lisbeth Finslo herself, who had been hidden under some bushes for almost a week, drained of life. At the same time my brain was reverberating from the conversations with Harald and Aslaug Schrøder-Olsen, while the image of Siv with her helpless hands around a haphazard bunch of flowers merged into the image of Vibeke Farang, her face much too old for her well-trained body. Above all this loomed the shadow of Camilla who, from what I could judge, had no more to do with any of this than Tor Aslaksen's relationship with her mother did. And as if this weren't enough, my mind was cast back to the main gates at Norlon, where the chain gang appeared as a nightmarish line of skulls against a toxic-yellow background.

I woke with a violent start. For a few seconds I had been drifting into sleep.

I placed my palms on the desk, stood up and went over to the basin, where I rinsed my face in ice-cold water, rubbed it until it was warm and red, and returned slightly more refreshed.

I called Karin Bjørge and asked if she was receiving soiled blankets for coffee. She said she even invited them to dinner.

I drove up to Fløenbakken, feeling as if I had sandpaper behind my eyes. Around me the town was metamorphosed into a garish, glittering carnival, people running around in much-too-skimpy clothing, smiling at one another insanely and not appearing to have any idea what was happening. My mouth was dry. I needed…

What I got was a long, soft kiss, two concerned blue eyes and a ham omelette with fried potatoes.

'You'll have to come and taste one of *my* specialities one day, Karin. Beans in tomato sauce and fried eggs.'

Afterwards we sat on her sofa, each nursing a cup of coffee. Birdsong drifted through the open balcony door, wrapped in the glass wool of traffic noise, so that we wouldn't be cast under a spell.

I told her everything, from the beginning to the end. She listened, mouth agape, her eyes seeming to widen further and further.

In the end we sat in silence, listening to the birdsong, the traffic noise and our own thoughts.

'I can understand that you feel depressed, Varg,' she said.

'What bother me most are the innocent victims: Kari, who, in perhaps the most vulnerable period of her life, is suddenly alone again; Siv, a victim of God-knows-what, maybe destiny, maybe something else; and Lisbeth – what reason is there for *her* to die in such a way? But worst of all – worst of all is the thought of Camilla. These are the cases that eat away at you and you can never get rid of them. The uncertainty. The not knowing, the fact that perhaps you will never know what actually happened.'

I focused away from the balcony door and onto her. 'Can you understand what stirs in the hearts of people who do whatever they do to young girls like Camilla?'

'No, but I remember often thinking the same way during the years we had Siren, my daughter ... well, you know.'

I knew all too well.

'I thought: why does she do such things to herself? What drives her to pump her body full of poison, destroy herself totally, at such a young age? And what do they think? The people who got her the drugs, who made so much money out of it, who used her ... and threw her life away? Is it evil, pure and simple? Or is it just stupidity?'

She made a gesture, towards the windows.

'And then I thought: are we actually any better? Aren't we filling the town full of poison, the country, well, in fact the whole world?'

'In that particular case, I hope it's only stupidity.' I followed her eyes across the town, which from a distance lay in a beauty bath of brown and grey smoke, dotted with black above the most congested traffic arteries. The sun inserted its sharp, testing needles into the fug, as if to take samples of the contents, but I doubted it would be happy with the results.

'But don't you think there is some connection between destroying a child and destroying nature, which was so perfect originally?'

'Yes, maybe, but this is so specific. And yet so up in the air. I mean, what did happen to Camilla?'

'What did he say, the man you spoke to?'

'Raymond Sørensen? It was the postman who did it. Why do you ask?'

'Because I once read a crime story where a crime had been committed in a house, but no one had seen anyone go in or come out. Then they found a letter in the post box, or something like that. At any rate, someone asked: what about the postman? Yes, they'd seen him, of course. He'd been there. In other words...' With a roll of her hand, she invited me to draw the natural conclusion.

'…It was the postman who'd done it. It was so obvious that no one had noticed.'

'Exactly.'

'I'm seeing her father tomorrow.'

'That's one possibility.'

I was lost in thought as more and more patterns formed in my head.

She gently interposed herself. 'Are you staying … over, for the night?'

I met her eyes. 'If we can get up in time.'

And we did.

36

I caught the ferry from Hatvik to Venjaneset and drove via Fusa to Hardanger, passing the old wooden church in Holdhus and the fish-rich lakes of Hålandsdalen, and meeting the Hardanger fjord in Mundheim. From there I followed the main road north.

Arriving in Hardanger at this time of the year was like travelling through a tourism manager's wet dream. The fjord was like a blue fracture in the terrain, the drifting morning mist like steam from subterranean saunas. The mountainsides rose like grey and green trampolines for the sunshine, which flashed to and fro, turning to white gold in the water, and patches of verdant light in the forest alongside the fjord. It had been a long winter this year, and the very last apple blossom lay like remnants of snow on the trees. Boatsheds and farmhouses, rowing boats, jetties and the white church on the horizon made it all the perfect fata morgana – a picture postcard sent to us by Tidemann and Gude, two romantic Norwegian artists, from the most beautiful of all worlds, where we were each other's tourism manager, all of us. Ah, bliss it was…

But in the boat-building yard in Omastrand lay a spanking-new catamaran, ready to be launched, a sign that progress had reached this part of the world too.

I parked by the disused general store in Røyrvik. Faded advertising posters served as a reminder of a shop that had buckled under the pressure of its competitors in Strandebarm and Tørvikbygd. Below the road a pebble beach formed a natural grey zone in front of the sea. I walked down and scanned the horizon.

In from the fjord chugged a little sailing dinghy, powered by an old-fashioned, two-stroke outboard motor. On board sat a man with long dark hair, wearing a ragged, washed-out T-shirt that had once been red and jeans cut off at the thigh. With him he had a four-year-old boy, red-haired, wearing khaki shorts.

The man squinted into the sun and shouted before the boat struck land: 'Veum?'

I nodded, and he waved as a sign that he had received the message. I was pleased. The arrangement had gone as planned.

The man stopped the engine, jumped ashore holding a rope and quickly secured the boat. He ran a hand through his hair, which was tied in a loose ponytail. His squinting eyes glinted brown as he came over and shook hands. 'Bård Farang.'

His voice was sombre and self-assured, and he radiated a kind of charisma that reminded me of Odin Schrøder-Olsen. He had the smile of a Raphael angel: big white teeth and pink lips. His skin was tanned, his hair almost black, and the only feature that marked him out as having passed thirty were the streaks of grey around his ears and the broad fan of laughter lines beside his eyes.

If he had been painted by Raphael, the boy would have been painted by Rubens, slightly podgy with the pale skin that came with red hair. He didn't look much like his father.

'This is Olav, the middle one.'

'So, you have three?'

'Yup.'

'Not counting Camilla?'

'Yes, I don't count her anymore.'

'Why not?'

'She's dead.'

'Are you sure?'

'Can you give me a good reason not to be? Is that why you've come?'

'No. I was just wondering, as you were so sure.'

He came closer. 'Listen. It might be possible to kidnap infants and bring them up as if they were their own, but not a normally developed seven-year-old girl who knows what her name is, where she lives, who her parents are and much besides. Perhaps even a bit too much, if you catch my drift.'

I nodded and looked down at Olav. 'This is perhaps not the right moment…'

He relaxed. 'No. I just have to do some shopping. I'll take the car, so I'll be quick. Will you wait here?'

'Yes, how far are you going?'

He pointed. 'Straight to Strandebarm. We'll be back in less than half an hour.'

He took the boy and an old-fashioned grey rucksack, as Norwegian as brown cheese, and got into the old, dark-blue Mazda estate parked by a turn-off up the road. Soon they were on their way, into the bay to Strandebarm.

I sat on the pebble beach, waiting, like an Edvard Munch painting.

They came back, parked the car and got out with a full rucksack. Olav held out a big, green apple to me with a juicy white bite taken out of it. 'Look.'

I smiled. 'Have you eaten all that?'

He nodded proudly and beamed at me.

Bård Farang put the rucksack in the boat and turned to me. 'Ready for the crossing?'

'Where do you live, actually?'

He pointed across the fjord to a small farm on a shelf a couple of hundred metres up the mountainside.

'And what's it called? Wuthering Heights?'

He laughed. 'No. Uren, Luren, Himmelturen. As in the old nursery rhyme.'

I motioned towards the car. 'Can you just leave it here?'

'Oh, yes. It's so old no one will give it a second look.'

I nodded across the fjord. 'There's a road to the ferry in Jondal, I take it?'

'Of course, but the fjord is the way to move around here, as in the days of yore. Besides, I like not having to be dependent on ferry times when I go to Bergen.'

'So, you do go to Bergen?'

'Yes. Now and then.'

'When were you there last?'

He made a vague gesture with his hand. 'Oh, a couple of weeks ago. Are you coming?'

When we had turned the boat's prow in the right direction and the engine had sputtered its way into a sweet spot, he began to point out places. 'Down there you can see the northern side of Varaldsøy island, with Bonde Sound to the west. To the east, Silde fjord flows into the mouth of Mauranger fjord, but it's already hidden by the headland there. Hamaren.' He pointed in the opposite direction. 'Vikingnes.' He pointed across the fjord. 'Grotnes.'

I jerked my head backward. 'And there's Hjartnes. I can hear we're in the *nes* part of Hardanger fjord.'

He grinned. 'Every other place name has a *nes* or a *vik* here. Headlands or bays, as you know.'

'Does it make every other inhabitant either a ness chieftain or a Viking?'

'It makes us mountain farmers, anyway.'

I stared ahead again. The closer we were getting, the steeper it seemed up to the farm where Bård Farang had settled. 'What made you move here?'

His tanned face twitched. 'A kind of weariness of civilisation and everything that comes with it. And by that I don't just mean Camilla. Even if it was obviously a symptom, as it were. Escape to the country is a common phrase, but for me it was a reality, and in fact I've thrived here.'

'I can understand that at this time of the year, but in mid-winter?'

He shrugged. 'It's fine, too.'

'It must be isolated though.'

'Don't you often feel isolated, over there?' He nodded backward, to the side of the fjord we had left behind us, as though that was where civilisation was.

'Yes, I do.'

'As long as I have someone who cares about me, we have each other and can live a simple, uncomplicated life … I'm happy. We have no problems apart from those nature gives us, and we have no choice but to accept nature. We are ourselves part of it. If nature ails, we ail. If it's healthy, we're healthy.' He motioned to Røyrvik again, the symbol of all that was wrong with the world. 'Everything has become so hard, so brutal and materialistic there. Money, money, money. Money determines everything. Time, time, time. I know, Veum, because I've been there, too. Where time's money and everything that can be done faster than yesterday is to the good. That's why we have computers of course, to save time. But the time we save we don't devote to ourselves, or others, or to something useful. If we did, all would be fine. No, we use it to make more money.'

'And by "we" you mean…?'

'Society in general, the economy, private individuals, whatever you like.'

'Including you, in other words?'

He beamed back. 'No, not anymore.'

We were across the fjord. Bård switched off the engine, landed and tethered the boat. He held it so that I could jump ashore. He lifted Olav and the rucksack over to me, secured the boat astern to an orange buoy and jumped ashore himself.

We were at the bottom of the road south of Jondal. Above us an aerial cable carried a small cart up to the farm. A green post box was attached to the outside of the cart so that they could avoid a wasted journey down to the road. The path to the farm rose as steeply as the cable.

Bård Farang put the rucksack in the cart and Olav on his shoulders. Then we started the ascent.

At first the path rose in gradual stages. We passed some scree where rocks had been placed to form a staircase, then we came to a steep cleft in the terrain. Here you had to hold on to juniper bushes and birch saplings, if your hands were free, and they had to be, because the natural steps formed by the mountainside were pretty steep. In the most difficult places, an iron railing had been bolted into the rock, but over the longer stretches you had to cope on your own.

Halfway up, I turned and surveyed the scene. The narrow road had shrunk to a cycle path. The boat in which we had crossed the fjord had become a toy. Beneath us Hardanger fjord lay like a yearning in your soul. And there was still a long way to go.

'Impressive, eh?' Bård Farang said above me.

'Hardly a place to bring the old,' I muttered.

'Oh, people lived up here until they were almost ninety. In the olden days.'

'My guess is they *stayed* up there then.'

'Yes and no, but they also managed to lower the coffins.'

'Blueberries, Pappa,' Olav shouted and threw himself forward off his father's shoulders, momentarily knocking him off balance.

'They're not ripe yet, Olav,' Bård Farang said. 'Look, they're barely red.'

'Sore tummy then?' the boy asked unconcerned.

'Mhm. A very sore tummy,' his father said, sending him a solemn stare.

We continued upward. We were approaching the shelf the farm was built on and gradually the terrain was changing. The cleft we were walking in widened and the ascent became easier. What from below had resembled a narrow ledge turned out to be a gently sloping and much broader plateau in the mountainside. A stone wall marked the boundary of the steepest parts and a palisade fence enclosed the property to the north and south. There was no need for a fence behind. The mountain rose steeper and darker than anywhere else.

We opened a metal gate and two children came to meet us: a five-year-old girl with her father's long dark hair and a toddler with white locks, a heavy nappy and a sceptical thumb in one side of his mouth.

'Hi,' said the girl to her father and stared at me with curiosity.

'Hi, Marthe,' Bård Farang replied.

He turned to me. 'This is Marthe and over there's our littl'un, Johannes.'

'Hello,' I smiled. 'My name's Varg.'

'Marthe,' she said, gauchely, as though I hadn't already twigged.

Johannes said nothing. He just gaped at me, wide-eyed as the whole of his hand followed his thumb into his mouth. I felt like the new chaplain and wondered how long it had been since he last saw anyone come up from below.

The farm comprised a white farmhouse and a red outhouse. Hay racks had been set up on the field in front of the buildings, and on the slope behind there were potato plots and large vegetable patches, some covered with black plastic. The plateau tapered gradually again north of the buildings, and from the heather slopes came a gentle bray from some sheep, as if to tell us they were still there too.

As we approached the farmhouse a woman appeared from the rear. She had soil on her hands.

She was a big, strong, red-haired woman with her hair tied tightly at the back, falling into a long ponytail down to her hips. Her skin was the same colour as her middle son's: transparent, dotted with light-brown freckles, and she had dry, cracked lips. She was dressed in the same outfit as her husband: worn jeans cut into Bermuda shorts, and a light-green T-shirt, bleached by the sun and washing. Clearly, she wasn't wearing a bra, and if I wasn't much mistaken, in her stretched belly was another child. With her fertile appearance, the warmth from her light-brown eyes and the soil on her hands she was Mother Earth in person, the Gaia age's happy version. When she smiled, I could see she was ten years younger than her husband, unless she had been vaccinated against wrinkles.

She splayed her palms in front of me. 'Sorry I can't shake hands. I've been weeding.'

'That doesn't matter.'

'So, this is Veum,' Bård Farang said. 'And this is my wife, Silje.'

We shook hands mentally with a direct smile at each other.

'There's water on the stove,' she said. 'Will you brew the tea, Bård?'

He nodded. 'I'll just chat with Veum first. I'll shout when we've finished.'

They smiled to each other as though they had just emerged from the registry office and had their whole lives in front of them. The children had started playing in the rocks next to the outbuilding. They were laughing loudly at something or other.

I looked past them, let my eyes wander across the green slopes, the stone wall and the thin birches on the outside, across the fjord, which had become a silvery shimmering metal strip, a couple of boats on it like dark rust, far below us and across to the mountains beyond, with Vesoldo in the north and Tveitakvitingen in the north-west.

It was a perfect picture. Almost too perfect. I hoped it would be equally perfect after I had finished talking to Bård Farang.

'Are you coming in, Veum?'

I nodded and followed him into the farmhouse.

37

It was like walking into a house from fifty years ago. The walls were painted in rural red, yellow and white. They were adorned with hand-woven tapestries in traditional patterns, black-and-white photographs of the farm in bygone days in black, varnished frames, portraits of people who had probably lived there and some amateur paintings of the fjord landscapes around us.

We each took a seat in a high-backed chair around a polished, oval table with an embroidered cloth in the middle.

There was no TV, but they did have a radio. The most modern feature of the interior was the dark-blue, push-button telephone on the wall – ensuring contact with civilisation.

Bård Farang fixed me with his gaze. 'Private investigator, wasn't that what you said yesterday on the phone?'

I confirmed with a nod.

'And you're investigating the old case?'

'No. I've been investigating a disappearance that took place last week. A young woman.'

'By the name of?'

'Lisbeth Finslo. Does it mean anything to you?'

'Nothing at all. Should it?'

'I hope not.'

'And you think this disappearance has something to do with Camilla?'

'I cannot exclude the possibility that there may be a link, yes. That's why I—'

'What is it?'

'First of all, I'd like you to tell me in your own words how you experienced what happened when your daughter went missing.'

'"In my own words". What do you mean by that? I was five hundred kilometres away.'

'In Oslo, I'm informed.'

'Outside Oslo. I was on a job-related course.'

'IT?'

'An introduction into new technology. But—'

'What do you mean by "outside Oslo"?'

'A course centre halfway between Oslo and Lillestrøm. Up in Gjelleråsen somewhere. I've been to so many places I can barely remember one from the other.'

'Gjelleråsen? That's definitely not far from Oslo.'

'Tell me, what has this to do with …? Didn't you ask me to talk about Camilla "in my own words"?'

'Yes, I did. Sorry, that was a digression. We can come back to it later.'

'Come back to…?' He scowled at me. 'When I returned, at the time, Camilla had definitely gone.'

'When did you find out?'

'Vibeke rang, early in the morning, hysterical.'

'Early in the morning? How early?'

'Listen, Veum, I have no idea what you're after, but the police checked my alibi thoroughly. As if I would have any reason to … I *could*'ve made it to the last flight from Fornebu to Flesland, but there were between forty and fifty course participants who were able to confirm that I was present and sociable, till well past midnight. But I couldn't have returned so early with a standard scheduled flight.'

'What about a private plane?'

He gesticulated exasperatedly. 'I can't fly.'

'Hm. OK.'

'So, there's nothing I can tell you, *in my own words*, about what happened. Vibeke and Camilla drove me to Flesland and waved me off. When I returned, she'd gone. And, bit by bit, as I began to hear about the details…' He leaned forward, the muscles of his upper body taut.

'Which details are you referring to?'

He leaned back again. 'There was nothing about it in the press.'

'No, but you're probably thinking about … your wife's visitor that evening?'

He studied me. Then he nodded and sighed. 'So, you know?'

'What went through your mind when you heard?'

He shrugged. 'It was quite a surprise. And terrible that it should've had an impact on Camilla.'

'Were you jealous?'

He grimaced. 'Jealous? Well, I'm not sure. The relationship between me and Vibeke had begun to deteriorate. And I don't blame her. I told you in the boat. Time, time, time; money, money, money. In those days I had too little of both. Now at least I have enough of the former.'

'Perhaps you'd also been…'

'If I had, it has nothing to do with you. And it had nothing to do with Camilla's disappearance, either.'

'How was it for you afterwards?'

'After she'd disappeared? It was a living hell. The police, the press, being chased from pillar to post, Vibeke always on the edge of a nervous breakdown. I tried to take it with more … more composure.'

'But it must've got to you, too?'

His face reddened. 'And how.' He hit his chest with a fist. 'It's still there.' He unclenched his fist and held out both hands. 'If I ever catch who did it, I'll strangle him in cold blood.'

'That's how much?'

'That's how much, yes. I loved Camilla … the way I love all my children. She was so trusting. When she was small and we went for drives in the car she always slept under a blanket on the back seat, never afraid that I wouldn't get her safely to where we were going or that I wouldn't wake her when we arrived. Often, she would lie awake in bed, even if I came home long after her bedtime, and then she'd always talk to me and tell me what she'd been doing and what she'd been talking about with … Mamma. And then she'd give me a good, long hug and finally go to sleep. And she did go to sleep, then, in thirty seconds.'

I smiled, as though I could see her in front of me.

'I realised during the first days – I resigned myself to the inevitable. When she didn't reappear and they didn't find her after dragging the nearest lakes and searching the area around where we lived, I realised that a crime had taken place. It made me wild with fury, but there was nothing I could do, at least not until the bastard had been caught. Afterwards I was a broken man … professionally. I never went back to the same routine. I was disillusioned, depressed … but instead of drowning my sorrows, as so many do…' He looked at me, as if I was an obvious case in point. 'Instead, eventually, the reason I came out here was because of my new lifestyle. Vibeke and I had separated. I began to take part in the alternative social movement, and met Silje during an environmental demo. And then … it was just us two. And in time there were more of us. Up here.' He looked around, clearly at ease with the situation.

'Demos, you say. Do you still go on demos?'

He nodded. 'It's the only direct social commitment I still have. But now, because of the kids, I usually have to go on my own.'

'Were you in town last Thursday, by any chance?'

'Last Thursday? If you're referring to the protest in Hilleren, in fact I was there, yes, during the first days.'

'You were?'

'Yes. Is there anything strange about that?'

'And you were there the whole time? You didn't go anywhere else?'

He bored into my eyes. 'What is it now? The woman who went missing?'

'Worse than that.'

'Worse? Is she…?'

'She's been found. And, yes, she's dead. As is her boyfriend. Tor Aslaksen – if the name means anything to you.'

His face tautened. 'Tor Aslaks— … *That* Tor Aslaksen?'

'Indeed.'

'And he's dead … too? When did that happen?'

'Last Thursday. And not just dead, but murdered.'

'Surely you don't think in all seriousness that I might…?'

'You just said if you ever met the person who'd taken Camilla, you'd strangle him.'

'But surely you don't think …? Do you think that it was Tor Aslaksen who—'

'Not directly. Maybe indirectly though. In your eyes. After all, he was the object of your wife's attention, if I can put it like that, when she should've been keeping a better eye on Camilla.'

'If I'd thought that, I would've dealt with him in 1979, Veum. Why on earth would I do it now, eight years later?'

'Right. What do you think happened to Camilla?'

He gestured with his hands. 'I have no idea. She woke up and went outside; that's the only possibility. No one would've dared come inside the house, with people around. Someone was waiting for her outside.' He opened and closed his fists, as if pumping extra blood to the brain.

Then he stood up. 'I'll just go and put the water on. For tea. If you want some.'

I nodded.

On his return, a propos of nothing, I said: 'You had a colleague at that time, who got your job when you finished. Bodil something or other.'

He eyed me suspiciously. 'Yes. Bodil Hansen, I assume you mean?'

'Was she on the course in Gjelleråsen?'

'Was she …? Yes, I think she was, in fact. Why?'

'Were you more than … good colleagues?'

'If we were, it's nothing to do—'

'She flies planes all over the place.'

'So?'

'Well, I'm just mentioning it. She took me up and showed me Bergen the other day, a bird's eye view of it. By the way, her name's not Hansen any more, but you probably know that.'

'In fact, I didn't. Imagine that. Actually, I haven't given her a thought for many, many years. Not until you just mentioned her.'

'She's called Schrøder-Olsen now.'

'Schrøder-Olsen? She isn't married to…?'

'Yes, one of them. Trygve Schrøder-Olsen. Junior, who's grown up now. The big, bad wolf of Hilleren himself.'

'Hmm.'

'By the way, Schrøder-Olsen has a sister, Siv. The first time I met her, she asked me: "Are you the little girl's father?" Have you ever met her?'

'Schrøder-Olsen's sister? Where on earth would I have met her? And why did she mistake *you* for…?'

'She's a little … She has brain damage. She had an accident in April 1979.'

'April 1979. That's more or less when…'

'Not more or less. Exactly the same day, Farang. The 26th of April.'

He arched his brows, shrugged and opened his palms, the personification of what's-that-got-to-do-with-me. 'I don't see the link.'

'I don't, either. Not yet.' A whistling noise came from the kitchen, and he was gone.

Soon afterwards he returned. 'The tea's brewing. If there's anything else you'd like to ask about, ask away.'

'No, in fact I don't think … Your wi … ex-wife, I mean, Vibeke. Do you have any contact with her?'

'Not any more. No, it's water under the bridge.'

'She's taking part in the Hilleren protest, too.'

He looked genuinely surprised. 'Is she? That's interesting. But she hasn't been there at the same time as me.'

'She's probably on the reserves bench as she has a full-time job.'

'How is she?'

'Fair to middling, I'd say. Even if Camilla's disappearance has been much more traumatic for her than it appears to have been for you. I mean, she doesn't have a new family. She hasn't had any more children.'

'Is that wrong too now?'

'No, no, no, not at all.'

We stopped there. We took the tea onto the front doorstep, the morning sun angling in over mountain and fjord.

The cups were blue and white, and there were home-made dill buns. The children were playing up in the meadow while Silje Jondal, Bård Farang and I enjoyed a quiet cup of herbal tea on a plateau high above Hardanger fjord one Thursday, approximately halfway through the second half of the 1980s, with a breeze coming off the sea, in fair weather.

We didn't talk about much more than life in these conditions. They seemed to be at peace and in harmony even though they had been cut off for almost ten days last winter because of the snow.

'What about when the children start school?'

'There's a school bus down below. It's no worse than how it used to be. Easier, in fact, because in those days there were no buses.'

'Do you go to Bergen occasionally, Silje?'

She turned to face me with a humorous glint in her eye. 'Not if I can help it. I send Bård to do any necessary jobs.'

'To the vinmonopol?'

'No, no, we don't drink, we don't smoke, we don't play rock…'

'Not even a bit of good old rock 'n' roll?'

'Rock's the music of the devil, Veum,' Bård Farang interjected with a grave frown. 'Noise.'

'Oh? Really?'

'And we've found peace up here.' He turned his eyes upward. 'We've become friends with God again.'

'Really? I had no idea you'd fallen out.'

'That's why I'm a firm supporter of environmental action.'

'Because…?'

'Because destroying the earth is like destroying God's gift to us. Clean air, bountiful sea, uncontaminated soil. He gave us all this with the creation and we … we've done our best to squander it, sully it, pollute it. I think, Veum, the only way to save the world from total ecological disaster is a comprehensive religious awakening from now to the end of the millennium. Because it's the only awakening that can get everyone to agree, despite all the political division. We have to become friends with God again, all of us.'

'No matter what he's called?'

'Whether he calls himself Allah or Jehovah, Christ or simply the Lord.'

I nodded. 'I think he has me in his address book, somewhere right at the back.'

'Under V,' Silje said.

I sent her a smile. 'Exactly. Under V.'

Afterwards I thanked them for their hospitality.

Bård Farang accompanied me down, ferried me across the fjord and waited until he had seen the car start before setting off and waving to me as he headed east again.

I sat in the car for a while, admiring the fjord, looking up to the mountain farm on the other side, thinking about the people I had met, who lived up there.

I inserted a cassette of genuine 1970s rock: Warren Zevon, and the only devilish thing about the music was one of the refrains: *Aah-ooooh, werewolves of London – Aah-oooooh, werewolves of London…*

Then I put the gearstick into first and drove back to civilisation. The trip was much too short. Civilisation is one of those places it takes much longer to leave than to return to.

38

In the mountains, halfway between Samnanger and Trengereid, just before the old ski lift station in Gullbotn, you see a sign saying you are entering the municipality of Bergen. If you arrived as a motorist from Uzbekistan, you would have the impression that in Norway even the cities are sparsely populated. The sole reason for having the border here was the expansion of Bergen in 1972, a result of Trondheim and Bergen competing over which city was Norway's second-biggest after Oslo. If you took the border seriously you would have to assume sheep formed the majority of Bergen's population.

From Gullbotn the E68 descends sharply towards Sørfjorden and disappears through a tunnel directly south of Trengereid. I turned off here, squinted my way through two of the darkest and narrowest tunnels in Vestland, and arrived in Vaksdal, where the long-time retired foreman of Norlon, Monrad Clausen, was spending the remaining years of his life. Sadly, it didn't seem as if there would be very many.

Monrad Clausen lived in a green house opposite the railway station with a view of Ulvsnesøya island, where there was no longer a reform school for delinquents but an open prison.

A white-haired woman in a blue linen dress, as if it were the middle of winter, let me in, but only after she'd conferred with Clausen, who was not her husband but her brother. 'He's got a bed on the ground floor,' she whispered as we went in. 'He can't manage the stairs anymore, so we've moved him down to the old dining room.'

She opened the door, and I realised that Monrad Clausen probably wouldn't manage much more than a few months. He was sitting in a narrow bed with four pillows piled up as a support for his back, his face the same colour as the pillows. He had shaved; the part around his mouth was like a battlefield before the Red Cross had reached him. His skin hung in folds over a lean neck, and the hands lying on the duvet were large and powerless, like porpoises on land.

When I entered, he glanced at me through dark, weary eyes.

I stood in front of his bed, ill at ease, like a distant relative on a courtesy visit. I leaned forward, unsure how good his hearing was. 'Thank you for granting me the time to talk to you.'

'Time?' he said with terse sarcasm. 'If it'd been the devil, I would've let him in.'

'Monrad!' his sister exclaimed and sent me an apologetic glance.

I smiled and she inclined her head. 'Would you like a cup of coffee, perhaps?'

'Please,' I said, and she left.

Monrad Clausen looked at me. 'And what would you be after?'

I saw the chair beside his bed, made a gesture and sat down without a formal invitation. 'I'm making some enquiries around some events at Norlon when you were the foreman.'

His mask tightened. 'Enquiries? Who for?' His voice was hoarse and rough, as though he had done a lot of shouting in his time.

'Erm, it's about the circumstances of Siv Schrøder-Olsen's accident on the 26th of April, 1979.'

'Oh, yes?'

'It's a bit difficult to explain everything, but there's some sort of connection with Tor Aslaksen's death.'

'Is Aslaksen dead?'

'Yes, he drowned last Thursday.'

'I'm out of touch, living here in the bush.' He studied his big working hands as they lay idle, like a disused factory. 'After I left, I moved out here to my sister's. She's a widow. She's lived up here since she was nineteen. It's a wonder she hasn't gone mad. In the past the train used to stop here, now it generally breezes past. If you want to go to town at off-peak times you have to catch the bus, even though it only takes half an hour by train. That's what they call environmentally friendly policies, the people who run this country.'

'Right.'

'Aslaksen, he was no slouch, you know. He and I were on the same side at Norlon. Do you know what the hotheads were intending to do?'

'No.'

'Listen. I was employed there from the very beginning, in 1949, and we worked there with that shit the whole time – hydrogen cyanide and much worse. Why do you think I'm in bed here, so out of breath that my lungs feel like stone and so weak-kneed that I can barely carry myself to the loo once a day?'

His sister came in and placed a cup of coffee beside me. The saucer rattled as she put it down and mumbled: 'Is he grousing again? But for me, he'd be in a home.' She lowered her voice a further notch. 'It's all the poison he's been inhaling all his life. It's gone to his brain—'

'What are you muttering, Margit?' growled her brother from his bed. 'Don't listen to her, Veum. She's not all there, the old haddock.'

She left the room, shaking her head and muttering. I tasted the coffee. It was weaker than the singing at the annual congregation of the Heathens' Mission House and you could count the coffee grains at the bottom of the cup. I made it five until I had to give up.

'At first they just released all the toxic waste into the fjord … straight into Vatlestraumen, the whole stinking lot. Then they decided it might be wiser to store it on land. They filled up an old well on the premises, until it overflowed. And do you know what they did then?'

'No.'

'They emptied the well whenever it got full, and transported it to some marshes they owned in Breistein, Åsane, and dumped it there.'

'Straight into the marshes?'

'Exactly. Aslaksen was against it. I was too. But what could we do? We weren't in charge, and if we made a fuss, we put our jobs on the line. And I was a shop steward. I had to think about the membership first…'

'But that night, a Thursday I think it was, the 26th of April, 1979, there was some kind of problem, wasn't there?'

'A secret document had come to light, about the pollution of the groundwater in Breistein. It was beginning to become an attractive area – one they could develop. The emptying of the well came to a stop, and we were summoned to an emergency meeting, at eleven at night.'

'Who was at the meeting?'

'Well, there was no meeting because everything went belly up, if I can put it like that. This is when the accident to young frøken Schrøder-Olsen happened.'

I leaned forward. 'But who was there when it happened?'

'Who was there? There was me, and Thomassen, but he's dead too. There were the Schrøder-Olsen brothers, Trygve and Odin, and then Aslaksen. He was the last to arrive, I remember. Except that we were waiting for the old boy, Schrøder-Olsen himself.'

'Hang on. When you were sitting there, did anyone leave the room?'

'Leave? Not that I can remember. But so many things happened at once that … I don't think so though.'

'Can you tell me what happened when Schrøder-Olsen and his daughter arrived?'

He thought back. 'Well, it must've been Odin standing by the window, watching out for them. He called out when he saw them. Then the next thing we heard was a scream and some shouting from down the stairs and everyone left. Well, Thomassen and I followed them. But by then it was all over. She was unconscious; later it turned out she had broken her neck, and it was a big drama. An ambulance came, and the old boy went in it with her. So there was no meeting that night. And wasn't until long afterwards.'

'But … do you have any idea what happened to Siv that evening?'

'No. She slipped and fell down the stairs, poor thing. A fat wallet doesn't help on such occasions. If you fall, you fall, whatever class you come from.'

'And there were no signs of trespassers on the premises?'

'Trespassers? A break-in, you mean?'

'Yes.'

'No. Everything was shut up and locked. Thomassen and I

made sure of that when we left. We were the last to leave, with Aslaksen. The brothers went to the hospital as well.'

'Surely there was a night watchman?'

'Not at that time. A company had taken over those duties and they had installed an alarm.'

'It might've been switched off while there was a meeting?'

'It was. We switched it on when we left.'

'Right. Any more you can tell me?'

He deliberated. 'No. What could there be? I spent my days working out there, surrounded by hydrogen cyanide, and now I'm here, in the autumn of my years, as the chapel puts it, and can you see any angels looking after me? Does anyone come from the Employers' Association bearing a gift as we approach Christmas? Have I got a king's medal for services rendered hanging on the wall? Nope. I just lie here shrinking. And soon I'll die. And the only person who will mourn my passing is … No, not even Margit. She'll heave a sigh of relief and say to herself: *Thank God, he's gone*. They can write that on my grave-stone, Veum: *Thank God, he's gone*.'

I smiled wanly. 'Harald Schrøder-Olsen's in a wheelchair.'

'Wheelchair. Old Schrøder?' He mused for a second. 'But I bet he doesn't get his lunch in plastic boxes from the community nurse, not him, and he gets medical help the moment he needs it. I'd imagine he has a private physio.'

'Not any more. But he did have.'

'There you go. What did I say?'

His sister opened the door. 'Here's your lunch, Monrad.'

'What is it today? Marinated floor cloths? In spinach sauce?'

She looked at me with an apologetic expression. 'They're so kind. They bring lunch three days a week and that's the thanks they get.'

I sighed. 'Well, I won't disturb you any longer. Thank you for your help, both of you.'

'It was a pleasure,' came the response from the bed. 'Give my best wishes to old Schrøder and tell him it serves him right.'

'What serves him right?'

'Ending up in a wheelchair, for Christ's sake. The wheelchair.'

I watched him as I left. He had sunk down in the pillows, as though about to disappear into them for good.

His sister accompanied me out. She whispered: 'He isn't always like that. You must've got him worked up. Sometimes he's in such a good mood that he sings.'

I eyed her sceptically. 'Sings what? The Internationale?'

'No, it's more like "Twixt Hill and Mountain".'

I thanked her for the information and concluded my visit. Down at the station a reddish-brown train passed, heading for Bergen. This one didn't stop, either. It rushed towards the town at 120 kmh, as though delivering an important message from Trondheim, news that they had extended their border by another chunk. The mayor would have a nervous breakdown. Bergen would never be the same again.

39

In Hilleren the situation was unchanged. The chain gang was sun-tanned and they were being fed liquid from large bottles with flexi-straws, like football players in the World Cup during the interval before extra time. Unless they had already reached the penalty shoot-out.

The heavyweights on the flanks glowered at me suspiciously as I approached, and it was abundantly clear how I appeared in their eyes.

I allowed my gaze to run from face to face, but I didn't recognise any of them. Vibeke Farang was at work, and neither Håvard

Hope nor Odin Schrøder-Olsen was at their post in the trenches at this stage in the conflict.

I felt uneasy. There were slightly too many loose threads, too many labels without a name on.

I looked down to the main gate of Norlon, through the fence and into the yard where the same ominous vacuum tanker was parked.

'Are you the little girl's father?' Siv had asked me, and two days ago she had said: 'I told Totto everything.' Totto who was synonymous with Tor Aslaksen and had worked here until a week ago to the day. Tor Aslaksen, who'd had a relationship with Camilla Farang's mother and probably Lisbeth Finslo too. A man with death as a visiting card, it appeared. A man with fate on his conscience. I would have liked to meet him personally. But, as so often before, I was too late.

My innate curiosity took me down to the gate, the two police officers and the same guard as last time. The man with the mutilated potato nose. He even appeared to recognise me.

I greeted him and asked if Ulrichsen was in.

'No, he's gone home.'

'Anyone else in admin?'

'Schrøder-Olsen himself is still there.'

'Could you ring him and tell him I'm on my way? Veum's the name.'

'That's fine. I don't forget a face like yours.' He unlocked the gate while I wondered whether to return the compliment.

He opened the gate enough for me to slip through while keeping a sharp eye on the chain-gang.

As I was walking to the entrance to the admin offices, he said behind me: 'I'll call them and say you're coming.'

'You do that,' I answered, and added under my breath: 'Let's see what he says to that.'

Without waiting for a reply, I mounted the five steps to the front door, opened it and stepped inside.

I tried to put myself in the situation that night. I was Siv, and my father had already gone ahead to the conference room. To the left was the door with the ridged glass and the sign: *PRO-DUCTION – LABORATORY*. Someone may of course have come out of there, but she wouldn't have got far enough to fall. If indeed she had fallen. No one had seen her fall. She could have been knocked down where she was found. On the other hand, her father had heard her fall, and she must obviously have had grazes or marks on her arms and legs from that fall. Why wasn't the case investigated? It was hard enough to reconstruct the past when there were reports. But when there was nothing but vague statements it was impossible.

I walked up to the landing from which, according to her father, she must have fallen. To my right was the tall window facing the yard and on the next landing the entrance to the administration offices.

At this point someone could have come charging down, without seeing her, before they met on the landing. She had screamed, the person had shoved her to the side, she had lost her balance and … I looked down the stairs … thud-thud-thud-thud.

Somewhere above me a door opened and I heard Trygve Schrøder-Olsen's voice. 'Hello? Veum?'

I stared in his direction. 'Yes?'

'What the hell are you doing here? Come up at once.'

'Thank you for the invitation,' I mumbled, carrying on up to the second floor.

Trygve Schrøder-Olsen stood in the doorway at the top, his shirt sleeves rolled up, his tie loosened and his hands down by his sides. He looked irritable and stressed, and his hair was a little out of shape – not much, but enough to be commented on at the annual shareholders' meeting.

'What do you think you're doing? Bluffing your way past the

guard in that way. I've given him strict instructions. Next time you try a stunt like that, I'll have the police remove you.'

'Why not try hydrogen cyanide? It's even more effective. Is this where the famous conference room is?'

He blocked the door.

'Have you got something to hide?' I asked. I shot a glance over his shoulder and through the door. All I could see was mahogany furniture, a table covered with green felt, and big piles of paper and bills. 'A handful of unfiled documents perhaps?' The walls were papered with silk in a classic pattern, like at Versailles or other estates. 'This is where all of you were sitting, wasn't it?'

He gesticulated angrily. 'Sitting when? And all of who?'

'That day in 1979 when your sister Siv had her tragic accident.'

I don't know why, but it was at this point the air seemed to go out of him. Like a rag doll, he stepped aside and let me in. 'And what business is this of yours?'

I kept the initiative. 'I spoke to your father on Tuesday. Let me just get this absolutely clear. The following people were present…'

He stared at me in desperation. 'Present? At the meeting?'

I continued: 'You, Odin, Tor Aslaksen, the main shop steward – what was his name again?'

'Thomassen.'

'And Clausen, the foreman?'

He glowered.

'And you were all waiting for your father.'

He nodded.

'The meeting was about…?'

He didn't answer.

'It was an important meeting, wasn't it? Very important?'

He nodded.

'What was it about?' I nodded towards the windows facing the yard, the gate and the chain-gang outside. 'The same as today? How to sweep the toxic waste under the carpet at the lowest possible cost and with the least possible fuss for the company?'

He flushed. 'Yes, OK. We had a difference of opinions. We were waiting for my father. No one knew which side he would choose.'

'Odin and you disagreed, I suppose.'

He sent me a triumphant look. 'No: imagine that, we didn't. This was *before* he got scruples. Odin and I were actually of one mind. It was Tor who ... It was Tor Aslaksen who was against, and he had Clausen with him. Thomassen, on the other hand, was the cautious kind, so he was ... waiting.'

'Let me get this clear. Tor Aslaksen was for a more ... what shall I say? ... defensible position, from a social point of view, while you and Odin were thinking about profit?'

He grimaced. 'If only it were so simple, Veum. At this point in time ... there were no defensible ways of disposing of the waste without huge financial consequences for the company. What we were discussing was storage possibilities. We'd always filled up the old well – under the manhole cover in the middle of the car park below – and stored it there. When the well was full it was emptied, but the discussion on that day was where to transport it. In those days ... We had received a report stamped SECRET, on the pollution of the groundwater in the area we used then as the main storage...'

'In Breistein, Åsane?'

'It...' He paused. 'Who told you that?' he asked angrily.

I didn't answer.

Our eyes met like two cars on a perilously steep hill. One had to give way to let the other pass. He cracked first. He looked past me, at the ancestral gallery on the wall behind me.

'Alright. So we owned a plot of land out there ... for which we had certain development plans.'

'Which were thwarted by the secret report?'

'Well, we had to find other ... erm ... options.'

'Which were?'

'Actually, this has nothing to do ... Why are you asking me all these questions, Veum? The people out there *know* all this. Surely you don't imagine Odin wouldn't have told them? Inside information,' he said in a bitter undertone.

'But at that time he was on your side?'

'Both Odin and I had top posts here. Then he suddenly gave up and left me...'

'Holding the baby?'

'With the responsibility.'

'Right. But on the day in question no decision was taken, was it?'

'No.' He ran a hand across his face. 'There was a tense atmosphere. We were waiting for my father. He'd had a drink, so Siv was driving. She'd just passed her test and was obviously driving more carefully than he would. So it took a while.'

'And you were all together in the conference room ... the whole time?'

'All together? The whole time? What are you getting at? We heard the car pull up and Odin went over to the window and saw it was them. "Here they are," he called. We breathed a sigh of relief, but then we heard Siv's scream at the bottom of the stairwell. I remember ... Odin turned to me, he was still standing by the window and our eyes met. His face was ashen. "What the hell was that?" he shouted and we ran for the door. And down below, at the bottom of the stairs, was Siv, lying in a heap. Since then, she's...' He threw up his arms. 'You know.'

'But that's exactly what I mean. Before this happened, you were all here together. None of you could've met Siv and...'

'No, no, no. Of course not. We were all up here. Besides, I've never believed anyone did anything at all to her. It was an accident.

She fell, screamed as she fell, and that was it. There were no signs of a break-in and no signs that we had any unwanted visitors on the premises.'

'But your father,' I said pensively. 'Your father still hadn't come up. He's the unknown, movable factor in this picture, isn't he?'

He recoiled with shock. 'What do you mean? Surely you don't mean to suggest that … This is preposterous…'

'But it's not impossible, is it?'

'Yes, Veum. Impossible is exactly what it is. Humanly impossible, unlikely, illogical and anything else you can think of with a negative prefix.'

'Inhuman?' I mumbled.

We glared at each other. In the end, I said: 'And the business matter. The waste problem. How did that go?'

'Badly. Why the hell do you think we've got a mob outside our main gates, Veum?'

'So, Tor Aslaksen didn't win the day with his views later on, either?'

'He was drawn into this other matter, wasn't he. They were at exactly the same time.'

'Which other matter? Are you referring to the Camilla Case?'

'Yes.'

'Your wife was a colleague of Camilla's father, Bård Farang, I've heard.'

'Bodil? You've heard, have you?' He was trying to sound sarcastic, but failed miserably. 'I didn't know her then. It's perfectly possible she was.'

'Perfectly possible? I suppose she must've talked about it?'

'Why? We never talk about … the past. Besides I've never been interested in … that kind of crime.'

'Not even on a human level?'

'What do you mean?'

'No, you don't have any children, that's obvious. What you

have is shares. I forgot I was talking to a pillar of the community. I apologise.'

'I think you should leave now, Veum. If you don't, I'll ring the guard and tell him to send the police in after you.'

'Do you know what I found out, Schrøder-Olsen? Little Camilla Farang disappeared the same night your sister Siv had her tragic accident here. And what's more, I think there's a link between the two events. And, as if that weren't enough, I think this link can be extended to include the deaths of Tor Aslaksen and Lisbeth Finslo a week ago.'

'Lisbeth Finslo?'

'And I intend to find out what this link is, even if I have to go to Breistein in Åsane. Is that understood?'

'Breistein? I don't understand a word you're saying, Veum.'

'Don't you?'

'But I will say you're…' He raised his voice. 'You're moving into dangerous waters, Veum. Don't go too far.'

'Should I interpret that as a threat?'

'You can interpret it as whatever you bloody like, as far as I'm concerned. You give *that* some thought.'

I looked around. The conference room did that to some people – gave them the strength and spine to threaten anyone. And such people were rarely without power. Before you knew what was going on, you were bankrupt.

'And as for Bodil…'

'Yes?'

'Well. Never mind. Leave now, Veum, or else…' He moved towards the telephone on a little corner table.

I raised a palm in defence and left voluntarily.

At the main gate I noticed that the guard still remembered my face. But next time he wouldn't let me in. Not without a royal decree, and even then it would still be doubtful.

I passed the chain-gang and surveyed the area. Up by the generals' green tent sat three or four people around a camping stove and a coffee pot, holding white mugs. One of them was Hårvard Hope.

When he spotted me, he quickly rose to his feet and came to meet me halfway, as though he didn't want the others to hear what we might talk about.

'What's this about now?' he said in a low voice, with a touch of irritation.

'Is Odin here?'

'No. What's this about?'

'Do you know where he is?'

He looked at his watch. 'At this time, you'll find him in the gym, I would say. If you hurry, at any rate. He's expected back here at six.'

'Which gym is it?'

He grinned. 'It's called Body & Soul and it's in Nygårdsgaten.'

'I doubt they're advertising Billie Holiday.'

'Hardly.'

'And if I've understood you correctly, that's where Vibeke Farang works?'

He nodded. 'But she closes at four today.'

'I haven't got anything more to talk to her about. Not today anyway.'

'Good,' he said abruptly.

'What do you mean by that?'

'It isn't good for her to have old wounds reopened. She'll never be free of them.'

'That's what happens when you experience this sort of drama. You drag it behind you for the rest of your days.'

'Well, it doesn't help when the outside world keeps reminding her of it.'

'Keeps? Have there been more people doing it recently?'

He shrugged. 'There's always someone. Journalists, gumshoes of various kinds, all sorts.'

'Do you know Bård Farang?'

'I know who he is.'

'He's an activist, too. He was here during the first few days, he told me.'

He looked away. 'Uhuh. Well, if he said he was, it must be true.'

I observed him closely. 'Are you and her…?'

He pretended he didn't understand. 'So, if you want to meet Odin, I recommend you go now, at once.' He nodded briefly, turned his back on me and walked back to the other activists, who sat with their heads together scowling in my direction as though I were a hydropower developer or worse.

40

Locating a gym in Nygårdsgaten, the town's most polluted thoroughfare, sounded like an ironic idea doomed to disaster. However, the studio had actually been in existence before exhaust fumes filled the streets.

Helse & Skjønnhet had been one of the town's very first health clubs, as they were called in those days, when they made do with using Norwegian company names. In the early eighties, following the new fitness craze from the other side of the Atlantic, with Jane Fonda as the guru, it changed its name and character to the more contemporary Body & Soul.

It was a change one could philosophise over until late in the night. On the one hand, 'body' was a lot more specific than *helse* – 'health'. However, 'soul' was, if possible, even more difficult to define than *skjønnhet* – 'beauty', and much more esoteric. One thing was sure, though: there were *no* pictures of Billie Holiday in the foyer.

Big purple letters on broad glass doors in red frames told me where the company resided. I followed the smell of heavily perfumed shampoo up to the first floor, where further broad glass doors led me to a combined reception area and cafeteria.

The tables in the cafeteria were round, white and plastic with matching body-shaped chairs. On a serving table there were Thermos flasks of tea and coffee. From a refrigerated counter you could help yourself to mineral water or a variety of salads, sliced wholemeal rolls with white cheese and salad, or mutton sausage and egg. On the walls hung large, pastel-coloured posters of aerobics athletes in tight-fitting costumes behind frameless glass.

Around some of the tables sat a handful of – to varying degrees of success – imitations. Everyone was in studied casual dress, a headband the same colour as parts of their effulgent outfits, which were so tight that some had considered it appropriate to tie a frotté hand towel around their hips to hide the fact that there was still a good way to go before they could emulate their idols on the walls. Most were very young: too young in my opinion to require any other training than sport outdoors. But I was too old to be entitled to an opinion on such matters. A generation and a half of the indoor fitness wave lay between them and me, and marathon runners were probably as passé as Elvis Presley in this context.

Nevertheless, I was met with an obliging smile behind the reception desk. The young woman sitting there would have looked healthier with less make-up on her face. How much soul she had I had no idea, but she had plenty of body, in the most felicitous proportions. She was wearing a tight white T-shirt with the company logo in pastel purple colours, decoratively sited on her breasts: *Body* undulated over one; *Soul* the other. Around her waist she had a slender, black leather belt to demonstrate to the whole world how slim and svelte she was, while the skin-tight, turquoise leggings in the same silky-wet look they all copied didn't leave a skin fold to the imagination, if indeed she had any.

'And how may I help you?' she cooed.

'Let me think about that.'

Her smile stiffened. 'Would you like a sample session perhaps?'

I resisted the temptation. 'Not today, thank you. Actually, I'd just like to meet someone who's training here. Odin Schrøder-Olsen. Is he still here?'

'Odin, yes.' She gazed down at the appointments book she had open in front of her. 'But he's probably in the sauna now. If you take a seat, he'll be out in ten minutes.' She motioned towards the counter. 'If you feel like anything, it's self-service. The price list is on the wall and you pay me.'

'Practical,' I said, and thanked her.

In fact, I was hungry. I helped myself to a salad, a bottle of Farris and a cup of coffee. I paid and found a seat at a vacant table.

The pastel-clad clients chose either to ignore me completely or regard me with condescension, as though wondering how I had been talked into buying *that* track suit. Most had perspiration dripping from their foreheads and damp patches on their outfits, but that was hardly because I made them nervous. The indoor temperature, combined with the weather outdoors, made lifting a cup of coffee a sweaty affair.

Via an invisible loudspeaker system, driving exercise rhythms penetrated the room, and every so often, through the two circular windows in a pair of red swing doors, I saw fitness devotees whizz past like figure skaters on ice. At any moment I expected to hear the sounds of a collision, but all I heard was the rhythmic thuds of muscle-training equipment, rubber soles landing on the floor and the occasional spring-loaded weight being let go too quickly.

After eating the salad, drinking the Farris and reaching the bottom of the coffee cup I walked over to the *donna* behind the desk and asked if she was sure that Odin really was there.

'Yes. He always has a cup of tea here before leaving. And a chat with people.'

'Have you worked here long?'

'No, but I've trained here for many years.'

'What type of training?'

'Karate,' she said, looking intently at me as if to see whether I wanted to find out how good she was.

'Do you know Vibeke Farang?'

'Of course. Do you?'

I nodded.

'But she's, like, more into bodybuilding.'

Like, more into. I never stopped being amazed by younger generations' modes of expression. Almost more than what motivated them to train the way they did.

'There he is. Odin! There's someone here who wants to talk to you.'

The red swing-doors swung back and Odin Schrøder-Olsen changed direction from the reception desk to me. He stroked dripping hair from his forehead, dried his face with a damp cloth and smiled his dewy, boyish smile. 'Veum? Still on the trail?'

'Yes, I am. I'd like to have a word with you.'

'Come on then. Let's sit down there.'

He helped himself to a cup of tea, I poured myself another cup of coffee, and we sat at the table where I had been earlier.

Other clients greeted Odin with a friendly 'hi'. Some even nodded to me. Now that it turned out I knew one of *them*…

He put his glasses on the table and ran a comb through his short dark hair, which was still wet from the shower and sauna. 'Are you still investigating the circumstances surrounding Tor's death?'

'No. The police have told me to stop. I'm not allowed to have anything to do with it.'

'Re-ally? And so why have you come to find me?'

'Well, to be a little more precise, I don't have permission to investigate the circumstances surrounding his death or his girlfriend's.'

'His girlfriend's? Is she dead, too?'

I nodded. 'But what I can investigate is the link he had with what has become known as the Camilla Case.'

'The Camilla Case?'

'Yes, do you remember it?'

'Oh, yes, of course I do. But I don't think I can help you with anything there.'

'Do you know Bård Farang?'

'Bård Farang … Yes. Right, he's with Greenearth, now and then. But he doesn't live … He lives somewhere in…'

'In Hardanger. I've spoken to him. Did you know he's Camilla's father?'

'No, I had no idea. But, to be honest, I haven't spoken to him much. He doesn't really belong to the inner circle, and our movement's grown pretty big.'

'But he took part last Thursday and Friday, he said.'

'Yes? That could well be correct.'

'Did you see him?'

He repeated the name again. 'Bård Farang, Bård Farang. To be honest, Veum, I'm not sure.'

'So, for all you know, he may well have been away from the action for a few hours last Thursday?'

'On the first day? There was so much going on, it was total chaos. Anyone could've been in and out.'

'Hm. You know Vibeke better then – his ex?'

'Vibeke … erm…'

'She works here and, from what I can gather, she's with your second-in-command, Håvard Hope.'

'Yes, right. That Vibeke. OK. Her name's Farang.'

'Camilla's mother,' I added.

'You know, Veum, that's news to me. I think … For so many

years my interests have been so focused on environmental problems that in a way I've had to push everything else to the side.' He smiled disarmingly. 'After all, there are limits to how much even an intelligent person like me can take on board.'

'Tell me about the poison then.'

'Which one?'

'The one at Norlon. And your position on it.'

'That could be a long story.'

'I have plenty of time.'

'More than I have.'

'My understanding is that you were on the other side of the fence at first.'

'The apple doesn't fall far from the tree, you know. Until someone kicks it away.'

'OK. And who was it who kicked you?'

He took a sip of the tea. 'To cut a long story short, Veum, Norlon has always dumped toxic waste. It produces synthetic acrylic fibres, using hydrocyanic acid and acetylene. There isn't much waste. But enough to create problems – long term.'

'And this problem was dumped down a well on the site, wasn't it?'

'Ah, so you know that. Yes, that's true. My father was very aware of this problem. He must have been way ahead of his time. The business was built on the plot of an old smallholding. If you go back to the Middle Ages, it probably belonged to Munkeliv monastery. At any rate, a natural well existed on the site. Very deep. They closed off the bottom with concrete and used it as a waste shaft for many years.'

'100% closed off?'

'There's no indication to the contrary. But at the end of the sixties the shaft was simply full. It was decided it should be emptied and the waste transported elsewhere. And this was repeated as often as necessary.'

'And this elsewhere was…'

'Well … I'm not sure if I should…'

'Breistein?'

'Ah, you know that, too?'

'I've heard rumours.'

'My father owned a big piece of land there.'

'And was there a disused well there, too?'

'No, but there was a marsh.'

'A marsh. Right. So, the waste was driven there and dumped?'

'Yes.'

'I thought you said your father was ahead of his time?'

'Well, this was near the end of his … Trygve took over the autumn he retired.'

'As a result of a conflict?'

'Yes.'

'You were on the management board at that time?'

'Yes, but not for long. It was in the wake of this very conflict that I had my … what shall I call it … my ecological epiphany?

'And what was the cause of the conflict?'

He frowned. 'Listen, to transport the waste we needed a vacuum tanker, the same kind that's standing in the factory yard ready to go now. Technically, this was a simple matter. We removed the lid over the well, sucked up the waste, drove to Åsane and got rid of it, and because we knew this was bordering on unacceptable practice, we did it after working hours. A couple of our most trusty workers helped. Trygve and I did too. Tor—'

'I'm beginning to understand why top managers earn such high fees. Was there a pollution allowance as well?'

'But then in the spring of 1979 this conflict arose. My father had got it into his head that he was going to sell the land. Houses were going up in Åsane, prices were rocketing. That was when Tor said: but what about the ground water?'

'He said that to your father?'

'To Trygve and me. We suggested quietly ignoring it, but Tor banged his fist on the table and said: "If you do, I'll go public." We had to … A meeting was called, late at night. Clausen and Thomassen were emptying the well when Tor went over and stopped them. There was a hell of a fuss and it ended with us having to call in my father as well. But then something else happened.'

'Your sister's accident. Siv.'

He gaped in amazement. 'Precisely. That put a stopper on everything. We screwed the lid back and had more than enough to cope with. Tor had his hands full elsewhere.'

'You're thinking of the Camilla Case?'

'Yes.'

'And you pulled out?'

'Yes. I had a few furious arguments with Tor, and we were never really friends again afterwards. But I did, of course, concede that he was right and bore the consequences. I pulled out completely.'

'While he stayed at Norlon.'

'He probably felt that was the best way to keep the situation under control.'

'But the relationship between Trygve and him couldn't have been very good?'

'You adapt. In business that kind of conflict is normal.'

'And what about … Trygve's wife?'

'Bodil? What about her?'

'Was there something going on between her and Tor Aslaksen?'

He put on a taut smile. 'I really don't know, Veum. My take was that…'

'I'm asking only in connection with other cases. Such as the Camilla Case.'

'Now I don't quite follow you.'

'It's where we actually started this conversation. Don't you re-member?'

'Yes, but—'

'Camilla Farang disappeared on exactly the same day as all this other stuff happening.'

'This other...?'

'With Siv. Tell me, would your father be capable of ... hurting Siv?'

'My father? Hurting her? Surely you don't think that ... What reason could he have?'

'What reason would anyone have? What happened that night at Norlon, Odin?'

'Happened? Don't ask me.'

'But you were there, weren't you.'

'Not at the bottom of the stairs.'

'No, because that's where your father was. And Siv.'

He rubbed his eyes, donned his glasses, looked at his watch, drained his cup and stood up. 'I'm sorry, Veum, but they're ex-pecting me in Hilleren.' He smiled apologetically. 'Pow-wow.'

I stood up. 'Think about what we've said. Consider whether there might be anything you've forgotten to tell me, something you might've repressed so deeply you perhaps don't even realise.'

He scrutinised me. 'Really? OK. I'll do that. But I doubt there'll be anything.'

'Think about it as if it's toxic waste, illegally buried in a place only you know. Perhaps that's the inspiration you need.'

'Perhaps, Veum.'

We walked together.

'Are you coming again tomorrow?' the woman behind the desk chirruped.

'Same time, same place,' he answered.

She didn't ask me if I was coming back. I made a note, on the debit side of her doomsday ledger. There was nothing wrong with her body. But her soul probably had a few stains. And she would never invite me to wash them off.

In Nygårdsgaten we parted company. I crossed the street to the car park in front of Grieg Hall. He walked to the multi-storey car park, but hardly to catch a bus. He was going to his, I suspected, catalytic converter-less VW, as if collecting antiques was an important part of his ecological commitment.

41

Breistein lay on the shadow-side of Åsane, a poor neighbourhood from time immemorial, where the greatest pleasure was to see the sun shine on Osterøy across the fjord. In more recent times they had been able to take the ferry to Valestrandsfossen and sunbathe en route. Before, they used to have to make do with fishing in the fjord and cultivating meagre soil for corn and potatoes.

Breistein still belonged to the more sparsely populated parts of Åsane. I passed the new Travpark in Haukås and followed the road through dark spruce forest down to the fjord. I was past the ferry point before I saw the big sign on the slope, parked my car at the edge of the narrow road and got out to examine the area more closely.

Building was at an early stage. Two large yellow bulldozers had been digging down to the bedrock, but the men driving them had long gone home. The plot behind the provisional wire netting was deserted and the locked gate announced: *BUILD-ING SITE – KEEP OFF.*

I hadn't planned to go in anyway. The impression I got from peeking through the wire was more than good enough. And I got some extremely useful information from the big sign describing what was going on inside: *A/S MILJØBO is building new, reasonably-priced, environment-friendly accommodation. IN-TERESTED? Contact…*

I scribbled down the telephone number I could ring if I was in the market for a flat, not that I was particularly attracted. But now I remembered the context in which I had come across Breistein. Unless I was much mistaken, it had been in a newspaper last Friday. Miljøbo had been named as one of the subsidiaries of Greenearth…

That was definitely one thing Odin Schrøder-Olsen had omitted to tell me.

With my cerebral cortex frowning thoughtfully, I drove back to Bergen.

One of the lightest days this year was coming to an end. The evening sun hung over Askøy municipality like a gold medal we had been awarded collectively for long and faithful service. In open-air restaurants froth foamed on top of beer glasses until mouths hoovered it up. On pavements people strolled, in couples or groups, at their ease, like lemmings on Valium. If there was a single person in town who had gone to bed willingly, it was because they had company.

I parked in the town's vegetable market, crossed the street and walked up to my office.

As I unlocked the door to the waiting room, the way the key turned should have caused alarm bells to ring. But perhaps I had been drugged by the beauty of the summer evening too. Or else the experiences of the day had clouded my powers of observation.

They came from behind the door, balaclavas over their heads. But that was all they had in common. The one who grabbed me by the arm and spun me round was strong and wide-legged, wearing denim jeans, a blue T-shirt and a light, red casual jacket. The one in the background wore elegant, light-coloured trousers, a beige overcoat and had a sagging belly. A broad red tie protruded from under the balaclava, like a tongue.

I half turned, unsure what they were after, when a ferocious punch to my neck turned summer to winter and evening to night in a few paltry seconds.

I should have become a meteorologist when I came of age. Or I should have read storm warnings more closely. Now the atmospheric pressure was falling so fast I lost consciousness. But someone was holding me up, in a strong grip. Someone who wanted more from me than just a blackout. Someone who was after something.

42

When I came to, I was sitting on a chair, tied and bound, with a tight, dark blindfold over my eyes.

I carefully moved my head. My neck hurt.

I tried my arms. They were bound at the wrists behind the chair.

I tried my legs. They were bound to the chair.

I was held fast, like an astronaut, but I had no idea where I was going. All I could be certain of was that the journey was going to be unpleasant. There was already turbulence.

'He's awake,' I heard – a rough, rusty voice, one forged from scrap metal.

Behind me I heard the sound of an iron drawer slowly closing. 'Interesting filing cabinet you have, Veum,' another voice said. A conspicuous one, preacher-like, a hint of refined Stavanger. 'I could make good use of it. If I didn't have so many other things to do.'

I grunted, still groggy from the brutal assault on my neck.

'I've been told you're quite the one for repartee, Veum.'

'You've been told wrong,' I mumbled, through the baked potato someone had stuffed into my mouth.

'Cake'ole,' snapped the scrap-metal voice, a model of brevity.

'What do you want?'

'I hear you've stopped drinking, Veum,' the preacher said.

'Oh, yes? Alcoholics Anonymous doing a spot check?'

No one answered, but my ears picked up a sound. A screw-top being opened.

My mouth went dry. 'Listen, I mean it. Surely, we can talk about this. What are you after?'

'Warm weather for the time of year, Veum?'

I clenched my teeth.

'You're sweating anyway.'

Yes, cold sweat.

'Feel like a drink?'

Yes! More than ever. But no. Not with Antabuse in my system.

'Welcome to the party, Veum.'

They held the mouth of the bottle against my lips. The smell of the cheap aquavit tore at my nostrils. I felt an acute discomfort, intense nausea, and the desertification of my mouth was a catastrophe.

'You can't ... force me.'

'No?' The preacher had come closer now. I could feel his hand in my hair as he yanked my head back and opened my mouth. 'You can choose how you want it. With or without teeth. But there's one thing you can't do,' he whispered, smiling audibly. 'You can't stop us.'

I wondered what he looked like. I would never forget his voice, but I wanted to know what he looked like, who he was and where he lived, so that I could haunt his bedroom when he was lying in bed and dreaming about the Gestapo.

He forced my head down lower.

I tried to turn my face to the side, but the hinges in my neck were rusted up. I wanted to bring my lips together, but the man standing in front of me was pushing the bottle so hard my front teeth were hurting.

With a gasp, I opened my mouth to breathe. He poured in the aquavit. A powerful punch to the stomach forced a sudden intake of breath and the burning liquid went down too, as if drawn into a deep drain by the undertow.

A numb resignation gripped me. There was less resistance to the next swig. The quantities were too large, and my throat stung as my stomach and insides contorted with cramp.

'What do you two want from me?' I choked.

'Let it work for a bit,' the preacher said above my head, and the bottle was given a rest.

'I'll have a slug myself,' the scrap-metal voice rasped.

'Not too much.'

'No, no.'

I heard the doctor from Hjellestad at the back of my brain: *Antabuse inhibits the enzyme acetaldehyde in the body, causing a whole series of unpleasant symptoms after the consumption of alcohol. I would strongly advise you not to drink, Veum ... advise you not to drink ... advv ... nnn ... t...*

'He's asleep!'

'Then wake him up again.'

A strong hand slapped me across the face, first from the right, then from the left.

My body recoiled. I mumbled: 'No ... I'm on ... med...'

It was like being at the dentist's. Head back, again, open your gob, something you didn't want in your mouth, gulp, gulp, gulp.

I felt the spirit running over my chin and down my neck and shirt. I was living carrion. Vultures were already attacking. I stank of corruption and death.

'Can you hear me, Veum?' a malicious voice whispered in my ear. I nodded and mumbled something even I didn't understand.

'You know you're about to go through hell, don't you?'

I nodded again, mute. I had tears in my eyes but the tight blindfold held them in.

'It's nothing compared with what you'll suffer if you don't bloody pack it in now. Is that clear?'

'Bl ... Bl ... p-pack *what* in?' I managed to stutter.

'All the muck-raking and digging you're doing. Is that clear?'

'M-m-m ... it's not ... I d-don't understand ... What do you want…?'

'For your own safety, Veum, I'll give you a bit of advice. And it's well meant. Take a summer holiday, go away, lie low.'

'Oh, f-f-for ... Are you t-two the p-police?' I slobbered.

'He's still the funny man, Fred. Give him another dose.'

'No. No…'

The dose was duly delivered; my body writhed. *Fred*. I had to remember that. I remembered Bjørnstjerne Bjørnson: *Fred er ei det beste*. Peace is not the best. Well, it may not be, but it would certainly do me.

I was ill, mortally ill. My skin was hot and dry, my heart was pounding like the drum in a janissary band on tour, transported by a steam roller. I could hardly breathe. I was as polluted with contaminants as the infamous Sørfjord. My head hung. I could lose consciousness at any moment. I felt as if I had the plague in my muscles: creeping, death-bringing plague. I was ill, mortally ill.

'Next time you'll be reading your own obituary at breakfast. Is that clear?'

C-c-l-lear. I couldn't get it out, so I nodded.

Breakfast? No breakfast at a moment like this! *Mother, give me the sun*. Fred is not the best, but he isn't as bad as the preacher. I would remember all this. I wouldn't forget.

Waffle hearts and worn lino. Dust balls like ostrich feathers. Frog's eye view from the skirting boards. Regaining consciousness in a storm. My eyes are open, the blindfold has gone. My arms are spaghetti; my legs are still tied to the chair.

Next time my obituary. Lie low.

But I couldn't get any lower. They would have to bury me first.

43

I was still lying on the floor with the chair on top of me. It took me what felt like three centuries to untie the knots. From the chair to the desk was at least forty kilometres. And only at the fifth attempt was I able to dial the right number.

'Yes, hello?'

'Ka-ka-karin?'

'Who's that? Do you know what time it is?' She was speaking into my wrong ear and sounded like Miss Piggy with a speech defect.

'It's me.'

'Varg? What's wrong with you?' Her voice circled around me and came from several places at once, like Indians on the attack in a 1940s John Ford western.

'Can I come to yours?'

'You sound so strange. You haven't been…?'

I licked my lips with a tongue that felt as if it had been nailed to my palate. 'No, but I need help.'

'Have you …? OK, then. I'll go downstairs and unlock. Are you driving?'

I laughed hysterically. 'No, no. I'll ring my chauffeur.' I dropped the receiver and lost the connection. I hoped she didn't think I had just slammed down the telephone.

I looked at my watch. A quarter past two. Outside, the night was so black it was blue, a Scheherazade night, full of adventure.

Then I rang, at the third attempt, my private chauffeur, on 990990.

'Taxi rank, good morning.'

'Happy Christmas. You're so cheerful at this time of the morning.'

'Sorry?'

I booked a taxi, and she said it was on the way.

I picked myself up, tottered over to the sink and held my head under running water well into the next century. It helped … a bit. But I was still more seasick than if I had crossed the North Sea in mid-December and had too much duty-free in the bar during the night.

I locked the doors behind me, and when I reached the lift I went back and checked both doors again.

The lift transported my stomach down while my head stayed on the third floor. It felt unpleasant, like being a jumping jack in the hands of a very small child.

The lift landed and – *boinggg* – my head bounced back.

I opened the doors and staggered outside, where the taxi was waiting, the exhaust pipe emitting angry puffs of smoke.

'Have you booked the taxi for today or tomorrow?' the driver asked, totally unmoved by my natural charm and the bewitching beauty of the summer night.

I ignored him and crawled onto the rear seat.

He eyed me suspiciously, but got in behind the wheel after patting the slim wallet he kept in his inside pocket. It was ready for some fodder, especially if it came in note form.

I gave him the address, two numbers out, it transpired later, and he drove me there with little more than a few frustrated grunts whenever he missed a wandering night owl he'd had in his sights.

When we arrived, I paid with a note and magnanimously told him to keep the change.

'Are you being funny or what?'

He held the note up for me. It was for fifty kroner, but the meter said 68:00.

I took out a hundred-krone note, turned it over to make sure it was the right one, passed it over and repeated what I had said before.

He put it in his wallet without comment. It was only when I was on the pavement and the taxi was up Fløenbakken that I realised he hadn't given me the fifty kroner back.

I looked around.

I was one block of flats too high up, and I needed a few minutes to orientate myself. But Karin was standing in the window waiting for me, and the ground-floor door was open.

Stumbling up the last few steps, I heard her voice. 'This is a surprise, Veum. Did you think I hadn't had enough after all the years with Siren as a daughter?'

My eyes swam up to meet hers. 'It's not what you think, Karin.'

'That's what she always said.'

I was now level with her. She was wearing a blue dressing gown, and I grabbed at her shoulders, not to embrace her, but for support.

She took two steps back and recoiled in horror. 'You reek of booze, Varg.'

I fell forward and hit my head on the floor.

'Agh,' I heard above me, then her hands gripped me under the arm pits and dragged me roughly over the door sill. 'What do you think the neighbours will say?' she wheezed.

'Are they up so late?' I mumbled.

The door closed behind me, and I felt as if I had been hermetically locked in. To keep hold of reality I seized her ankles.

Slowly I climbed up her bare legs, gripped her knees, the back of her thighs … 'Varg!' she said and held my hair.

I stopped climbing, forced my head back and met her eyes. They were two thousand metres above me, where the oxygen was so thin she had to wear a mask.

'It's not what you think, Karin. Two men did this to me. Look.' I let go of her thighs and held up my hands so that she could see the marks from the tight ropes.

I shouldn't have let go.

I fell back down and this time I didn't get up.

This time I was out cold.

44

I was floating in a sea of darkness.

In the distance I heard her voice. 'Make him vomit? And then black coffee. OK.' Then the clunk of a receiver being replaced.

I was an old man. I had to be accompanied to the toilet. But I wasn't allowed to sit. They forced me onto my knees, bent my head over the bowl and told me to stick a finger down my throat.

I was an old man, with no powers of resistance, so I did what they said.

I gasped for air. My stomach was hung out to dry on the toilet bowl and it was only when I was on my feet that it moved back to its normal place.

The old man does what he can. One arm there; the other there. That's right, like that. The belt buckle, right, the zip, there we are. Did she touch me? It must have been by chance because she doesn't do it again.

The *smell* of clean bed linen. 'Sleep now, Varg.'

I sleep. For a long time. I dream. Too much. When I wake I am soaked in sweat and a fresh coffee aroma is wafting through the whole room.

There is a white cup on the bedside table. Steaming.

She is sitting beside the bed. She is wearing a red-and-white T-shirt, tight jeans, her eyes are tired and there is no lipstick on her lips. 'I've called everyone and told them I'm ill,' she says.

'What's wrong with you?' I ask.

'You,' she answers with a smile.

I drink two cups of black coffee and fall asleep at once.

The next time I wake the day has gone. She is standing in the doorway, wearing the same clothes. 'Are you hungry?'

I give that some thought. 'I think so.'

'I've made some food.'

'Perhaps I should have a shower first.'

She nods and is gone.

I stand in the shower for a generation or two until there is no more hot water.

There is a man's dressing gown hanging from the inside of the door. It is so new the price ticket is still on one pocket. It is brown and green and makes me feel as if I was enjoying the sun in a protected forest when I put it on.

There are two glasses, each containing a toothbrush.

Like in Upside Down Land, I cleaned my teeth before eating. I ran a hand through my wet hair and tried to focus on the mirror. But it kept moving. I was still dizzy.

I went downstairs to a set table, cloth and everything, like a convalescent in a care home. But I didn't eat as much as she had hoped and afterwards I couldn't remember what I had eaten.

The sunset stole across the country like a thief of the night, removing all the contours, and the town was wrapped in soft, blue silk paper and sent by express to the following morning.

The music came from far away. 'Mood Indigo' was being played on a velvet clarinet.

We sat beside each other on the sofa. She snuggled carefully inside my arm as if fearing she might bruise me.

'What day is it today?' I asked.

'Friday.' After a while she asked tentatively: 'Are you ready now to tell me what happened?'

I nodded and told her.

Afterwards her face was taut and stern. 'That was what they did to Siren too.' She clenched her small fists. 'I don't know what I would've done if I'd found out who they were. It's in situations like this that I understand how it's possible to kill.'

'I survived.'

'But Siren didn't. They might just as well have killed my own child.'

'I understand.'

'What are you going to do?'

'Go to the police.'

She looked at me askance. 'That sounds sensible,' she said in an unconvincing tone.

'Yes, doesn't it,' I said. Easy as ABC, except that I was VV.

'Do you feel better now?'

'Like the open country after a hurricane. But a rescue team is on its way.'

'Do you want to have a nap?'

I nodded. 'Mood Indigo' had morphed into 'Night and Day', and the clarinet was now a saxophone, while a piano was playing the melody like raindrops on a window pane. My God, how I longed for rain. I stood up and stretched my sore muscles. I had cypresses behind my eyes, lemon peel in my mouth and acid in my blood.

She supported me into the bedroom and asked whether I wanted to sleep alone, tonight as well.

I sit down on the bed, my dressing gown draped loosely over me.

She stands in front of me, and I answer: 'No, not tonight.'

I undo her trousers around the waist and slowly take them off. She raises her arms and pulls her T-shirt over her head. She has nothing underneath.

'But I don't know if I can,' I mumble.

'I don't expect you to,' she says softly, and lies against me like cherry blossom falling from the tree after flowering is over.

She wraps her arms around me and smells close and sweet, like the scent of summer on a day the swallows are flying higher than ever before.

And after a while it turns out I can after all.

45

On Saturday and Sunday, we fluttered like butterflies beneath the clear, dew-free glass cloche Providence had placed over the town, labelled 'pre-summer'.

The poisoning had eased. My strength returned. I ate like a wolf, emptied the town's stocks of Farris, tempted fate and kissed like a seventeen-year-old who had never done it before.

On Monday morning I went to the police and asked to speak to Jakob E. Hamre.

He received me with, if possible, even greater reticence than ever. He looked overworked, stressed and disgruntled, with dark bags under his eyes and, for him, conspicuously dark stubble. His tie and suit jacket were slung over the back of a chair, and his shirt looked as if he had got it back from the dry-cleaner's with an apology that there was nothing more they could do for it.

'Veum?' he said, impatiently meeting my eyes. 'I have no time for you. I have two unsolved killings on my plate, and no one has had any luck with them so far. I don't need *your* help. What do you want?'

'To report an assault.'

He closed his eyes and opened them again. 'Off you go. Two floors down.'

'It's connected. With everything you're doing.'

'Everything *we're* doing. To be precise, Veum. *We.*' He leaned back in his chair, rubbed his fatigued eyes, pointed to a chair and said in the same transparently sarcastic tone: 'Tell all, Veum, please tell all.'

I told him, and he listened in silence, without making any notes.

After I had finished, he said: 'Two men, you say? One spoke with a Stavanger accent? And they told you to lie low. Go on holiday. I couldn't have put it better myself, Veum.'

'They were there on your behalf, you mean?'

He smiled thinly. 'Do you wish to report the matter?'

'Yes, but—'

'Do it downstairs. I have no bloody time for—'

'Don't you understand that all of this is connected, Hamre?'

He leaned forward and snapped: 'The last time I talked to you, you promised to stick to the Camilla Case. All this other stuff you're alluding to—'

'But they keep popping up. All these cases are linked, Hamre. The Camilla Case, the Norlon business and the murders of Tor Aslaksen and Lisbeth Finslo.'

He stood up, his face crimson. 'Tell me what we've bloody missed then,' he yelled. He stared at me as the colour slowly drained from his face, as if it had been dipped into a chemical potion. He slumped back down. 'I'm sorry, Veum. Forgive me. But I haven't been outside these walls the whole damn weekend. Let me hear what you have to say.'

'I'll start at the beginning. That is, with the older of the two cases. Little Camilla goes missing one evening in April, 1979. Her mother, Vibeke Farang, is having an affair with Tor Aslaksen, who visits her, to put it politely, the night Camilla disappears. Tor Aslaksen has to go to a late-night meeting because they have some disagreement regarding the disposal of toxic waste. Present at this meeting are Odin and Trygve Schrøder-Olsen, two employees and the boss himself, Harald Schrøder-Olsen. That is, he is expected and is being driven by his daughter, Siv. As they arrive, something happens. Siv falls down the stairs – possibly pushed, possibly knocked down by an intruder, possibly an accident. Whatever the cause, she breaks her neck and her life is in ruins.'

Hamre has leaned forward with an intense expression in his eyes. 'Yes, so?'

'Siv has brain damage. She's still … She lives in her own

world. But the first thing she asked me when I met her for the first time, ten days ago or so, was this: 'Are you the little girl's father?'

'Bård Farang?'

I nodded.

'She mixed you up with Bård Farang? She must've met ... Could Bård Farang have been the intruder you just mentioned? No.'

'No?'

'If this happened the same night as little Camilla disappeared, Bård Farang has an alibi.'

'You guarantee this alibi, but there's one thing about it...'

'Which is?'

'Bård Farang was at a seminar in Østland. I'm sure you re-member that. At this same seminar was a young female colleague called Bodil Hansen.'

'Yes?'

'This Bodil Hansen was a keen amateur pilot. Small planes. I have a feeling she and Bård Farang were closer than anyone cares to admit.'

'Have you spoken to her?'

'Yes, but she has a different name now. She's married to Trygve Schrøder-Olsen at Norlon.'

He closed his eyes to think. 'But ... but...' He opened them again. 'It's only in Agatha Christie novels that people create false alibis like that. The statements were cast-iron ... How long do you think it takes a small plane of that type to fly from Oslo to Bergen – and back again?'

'Cast-iron statements ... from a crowd of pissed seminar par-ticipants?'

'And what would he be doing here ... kidnapping his own daughter?'

'No, of course not. But let's suppose he had a mission, at

Norlon – industrial espionage, environmental activism, what do I know? And suppose Bodil Hansen-as-was helped him. Imagine the shock he had when, back in Østland, the telephone rang early in the morning and he was told his daughter was missing – while he was a few kilometres from the crime scene but not actually there.'

'But what has this to do with Tor Aslaksen and Lisbeth Finslo?'

'Tor Aslaksen is the key figure here. He was mixed up in the Camilla case. He flew with Bodil Hansen, now Schrøder-Olsen, and I do mean *flew* – he piloted the plane. He worked at Norlon. And he was the first of the two to be murdered.'

'And *why* was he murdered?'

'Because he knew something. Something he'd decided to tell a neutral person. Me, to be precise.'

'Really?'

'Lisbeth Finslo was simply the mediator. She and Tor Aslaksen were in a relationship. He'd begun to get involved in something that worried her. We have her daughter's word on that. Lisbeth had got to know me. It was probably her who suggested he should contact me. He wants to do it as discreetly as possible because there are important people involved, and an opportunity presents itself when Lisbeth has to show me round Pål and Helle Nielsen's house. But then someone got in before us. Someone who sent Tor Aslaksen on a one-way trip, to the bottom of the pool, never to float back up, if you know what I mean.'

'Poetic but accurate, Veum.'

'Lisbeth is shocked and runs out … into the arms of the man who kills her.'

'Or woman?'

'Or woman, yes. There's a fracas and fate deals her a mortal blow. She's dragged into a car and driven to the nearest dumping ground – in Bønestoppen. End of story. Another instance of mediation turning out to be a thankless task.'

Hamre mused. 'That's not impossible, Veum. It explains most things. Even the glove fibres.'

'Glove fibres?'

'We found fibres of leather gloves under Lisbeth Finslo's nails. Naturally enough, the person who broke in was wearing gloves.'

'But there was no sign of a break-in.'

'No, but anyway. The trespasser moving around the house would wear gloves.'

'And there was a key, to the swimming-pool door.'

'Oh, yes?'

'Schrøder-Olsen senior had one – he used the pool for his physical training. Lisbeth Finslo was his therapist.'

'Bård Farang couldn't have got his hands on it?'

'Not unless he had a co-conspirator – this time, too.'

'Don't take it for granted that your first theory is right, Veum. You have been wrong before, if I remember correctly.'

'Can I go back to Norlon for a moment?'

Deep furrows formed in his forehead as he raised his eyebrows. 'Of course.'

'Harald Schrøder-Olsen owned a plot of land out by Breistein where Norlon had been dumping its toxic waste for years. Before I came up here this morning, I dropped in on the local property registry.'

'Did you now? Were they awake so early in the morning?'

'Both eyes were open anyway. And they helped me to the best of their abilities.'

'And so you found out…?'

'The property in Breistein was transferred by Harald Schrøder-Olsen around two years ago, according to a conveyance deed signed on 8th May 1985 and ratified ten days later.'

'I see. To whom?'

'That I already knew. Through the chairman, to a share company calling itself A/S Miljøbo.'

'Miljøbo? Sounds fashionable. And the chairman is?'

I paused for dramatic effect. 'A lady by the name of Bodil Schrøder-Olsen, née Hansen.'

'Well, I'll be damned.'

'I said something along those lines too, Hamre.'

46

We sat looking at each other. We had drunk our respective chalices and we were both wondering if they had been poisoned.

I cleared my throat. 'I think I've established some kind of contact with Siv Schrøder-Olsen, Hamre.'

He arched his eyebrows. 'And how old is she now?'

'Twenty-six. But mentally four or five.'

He shook his head. 'An impossible witness. The prosecuting authority wouldn't touch her with a barge pole.'

'I could try and talk to her, ask her if it really was Bård Farang she saw that night. If such a direct question would have the required outcome.'

He made a sweeping gesture with his arm. 'I could have some of our child crime specialists talk to her. They might get somewhere.'

'Let me try first. I already have an understanding with her, I think.'

He stared at me. Then he shifted a pile of papers as if to show he had taken a decision. 'OK. But tread lightly, Veum. She can never do more than point us in the right direction. She can never be used in court.'

'I understand. What about Bodil Schrøder-Olsen?'

He laid so much gravity in his voice that it sounded like a

monotone. 'I'll look through all of this one more time, Veum. I'll consider everything you've said, about Tor Aslaksen's role, and Lisbeth Finslo's, but leave this to us, OK?'

'Message received loud and clear. Over and out.' I stood up.

He raised an index finger. 'One more thing, Veum, before you go down and register your complaint…' He left a pause long enough for me to protest, but I didn't. 'Does the name Birger Bjelland ring a bell?'

'Not loudly enough for me to hear. But there's something familiar about it.'

'A so-called businessman. He operates in a legal grey area. Let me put it like that.'

'And?'

'He's originally from Stavanger. That's all.'

I sent him an ironic smile. 'Do you want me to pass this onto the department downstairs or will you take it up with them directly?'

He grinned. 'Let them find out under their own steam, Veum. Then we'll see how good they are.'

'I fear the case has already been shelved then,' I said and left for the ground floor.

I regretted entering the moment I arrived. The duty officer wasn't exactly the sharpest pencil in the drawer. More like one of the rubbers. He was pleasant enough, but it took me fifty minutes to file the complaint and leave.

Then I walked down to Strandkaien.

Outside my waiting room I stood listening with one ear to the door for anything unusual.

I didn't hear a sound, so I cautiously let myself in.

I repeated the procedure with the office door, but there were no unexpected guests hiding in there either.

On the floor by my client chair were the ropes I had been trussed up with. Spread out in a fan from the grey filing cabinet were my papers, just as one of the assailants had thrown them, and the tap over the sink was dripping; I had forgotten to turn it off properly.

I did now, then pushed the piles of papers into a corner and decided to attempt a tidy-up when I had the time and mental space.

The light on the answerphone was green. There was a message waiting for me.

I rewound the tape and listened.

'Veum?' It was a woman's voice. I recognised it, but couldn't place her until she said who she was. 'This is Silje Jondal. I'm married to Bård Farang.' She paused again as though expecting the answerphone to interrupt her, or maybe because she was unsure how she was going to continue. 'Erm … Have you seen Bård? He went to Bergen right after you left and today … that's Saturday … I still haven't heard a peep fr—'

She was interrupted by the tone and a voice saying her recording time was up. After the tone she returned. 'Hello? Yes, well … would you be so kind as to ring me if he hasn't … if you … as soon as you can?' Long pause. Then she put down the receiver without another word. But the sigh she heaved before ringing off reached all the way from Hardanger last Saturday to Bergen today.

I let the tape run, but there were no more messages, so she hadn't rung back.

I switched off the answerphone and stared at it. Bård Farang in Bergen from Thursday? And he hadn't contacted her?

We were approaching the end at a gallop now. The moment of truth was right around the corner. But which truth and which corner?

I dialled the number of the Hardanger mountain farm. She answered after one ring. 'Yes? Hello? Bård?' came the impatient reply.

'Veum here.'

'Ohh. I was hoping it would be … Did you get my message? Why haven't you called before?'

'I was … a bit tied up. I only got your message just now.'

'Oh, but then—'

'So you still haven't heard from him?'

'No. No, I haven't.' Her voice was muffled in the way that heavy rain blurs visibility through a car windscreen. I realised that she was crying and it was the tears that were breaking up her voice. 'This has never … Nothing like this has ever happened before, Veum. I'm scared out of my wits. I'm so frightened that something has happened to him. The children … I can't concentrate on anything. I just sit by the phone waiting.' In a sudden burst of aggression she shouted: 'You did this to him! It started when you came here. Afterwards he was in a different world. And he left the same afternoon.'

'On Thursday?'

'Yes.' In a meeker tone, she added: 'And you haven't … seen him?'

'No, but I haven't been out much recently. I've been … unwell.'

'Oh.'

'You have no idea where he could be, who he could be staying with?'

'No…'

'Parents? Family?'

'Not in Bergen.'

'Old friends?'

Silence.

'Girlfriends?'

She hesitated. 'Have you met his … ex-wife?'

'Vibeke? Yes. Do you think he could be staying with her?'

'I don't know. They went through an awful tragedy together. And I-I suppose that's why you visited him?'

'Yes. I won't deny it. But don't you think it strange that he hasn't called you?'

'Yes.' She was crying quietly.

It was harder to console people over the telephone than when you could just put an arm around them. 'Would you like me to try and find him for you?'

She sobbed. 'I don't know. But if you do see him, could you tell him to call me – without fail?'

'Yes. Of course, I will. There's a possibility he's involved with the demo in Hilleren, and if things have started to come to a head there, he might be one of those chained up and therefore unable to get away. To phone you, I mean.'

I had sown a seed of hope in her voice. 'D-do you think so?'

'It's by no means impossible. I can go there later today. I'll look for him, and if he can't get away, I'll phone you back ... with love from him. Alright?' I tried to sound much more optimistic than I felt.

But she accepted it. 'Oh, thank you so much. Then you'll ... one of you'll phone?'

'One of us, yes. One hundred per cent certain. Take care.'

'Bye.'

I sighed out loud as I rang off. Yet another person I was going to disappoint. Someone else I was going to bring a different message from the one she was expecting. Another seed sown that would never flower.

I called Vibeke Farang. No one picked up.

I called Body & Soul. She was on holiday.

Then I walked home, took my car and drove south via Skansen.

The sun hit me in the eyes, like the sceptre of some insane monarch. Summer had seized up, a sign that the times were in disarray. I was on my way to talk to Siv.

47

I heard him before I saw him, in one of the first bends after passing Blomsterdalen. His old VW Beetle sputtered like an angry pressure cooker shortly before exploding. I hooted my horn, indicated right and pulled up, trying to catch the eye of Odin Schrøder-Olsen in the oncoming lane.

In my rear-view mirror I could see him performing the same manoeuvre. We got out of our respective cars and met halfway, like two liberated agents in a swap at a Central European border.

'What's up?' he said.

'Anything new?' I said at the same time.

He gestured for me to continue.

'I mean, have you remembered something?'

He appeared to be irritated. 'About what?'

'What we were talking about the other day.'

'I can't dig up the past, Veum. I have more than enough on my plate with current issues – now things are hotting up out there.'

I looked towards Store Milde and then back at him with an interrogatory expression.

He grimaced. 'No, no. At Norlon, in Hilleren. It's moving towards a head-on collision.'

'Why?'

'Because time has run out, and no one's capable of listening to sense.' He thumbed over his shoulder. 'I've just come from there – a last-ditch attempt to find a negotiated solution.'

'Who with?'

'With people who should know better. My father, who could bring his seniority to bear on the conflict, and Bodil.'

'Bodil?'

'She's involved whether she wants to be or not.'

'Because of Miljøbo, you mean?'

'So, you've heard about them?'

'Recently.'

'But, first of all, she ought to tackle Trygve … properly.'

'There was no outcome?'

Bitterly, he stared past me. 'No, and this morning the vacuum tanker driver was in position. All hell's going to break loose today, Veum. I'm pretty sure. Are you coming?'

I deliberated, but not for long. 'Yes, but first I have to talk to your sister.'

'Siv? No one talks to her.'

'I'm going to try anyway.'

He sent me a resigned look. 'If you have nothing better to do with your time, fine.' He nodded, turned and walked back to his car.

I called after him. 'Have you seen Bård Farang this weekend?'

He turned and nodded. 'Yes, he's been in Hilleren most of the time.'

'Most? What do you mean by that?'

'None of us is at it twenty-four hours a day, not even us lot. That's all.' He dismissed me like a buttoned-up spokesperson at an embarrassing media conference.

Before getting in my car, I detected a change. The wind was picking up, a strong, warm south-westerly, seething with re-pressed energy. It tousled my hair with the passion of someone who hadn't seen me for years.

I stared into the teeth of it. The sky was still blue and the sun as magnificent, but small white clouds were drifting in from the sea, like sheep fleeing an invisible grass fire, faster and faster by the minute.

I got in the car and drove on.

I turned up towards Fana Folk High School and parked behind a blue Mazda estate. As I locked my car, it struck me that I had seen the Mazda somewhere before, and not that long ago.

I walked to the gate and hurried up to the old timber house.

Aslaug and Harald Schrøder-Olsen were at the garden table, in an intense discussion. When I rounded the corner, they shut up like oysters and watched me, as friendly as two unaffordable meals on a menu.

'Isn't Bodil here?' I burst out.

Aslaug Schrøder-Olsen retained her cultivated manners. 'No, she's left.'

Her husband immediately cut her off. 'And what has that got to do with you, Veum?'

'Well, I just heard she was here.'

Aslaug Schrøder-Olsen visibly clenched her lips. Her husband said: 'This is a private conversation, and we don't want you sticking your big nose in.'

'Erm…' I instinctively held my nose. 'And Siv? Would it be possible to…?'

'No,' he said categorically.

She looked at her watch. 'Soon be one … She should be back by now.' She cast a worried look towards the arboretum and half rose to her feet.

Harald Schrøder-Olsen closed his eyes to hide his anger, and I said: 'Then I won't disturb you any longer. My apologies.'

She was unhappy. 'Veum, if you see her—'

'I've said no,' her husband interrupted. 'I could sue you at the drop of a hat.'

'On what basis?' I said, and left them without waiting for an answer. He could sue me in heaven for all I cared. The angels were on my side.

For a moment I wondered whether to drive to the arboretum and then walk, but I decided not to. Instead, I jogged there.

I had an unpleasant sense of unease in my body, and now I knew who the dark-blue Mazda belonged to. It was Bård Farang's. But where was he? With Bodil or … on the same mission as I was?

I received the answer at the top of the hill just before the mini-arboretum.

He was heading towards me, panting, as though he had just discovered another hole in the ozone layer. On recognising me, he pulled up abruptly and looked left and right as if considering whether to make an escape.

'Bård,' I yelled to stop him.

Then he broke into a run, straight towards me. 'It's too late. We have to call an ambulance. I only wanted to talk to her, to hear about Camilla. They're going to kill us all.' He was wild-eyed and his voice trembled with desperation.

I could feel my blood freeze. I grabbed his arms and shook him. 'What are you talking about? Has something happened?!'

He pointed towards Lake Mørkevatn. 'In the water ... She...'

I gaped at him. His hair was dishevelled, his face haunted and twitching. The composure I had observed in him in Hardanger had disintegrated. All that remained were bare, raw nerves, an exposed minefield. 'You don't mean...?'

He nodded furiously.

I let go of him and pushed him in the direction I had come from. 'Do you know where her parents live?'

He shook his head helplessly.

'The brown house opposite where you're parked. Tell them. Get them to phone ... Say I'm down here trying...'

I didn't know what I was going to try. All I knew was that I was more frantic now than I'd ever been. I left him there, in the middle of the road, like a child who had lost his way.

Before rounding the next bend, I quickly glanced back. He was heading in the opposite direction.

I raced past the Crown Prince oak and onto the path down to Lake Mørkevatn, which lay between the birch trees like a blind eye.

I came to a halt at the edge.

The water lilies floated like clumps of clotted blood in the water, and there, under the dark-green surface, I saw her.

She was lying on her back, in the shallows, eyes open, as though only resting.

But the whole of her face was underwater, the flowers from the bunch she had just picked were scattered across the lake, a gauche farewell from the grave.

48

I waded in, with the water up to my knees, grabbed Siv under her arms and pulled her ashore. Her dress hung from her like seaweed.

I laid her down on her stomach, lifted her from the middle and emptied her lungs of water. Then I turned her onto her back, opened her mouth and placed mine against hers.

I breathed life deep into her, raised her face and looked into her open, lifeless eyes. All I could hear was the wind gusting through the treetops above us: the universe breathing.

Again, I felt her cold lips against mine; again, I blew air inside her.

I glanced around. No emboldened boys on the other bank today either, just one audacious boy on this side.

I groaned aloud –

– and kissed her,

again,

and again,

and again…

Her eyes were glazed, her skin was bluish-white, her lips were like dead snails, stomach up. Her flowers were still floating on the meniscus of the lake: freshly picked buttercups, bluebells, anemones and whatever all the others were called. But her hands had opened to embrace eternity and she was no longer a small girl in a much-too adult body. Life had caught up with her, and she was what she was: a young woman who had died well before her time.

Now I could hear the sirens, in the distance.

With tears in my eyes, I didn't concede that I had lost and continued to try to breathe life into the dead doll. But she was a statue who had been knocked over when death seized power. She would never stand on the plinth and offer flowers in her podgy hands to anyone again.

I heard voices and the sound of running feet.

Young men in grey uniforms with the Red Cross badge on their sleeves slowed down when they saw us.

Still kneeling, I looked up at them, as though they were messengers from a battle I hadn't heard of.

The first looked concerned. He placed the stretcher against a tree trunk and another bent down, held her wrist and searched despondently for a pulse. Then he straightened up with an expression on his face that suggested he was suffering from back pain. 'This is a case for the police,' he said above my head.

I placed my mouth against hers and tried once more to bring her round.

Behind me, a soft voice said: 'It's no use. It's too late.'

I raised my face and looked directly into Siv's eyes. All I saw was my own reflection. She had taken her secrets with her to wherever she was going.

I got up, awkwardly mumbling: '"Too much of water hast thou, poor Ophelia. And, therefore, I forbid my tears."'

'What did you say?' asked one of the Red Cross lads, a sun-tanned face wreathed by blond curls.

I just shook my head and didn't answer.

'Do you know her?'

'Yes.'

'Petter's ringing the police now, from the car. We'll have to wait here.'

'She isn't going anywhere.'

'No.'

*

The police came as though blown by the wind. It was increasing in strength. Now it was howling in the treetops around us, like a lost soul, whipping up the water of Lake Mørkevatn into small, choppy waves and washing her flowers ashore as spoiled evidence.

Hamre came in the second group, before they had secured the crime scene. The look he sent me was like the speech he had given me the previous day. It contained everything he had not managed to say. But the content was concise: 'Who is she?'

'Siv Schrøder-Olsen. I arrived too late.'

'As usual.'

'Mhm.'

He left me and whispered instructions to his colleagues.

I didn't move from where I was standing, as though I had been planted there, too. A rare plant: Lupus vargveumus. Extremely short flowering period. Likes to appear beside corpses. Withers quickly.

Hamre came back. 'Anything you can tell me?'

'I arrived here … forty minutes ago. I met Bård Farang on the road. He was wild-eyed and told me she was down here.'

'Bård Farang?'

'Camilla's father.'

'Are you saying *he* found her?'

'Yes. But he left her.'

'Left her where? What do you mean?'

'In the water. I pulled her ashore.'

'Left her in the water without examining to see if she…?'

'Seems so.'

'Where is he now?'

'Wasn't he up with the Schrøder-Olsens?'

'We haven't been there yet. Wasn't it them who called the ambulance? Why aren't they here?'

'He's in a wheelchair. Shock? I don't know. Perhaps she can't leave him.'

Hamre beckoned an officer over. 'Sæve. Drive up to…' He looked at me. 'Where do they live?'

I explained.

'Ask if there's a man called Farang there. Bård Farang. If not, organise a search for him. Have you got a description, Veum?'

I described him as well as I could and added the make and colour of his car. The officer noted everything down and hurried off.

Hamre shook his head as if to emphasise what he thought about all this.

'And me?' I asked.

'You? You can go to hell, Veum. You'll find a few corpses there too, if I know you.'

I looked over at Siv for the last time. But she was out of sight. They had covered her with a grey blanket. Under it she was sleeping the big sleep, and if she still had nightmares, there was no solace. No one was going to wake her. No one was going to hold her tight.

I left.

I was up on the road before the significance of Siv's death struck me, like nausea. If someone would go as far as this, then the content of what Siv had said was more important than I had assumed. In that case it tied the threads between the three cases even tighter.

But *who* was it? That was still an open question.

Back at my car I looked around.

Bård Farang's car was gone.

I looked up at the Schrøder-Olsens' house. It stood there, bathed in the early afternoon sun, with no indication of all the commotion there must be inside right now.

I didn't feel like going there. I had other confrontations to find.

I got in the car and drove to Hilleren.

Dark-grey cloud systems were building over the sea, like barricades to the summer. The ceasefire was over and a storm was brewing.

And in Hilleren it was as Odin had predicted. All hell was about to break loose.

49

It was like entering a battlefield; both sides had assembled for the final, decisive push, with an undermanned buffer zone in the middle.

The demonstrators had summoned all their reserves and numbered between a hundred and two hundred people. Inside the gates to Norlon the workers formed a defensive ring around the big, sinister vacuum tanker, the way that soldier ants gather around the queen to protect her against intruders. Between the gates and the demonstrators there were ten uniformed officers looking sombre. Up on the road two additional officers were trying to keep the rubbernecks at a distance, while representatives of the press and the media were waving their cards and demanding safe passage. It was like on the first day: the TV cameras were back, as were the portable recorders, press photographers on the Golan Heights east of Norlon, and journalists with sensation-hungry faces already writing down their first impressions of the atmosphere.

I parked by the side of the road and avoided the sentry post, in the wake of two journalists.

The mood was tense and irritable; nerves were on edge. Rhythmic slogans were chanted. 'NO TO POISON! DOWN WITH NORLON! NO TO POISON! DOWN WITH NORLON!' The demonstrators hooked arms, chain after chain, until they formed a compact, moving carpet.

Detached from the others, some way up the slope to the green command tent, I saw Håvard Hope and Vibeke Farang in a furious discussion. The slogans they were shouting were not in unison with the others, but they were screaming them at each other.

He grabbed her arm, but she pulled it away as her face contorted in a mute scream.

Odin Schrøder-Olsen came running down from the tent. He stopped beside them and said something. For a moment they stood there on the slope like three field commanders in a final consultation, unable to agree on where to attack.

Vibeke Farang shrugged her shoulders and pointed to the demonstrators below them. Håvard Hope shook his head and made a vague gesture with his hands. Odin stood, slowly trying to gain an overview of the situation. Then his eye caught mine. At first it moved on as though it hadn't seen me. Then it returned and fixed me with a stare.

I made a sign to him.

He pretended not to understand.

'It's important,' I shouted, and ran towards him. 'It's about Siv.'

He said something to Vibeke Farang and Håvard Hope, and took a diagonal path down to me.

'What was it you shouted?' he asked, still several metres away.

'Your sister, Siv. She's…'

'Yes? Spit it out, man.'

'Dead, Odin. Dead.'

He looked at me in an amused daze, as though he thought I was teasing him. 'But you were going to talk to her, weren't you?'

'I didn't get there in time.'

'What do you mean? But how? She couldn't just … die.'

'I'm afraid she could.' I half turned to the factory. 'Is your brother down there?'

'Yes, I think so. Bodil's just arrived. I suppose she'll tell him what's happened.'

'If she's just arrived, I doubt she knows yet. So, you can slip in, can you?'

He smiled wearily. 'Especially trusted people can.'

'Can you?'

'Me?' He ran a hand through his hair and straightened his glasses, unsure. 'Yes, I probably can, so long as I don't take a bodyguard with me.'

'Shouldn't we tell them?'

'Yes, but what did she die of?'

'She drowned. If we can see Trygve and Bodil down there, I won't have to repeat everything.'

'OK. Come on.'

The shouts from the demonstrators became louder as we approached: 'NO TO POISON! DOWN WITH NORLON! NO TO POISON! DOWN WITH NORLON!'

In the middle of the crowd, I glimpsed the untidy hair of Bård Farang, but I had no time for him now. He had come here to stay to the bitter end, I was fairly sure of that.

We edged around the crowd, and some of the closest demonstrators started a new resounding refrain: 'O-DIN! O-DIN! O-DIN!' If Saint Olav had heard them, he would have thought his life converting Norwegians to Christianity had been in vain.

Odin raised both hands as a sign that they should stop that particular chant.

The ten police officers stood with their feet firmly planted in front of the gates. The petrified guard inside stared through the wire netting. On the loading ramps sat a group of workers, drinking coffee from a Thermos, while another group were prepared for action by the vacuum tanker. From open car doors came the sound of rousing music.

A higher-ranking officer with a dark moustache and as many facial expressions as Robocop extended a palm and said brusquely: 'Halt! No unauthorised personnel are allowed in.'

Odin ignored him and addressed the guard. 'Åsebo, call Trygve and tell him I have to talk to him.'

The guard nodded and went into the sentry box.

To the policeman, Odin said in a low voice: 'The administrative director, Trygve Schrøder-Olsen, is my brother.'

Åsebo shouted through the open window: 'What's it about, he says?'

'Tell him that Si— ... tell him it's about a death in the family.'

The guard turned back to the telephone. Immediately afterwards he came out and nodded to the police officer. 'Let him through.'

'And him?' The officer pointed to me.

'He's with me,' Odin said.

The policemen let us past and formed a new ring behind us, ready for sudden attacks from the crowd as the gate was opened.

'O-DIN! O-DIN!' the crowd chanted behind us, and reverberating applause accompanied us through the narrow opening, before the gate was slammed shut.

I turned round and looked back.

The crowd was cheering and chanting: 'NO TO POISON! DOWN WITH NORLON!'

Håvard Hope stood alone on the slope, isolated from the others. I searched for Vibeke Farang. There she was, merging into the crowd, heading straight for her ex-husband...

Now she was close and he turned towards her. She said something and he nodded.

Then he put his arm around her and together they faced the gates again, joining in with the chant: 'NO TO POISON! DOWN WITH NORLON!'

'Are you coming?' Odin said behind me.

'OK.'

We crossed the yard. Some of the workers glared at Odin, a couple of them dropped inaudible comments, and most watched us until we were inside the building.

'He's probably in the office,' Odin mumbled.

I followed him up the stairs to the administrative offices, the same stairs his sister Siv had fallen down eight years previously, a fall that had now lost its significance.

I looked out through the tall window, straight at the vacuum tanker, which was facing the gates with its back to us, beside the rusty cover hiding the old well where the poison was stored.

At that moment, precisely that moment, I knew what I had spent far too long hunting for in the dark. I had found the last piece of the jigsaw. Now all I had to do was find where it fitted.

But Odin was already half a floor ahead of me, and I had to run to catch up.

We entered the offices where I had first met Ulrichsen what seemed like an eternity ago. The same two guardian angels stood at the entrance: the warm, early-summer's day and the chilly autumn evening. When Odin stepped inside, with me hard on his heels, they looked upon him as if he were Satan in person, descended from the heights, with me as his prophet.

'Hello, ladies. Is Trygve in?'

The older of the two answered: 'The director's in his office, yes.'

'And Madam Director as well, by any chance?' Odin said sarcastically, walking past them and knocking on the door marked

Trygve Schrøder-Olsen. He gave them ten seconds to brace themselves in case they were busy doing something private. Then he walked straight in and beckoned me to follow.

I winked at the young blonde and sent a deferential look to the martinet. Inside the office, I quickly closed the door after me and stood in front of it like a mercenary occupying a government building.

Bodil and Trygve Schrøder-Olsen were sitting on opposite sides of the director's desk, but not so far apart that they couldn't hear what each said without shouting. In a sudden aberration I tried to imagine them in bed; after all they were married. But I couldn't. There was something distanced and business-like about them that made it impossible.

'So you got down then?' I said to Bodil.

She answered with an almost imperceptible curl of the top lip.

Her husband rose from behind the desk. 'What the hell is this about, Odin? Why's he here?' I bowed courteously, to thank him for his attentiveness, as he continued: 'What death in the family are you referring to? It's not...' he lowered his voice and raised his eyebrows '...the old boy?'

'No, Trygve,' Odin said softly. 'It's ... Siv.'

There was a silence. The only sounds were Bodil's sharp intake of breath, a telephone ringing – and being answered – in the distance and the faint echo of the chants outside: 'No to poison ... Down with Norlon...'

Trygve Schrøder-Olsen stared at his brother and had to grip the edge of the desk. 'W-what do you mean ...? Is Siv...?'

Odin half turned to me. 'Veum brought the news.'

'Veum? Why?' He pointed angrily at the telephone. 'Why didn't anyone...?'

'He'll have to tell you himself.'

'It's only just happened,' I said. 'No one's got that far yet. I don't know how your parents have taken it. I only ... found her.'

'Found her?' Trygve echoed.

'Where?' Bodil said in a weak voice.

'In Mørkevatn,' I answered. 'Drowned.'

'In Mørkevatn?!' Trygve said with irritation, as if it were an extremely unsuitable place.

'An … accident then?' Bodil queried.

'Misfortunes seldom come singly,' I answered cryptically.

I cast my eyes over them: Bodil's delicate beauty, hardened by ambition, Trygve's brusque authority, beginning to show cracks, and Odin's almost feminine sensitivity behind his round glasses. They had one thing in common. Not one of them shed a tear for their drowned sister and sister-in-law.

'Can you tell us the whole story now, Veum?' Odin asked.

Trygve looked at him. 'Don't you know any more than this, either?'

Odin shook his head. 'He wanted to tell us in a plenum, as it were.'

Trygve gazed at the window. 'As if we didn't have enough on our hands.'

Odin pointed in the same direction. 'You brought that on yourselves. You should've listened to me before.'

The noise outside had grown much louder. The chanting of slogans was even more concerted, and there was an ominous cracking sound, as though something heavy had been laid against the gates.

'Can we stop talking about that now?' Bodil pleaded. 'So that we can hear about…' She looked at me.

'There isn't much to say,' I said. 'I wanted to ask Siv about something. Something only she knew.'

'Siv knew nothing,' Trygve said with irritation again. 'What you say is just rubbish. She wasn't right in the head.'

'I said the same,' Odin said. 'Even if I used different words.'

'I wanted to try anyway,' I continued, as stubborn as a diver in mid-dive. 'But it was too late. For me.'

'For you?' Odin queried. 'Do you mean that someone else…?'

'I met Bård Farang there. Actually, it was him who found her.'

'Bård Farang? But what was he doing there? What did he have to do with Siv?'

'Perhaps she recognised him?' I said inquisitorially.

'Recognised him?'

'Now let there be an end to this nonsense,' Trygve broke in. 'I don't have time to stand here listening to rubbish.' He grabbed the telephone. 'I have to ring home and—'

'Wait,' I said. 'Not yet. Put down the phone.'

Strangely enough, he obeyed.

'He hasn't had a chance to tell us anything yet,' Bodil said, staring stiffly at me.

'There's not very much more to tell. Bård Farang said she was in the lake. I ran down … and found her. She had drowned in Lake Mørkevatn. In the shallows.'

'In the shallows,' Bodil repeated automatically.

'So, it wasn't an…?' Trygve left the sentence unfinished.

'It's very unlikely that it was an accident,' I nodded. 'Unless she had felt unwell, of course. But I don't think that was the case.'

Odin made a vague gesture with his hand. 'But *who*…?'

I sighed and took all three of them in one sweeping glance. 'Yes, who do you think?'

They exchanged looks. Odin shrugged. Trygve shook his head, annoyed. Bodil sent me another stern glare, as though she wanted to force the answer out of me.

My gaze stopped at Trygve. 'By the way, Birger Bjelland sends his regards.'

His jaw dropped. 'Birg … Bjelland? What do you mean?' Big beads of perspiration formed on his top lip and red blotches appeared on his neck.

'You have business connections with Birger Bjelland, don't you?'

He fidgeted with the inside of his shirt collar. 'Yes, peripherally, but…'

'He sends his regards and told me to say he wasn't tough enough. Send someone else next time.'

He was rocking on his heels now and it wouldn't be long before he was on his back, stomach bared, open to all attacks. 'Did Birger Bjelland really—?'

His wife interrupted, in a voice like clinking ice cubes: 'Trygve!'

He peered up at her, like a well-trained dog, and nodded.

She turned to me. 'What does all this mean, Veum?'

Thoughts danced on my brain like hail on a corrugated tin roof. The din was so great I could barely collect them. Slowly, I said: 'It means that in some way or other all of this is connected with Miljøbo.'

She smiled acidly. 'Really? In which way?'

'Well, I…' I ran my eyes over them. All three waited for an answer. 'You're the chairman of the project, aren't you?'

'So?'

'You're responsible for its success, aren't you?'

'Financially, yes. But I don't own it.'

'No? Then who does?'

I didn't receive an answer to that question. At that precise moment there was a loud crack outside – a bang, such as when a steel construction breaks; and at the same time a huge cheer rose from the demonstrators and then, like a thousand banners flapping in the wind, the sound of running feet.

'What the hell…?' Trygve shouted, and charged towards the window.

'What was that?' Odin said, following him.

Trygve turned to Bodil. 'They've broken down the gates.' He pointed to the telephone. 'Call the police.'

'But they're here.'

'They need reinforcements. Oh, my God.'

He turned back to the window. Beside him, Odin recoiled at the sight.

I joined them at the window.

It was shocking to behold, like seeing a concrete dam break and cascades of water streaming out and smashing everything in their path.

The broad gates were torn off their hinges, and the demonstrators poured through in a flood. They stormed towards the vacuum tanker, where the defensive ring of workers was overrun, like the back line of a junior XI against the Brazilians.

Behind the demonstrators came the mythical Wild Hun – the media folk: TV cameramen and radio reporters, journalists and press photographers. This was the event of the century this week, bigger than the Battle of Stiklestad in 1030 and more exciting than the cup final.

The ten police officers didn't have a chance. They were brushed aside in the same way as the gates, and now they were trying to work their way through the demonstrators from behind with raised truncheons. One of them blew a whistle and from the main road two officers came running down, as though they would be able to make any difference.

'What are they trying to do?' Trygve groaned.

'They're hijacking the truck,' Odin shouted, with a mixture of triumph and horror in his voice.

The truck was already surrounded. The driver was forcibly dragged from the cab and laid on the floor like a vanquished bully in a youth club. A hand rose in the air, holding something that glinted in the sun.

'The ignition key,' Trygve groaned.

Two figures clambered into the truck. One had long dark hair tied in a pony-tail at the back. The other was as supple as a panther, with zebra stripes in her hair, collected in an untidy bun on top. I was in no doubt as to who they were: Vibeke and Bård Farang.

'Bonnie and Clyde,' I muttered.

'What?' Trygve barked.

The vacuum tanker started up with a roar, and the demonstrators scattered to the side, cheering.

Behind us, Bodil was on the telephone.

Odin turned to her. 'Is that the police?'

She nodded.

'Tell them to be bloody careful. That truck is a bomb. It could raze the whole of Bergen.'

The big truck swung slowly towards the gates.

The police officers stood in front of it, but Bård Farang stepped on the gas pedal and accelerated towards the opening.

At the last moment the officers threw themselves to the side, the truck skidded through where the gates had been and was on its way up to the main road, the engine revving madly.

Odin grabbed my arm. 'Have you got your car, Veum?'

'Yes.'

'Come on then. Let's follow them.'

Trygve hung onto his arm. 'Odin, stop them for God's sake. Stop them. This is a catastrophe.'

I met Bodil's eyes. She was standing over the telephone like a plaster statue, still holding the receiver. But she wasn't speaking and she wasn't listening to what was being said at the other end, either.

Odin detached his arm from his brother's grip, and we sprinted down the stairs.

'Wasn't that Bård Farang?' Odin wheezed.

'Yes,' I panted back. 'And he has a lot of scores to settle.'

50

In the yard there was a dangerous stand-off between the demonstrators on one side and the police and the workers on the other. The cavalry had done their work. Now it was the time for close combat.

We gave them a wide berth. Inside the smashed gates, Håvard Hope stood with his arms hanging by his sides and a totally dazed expression on his face. When he saw Odin, the shortest fuse I had seen for years began to hiss: 'Can you see the consequences now? This will blow the whole of the environmental movement into smithereens. Are you aware what that truck can do?'

'Shut up. We'll stop them.' We ran past, and Odin added: 'If we can. Where the hell's your car?'

I pointed. 'Up there.'

I could taste blood in my mouth and my heart felt like a heavyweight boxer trying to pound his way out through my ribs. Odin was ten to fifteen metres ahead of me. 'The grey Corolla,' I yelled.

We arrived. I unlocked the car, dived behind the wheel, opened the door on his side and revved up before he had closed it. 'Did you see which way they went?' I gasped.

'There.' He pointed towards Håkonshella.

'OK.' The tyres screamed as I shot off and skidded into the carriageway like a wounded animal. We were heading for the ditch, but then the front wheels gripped the tarmac and I had the car under control. We were doing eighty before I had changed into third and we entered the bends like a jet fighter.

'What do you reckon they have in mind?' I asked.

'No idea. I just hope we catch them up first.'

'What did you mean by a bomb?'

'Exactly what I said.' We passed the Håkonshella turn-off and continued towards Alvøen. 'If the truck was full, it contains half a tonne of concentrated hydrogen cyanide waste. If that were to explode after a collision in Bergen city centre, it could develop into a cloud of gas that would kill everything within a radius of ten kilometres, in a minute or two.'

I cast him a side-glance. 'Are you serious?'

'Of course I'm bloody serious, Veum.' Odin's face was pale and drawn. 'They're driving around with an atomic bomb behind them.'

I gave a hollow laugh. 'I think I can hear the newsreaders now. *"This is the news. At six-thirty this evening Bergen was obliterated…"* Do you think that would make people in Trondheim or Oslo react?'

'This is not a laughing matter, Veum.'

We passed under Sotra Bridge. 'Gallows humour, Odin. Laughing from the scaffold.'

At the start of the Godvik bends, two cars were in the ditch and a handful of people were pointing angrily towards the town. '"Kilroy was here",' I mumbled laconically, and steamed past them as though they had guardian angels.

The hairpin bends between Godvik and Brønndalen had slowed them down. As Sotraveien came into view in front of us we had the vacuum tanker in our sights for the first time. We did a hundred down Lyderhornsveien towards Vadmyra and Loddefjord Torg. Metre by metre we were catching up with them, and I could see my licence fluttering off to Sotra if there were speed traps in the area. A blue light flashed down by Bjørndalspollen.

'I hope they don't set up any bloody road blocks,' Odin shouted.

'Perhaps they'll use stingers?'

'The tyres are too solid and, besides, if it careers out of control and crashes into another car … *pouff.*' He illustrated the explosion with his hands.

'Perhaps it's a stupid idea to follow them? Wouldn't it be better to go to Hellesøy and hope for the best?'

But I kept going. The truck thundered through the valley like a tank. Bård Farang held his hand on the horn and didn't care what colour the lights were. Pedestrians jumped aside as if afraid to be caught in the slipstream, and panic-stricken motorists sat clinging to the wheel, as if they were red-and-white lifebuoys. And we followed in the wake, like a delayed echo.

The police had halted all the traffic at the Bjørndalspollen crossing and they displayed a *STOP* sign, as if it were an ordinary traffic control. But Bård Farang wasn't interested in knowing if all the truck's lights were working, and we passed the police doing ninety and gesturing with every available limb that we were in pursuit. In the long, gentle bend leading to the Bjørndalstræ crossing I could see four or five blue lights in the rear-view mirror. Through the crossing and alongside Lake Liavannet we were like a funeral procession on the way to the last ferry, travelling at far too high a speed. *Good evening, this is the news. No survivors have been found in Bergen from the...*

'What are they thinking?' I groaned.

'No idea. What did you mean by ... he has a lot of scores to settle?'

I concentrated on keeping the car on the road. Then I said: 'Haven't you worked that out yet?'

'No.'

We were approaching the populated district of Nygård now. The vehicle in front showed no signs of turning off. It followed Kringsjåveien around the headland and into the district of Laksevåg. We had the whole of Bergen city centre in front of us, the Fløien and Ulriken mountains and the sky, from which the sun had suddenly departed, as though it couldn't bear the sight of the town's demise, either. High, high up, grey-and-white clouds had drawn the curtains and abandoned the town to its fate.

Cars had pulled up by the kerb and half on the pavement in both directions, as though a track had been ploughed down the middle for the insane funeral procession from Ytre Laksevåg.

We were close to Puddefjord bridge and the city-centre turning. But the truck didn't take this one, either. 'Steering wheel must be jammed,' I muttered.

They continued along Carl Konowsgate, into Michael Krohnsgate, and at the same lethal speed to Danmarksplass square.

'Oh, my God,' Odin exclaimed. 'I hope they've managed to stop the traffic there.'

They had. We thundered through the worst traffic junction in the Bergen region, along an espalier of blue lights and makeshift police road blocks, over a crossing and into Ibsens gate, towards Landås and Haukeland Hospital.

'Do you mean that about the cloud of gas?' I asked.

'Do I mean it? I'm deadly serious. If that truck blows up, even Haukeland Hospital won't be able to cope.'

As though it had suddenly occurred to Bård Farang that he had to comply with some traffic rules, he abruptly indicated left at the crossroads between Ibsens gate and Haukelandsveien, skidded round the bend and disappeared down the tunnel beneath the hospital as though he was delivering an acute admission to the lower ground floor.

I also went into a wild skid, turned round once, then twice more, until I had the car back under control, changed down, steered the wheels into the bend and set off in pursuit, ahead of the nearest police car.

The truck had a substantial lead now, but by Årstadsvollen we were back in contention.

Odin clung to the dashboard and leaned forward. 'My God, Veum. If they're going to do what I fear they will…'

The same thought struck me. 'You mean … Svartediket?'

'Yes, I do. Jesus.'

And we were right. At the end of Årstadsveien the truck cut across the pavement into Svartediksveien. It squeezed past the tree growing in the middle of the Lappen junction and then sped up Tarlebøveien.

'What about the barrier?' I shouted.

'Won't hold them up for a second,' Odin replied.

With a crash the truck drove into the barrier closing Isdalen to traffic. For an instant it looked as though it had checked the vehicle. Then the truck expelled an extra puff of bluish-grey smoke from the exhaust pipe, roared like some prehistoric creature and smashed the solid boom into smithereens. A cloud of dust rose from the gravel behind as it raced on, up Golibakken hill and into Isdalen, fifty metres up the slope above Svartediket, the main reservoir for the town's drinking water.

51

Isdalen divides the Fløien and Ulriken mountains like a Canadian valley, surrounded by spruce trees, with the huge lake of Svartediket in the middle.

Originally it was only the furthermost valley floor up towards Kjeften and Trolldalen at the back of Ulriken that was called Isdalen, but the name had come to embrace the whole of the valley that used to be called Våkendalen. Våkendalen had been reduced to the sheer ascent to Tarlebø in the north, while Hardbakkadalen climbed steeply in the north-east and led to Borgeskaret, which had been the traffic artery and postal route since as far back as King Sverre in the late twelfth century. Until the early 1950s the furthest farms were occupied. Now the valley was deserted, apart from the constant criss-crossing of runners and hikers, dog-owners and tourists.

The valley had kept the appearance of a wilderness. Standing on the furthest bank of Svartediket, it was hard to imagine that you were within walking distance of Norway's second biggest city.

The green vacuum tank tore through this valley like a lobotomised bull in a china shop. Bård Farang kept his hand pressed down on the horn so that walkers and runners could jump aside and not end up as flat as worn trainers. A barking Alsatian went for the intruder and only escaped being crushed into meat stew *avec* tail by the intervention of its owner, who grabbed its collar and yanked it back.

On it went, down the narrow gravel track like a snowplough over a covered mountain pass, and we kept our distance in the haze of dust behind. The winding road suited the Corolla better than the truck and ascending the tortuous hairpin bends in the middle of the road we were so close to them that I had to brake. 'Is there any chance of us being able to stop them?'

'If only I knew what they were planning,' Odin answered. 'If they've come here to drive into Svartediket, the drinking water would be contaminated for months.' *Here is the news. From Bergen it is reported that the whole of the town is in A&E having their stomachs pumped after...* 'But the greatest danger is still the explosion. A cloud of gas with the wind from the valley behind it would not only affect the centre of Bergen but large parts of the Fana district as well.'

Sparks flew from the low concrete wall bordering the road as the truck squeezed through the tight final bend. In a flash I saw beyond the truck, to the next bend, where a group of between twenty and thirty runners reacted individually, some by throwing themselves over the concrete wall down towards Svartediket, others by scrambling up the juniper-clad mountainside for their very lives, while others stood paralysed in the middle of the road.

The truck swung from side to side, more sparks flew, and beside me Odin screamed: 'We've had it now, Veum. Holy shit!'

I jammed the brake to the floor and wrenched the wheel to the left, skidding like a rally car in the last bend before the tape.

To avoid the paralysed runners Bård Farang drove in a straight line. The truck seemed to be trying to climb the mountainside like a track vehicle. It took juniper bushes with it, snapped trees like matchsticks and crashed into a rock face with a bang that made the mountains around us sing.

Under my wheels the gravel crunched like teeth breaking, before we too came to a halt. There was a stench of burned rubber and oil, and pure petrol was coursing through my veins. I was on the point of exploding into a mushroom cloud as well.

Then there was silence.

We found ourselves in a sudden vacuum, an airlock in time. Blood roared in our ears and all we heard was our own pained breathing.

I had closed my eyes waiting for the bang and the catastrophe. But nothing happened.

I opened them again, raised my head and saw the truck.

It was standing at an angle with the bonnet in the air. One front wheel was spinning, in perpetual motion, making a sick, whining sound, like the whimpering of an injured animal.

Out tumbled Bård Farang, from the driver's seat, clutching his head. He turned to the open door and reached up a hand. Vibeke Farang grabbed it and followed him down.

Behind us police cars screeched to a halt, two of them so close they collided.

Bård Farang pointed up the mountainside, where a steep path led up to Midtfjellet. Then he dragged Vibeke Farang up with him. She was holding one knee and obviously limping. But they were still at large. Bård and Vibeke Farang, environmental activism's Bonnie and Clyde.

I turned to Odin. 'Shall we try and stop them?'

He sat staring after them apathetically. Then he shook his

head. 'The police will catch them at the top. The most important thing was the truck.' He undid his safety belt, which had left a dark-blue stripe across his collarbone.

The first officers on the scene were already past us and on their way after them. They didn't have a chance. They wouldn't even reach the top.

Good evening. This is the news. At six-thirty this evening Bergen escaped being totally obliterated when a couple in a vacuum tanker full of industrial toxic waste… I switched off the voice in my head and searched impatiently for another station.

A surly policeman subjected us to close scrutiny. 'This is not going to be cheap, I can tell you. Your driving licence and papers? Thank you.'

A runner in her early forties, in a red T-shirt and big glasses came up beside him. 'We work at Haukeland Hospital. Is there anything we can do to help?'

I pointed to the police officer. 'First aid urgently required here. A tight compress, between his ears.'

Behind me, Odin burst into hysterical laughter, as if someone had said something funny. As if there could ever be anything at all to laugh at again.

52

The following hours were full of drama. The valley was closed to all traffic. A fire-service helicopter sprayed the wrecked truck with foam, and the crew, in full protective gear, took air measurements to check for possible leaks, climbed into the cab and switched off the ignition.

The people beyond the truck and those further down had to take a different route home this evening, via Tarlebø and Blåmanen. The Haukeland Hospital sports team had a produc-

tive Monday afternoon: sport plus some first-aid practice on ter-
rified walkers, and runners with sprained ankles and the initial
signs of shock.

Bonnie and Clyde were brought down from the mountain.
Bård Farang in handcuffs. Back down in the valley, they were es-
corted to a police vehicle and driven away, without so much as
a single look between us.

'So it *was* Bård Farang who...' Odin said beside me.

'Do you think they were in it together?'

'In what?'

'The ... business with Tor ... and everything.'

'Hm.'

I watched the police vehicle as it drove off. Bård Farang ... I
couldn't help but think of his new wife, Silje, and his three
children, Marthe, Olav and Johannes, fatherless and abandoned
on a mountain farm high above Hardanger fjord, with a view of
distant mountain tops and little else. I wondered what had made
him leave them and visit his first wife. Was it because they had
experienced tragedy together that it naturally brought them back
when the crime finally had to be avenged? And had it been me
who unwittingly put him on the right track? Or were there other
reasons?

We briefly reported back to the still-surly policeman, who
realised that we could hardly be held responsible for what had
happened and accordingly let us leave the valley without any
charges.

The police directed us to the nearest turnaround for the car,
by the old quarry before the Tarlebø ascent. There we had to
wait until most of the police cars had turned.

It was conspicuously dark when we left Isdalen, but that was
not because it was so late in the day. The bank of cloud that had
drifted over Bergen this June evening was of beaten lead.

As we passed the shattered boom in Golibakken, Odin said:

'I'll have to go and see my poor old parents. It must've been quite a day for them, too.'

We turned into Årstadveien, and I said: 'I can drive you there. I have something to ask your father anyway.'

'Oh? What's that?'

We were both in slow-mo this evening, and it wasn't until we were out of Haukeland tunnel that I answered, indirectly: 'How bad is your father's state of health, actually?'

'How bad? Surely you must've seen for yourself? You don't suspect him of…?'

'No, I was just wondering. Some people can be surprisingly agile, despite being in a wheelchair. And what I witnessed the other day was that he was in fantastic form, considering his age. At least as far as his upper body is concerned.'

'Absurd.'

'I've even known people who have found it so agreeable to be spoiled that they've chosen to stay in the wheelchair, when in reality they were healthy.'

'Not my father, Veum. I can vouch for that. He would never have managed to sit still.'

'No?'

'No.'

We drove down Birkelund hill. The central parts of what had once been Fana unfolded before us, like a quilt appliquéd with silver in the false dusk. The cloud was so low now that the peaks of mountains were lost, and over Nordås there was a hazy mist, like a protracted yawn in the open landscape.

'You said,' Odin resumed cautiously, 'that Farang had a lot of scores to settle.'

'Yes.'

'Was that why he – and Vibeke – went on this crazy venture?'

I nodded slowly. 'As a kind of revenge, maybe. Against Norlon, or against society, all those unknowingly happy people who in some way were still complicit in what happened to their daughter.'

'I don't understand what you mean. The toxic waste scandal would have affected Norlon primarily, wouldn't it?'

'Probably. And the waterworks.'

'But no one at Norlon took the life of their daughter, did they?'

'No?'

'No?'

'And you're sure she *is* dead?'

'That's what everyone's assumed, isn't it.'

At the lights in Paradis we waited on red, as if we still hadn't been found to be worthy enough to be allowed in. But then we were forgiven and they were green, and as we bore left to Hop, I said quietly: 'Tor Aslaksen killed Camilla Farang.'

'What?' he shouted. 'I refuse to believe … You'll have to tell me more,' he added more calmly.

Another set of lights, another wait.

'It's the obvious solution. As obvious … as the postman no one saw because he was simply there.'

'What *are* you talking about, Veum?'

'Listen. Tor Aslaksen has a dalliance with Vibeke Farang while her husband is in Østland, at a seminar. But he can't stay long because of the ongoing conflict at Norlon. And then he promises Vibeke he'll take the Farangs' car so that he can deliver it to the garage the following morning.'

'Ye-es.'

'Let's assume that little Camilla wakes up, hears noises, gets out of bed and sees what's going on. Perhaps she thinks, as children often do in such situations, that something terrible is happening to her mother. She seeks comfort in the only place she can find – with her father.'

'But—'

'But, you're quite right, he's not there. The *car*, however, is, and she associates this primarily with him – and the blanket on the rear seat, which she usually wraps around herself when she sleeps. It gives her a sense of security. She thinks.'

'Are you saying she went to sleep in the car? And that it was unlocked?'

'It must've been. Because when Tor Aslaksen drove off a little while later, she was asleep on the rear seat.'

'But are you saying that he found her there and he …? I refuse to believe that. Not Tor.'

We were on our way to the Rådal junction now. On the left was Lagunen shopping mall, where people sat for ages in car queues: customers going in, customers coming out, employees going in, employees coming out. If you miss the security of sitting in a line of vehicles, you should visit Lagunen, at any time of the day.

In front of us were two new sets of lights.

'When I said that Tor Aslaksen took Camilla Farang's life, I should perhaps have expressed myself more clearly. I don't mean he did it deliberately. He did it unwittingly.'

'Hm.' He sounded disgruntled.

'And by that I simply mean he didn't see the little girl sleeping on the rear seat, but drove directly to Norlon, parked to the right of the gates and hurried into the crisis meeting without noticing anything. Are you with me?'

He nodded with a sceptical expression on his face.

'Then your father arrives … and Siv.'

'Uhuh.'

'All of you are in the conference room waiting. Also, Tor Aslaksen.'

'I see.'

'Perhaps the sound of your father's car wakes Camilla. But now she's disorientated. She gets out of the car. She's somewhere she's never been before. Then she sees a door, lit windows. She walks in that direction. In the window between the floors, she sees a young woman, Siv. She might've thought it was her mother. Perhaps she associates her with security.'

'Siv? Security?' He smiles wistfully.

'She waves to her, runs towards her, catches her eye and then … she is literally swallowed by the underworld. She falls straight into the open well, behind the vacuum truck. And this is what Siv sees. The little girl vanishes into thin air. That's why she screams and turns so abruptly on the stairs that she loses balance and falls. And has the terrible accident. That's why, even now, eight years later, she still talked about "the little girl". "Are you the little girl's father?" she asked me the first time I met her. "I told Totto everything," she said the next time. I don't … I don't think Tor Aslaksen discovered the link until this year, when he connected what Siv told him with the mystery that had plagued him, like everyone else involved, for so many years.'

Odin sat in a deep silence, without saying a word.

We turned off Flyplassveien and headed for Blomsterdalen and Hjellestad.

Then he spoke. 'And then what?'

'He confided in his girlfriend, Lisbeth Finslo, wondering what to do next. He didn't have a shred of evidence, and it was highly unlikely that they would find any remains of poor Camilla in the well, after so many years of draining it.'

'Evidence? You can't talk about evidence, Veum, when there was no crime committed.'

'One could maintain that it was negligent manslaughter in that the well was uncovered and there was no guard posted. For which A/S Norlon is responsible.'

He threw his arms in the air.

'Besides which there was another sin committed. That of

silence. No one said anything afterwards when calm had re-turned. Which meant that Vibeke Farang and her husband were left to live in uncertainty. It must've been like an iron ring around your forehead, getting tighter and tighter with every day that passed. This silence was so serious that when a certain person suddenly discovered this year what lay behind it – i.e. Tor Aslaksen – then he was muzzled for good.'

'He was muzzled?'

'Because in the meantime the need for silence had become confused with a hunger for profit.'

'Profit for whom?'

By the marina in Kviturspollen we turned into Mildeveien. The forest was close here on both sides of the road. The trees leaned forward like concentrated jurors, listening but still unable to see the link.

'This is where *I* come into the picture. Lisbeth Finslo had con-tacted me…' I nodded ahead '…at Hjellestad Clinic. She had promised Tor to arrange a meeting with me, as discreetly as possible. The opportunity that offered itself was setting up the house-watching arrangement for Pål and Helle Nielsen. But in the house, by the pool, Tor Aslaksen was caught off-guard. Someone had been waiting for him. In other words, someone with access to a key.'

'My f-father?'

'Possibly. There was a fight. Tor Aslaksen was knocked uncon-scious and pushed into the pool, where he drowned. But then Lisbeth and I showed up. At this point I'm still not sure what really happened. Perhaps your father had heard us arrive. Perhaps he was already outside. In any case, he was cool enough to wait, to see what was going on. And was surprised when Lisbeth ran out of the house in panic – straight into his arms.'

'And my father's supposed to have done this from his wheel-chair?'

'How would Lisbeth have reacted if he was the person she met outside, out of his wheelchair and as frisky as a foal? Would she have gone with him?'

He didn't answer. We had arrived at the house.

I turned up the narrow road to Fana Folk High School and the arboretum.

I parked and we got out of the car.

We surveyed each other across the car roof.

'Will Trygve be up there, do you think?'

'If he's back from Norlon, he will be. That's what I'd assume.'

'And Bodil?'

'Probably. Why?'

I rested my gaze on him. 'Because it could be interesting to talk with all of you together.'

He smiled stiffly. 'Like Hercule Poirot with all the suspects assembled in the library?'

'That sort of thing,' I said.

Then we walked up to the house.

53

We rang the main bell.

Immediately afterwards we heard Harald Schrøder-Olsen's voice in the speaker beside the door. 'Who is it?'

'Odin. Let us in.'

'Us? You aren't alone?'

'I've got Veum with me.'

There was such a long pause that it was noticeable. In the end, however, the door lock buzzed as a sign that we could enter.

I hadn't been this way before. There was a strong smell of old wax and select varieties of wood in one of those exclusive, solid hallways with which prominent Bergensians like to confront their guests, to make them feel inferior well before the first glass of sherry.

A broad mahogany staircase, covered in the middle by a Persian runner, led up to the main floor, where Odin walked ahead into the same room I had been in before, with the graduation photograph of Siv on the piano and glass doors leading onto the patio.

Harald Schrøder-Olsen sat in his wheelchair by a small, round table. On the other side, in a chair that looked a great deal less comfortable, sat Trygve. On the table were two tall glasses containing contrasting quantities of a mahogany-coloured liquid. At the opposite end of the room was a television set showing a poor American comedy film with the sound turned off. If possible, this seemed to make it even less amusing.

Odin impetuously turned to his father. 'Pappa. About Siv…'

Their eyes met. But they didn't shake hands or touch. There was no hugging in the Schrøder-Olsen family.

I looked at Trygve. He was in a terrible state, as if he had been sitting there and drinking whisky for two days without even going to the toilet.

'Isn't Mamma here?' Odin asked.

'She's gone to bed,' his father answered. 'Bodil's with her. The doctor's given her an injection. I'm afraid this has been too much for her.'

You can take it all though, I said to myself.

He motioned towards the television. 'We were headline news this evening.'

'Siv?'

He shook his head. 'Norlon.'

Trygve stirred, as though someone had pushed him.

'Could be worse,' I said. *Good evening, this is the news…*

'Worse?' Trygve mumbled.

Schrøder-Olsen senior glowered at me. 'And what brings this gentleman here on an evening like this?'

'The truth, Schrøder-Olsen.'

'The truth about what?'

We glared at each other. A cough came from the doorway. We all looked at Bodil.

She stood there, as black as a tarantula, in such a tight-fitting jumper and trousers that I wondered what she was celebrating. But her face was clad for mourning, grave, without a hint of a smile. She nodded. 'I thought I heard…'

'How is she?' her father-in-law asked.

'She's asleep now.' She looked at me as if wondering which branch of the family I represented.

I gestured towards one of the free chairs, to suggest she could take a seat.

She bowed ironically and followed my suggestion.

Odin stayed on his feet. 'Veum has something he'd like to ask you.'

'Does he now?' she said sarcastically, shifting her gaze first to Trygve, then to her father-in-law.

She had brought a new atmosphere into the room, a sense of imbalance, and it struck me that they were like characters in a Greek family tragedy, from a distant Phoenician royal house. The strangest ideas went through my head, and I stared at Harald Schrøder-Olsen thinking: *Has she served you your sons on a platter?* And then at Odin: *Or was it you she always wanted?*

Schrøder-Olsen senior leaned forward. 'The truth about *what*, I asked you, Veum.'

'About Siv. About Camilla.'

'Siv's dead.'

'But how did she die?'

'She drowned.'

'All by herself?'

'Is there anything to suggest otherwise?' He cast around. 'Is there?'

No one answered.

'We're short of a few people,' I said.

'Who?'

'Tor Aslaksen. And Vibeke and Bård Farang.'

Bodil and Trygve exchanged glances. No one else reacted.

'But all three of them are unable to come. For different reasons.'

Still, no one said anything.

I focused on the man in the wheelchair again. 'We can start with Camilla.'

'I don't know anything about anyone called Camilla.'

'Why didn't you react when I mentioned her name then? Just now, with Siv's? Why didn't you react to the names of Vibeke and Bård Farang? You know as well as I do which Camilla I'm referring to.'

Trygve stirred again, like one of Frankenstein's monsters slowly coming to life.

Bodil snarled: 'How dare you, Veum. What gives you the right to come here and—'

'I've given myself that right,' I interrupted her. 'On Camilla's behalf. And on behalf of all the others.'

Trygve grabbed blindly for the whisky glass, lifted it to his mouth and took such a long swig that I actually felt the effect myself. He put down the glass and raised his eyes. They were darker than night.

Silence reigned until I spoke up again, focusing on the head of the family. 'You and Siv drove to Norlon that April evening in 1979 when Camilla disappeared. What did you see?'

'I…' He made a grab for his glass and took a large swig. He didn't offer whisky to anyone else, as though he thought we were too young or knew it wouldn't do us any good.

'Let me refresh your memory. An open well perhaps?'

He pursed his lips.

'You and Siv. Did no one else react?'

His lips moved soundlessly. The veins in his temples bulged.

'Sorry, I didn't hear your answer.'

Bodil broke in again. 'Veum!'

The old man mumbled: '"Shouldn't we close it, Pappa?" she said.'

All eyes were trained on him now.

'I replied: "No, we haven't got time." So, we left it open. I was on my way up the stairs, as I've told you so many times before, when I heard Siv scream. She screamed before the little girl disappeared from sight, as if to warn her, and I looked out…' He shifted his gaze. 'I saw it happen, Trygve.'

His son nodded, without a word.

'And it was my fault. All mine. I left the well open and I failed to do anything … afterwards. It all happened so quickly. Siv fell, down all the stairs and lay unconscious … I was in shock, I think. A double shock. It was only when I was in the ambulance that I realised what had actually taken place. And I knew, I knew, there was nothing else we could do. It was too late.'

I turned to Trygve. 'And no one else saw anything?'

He answered in a monotone: 'No. The pumping stopped when Siv fell. I mean … it wasn't restarted. The lid was put back on and the truck drove away … with the waste. Later the well was filled again. That's all I know. I've never considered whether it would be possible … Can you …? Is it possible to still find her remains down there?'

'I don't know how far pathology has advanced or how thorough you are when you empty the well, but I doubt it.'

I moved back to Bodil. She had gone quiet, after this. 'Little Camilla was allowed to rest in her private grave, for all eternity. No one wanted to have any more publicity surrounding this matter. Least of all you, Bodil, who wanted to avoid any possible attention regarding Norlon and toxic leaks, such as in the marshes by Breistein.'

Her jaw fell. 'Was I supposed ...? What could *I* have known about the Camilla Case? I hadn't even become part of the family when all this happened.' She looked at her apathetic husband. 'Was I, eh? Trygve?'

'No,' I said. 'Because you were at the seminar in Oslo with Camilla's father.'

'Yes, I was. Hundreds of kilometres from Bergen.'

'You gave each other the perfect alibi, you and Bård Farang. It's almost as if you had a bad conscience about something.'

She waggled her head slowly from side to side as though saying no to a little child.

Trygve looked up again. 'When was this?'

'In 1979,' I said. 'In April. Your sister, Siv. Do you remember?'

'Yes.' He looked at his wife. 'That's correct. At that point I hadn't even met...'

'Let's stick with the Camilla Case a bit longer. We've established that Siv saw what happened to her. And that you did too, herr Schrøder-Olsen. Was anyone else in a position to see?'

They eyed each other.

'Those of you in the conference room.' I zoomed in on Odin. 'You, for example?'

'Me?'

'Yes, you. According to several statements you were standing by the window, watching them arrive.'

Trygve nodded. 'Yes, you were, Odin.'

Odin glowered at him. 'So?'

Trygve spoke in a slow drawl, as if on dope. 'And when Siv screamed, from the stairwell, you were still by the window. I remember seeing you recoil, not as if you'd heard something but as if you'd *seen* something.'

I took charge of the conversation again. 'And, at that time, you were still on the other side. When this happened to Camilla you immediately grasped the consequences for yourself and the whole family. At this point your mind was still on profit.'

He glared at me with manifest derision in his eyes. 'And that's why – since then – I've devoted my life to the fight against toxic leaks and other abuses of nature and the environment?'

'Yes.' I nodded gravely. 'Yes, I think so. Precisely for that reason. Driven by your conscience rather than idealism.'

He studied me from the corner of his eye, as though wondering which planet I came from. 'And what reasons would I have today for maintaining this silence you just spoke about?'

'Still profit.'

'But I've left all that shit behind me, Veum. Are you a bit slow on the uptake or what?'

'You've left it behind, unless I misunderstood what you said the other day, with your honour and an advance on your inheritance intact. Isn't that so?'

He abruptly studied his feet.

'Your share of the inheritance – an apparently worthless plot of land by Breistein, thoroughly polluted with dumped toxic waste. And it was then, when you took over the deeds in 1985, I believe, that the great transformation took place in you, Odin.'

He didn't look up, but I could see him fighting to keep his face under control, as though he was examining himself in the mirror in the morning and couldn't bear what he saw. 'The great ... transformation?'

'Actually, I believe you when you say you've devoted your life to the environmental movement. And that you were committed to it from 1979 to eight-five. Let's say that.'

'I'm still committed to it.'

'But I also believe you were trapped by your own past, the environment you grew up in, the influence of these people...' I made a sweeping gesture towards Trygve and Harald

Schrøder-Olsen without dignifying them with a glance. 'And by the person you really were until Camilla's terrible accident. When, in 1985, you suddenly found yourself with, on the surface, an extremely valuable piece of land, the old hunger for profit returned, like some inherited contagion in your blood. Do you understand what I'm saying?'

'I—'

'Perhaps you still think you're fighting for a holy cause. But you've launched a kind of model for environmental supporters under the name of Miljøbo, on precisely this plot of festering land. That shows a lack of self-respect.'

'The intention was to—'

I interrupted him. 'With enormous potential for profit in a market requiring passion or idealism. It's what we might call eco-capitalism, to coin a new word, isn't it?'

He was still studying his feet.

'What are you looking for, Odin? Your lost honour?'

'Listen, Veum—'

'No wonder Mr Activist has been so passive in the Hilleren campaign. You were even *against* it, Håvard Hope told me. It wasn't because the family name was involved. It was for quite different reasons.'

'What are you talking about?' Harald Schrøder-Olsen interposed.

'We're talking about the fact that your son, Odin, has three lives on his conscience.'

'Three lives! Odin? Don't…'

'It's true.'

Trygve reached for his glass again, but knocked it over. The contents ran across the table, but no one was looking, and no one made a move to wipe it up. All eyes were on Odin.

'Odin?' Schrøder-Olsen senior's voice fell like an axe.

Odin's face was grey. His eyes were swimming. 'It's not as you imagine. I did it to protect…' His gaze moved to his father, but he couldn't keep it there.

'Protect?' his father barked. 'I don't need any protection. I can protect myself.'

'You could once,' his son said feebly.

'So how did it happen?' I said. 'You followed Tor Aslaksen to the house in Kleiva—'

'Followed? Do you think I'm psychic? How could I guess when they'd arranged to meet you?'

I hesitated for a second. 'No?'

'I was *there* with him. We were going to talk to you. Don't forget that for Tor I was a childhood friend and an activist. It was me he confided in first. But I said we should wait. I was thinking about my father. It was him this would affect.'

'Skip the sob story now, Odin. Keep to the facts. Did … did Lisbeth Finslo also know you were there?'

He nodded. 'I spoke to her.'

'After you'd … while I was upstairs?'

'I told her it'd happened before I arrived. It must've been my father who—'

'What?' Schrøder-Olsen senior shouted.

'Yes, because of the key, of course. I used the same fiction on him as you just used on me in the car, Veum – he was better on his legs than he pretended to be. I told her to meet me outside, this was a family matter, we should keep you out of it, drive up to the house and talk to him, be as gentle as possible before handing him over to—'

'Gentle was the word. So gentle that you killed her, too.'

'It was—'

'To protect your profits. Don't tell us otherwise. When you killed your own sister today it was hardly to protect your father, was it. It was all about you.'

Harald Schrøder-Olsen knocked over his glass, grabbed the

arm-rests on the wheelchair, lifted himself up and held the position, his torso quivering like a gymnast's on the pommel horse before the final all-decisive routine. 'Siv?' he roared.

'She'd begun to start blabbing … to far too many people,' Odin yelled. 'First Tor, then Veum. And Veum had been getting much too close. The whole project in Åsane could've gone up in smoke. I got … I got Bodil to contact an … acquaintance to see if he could … help.'

I pointed to Bodil. 'Birger Bjelland. I've kept a note of his name. He'll be hearing from me in due course.'

She remained professional, as if the assault had been a minor matter that could be repeated if so desired.

'But that didn't help, either,' I continued. 'So, there was only one way to be sure.'

Odin threw his arms in the air. 'It was no life, Pappa. She was unhappy. She wasn't our old Siv.'

'Unhappy? Are you calling Siv unhappy? You miserable worm. You miserable bloody wretch. Who gave you the right to judge?'

I leaned forward, fixing Odin with a cold stare. 'So now at last they all know the truth. Camilla's parents. Lisbeth Finslo's daughter. Tor Aslaksen's mother. Your own mother. All those people who had no one to protect them. All of them have an answer to their questions now.'

There was a pause for a moment, as though everyone was searching for something, anything, to say. Odin stood in the middle of the floor like a wax figure. Trygve blinked, and finally I understood what his problem was. He was quite simply plastered. Bodil had no time for any of us. She stood up and tossed back her head like an offended princess.

I mused on what Aslaug Schrøder-Olsen had said, that having children was like sowing bulbs: some were damaged by the frost and their growth was held back; others grew and thrived, apparently perfect. I thought of Vibeke Farang and the pale-red skerry flowers; and perhaps that was how it was: the most attractive flowers were the ones with the bitterest scent…

Harald Schrøder-Olsen broke the silence, pointing at his son with a prophet's finger and cursing him roundly: 'Be gone with you. Take him, Veum. Drive him to the police station and tell them everything. Everything. About Camilla, too. As for you…' He glowered at Odin. 'I never want to see you again. Never! Have you got that?'

Odin nodded obediently, five years old, with tears in his eyes.

Then his father swung his wheelchair round and sat with his back to us, waiting for us to go.

Odin looked at his brother. Trygve hiccupped, unable to focus on any of us.

He looked at Bodil. A frigid smile passed over her lips and was gone before anyone realised it had been there. She discretely shrugged her shoulders and glanced at the door.

Odin followed her eyes. Then he trudged slowly in the same direction, without looking back or saying another word.

When we emerged outside, it had begun to rain. We were soaked before we reached the car.